NELIEM

CLARE DI LISCIA

Month9Books

Trade Paperback ISBN: 978-1-948671-37-8
ePub ISBN: 978-1-948671-44-6
Mobipocket ISBN: 978-1-948671-46-0

Published by Month9Books, Raleigh, NC 27609
Cover Designed by AM Design Studios

Month9Books

Dedicated to my beloved Nonna,
A living inspiration.

NELIEM

CLARE DI LISCIA

A gainst the suffocating dust under the gazebo, a thousand promises fade. The floorboards creak, the planks just above my head bending, sinking alarmingly closer. I should have chosen a better spot, somewhere away from the heat and the flies, but the violins were already tuning, and the crowds were flocking toward the square like scattered sheep.

I shut my eyes to the sight of Micha holding that girl's hand. How bright with pride my friend's face beamed, how his body twitched for the music to start. I'd rounded the corner, bursting to tell him of releasing my eagle and that we should skip the ceremony altogether. I'd been so excited, I'd overlooked how he'd dressed. His hair cut short and his hands, always smudged with ink, spotless.

A memory, already so faint, sprung in my mind and brought tears to my eyes. It should be me waiting for my intended before the crowd. Someone taller and blond and with his gaze fixed only on me. My heart raced, every beat a stab as I fled like a coward, rushing to hide away and die.

Last year, there had been a band, and the air was sweet with hope. Not one speck of dirt was under my nails, and three perfect lilies were entwined in my hair. Today is different. Today I want to drift away and float in the wind, rise with the sun, soar against sky and earth far from here. But the starting bell chimes, and I wilt back to the ground.

The azaleas part and a thin, dark form slinks closer. It's Etta. She's left her father's side to find me. Scrunching up her forehead, she gives me that look that I love so well. "You're so much prettier than Nillia, Oriana."

Nillia.

"I don't think of Micha like that." It's true. Our friendship is solely based on our strength training and disdain for our enemy. But still, he should have had the decency to confide in me.

Weeks of him being too busy to practice, too much work at the printers with the embargo now affecting neighboring Odessa as well. Talk of a united island strike. A revolt to show all pagan Untouchables controlling Madera that our voices would finally be heard.

Excuses. Lies.

My dagger strikes the ground compulsively as the last chair, adorned with fresh daisies, is lifted for all to admire. Its strength vibrates with every thrust, and my weakness washes away.

From the moment I clutched the blade, it's always been this way, transforming what was once a pathetic girl frightened of her own shadow into someone her own people feel skittish around. Someone too daring, too outspoken, defying her enemy at every turn.

A whiff of soap makes me turn as Etta pries closer. "Will the wedding party pass out candies?"

"Only for family." Lifting myself from under the gazebo, I gaze toward the orchard, dreaming of an apple cake, and almost miss the procession. The chosen are adorned in scarlet, their hair braided tightly in the tradition that tells everyone that they are no longer girls; tomorrow they will be wives.

My own mother stands with her sisters and the rest of the married women from our village. Everything in me tightens. The wind picks up, lifting the voices higher so that the whole world can hear. The harmony is what water is to a dying man, perfect and utterly unbearable. The truth sears through me as I stab my dagger deeper at the soil.

There will never be anyone singing for me.

On cue, Etta's stomach rumbles. By the way her gown drapes over her shoulders, sagging, I know she's lost more weight since the cane embargo. I narrow my eyes at the orchard, unable to stand the sight of her sharp bones poking out of her arms.

If she can wait until tomorrow and doesn't mind a bit of dirt or eating off someone's discarded plate, there will be plenty of pickings.

"Last year everyone got candies. I got two caramels and a chocolate." She licks her parched lips and in her smallest voice whispers, "I would like a caramel."

Etta clears her throat with a rasp. I know what she needs. There will be no one in the orchards picking fruit. As our festivities end, the Hugganoff rulers' celebration begins. We all call them Untouchables, since they are too superior to touch. They pay homage to their false gods with fireworks and proudly display every picked rose and tulip for miles over their doorways. Ancestral ghosts are offered bowls of choice fruit, which will go untouched, by every doorway. Slaughtered lambs and goats roast on skewers, and savory vegetables simmer before an open fire. It's all calculated to make us Outcasts, the last of the true believers, feel more worthless.

The dagger jerks as if telling me to proceed. I get up, thinking of only one thing: the unattended apple orchard brimming with fruit. Untouchable fruit. Fruit we pick for them, wash for them, and serve them, feeling lucky to eat a bit of core and seed.

"Wait here," I order Etta. And for a moment, a wave of panic engulfs her.

She yanks my hand, tugging hard. "Don't." At a loss, her eyebrows arch. "Oriana, you know it isn't safe."

Etta doesn't understand how the dagger helps me overcome weakness. It would be too difficult to explain how I'd be dead a dozen times if it hadn't been for my treasured possession. Instead, I wink, shaking her off. "I never get caught."

To prove it, I toss my dagger midair and catch it like a boy. Then, in one fluid movement, I leap over the wall that separates our Outcast village from the Untouchable part of town. My feet gain momentum, and I sprint until I see the outline of the orchard calling to me, beckoning me forward. I unravel my knapsack, knowing that it will soon be filled with choice apples.

A hawk flies overhead, its call a welcome relief from the celebration that had me hunched over and cowering like a frightened animal. I scan the area, counting the steps that will deliver me there and back. The dagger in my pocket electrifies as in warning. I flinch just as a twig breaks behind me; a glimmer of red hair and a long shadow causes me to run in the opposite direction, away from the orchard, as panic takes over.

When I get to the south wall, I race across the field headed toward the sea. Before I clear the field, I realize too late that it's a trap. I have been herded like a sheep, far from the few scattered homes, toward the deserted cliffside where no one will hear my screams for help. Another boy with flaming red hair stands behind a tree waiting for me; I recognize him from the market. I can smell him, sweaty with a tangy sweetness that can only mean one thing. He's been eating apples and waiting for some starving girl foolish enough to think she could steal some fruit.

I reach for my dagger, strength pulsating so deeply that I nearly drop it from my sweaty palm. Then, the voice of the boy of my dreams, whispers, "*Hold it steady, Oriana. You can do this.*"

I tuck all fear down deep within me. Later, I tell myself; later I will worry.

My would-be attacker's breath hitches in the back of his throat, excited that his plan has worked. The first boy, obviously his brother, clumsily rushes toward us. He stumbles and curses loudly, determined to catch up.

I don't bother to look for help. I am too far from my village and with the celebration underway, even Etta couldn't convince anyone to come find me.

I bite the dull end of the blade to free my hands, and dive under a thistle patch full of thorns and splinters, making my body twist. Down below, waves crash violently. The sea here has a fierce current too strong for most to master. The boy hesitates, eyeing the thistle patch warily. Unlike me, he wears new clothes, a bright jacket and tailored trousers, no doubt for his ceremony later tonight.

My throat going dry, I edge closer to the cliff, a fresh cut on my hand oozing blood. The Untouchable follows. He pretends to be brave, but the moment his hand brushes against the splinters, he cries out. He stops to suck the gashes, and his jacket catches and rips. His look of resignation says it all. If it were only him, he would give up, go home and fabricate some excuse why his new jacket is now ruined. But his taller brother, with the grace of a drunken mule, finally manages to catch up, his velvet trousers stained and torn from falling so many times.

When his eyes catch mine, he sneers, flashing his crooked teeth. Holding his thighs for support, he gasps, "For an Outcast, you're fast."

My mother says there are worse names to be called than Outcast. But right now, all I'm thinking is that there are two of them and one of me. No matter how many times I play it in my head, I can't win. The weaker one, a trickle of blood soaking his shirt, moans, "She's not worth it."

The taller brother, the one who chased me, touches his privates and shoots a devious look. I process their exchange with a shiver running down my spine. These boys don't intend to beat me or humiliate me. They intend something far worse.

Everything in me trembling, I drop the dagger. It stabs the ground just above my feet. While they gawk in triumph at the surrendered blade, I step back, inching further toward the ledge.

"Smart move. It'll go easier for you if you don't put up a fight," laughs the tall one with the stained trousers, who climbs unsteadily up the crumbling wall once used to prevent people accidentally falling off the cliffs. His arms are so long that all he has to do is reach down and it's over.

"Oh, Neliem … don't you fret." The shorter one, who should have had the sense to flee, hisses.

I get called that a lot. Neliem is an Untouchable name of a hero from long ago that means "he who would fight to the death." Legend states he offered guidance to the broken and poor of spirit using a dagger like mine to overcome evil. Since I'm only a skinny girl who happens to be fast on her feet and good with a dagger a boy who died taught her how to fight with, I wear the name as a badge of honor.

His plait coming undone, the dimwit sloppily scoops down toward me, his foul breath commanding, "Come here."

The boy's voice in my head whispers, "*Fight.*"

In answer, I flip and kick the redheaded boy hard in the face. He stumbles back, his face red with shame at being bested by a girl who will, one day, if she is lucky, clean his bedpans. But I do not stop there. In one fluid move, I collect my dagger from the ground and release it full force. It flies true to its mark, slicing off the shorter one's ear before impaling firmly in a tree.

With blood pouring down his neck, the shorter one screams, ready to bolt, as the taller one sizes me up. We stand at an impasse with me cornered against the ledge, nowhere to run, and my dagger out of reach. And I still want those apples.

The same hawk as before swoops down, its wingspan casting a wide shadow over where we stand. It's a sign from Neliem himself.

Without hesitating, I glide like a dove. I am like my namesake, who does not fear death, but overcomes it. The rush of adrenaline takes over, pushing me to do what no normal girl would. Every muscle in my body throbs as I dive off the cliff and soar into the endless blue waves. I am light and dust and magic. No fear, just pure elation.

Less than an hour later, as the fireworks announce the start of the Untouchable ceremony, I share three perfectly ripe apples with Etta on her porch. Etta eats greedily, even swallowing the hard peel in careful, tiny bites. Distracted by the delicious apples, she doesn't bother once to ask why I arrived at her door completely soaked through my undergarments, the tips of my hair still dripping wet and without my cherished dagger that the Untouchables must've stolen before fleeing home.

Once done, we begin our ritual prayers. As Etta lights the candles, praying for her mother and father, I think of the boy of my dreams. Hiding my eyes, I whisper the blessing, wondering for a moment if I made the whole thing up, conjured up someone who never existed.

2

I don't eat the last apple until a full week after my escapade on the cliff. It's by far the largest and juiciest, but it doesn't remove the sting of not being able to retrieve my dagger.

With an indescribable ache in my bones, I notice that my mother has unexpectedly set a new dress and a ribbon on my dresser. Last night she insisted I bathe, even though Sundays are reserved for proper bathing. A hot bath means two unnecessary trips to the well, plus all the boiling and excessive soap usage. I stare at the dress from the only mirror in the house, wondering who it belongs to. Usually dresses this well-made are sold.

All week, noisy neighbors have been trotting in and out, inquiring over ordering a gown. They chatter mindlessly about the embargo and how we might face yet another famine. If Micha were here, he would call for action, spreading his pamphlets at every door, demanding that all of us in Madera unite with the neighboring islands of Odessa, Phillma, Cortos, and Waria for equal rights against the mainland of Perla Del Mar.

But Micha is not here. He's in Odessa with his bride, planning to work for his uncle's printshop. The short note he left has already been torn into bits and used as kindling.

I can feel the wind pick up through the broken glass in my window. The Prince's proclamation, nailed to the gates, rattles mercilessly. Some say it is what stands between my people and certain death from Untouchables. A sworn promise of protection by the gracious, most sovereign Prince Philippe. But the faded cut on my arm says it's merely wasted ink.

It is the last day of the pagan Untouchable matching ceremony, during which an Untouchable male may choose whomever he desires. This means a half-day at the prison we use as a school, so we are all dressed a bit nicer than usual. The ceremony comes from an asinine legend where the groom rides on his horse through villages and selects a bride simply by tossing her on his back and stealing away into the night to do whatever he pleases.

Swallowing, I run my fingers down my dress. It's not new; it's someone's hand-me-down, like everything else in my closet. I lift the soft blue fabric and admire the flawless stitching, the way my mother has sewn it to fit my small waist perfectly.

Tracing over the ribbon, the silky texture beneath my fingertips feels like rose petals. I know it was made with love. Or, I should say, the only way my mother knows how to show love. Now it is the only love I'll ever know. The season is officially over, making me the oldest unmarried girl in our village. The only one left without anyone choosing to claim her.

Absentmindedly, I reach under my pillow, only to find my dagger still missing. The day after the attack, I heard those boys were seen by Dr. Wenloe, the traveling doctor who makes regular rounds of all the towns and villages and sees us Outcasts if time permits. Both had black eyes and cut lips. The shorter one with the missing ear was walking with a limp, and the other had a dislocated shoulder and five cracked ribs. I couldn't help but feel a perverse sense of justification tickle down my spine thinking that their parents had had the last word, beating them senseless for ruining their clothes.

A gentle tap on the door interrupts my daydreaming. I slip the dress over my head and, avoiding the mirror, turn to the doorway.

My mother fusses like a mother cat over her kittens. "Your eyes will look blue today. Like your dress."

I sit down under the pretense of doing my stockings. I have no interest in my eyes or any other feature, but she persists. She reaches for my hair, thick with curls and the only similarity we share. "Let me do your hair," she says. "It's so pretty."

The memory of Nillia adorned in scarlet with proud fathers and uncles and male cousins parading the chosen on chairs toward the quarter square, sends a fresh wave of nausea.

There will never be anyone singing for me.

So, I close my eyes and accept the scraps of my mother's pity, all the while biting back the sarcastic remark threatening to deflate her. Not today. Let her pretend that someone might be interested if I wear her silly dress and have nice hair.

Since I am now seventeen, a trade will be selected for me in the few remaining days of school. It will probably be something I detest, like cleaning or cooking for a rich, Untouchable family who won't even bother to feed me properly. Then, as the days grow colder and if there remains an odd-numbered Outcast boy from a neighboring village, he will reluctantly accept me rather than have no one.

Just dwelling on the unfortunate Outcast boy who will lower his standards to bond with a girl known as 'Neliem' makes me almost pity the poor sap and wonder if perhaps my escape skills will not be entirely wasted.

I laugh hollowly, and my mother momentarily stops braiding my hair. Avoiding the mirror, I follow her orange-brown eyes to the small altar erected at the far corner of my room. She has collected coins since my first blood to set aside for my wedding chest. Nothing too fancy, just the necessities: a veil, clean stockings without holes, and one pair of spotlessly white shoes.

Now the chest lies closed, a layer of dust covering the lid. I can think of a dozen better uses for the money. Perhaps a goat, one that's been fattened.

Before I can protest, she reads my thoughts, patiently tying the last ribbon. "No, Oriana, those are for you," my mother insists. She gets up and takes the items out as if they were woven with golden thread, gently placing them on my bed for me to admire.

I ignore them, choosing to stare outside while she does my stockings. I wonder who would choose me instead of a goat that can be milked and provide delicious, fresh cheese every evening.

I tell the truth. "I would take the goat."

Mother only shakes her head, knowing the price that 'Neliem' comes with. Not even Micha, who was a kind-hearted friend, could be swayed. The bell in the square finally rings, beckoning us Outcasts to venture out. Outside our broken fence, the constable strides by, nodding toward our home, but I ignore him. Never once has he attempted to come to our aid, even though the evidence of wrongdoing is constantly before his eyes.

Prince's proclamation, my eye. If I should ever have the fortune to meet this overfed, delusional man, he'll get more than an earful.

My mother walks me to the doorway, her eyes on the road, and kisses my cheek. "Today is a good day."

I stare at her, dumbfounded and wondering what's gotten into her. Respectfully, I bow and wipe the kiss away. I don't like kisses or hugs. Not that I've had many. None from Micha. But he did once hold my hand to keep me steady when my shoe fell off, and I almost stumbled.

As I cross the pathway, I spy Etta. I hurry toward her, and place her small hand in mine. Since the day of the near assault, I've been on high alert. My fingers ache for my dagger, remembering the smooth metal and faded etching. I stuff my other hand in a pocket and suspiciously scan the crowd of students, making sure there isn't an unfamiliar face. The unpaved walkway and overgrown hedges could easily conceal someone. Sensing nothing unusual, my shoulders relax, but my fingers still itch. Tonight is as good a night to find those Untouchable boys, and retrieve my dagger as any.

Today, Etta is practically jumping up and down, her shoes

polished so brightly that the glare stings my eyes. She exclaims in a cheery voice, "They are coming to the school today. They say their final matches will be made there, at school. Three today, three!"

A wave of dread washes over me. She shouldn't care what Hugganoffs do. All they care about is subduing and conquering, while my people want to bless everyone as they starve to death. This event isn't for us unless Matron takes pity and offers us some fresh fruit to compensate for wasting the better part of the day watching students who torment us make their choices out in the scorching sun.

"Maybe we will get an apple." I try to force a smile.

Eager to get to school, she skips happily ahead. I can't help but frown at her stick legs. Etta's only a year younger, but she's so much skinnier than me. Her fair hair is neatly combed, her face scrubbed so that her pink cheeks and yellow eyes stand out. With a bit more food, if she hadn't the misfortune of being born the year of the famine, she would be beautiful with many admirers. With fourteen girls in her year and only five boys who survived, Jerris, the baker's son, is probably her only bet—he's made several grass bracelets that dangle from her wrist. It's been years since he made one for me. The long ribbons in her hair jiggle as I count her steps.

One, two, three, four, five, six. Stop. Little jump, and a skip. One, two, three.

Etta stops at the school post, her bright yellow eyes glistening. "What do you think?"

All I truly want is this day over. I pray that all three of the matches end in double suicides. And if that doesn't happen, I fervently hope that their children are born deformed or mute so that they can't taunt and ridicule my people. Poking my shoe in the dirt, I imagine one infirmity after another plaguing them mercilessly until they beg for the swift hand of death.

Etta doesn't wait for my response. "I bet the boys are handsome, Oriana. I bet they're so handsome that just looking at them will make my heart ache."

Feeling that today would be a good day to return home and feign illness, I watch hopelessly as she goes inside and bows to Matron, who carefully inspects her hands and face. Matron wears her usual frown as her beady black eyes narrow, searching for the smallest imperfection to send her back home. Once cleared, Etta scurries into the schoolyard to take her place in line.

I stare at my nails, wishing I had had the forethought to dig into dirt or something even worse. But it's too late. Matron inspects me for flaws. When she reaches for me, the fresh memory of her calloused hand slapping me causes me to jolt back. I snap, "Don't touch me."

Her wrinkled mouth drops, but no insult or slap ensues.

Refusing to bow, my skirts rustle just as the wind picks up. I rush to join Etta, knowing that I might get a rap on the head for my insolence later, but I don't care. I'm so preoccupied, I don't notice the foot sticking out until it's too late.

My ankle twists painfully, and I drop. Neliem stirring, I catch myself easily before I go face first into the puddle. With speed, I brace my arms and pushing up, avoiding a kick from a shiny white sandal. A chorus of giggling ensues as I jump to my feet and scurry to my side of the courtyard.

Matching day indeed. Taking my place, I brush the dirt off my hands, not bothering to search for my attacker. Reporting it will accomplish nothing. Instead, at the chosen time, I'll match any blow they give me, leaving them huddled on the ground moaning in agony.

Together, us Outcasts stand perfectly straight in line, not moving under the burning sun, for what seems hours. Sweat from my scalp runs down my back. A fresh wave of dust flutters over the courtyard and my stance shifts. On the Untouchable side, the water bucket is being passed. When it's our turn, a boy spits in it before turning it over, the water seeping into the dirt.

For a moment, I think I might faint. Etta, a ball of nerves, keeps peering around the crowd toward the commotion up ahead. A small group has gathered to inspect some of the Untouchable girls.

Wiping my drenched forehead with my mother's handkerchief, I notice the dark circles under Etta's eyes and feel a twinge of guilt. Up ahead, three tall blond boys dressed in formal attire take their time talking to the dean. By their posture and the ridiculously expensive clothes they wear, I can tell they are from the mainland. One smiles in my direction, and I quickly narrow my eyes and check to see: dark tailored trousers and fine leather shoes. The foot that tripped me was pale and wore white sandals.

To my left, I spot one very pretty Untouchable girl with lush blond curls and a pink dress that shimmers in the blistering sunlight. It's her shoes that make me stare. She eyes me coolly, prepared to toss an insult, but the dean strolls by. Two boys lag behind him, one prodding the other into action.

At the other end of the courtyard, Matron, now finished inspecting Outcast children, announces, "Today we will have three Matches, the last of the season. And from three cousins, no less."

As if expecting her name to be called, Etta straightens her posture, showing her lovely neck. I wince and spot a bit of shade to my right, concealed perfectly by a fig tree. It would be too easy to escape the Untouchable mating ritual and not be found out.

Up ahead, Jerris waves, trying to get my attention. He stands tall, stubble on his chin, his soft brown eyes by far his best feature. His brother Rathe is up ahead, tormenting a girl by pulling her braid every time she turns. Jerris. One of five. Not a bad choice. We would always have fresh bread. I glance back at Etta, who's stopped breathing, her nails cutting into her palms as she stands on her tiptoes.

One of the boys up front has picked his match and holds her hand gracefully. The girl has long wavy hair and sad, brown-green eyes. I think her name is Tanya. Something about her expression makes me gawk. The smile on her face seems forced, and she flinches away from him as if he had the pox. The boy, either not aware or too dull to care, takes her aside and they leave to conduct the short ceremony with her family.

At least she was spared a day of tedious schoolwork. The second boy makes his choice, the blond girl in the pink dress. Overjoyed, she jumps up and down while he holds her somewhat stiffly and they join the other couple.

Matron clears her throat. "Ezra Mercer will make his choice."

The sun's fierce and I can't make out his face, just pale blond hair that brushes against his shoulders. I don't know why exactly, but my mind flashes to the two redheads who chased me last week. What they planned for me was something other than a beating, and I'm sure that as soon as they heal, they will be back for more. I pray the bruises their father pounded into them will cause them to be slow and sloppy.

The last Untouchable purposefully steps down the center of the rows. The wind shifts and a dove dives into the courtyard, holding everyone's attention. Seizing the moment, I quietly duck into the bit of shade and lean flat against the cool wall. My blue dress blends into the blue wall, and the rip in the gate is wide enough to slip through without anyone being the wiser.

A pained murmur cascades from the Untouchable side. Breaking the invisible barrier that has separated our two sides for as long as I can remember, the last match is not on the left-hand side of the rows. He's now walking with the dean on the wrong side, the Outcast side.

Only one explanation comes to mind: he must be dimwitted. Etta runs her fingers through her hair. The boy's foot halts just when he reaches her. I'm certain that she's about to faint. Her back is as straight as a post while he lingers. The scoundrel, a full head taller than the dean, tilts his head and shields his eyes with his hands, searching up and down the rows.

Cooling off, I study him. Interestingly enough, he doesn't seem as menacing as the rest of his people. Not a trace of malice or hostility. None of the familiar jeers or bullying that Hugganoffs are famous for, just puzzlement. His lean frame has likely never known a hard day's labor. His gaze sweeps one more time down the length of the line. Not finding the object of his desire, he settles on Etta's bright, over-eager face.

I'm unable to fathom what's about to happen. Can this be true? An Untouchable picking an Outcast? My hands go numb. Of course, it's happened before, once or twice. Not often. But she's so gullible and defenseless. I should do something, anything to make him stop.

The teachers stand with politely frozen expressions. Only Dean's teeth clench, his expression alarmed, reminding me of the time someone started a fire and one of the classrooms nearly burned. Matron, paler than normal, points her black eyes toward me. I tighten my fist, thinking that it's another cruel joke, making easy sport of us Outcasts. My blood boils. I'm half hidden in the shadow watching, my heart nearly thumping out of my chest.

On cue, Ezra steps back. It's clear that he isn't picking Etta. They're just talking, and he's taking the time to set her at ease, so she can speak clearly and tell him whatever it is that he wants to hear. He says the word 'friend,' and I step out of shadow into blistering sunlight. The wind picks up, and I inch closer to Etta, who converses with this stranger as if he's some long-lost acquaintance. All the tension has left her shoulders, and for some strange reason, she's laughing, her hand over her mouth.

Whoever he is, he's wasting valuable school time. There's a new set of weapons I wish to draw before noon. His gaze immediately turns to my hands and our eyes connect. Soft blue, like the sky after a downpour. I shiver. The hostile gaze of several Untouchable girls shoots daggers into me.

Etta's fingers gently stroke mine. "Oriana, Ezra was just asking about you …"

Never have I wanted to hear the clang of the bell so badly. My heart thumping hard, I search the teachers, but they're not moving. Neither is Dean or Matron, who appears frozen where she stands.

Everything stops when his hand reaches for mine. The air, the wind, the sun, it all freezes. All that exists is that hand. And it's perfect, except for one torn nail. Nine perfectly manicured nails, one slightly less than perfect. Then the most flawless hand ever created touches mine. Instinctively, I wipe my sweaty palm on my dress and inch away.

He persists, holding his steady hand out to me, a visible sheen of sweat on his brow asking a question that only I can answer. Behind him, the woman whose job it is to clean the school's sewer limps toward the bathroom with a plunger and bucket.

There are fifteen paces between her and me. Fifteen, fourteen …

Her head is lowered, a tangle of frizzy white hair escaping her braid. I hold in a gasp, for some reason unable to take my eyes off her. Thirteen, twelve. There is no ring on her finger and her shoulders sag, a small hump forming on her back.

I shiver out of reflex. It takes me a moment to realize why. That woman is me in a few years' time. And this boy's hand is the closest to a chair ride to the gazebo I will ever get.

My mind spins a thousand thoughts, all incoherent and wild, tumbling over each other like a deck of cards. I see myself running most of my life, running from everything this boy stands for: being hunted for sport, treated like garbage, picked on and ridiculed for being poor and an Outcast. But far worst of all, starving while they tossed good food away before my eyes, making me dig like a rat in the trash for their scraps.

Everything his hand offers I have hated and sworn nightly curses at to lull me to sleep. The woman trips, her bucket of waste spilling over her, and I wince.

Ten paces separate us.

Sensing my discomfort, Ezra leans closer. The scent of mint and lime and something familiar fills my nostrils. Only once in my life have these people not bitten, kicked, or thrashed me within an inch of my life. And since it was so long ago, I honestly question the memory. Perhaps it was merely some fairytale where the poor beaten girl finds a moment of peace.

But now this.

Not flowers at my feet, but this almost-perfect Untouchable hand. And, miracle of miracles, he offers it freely to me. Me.

Neliem.

And I know only this: whoever this boy is or isn't, he will not mock me. Never again. My hand, no longer numb, somehow moves and clenches his. Just as strong. Just as determined. A strange spark of energy flares when we touch.

Neliem.

And then he smiles, a broad, beautiful grin, and holds up our hands for all to marvel and gasp at. Every mouth from the Untouchable side is gaping. The teachers immediately start calling in the students by order.

My side of the line remains standing, their faces no better at hiding their shock and utter bewilderment. Only Etta has the decency to smile and clap politely before following her line to class. Her skirts whirling, she turns and blows me a kiss that I register a moment too late.

A feeling of weightlessness encompasses me, my legs limp, my face cold even with this heat. Slowly, everyone disappears, leaving us alone for the first time. I don't know what to say or think or feel. The woman is gone, probably washing the muck off her clothes, but it doesn't matter anymore. Whatever emotion possessed me to accept his hand has vanished.

Behind the school gate, I spy a carriage with two large horses bristling in the scorching heat. Three crows flying overhead caw a screech that sears right through me. The driver shakes the reins, squirming in his seat, anxious to drive us to our homes for the ceremonies.

Where the bonding will be sealed.

The bile climbs up my throat. Feeling ill, I gulp. For a second, my grip on his hand falters.

Ezra nudges gently. "Take all the time that you need, Oriana. I know this is a bit of a shock …"

I imagine Neliem on his majestic stallion stealing his bride: his long hair wild in the wind, his face a mask of strength, his outstretched arms encompassing the world in their grasp.

Reining all my strength, I steady my wobbly knees and inhale. I am not afraid. I am Neliem. It was me who threw herself into the deepest part of the sea where the waves were too fierce for any Untouchables to dare follow. And I will not waver. Not now. Not ever.

Unexpectedly, his fingers glide up my face in a way no boy has ever touched me. It tingles and spreads a fire that threatens to consume all in its wake. I jerk back, swatting him like a fly. Calmly, he touches the spot I struck—it's redder than I expected. But he doesn't seem the least offended. Instead, he laughs. "Forgot about that right hook."

He winks, making his soft eyes glisten moonlight and lullabies, before offering me his arm. At that moment, I know this is no mistake.

I have bonded in the schoolyard with an Untouchable.

3

The carriage moves like a half-dead mule that no one troubled to shoot. With its rattling windows and jittery floors, we press snuggly against each other. Foul pagan air burns in my lungs. Ezra, wedged between the sad girl and me, leans back in his seat. Then a wheel hits a rock. The moment my head hits the ceiling, Ezra's gentle hand cups it without asking.

His touch is as unexpected as it is unwelcome.

"Careful," he calls out to the driver, his eyes never leaving mine. There's that spark of energy again between us. The one I can't place. The cab shutters, the wheels crushing against the loose gravel that outlines the dirt path toward town. His breath tickles against my earlobe as he raps for the driver. "Go slower; there are women here."

His admonition comes off softer than spun cotton.

I'm flooded with questions. He seems tame, docile even. But he's Untouchable, descended from the Hugganoff conquerors who subdued my people. Which means pagan. Practitioner of black magic. Worshipper of ancestral ghosts. And I shouldn't be here. It's all too frustrating as I clench my fists, willing my dagger to appear. I turn away, refusing to look at him. My head's fuzzy enough without those blue eyes seeping into mine.

I attempt some distance and press my back against the side of the carriage, as far as I can be from this Untouchable. But it's impossible. Ezra, his arm against mine, draws closer until his warmth presses against my flesh.

I loosen my collar and form a plan, a means of escape. There's a door and two windows, but one window's barred, the other too small for a skinny girl to wiggle out. Outside, the driver whips the horses and the carriage picks up speed.

My skin prickles, the tingle spreading. He's too close, and I have no intention of throwing myself out of the carriage. I steady my breathing, attempting to appear relaxed, but it's harder than I imagined. There are too many people in this confounded carriage, and I can't quiet my nerves. I glare directly at the other boys. Cousins. They seem to resemble him, but don't have the soft blue eyes. Their eyes are harsher, darker, harder to read. But if I'm forced to endure their company, I might as well figure out my enemies' weaknesses. Their faces are tense, and perfect beads of sweat form on their fine clothes. Nervous, yes. Scared? No.

The boy with Tanya isn't pressing against her—he occupies the seat directly in front of her. I think he's the one that had to be pushed to make his choice. The smile has left his face, as if his mistake has suddenly dawned on him. Maybe he isn't as dim as I thought.

The other cousin is named Henric. The girl in pink, who might've been the one who tripped me, hasn't stopped singing out his name. Unashamed, he ignores her and stares right at me. His look is neither warm nor inviting. Henric's steady gaze wanders up and down me like I'm some animal on display and he hasn't decided if I bite.

I clench my teeth tighter, and he flinches.

The leaner boy, closer to the barred window, clears his throat as if he might know me. I notice that his ear has a cut and fading bruises mar both his knuckles. That's when I see a gold pinkie ring with an "M" elaborately etched above the Prince's insignia. All three boys have the same one.

From my studies at school, I know the significance. The mark of the loyal families who stood by Prince Philippe, the last of his line, during the time of civil unrest. Escaping a coup, the prince fled the capital by hiding under a hay barrel. His second cousin was bent on destroying anyone bearing the Hugganoff name. Only a few noble families in the southern city of Playa Del Sol offered support, rounding up those who wanted an end to tyranny. Allowing, for the first time, for my people to not be butchered. I push away any thought that these boys are anything like their fathers.

The girl with the pink dress fusses over Henric, attempting to wipe some of the sweat off his brow. Instinctively he nudges away, averting her touch. "Henric, will we eat now or later?"

"Later," he huffs before returning to ignoring her.

I study him, knowing his not-so-subtle secret. Not that he's definitely the better-looking one of the three, but that something lies in wait under the surface. Just like me. The intensity of his stare penetrates me once more, but I stare back, unaffected. If anything, I'm amused.

Tanya's fingers tighten and release too many times to count. I'm still not sure what she feels for her mate, if anything. He's the one who seems to recognize me, but from where, I have no idea.

When Tanya's not playing with her fingers, she keeps pressing her hand over her skirt, smoothing the fabric as if attempting to shield her skin from catching a glimpse of sunlight. The carriage jolts, abruptly stopping in the Untouchable part of town. I've never once been. The distinct fragrance of rosemary and jasmine assaults my senses as the carriage door flings open and a chubby woman wearing a red apron comes rushing out of a home, her arms open.

Behind her, I gawk at the house. It's beautiful, with a perfectly manicured garden bursting with countless flowers. Tanya's betrothed helps her and gives me a sly wink. I stifle a gasp and stare at Ezra, realizing that we're all expected to come out for the ceremony.

He gives me an apologetic nod, almost as if he realizes I find his traditions barbaric. I scan the house suspiciously, not wanting to take a step anywhere near it.

I fully understand what this is.

An Untouchable ceremony, and therefore, a pagan ceremony full of demons and sorcery and all forms of debauchery.

As an Outcast, I am forbidden from having anything to do with it. Carefully, I take one step out of the carriage, my mind calculating how best to escape. I cannot be far from my home and could run, dash away.

Sensing my unease, Ezra lingers at my side. "It's nothing more than a simple bonding ritual." Then, he lowers his voice so that I strain my ears to hear. "No blood-letting."

His soft hand grazes mine for the briefest moment, calming my nerves enough that I don't go racing for my life. I hesitate, eyeing the house apprehensively. It seems innocent enough, with bright orange shutters and a roof that's never known a leak. Also, it's disturbingly big, probably several rooms, and I bet Tanya's never once had to clean any of them. I register the neighboring homes. They resemble each other with only an exception of larger or smaller front gardens, yellow or red roses—nothing more to distinguish them apart.

The woman bows and greets us, "Thank you for this honor."

The glint in her eye catches my attention, and I step back, bumping into Ezra. Henric and the others briskly pass, accepting the invitation without so much as a nod.

"Oriana?" Ezra lowers his head and whispers, his eyebrows arched. "It's all right to be scared."

I am two steps away from slapping his handsome face and kicking him to the ground.

"I'm not scared," I scoff, jerking my shoulder and hiding the truth. I would gladly throw myself over a dozen jagged cliffs before facing whatever is inside of this Untouchable home crawling with ancestral ghosts. Scanning the pavement, I search for a weapon that can be easily hidden and used when the opportunity arises. My prayer is answered in the form of a bent, rusty nail on the ground. Without drawing any attention, I scoop down and hide it in my palm before tucking it away in my pocket.

Ezra attentively hovers over me, his minty freshness distracting. Pretending to adjust my skirt, I scurry past him.

But it's no use. He stands protectively over me, whether shielding me from some ensuing attack or just being overly familiar, I can't figure out. A tingle spreads where his breath flutters across my neck.

"I think I'm supposed to be there," I murmur, an unfamiliar emotion threatening to surface. The girl who would sooner kick me out of the house catches a look from Ezra before moving aside.

Ezra nods and reluctantly moves. Before I turn to go, he pauses to place a lock of my undone hair behind my ear. It's something that I've done for Etta hundreds of times, but this feels different somehow. More intimate. Without waiting for permission, I follow the blond girl to the open room and the door slams shut behind me.

The window closest to me is barred, and for a moment, I think I've been caged. First the carriage, now here.

The room is so beautiful that I almost forget to count the exits. Fifteen paces to the closet, ten to the window, fourteen to a door that most likely leads to the bathroom, which means indoor plumbing which means money. Dozens of dolls with perfectly curled hair outline one wall, their glass eyes following my every move. But not one ghost lingers about.

Strange.

There are no sharp edges or anything that I can use as a better weapon except for three sharpened pencils on her desk. The pencils would be too difficult to conceal, leaving me with the rusty nail.

Every inch of this room sparkles in shades of pink and lush cream colors. The richest fabrics adorn her bed and windows and the rug by the side of her bed is so thick that for a moment I wish to kick off my shoes and rub my feet against it. I'm so entranced that I barely notice when the girl with sad eyes stumbles against her bed and lets out a heartfelt sob.

The blond girl crosses her hands impatiently. "Stop the theatrics, Tanya."

The girl's face is drenched in tears as she whimpers, "Don't look at me like that Cassia, you're the only one who wanted this ..."

Tanya sobs so forcibly that I find myself looking for a handkerchief. I open a drawer and find a dainty one, with five others perfectly ironed with her initials, T. S., underneath.

"What are you bawling about? He's handsome and rich. You act as if some fisherman's son bonded with you, not a rich man's only son."

Realizing that I'm still in the room, Cassia stops complaining and darts a hot look that speaks volumes. Without Ezra at my side, she allows the full extent of her scorn to surface. Little does she know that in half a breath, I could have her on her knees begging for mercy if I so choose.

Tanya moans, "I don't love him ... I don't love him ..."

Cassia, unimpressed, huffs, "It's done, Tanya. He offered, and you accepted."

"I would have been beaten if I hadn't." Tanya eyes the door cautiously. "My family suspected I wouldn't and locked me in last night. Screaming at me about duty and honor ... and ..." She gulps down a hiccup, then grunts, "No dinner was served, just broth."

It's nice to know that Untouchable girls are also beaten and go to bed without supper. I'd always wondered. And, true enough, what she says is accurate. Even I couldn't help but notice the barred window and the lock outside the door.

Tanya finally acknowledges that I'm in the room when I press the handkerchief to her side. "Orsis?"

I correct her, "Oriana."

She smiles and pats her bed, inviting me to sit closer. "That's right."

I'm already in the perfect spot, my back to the wall to allow easy access to the door and so I'm not taken by surprise. But hesitantly, I shift closer on the bed. I finger the nail in my pocket, wondering if I could excuse myself and sneak out another window.

Cassia, becoming increasingly agitated, huffs, "Dry your face and pinch your cheeks or maybe he'll change his mind. He's the best looking of the three ..."

I raise an eyebrow, almost wanting to object. Henric's definitely the better looking. Then I think of Ezra's gentle eyes. The ones that remind me of the sky. A sharp knock on the door quickly commands our attention.

"That will be Landis, act the part ..." Cassia pinches her cheeks for good measure. "There, all better. We're all ready."

Cassia sings the last part out like a lark awaiting her lover. I wince a bit. This is nothing more than a stupid game. The door creaks open and Landis stands at the threshold, gawking at the three of us. I might be imagining it, but his gaze seems to linger on me the longest before shifting to Tanya. Some of the tension has left his face, but his eyes hold apprehension. He definitely suspects more than he's willing to say. It reminds me of standing at the ledge of the cliff, debating diving or staying put and taking my punishment.

Landis braces his stance, the crease never leaving his forehead. "Tanya, you can change your mind. My own mother changed her mind twice before wedding my father."

Playing the part better than I thought she could, Tanya gets up, her face a perfect mask of unspoken joy. "And deny myself the happiest day of my life?"

Landis's shoulders relax, but he's not what holds my attention. Standing off to the side, Ezra's eyes are blazing hot coals into mine. It's nothing like the brutes who wished to assault me. This look is unlike any I have ever experienced. It's deep and powerful, like unspoken thoughts too personal to utter out loud. Without thinking, I tug my collar higher up my neck, my cheeks burning.

I shake the sensation off, unsettled enough to make my way out of the room, trying not to run, trying not to count, just trying to appear normal. Just as I scurry past him, Ezra catches my waist, those warm, perfect hands pulling me closer. His nose barely brushes against my braid, his finger traces a pattern of something I can't place on my shoulder. "Oriana."

My eyes close and I think of summer. A meadow covered in daisies. The wind sweeping through my hair.

His hold loosens, but I don't move. A thought tickles at the back of my mind. The image of butterflies fluttering aimlessly in glass containers. And my eagle, my beautiful, perfect eagle, flying away, never to return.

I snap my shoulders back and turn to face him when we're interrupted by Tanya's mother. She places a garland on her daughter's head and murmurs some words too soft to hear.

In front of us a fire pot burns, and a sweet, sickly stench fills the room.

I suppose it's the mating ritual where they tear off their clothing and bow down to one of their false gods before plunging a dagger into their hearts. When that doesn't happen, I peer closer, curiosity getting the better of me. Landis and Tanya pour water over the flame at the same time. It fumes then sizzles, sending a wave of gray smoke in the air. It smells like cinnamon and burnt paper. They bow three times, and the smoke darkens, forming an image on the white wall.

I step closer.

Tanya's mother clasps her hands, her knuckles shockingly white as the image takes shape.

"It's a ring, a ring … the sign of a happy marriage." The woman stresses the word *happy* emphatically before she whirls around like a child. I stand transfixed, staring at the image that no longer looks anything like a ring. It's oval and has a tail that snakes to its side.

Mesmerized, I puzzle out the image.

Generously, Tanya's mother offers some refreshments that Ezra refuses with a shake of his head. He stares intently at the image as Henric leans closer and whispers, "Two weeks."

Noticing me, Ezra nudges Henric away as Tanya, now transformed into the perfect bride, chats away with Cassia and Landis like this was all her idea. But I couldn't care less what they're gossiping about. Ezra shifts his stance, his feet restless. I know the feeling too well. The urge for speed and flight, like racing a kite the first day of fall.

His intent gaze locks on the not-too-happy couple with a look that could be confused with revulsion, the space between his brows pinching tight.

He's upset. I can't help but glance down at my old dress and wonder if he's having second thoughts. Then I think, of course, he's having not only second but third thoughts. Frowning, I try to distract myself with the idea that I don't care either way. The truth sears hot in my chest, disturbed by the notion that I've disappointed him somehow. Neliem in me shouldn't care in the least. It should relish his rejection as yet another sign of our incompatibility. But for some, unexplainable reason, part of me does.

Through the wide-open window before us, a gentle breeze lifts into the room, upsetting some papers on the table. Ezra's long blond hair sways like feathers, and I think of my eagle soaring majestically in the endless sky. If my face had been tilted just a fraction to the right, I would have seen it, seen how Ezra seems familiar. For a moment, the urge to reach out and run my fingers through his hair overtakes me. Outcast hair is thicker, curlier, and sometimes so coarse that I've broken my share of combs trying to tame Etta's wild mane. But Ezra's hair seems silky soft, smooth as a feather and as delicate as rose petals.

My fingers twitch.

Catching me off guard, Ezra asks, "Are you thirsty?"

Without hesitating, he offers me a full glass. A wave of tension rolls down my body, knowing what it is.

Sacrificial blood.

Ezra arches a knowing eyebrow as if I'm the one being foolish and takes a sip. Reluctantly, I smell it before bringing it to my lips.

Water. I drink it down greedily in one gulp.

The corners of his mouth lifting, he motions to the ceremony. I watch skeptically. I have just accepted an Untouchable's bond and find myself in the part of town I've been curious to enter for most of my life. And yet, other than Cassia's blatant hostility, no one has tried to harm me.

Not even Tanya's mother, who stinks of some herb I can't place. Ezra's face searches mine for some sign of what I might be thinking. "The ritual opens the bond, but it's not for two weeks that it's sealed."

It seems barbaric. I glance quickly at Landis, then at Tanya, who's showing everyone the image on the wall, commenting on the size. "Aren't they wed?"

Ezra smiles, then whispers, "No."

"Then why do it?"

"It's how we do things. I suppose the time is allotted to make sure that it's a good match."

"What happens if it isn't?"

"He can send her back at any time during this sealing period."

"Oh." So, I might be home in two weeks, and this could be nothing more than a bad memory.

He stops staring at the oval that's starting to fade and looks me up and down, sending a quiver to my gut.

"But don't worry." The tip of his finger traces the lace on my sleeve, making my skin hot. "Ours is different. We're skipping this part and making it official. No give backs."

I blink, confused.

He explains, "You won't be returning home in two weeks or two years or twenty-two …"

What was meant to reassure me makes all the blood drain from my face.

"Oriana?" His voice is smooth like rich velvet, but I don't trust it.

And regardless of how his hair might feel, I tighten my grip on the nail. "I said I'm fine."

The only door within reach is unfortunately blocked by a table loaded with enough food to feed fifty of my people. The stench of incense tightens in my head like a vise, causing my temples to throb. It's all too much. I open my mouth to scream, to tell these people what I really think of them, how much I hate them and their stupid ceremonies and how I pray every night for their pagan gods to wage war and annihilate all of them.

As if somehow aware of the volcano that's about to explode, Ezra lifts my hand and raises his voice. "We go to Oriana's home next."

He addresses his cousins formally, all but ignoring the gawks and stares that burrow into every inch of my flesh. Tanya's mother tenses, her neck resembling a plucked chicken's, but she swallows back the complaint. Softening her voice to a dull rasp, she whispers, "But, I thought …"

The woman stares at the feast she's prepared.

Dismissively, Ezra waves his hand. "The food will be distributed to the poor. Arrangements have already been made."

This means my people will eat tonight.

Cassia's face falls, the contempt she holds for me more palpable than ever. But she masks it with a sweet smile that pinches her cheeks. And I know why. By placing my ceremony before hers, she's been slighted. Her voice scratches like fingernails on a blackboard, "Must we, Henric, my darling?"

But Henric doesn't bother to acknowledge her. His gaze is locked on Ezra. It's as if the two are speaking without words. I watch, mesmerized by the power play, which Henric concedes silently with a stiff nod. Cassia, furious, stomps her feet like some spoiled brat. In one fluid motion, Henric grabs her arm and pulls her back to the corner of the room, out of earshot.

An image of the horseman galloping into town to select some wayward female before riding off brings a smile to my lips. I can't help but wonder if he rode back to toss her aside when he was through. These Hugganoffs truly are savages. My people, although poor and feeble, celebrate a wedding feast for three entire days and there's none of this trial sealing for two weeks to see if it's a fit. It's all or nothing.

Ezra catches my smile. "Something amusing?"

"Thinking of the horseman mating ritual." Then, sweetly, "Your people are spur of the moment."

He stops mid-stride to drink me in. "Not all of us. Some of us know exactly what we want and always have."

Startled, I wipe the sweat off my palms, glad for the first time that I have a mother who troubled herself to make sure I looked presentable today, even though it's just a hand-me-down dress and shoes without holes. The thought of my mother and what this news will do to her is almost too much to bear. I feel queasy just imagining her face.

I force my feet to move when Henric opens the door, allowing a loud burst of wind to sweep into the house. For the first time, he's not scrutinizing me like I'm some animal on display. His attention is on the back wall. Instinctively, I turn to catch one last glimpse of the fading smoke ring. Unexpectedly, the pot boils over, splashing drops of glistening red tea against it. I gasp, holding my throat as I finally realize what the image is.

It's a noose.

A noose with blood splattered against it.

My knees weaken. Holding me against his chest, Ezra steadies me before helping me inside the carriage. The driver slams the door, and we're off.

If he were anyone else, I would collapse against him. Only pride prevents me from making a fool of myself. Instead, I lean against the carriage cushions, still in shock. Closing my eyes for a second, I force myself to keep a clear head.

Back in the Outcast part of town, with dirt roads and shanty homes falling apart, small children play in the mud and stray cats meander up and down the street. Here, I don't have to contemplate the meaning of pagan ceremonies or the faded image of a noose with blood. Shame washes over me. I don't want to get out of the carriage and claim these miserable people as my own. Cassia grimaces, covering her mouth with a dainty handkerchief as if the very air's contaminated.

My nosy neighbors gather, some peering from doorways of rotten wood with peeling paint, others spying from shuttered windows to gaze at the magnificent carriage that has never once been on this side of town. Even these weathered horses resemble stallions here. I think I spot Etta behind her cracked window, staring, probably wondering what has happened. I wave a bit, trying to convey confidence, even though nothing could be further from the truth.

Ezra, oblivious to his surroundings, gets out first, offering me his arm. I take it willingly, too stunned to shun him. Somehow, he seems unaware of the slum he has driven into, as well as of the unfriendly gawks and stares of half-starved people that seem to burn holes in all his finery.

Behind me, Tanya wrinkles her nose. Irritatingly, she makes even that look adorable and ladylike. The anxiety builds with every step I take, my miserable life flaring before my eyes. I am poor. Poorer than my neighbors. We rent a small shack that is in desperate need of a new roof. My mother sews to earn her keep, and when those jobs are scarce, she's reduced to washing laundry for Untouchables. I have no memory of my father, just scattered images of a warm smile and bright eyes. I wish I lived in one of the better homes, or by the sea—anywhere but here. The weight of everything wrong with me pounding in my heart, I step up to the broken gate, which Ezra holds as gracefully for me as if it were etched in gold.

Before I can offer up some excuse, he speaks. "Thank you for inviting us into your home."

For a moment, I think he's joking, but his eyes hold pure skylight. It nearly breaks me. Here he is, when he could be anywhere. The thought makes me shake for an entirely different reason. Tears swelling behind my eyes, I prepare to beg him not to allow anyone inside.

Instead, he gazes thoughtfully toward the sky. "A rainbow. It's a good sign."

I turn, and my jaw drops. Before me is the most beautiful rainbow that I've ever witnessed. Every color illuminates clearly, encompassing the entire horizon above the sea.

Ezra grins that shy, boyish smile and without meaning to, I lean into him. "There shouldn't be a rainbow, not this time of year, not with the heat …"

"And yet there is."

And for the briefest moment, I believe. I believe in happy endings and butterflies in glass jars and my magnificent eagle returning.

Of all the possibilities I envisioned happening today, being selected as the bride of a Hugganoff was never one. Perhaps it's the lingering effect of the rainbow, or the fact that he doesn't seem disturbed by the gutter I live in. It pushes me to hold my head up a little bit higher and follow him inside. Behind me, Tanya's at my heels, probably trying to avoid my neighbors and escape Landis at the same time.

Ezra turns abruptly, signaling Henric to approach.

Henric emerges from the carriage slowly but purposely. He doesn't make a show of the dried-out garden or the broken fence. He could be in the middle of an oasis the way he stands tall and proud. I have no doubt that there isn't a thing that this man does unintentionally. "She has a … headache."

Ezra narrows his eyes toward the carriage. "Then tell her to come out for some fresh air. That is not a request."

Henric, not skipping a beat, forcibly retraces his steps and drags Cassia from the carriage. Instead of approaching my home, however, they wait in the garden. Ezra relaxes noticeably before planting a soft knock on the door. It's so gentle that I'm positive that my mother will never think to open it. But the shuffling footsteps indicate otherwise. Clenching my fists, I brace myself for the hysterics. Perhaps she will disown me, toss me to the streets, tear her clothes and rub ash on her face for a fortnight. Holding my nail, I imagine using it to claw myself out of this mess.

The door flings open, and my mother finally appears. Her clothing is fresh, not what she was wearing this morning. And her hair's washed, which means two laborious trips to the well. Worst of all, a table full of refreshments, which we could never afford, signals that she was expecting guests.

"I was wondering what took you so long." Her grin broadens, ushering everyone in.

For the third time today, my mouth drops open, the nail falling out of my hand. Ezra steps inside without hesitating, his eyes curiously taking everything in. The shock of my mother's reaction has left me weak and confused. My stomach hurts, and my clothes reek of forbidden Untouchable incense. The men enter stiffly as I go at once to my room with Tanya in tow. All her fears seem momentarily wiped away as she stares with big eyes at my sparse room, catching every crack and stain on the wall.

From the open window, Cassia's still in the garden, and for the first time today, I'm relieved. Being spared from the embarrassment of at least one Untouchable dissecting my home seems a great thing.

Grasping the lever, I close the window and steady myself for what lays ahead. Tanya makes herself comfortable by sitting on my bed and playing with an old doll that's missing both legs. I glance around, noticing that some of my things have been moved.

Outside my door, laughter erupts as glasses clink. My mother is laughing with pagans, which seems more than odd. She never laughs. Ever.

I turn to Tanya, trying to determine how big of an enemy she is. She's pretty, but not alarmingly so, and I don't have any memory of her taunting or hurting me.

I test the waters. "There's been some mistake."

She nods, finding an old diary that I quickly tug out of her hands. "I feel the same way."

"Is this some sort of joke?" I have to ask, dreading the answer.

She blinks those hazel eyes, which now seem more green than

brown. "Not for him."

Her gaze drifts out the window, toward the mountains, which I ache to climb.

I try again. "I don't know him."

"My grandfather owns spice ships. The Mercers want spices. That's why I'm here." She rubs her hands, and then, without asking permission, uses some of my hand salve generously over her hands and arms. "I am too poor to say no."

I have to bite back the chortle threatening to erupt. She lives in the largest house I've ever stepped foot in, with servants and more luxuries than I have been privy to my entire life. Meanwhile, I wallow here in poverty and would have until the day I died, if it hadn't been for Ezra.

"My uncle swore that if I didn't ..." Tanya trembles, her voice breaking as her hand slides up her throat. Without having to guess, I know something sinister was planned for her if she dared refuse. I recall the noose on the wall clearly, wondering what it signifies and unintentionally fingering my own neck. For the first time in my life, a hint of compassion pangs in my heart for this Untouchable girl with sad eyes.

But I don't have a moment to lose; I need answers. "Tell me what you know of Ezra. I need to know ... I don't remember him at all." I try to concentrate, straining to remember a chance encounter that didn't involve me running for my life. "Perhaps school, the market ..."

I bite the tips of my fingers, desperate for answers, anything to make his intentions clear.

"He's nice. Polite. Doesn't talk a lot. He graduated a year ago ... or two ..."

My shoulders drop; it's what I originally suspected. She's utterly useless.

"And?" I don't bother to hide the edge in my voice.

"He told his family months ago. Everyone has been trying to talk him out of it." Glaring at the door, she whispers, "Especially his brother."

At the mention of his brother, a spark lights up in her eyes. The green blinding, the brown all but gone. Intrigued, I lean forward. There is definitely more, something she's not saying. Suddenly bored, Tanya plays with a stray ribbon, frazzling its ends with her nail. She hangs it above her head, catching the light. I feel Neliem awakening. "Really?"

"Don't worry, Ezra wouldn't listen to anyone."

The hint of compassion I felt earlier for her is completely gone. I hate her. And she has no business in my room touching my things. I yank the ribbon out of her hands, hoping it burns and cuts, leaving a hideous scar that gets infected and needs to be amputated.

"As well as Landis." I hope the dig about her mate makes her squirm.

But she just wiggles onto her belly, her eyes dancing around the room, her mind elsewhere. If she's even slightly offended, she doesn't give anything away.

"You know, I've never been in an Outcast's home. I mean, *inside*. It's not what I expected at all. It's so clean."

I want to strike her, then kick her, then tear out every curl from her scalp until she's bald and bleeding. But the sharp knock startles me. Desperately, I reach for my trusty nail, but it's gone. Feeling helpless, I stare at the door. It doesn't even have a lock. I swallow the lump in my throat and scowl. "He doesn't want to do the two weeks waiting period; he wants to have the real ceremony. Is that allowed, or legal?"

Her eyes return back to a dull brown. "Does it matter?"

Another knock, sharper than the first, causes the entire doorway to shake and tells me that my time is up. I somehow manage to get to my feet without pouncing on Tanya.

Completely unaware of my dark thoughts, she dares to smile. "Oh, and he's been in love with you since any of us can remember."

I stumble, almost twisting my ankle, but manage to open the door without falling. The first thing that assaults me is my mother's beaming face. I flinch back when Ezra scoots past her and reaches for me. His hands are steady, though a hint of worry creases his forehead.

"You were in there forever." His voice is whisper soft, but the panic is as transparent as glass.

Sensing something amiss, he shifts his gaze at Tanya suspiciously. She dutifully crosses the threshold, taking her place as witness, then double backs and tugs Ezra outside.

"That's for later," she teases, and my stomach drops.

My mother closes the door firmly, taking time to prolong my humiliation. Her grimace says what her words won't. I am unsuitable, too plain, too skinny. She motions to the bed, and I sit. My gaze drifts out the window; I'm hoping that my eagle returns to rescue me. When my mother changes my shoes, I realize that I had been wearing my new stockings the entire time.

My wedding stockings.

Quickly, she grabs a dress from my wardrobe that wasn't there this morning. She wiggles off my old dress, shaking it off as if it was nothing more than garbage.

I am about to call this charade off when she speaks. "You will listen to him."

"I'll do as I like."

She stops her fussing and pinches my arm. Hard.

I jerk back and watch the tender flesh turn spotty red, the mark where her nail caught nearly bleeding.

A knock rattles the door, nearly shaking it off its hinges. I hear Ezra's calming voice loud and clear. "Is everything all right?"

I bite back the scream threatening to rip out of my throat.

My mother gets to the door first and whispers something about my nerves. She closes the door and pulls the new dress over my head, puffing out the fabric that's lacking that familiar musky odor. Not old. Not a hand-me-down. A new dress. My first. And it's my wedding gown.

Tanya, breathless, enters, forgetting to shut the door. Her eyes widen, her lips stained with wine. "I've been sent to help."

I blink back the tears and regain my composure.

Outside the door, the witnesses approach. I stifle a moan, willing my hands not to shake. I think of all the times I averted death. Countless times. Too many to number. And yet, even faced with my mother's wrath, this I cannot do. I cannot go through with this false ceremony.

Tanya helps me up, gliding effortlessly as my mother fixes my veil, making sure to cover every inch of my face. They leave to take their places, and my feet are glued to the spot right before the threshold.

Cassia cackles like a crow from the window. "She's backed out; I thought as much."

Rage pulsating from every muscle in my body, I step outside my room. My mother places a sweet bouquet of morning spring flowers in my hands with a sigh. Costly I think, wondering what else could be in store.

"You look beautiful," my mother exclaims, a bit too brightly. She catches Ezra's stare and pales. I turn to see what he's gawking at and notice that he's found the latest mark of her disapproval. Self-consciously, I cover it with my sleeve as she readjusts my veil.

My mother glances nervously over my shoulder. "He will take care of you."

Behind me, the priest fumbles through his book of prayers. He's probably never presided through one of these in his lifetime; a bond of Untouchable with Outcast.

When Ezra's hand reaches for mine, I stare through the veil into his eyes. Soft blue with specks of white. Such an unusual color. I swallow hard and focus. What kind of trap is happening: think Oriana, think. I close my eyes and imagine all probable outcomes.

One: I race for the door and take my chances. Of course, the new dress doesn't allow for me to run at full force, and with Henric standing guard outside, something tells me that I won't get far.

Two: I leap out a window, and if luck is on my side, I make it to the beach and swim away to safety. Only days later will my body wash to shore. Perhaps the gown might even be salvaged.

Which leaves my third option: I go along with this sham and take my chances. Like the first leap into the abyss, the skies clear, the waves inviting. All I need to do is push off.

When I open my eyes, I immediately notice how the entire house seems altered. Cleaner, brighter than normal. The delicate aroma of flowers and expensive food smells like a bit of heaven. An open bottle of wine is at the table, chilled for the celebration. An unheard-of luxury. The obvious unnerves me: Ezra must have paid.

A small pot of incense burns to the side. But it's not an Untouchable stench. It's sweet. Orange blossom. This leaves the culprit responsible for all this facing me. My intended. The food set out has been nibbled on. I can't help but wonder how my mother prepared all of this when it suddenly dawns on me. She must've known for weeks to have carried this out.

Weeks that my mother had refrained from pinching and slapping me.

The priest clears his raspy throat and for a second, I'm positive the phlegm will climb up and splatter all over me. Instead, his weathered finger presses on a prayer somehow suitable for this bonding ceremony. His face creases as he murmurs under his breath to Ezra, "Are you sure of this?"

The realization that my own people think so little of me makes Neliem quiver furiously. A flame ignites in the pit of my gut. But Ezra, his face intent, nods. Not a long, over-exasperated nod, but a short, quick answer, as if it wasn't even a real question. My heart stirs, my hand warming in his. Behind us, Cassia and Henric stand in the far corner of the house as rigid as statues. Below that fake smile, there is a visible red mark on her arm where Henric must have grabbed her.

Two small garlands are placed on our heads, pressing down over my veil so that I can barely see what is happening. The priest raises his hand for a silent blessing. Under my veil, the air is suffocating, hot and dry and causing my skin to crawl. It takes everything in me to focus against the pounding in my head and heart.

"You may kiss the bride." The words shatter me awake.

I stumble back, my knees weak. Ezra lifts the veil with that quizzical look on his face. My mother rushes to remove the veil, folding it carefully in her arms, preserving it for some reason. Then I remember. The veil is always made into the first child's christening outfit.

Ezra leans closer, softening his lips, that familiar scent I can't quite place lingering. He's about to do something dangerous but thinks better of it and paces back, satisfied. "Think you've had enough surprises for one day."

Startled, my jaw drops. And I would probably have slapped him it wasn't for the fact that I can't move my hands.

"I hope you don't mind." He motions toward the incense that's drenched the entire room in citrus fragrance. I'm too startled to object as he guides me toward the flame, his hand over mine as we tilt the silver goblet and water splashes, an image forming on the wall.

My mother stands alarmingly close, holding her breath.

Outcasts don't believe in Untouchable signs, or fortune tellers, or false gods. Untouchables pay a coin to ensure an ancestral ghost protects their journeys over water. Their omens, both bad or good, are meaningless.

But just the same, my chest tightens.

Instead of pinching me, what my mother should be doing is tossing the lot out for contaminating our household. Instead she waits, little beads of perspiration forming on her brow. Tanya steps up, staring with those big sad eyes. "It looks like …"

Even Cassia inches closer, squinting, then frowning, a deep grimace forming on her pretty face as she grinds her teeth.

It must be much worse than a noose, I tell myself, refusing to so much as glance at it.

Ezra lets out a soft sigh, a smile creeping across his lips. And something in me lifts.

"It's a heart, a beautiful heart." My mother gasps, jumping up and down, relief washing over her. I'm too shocked to register it as both Henric and Landis congratulate Ezra with warm hugs and pats on the back.

I finally turn and stare at the image on the wall.

It looks like a heart, but I refuse to believe it.

I find my voice. "It looks like a lump of fat."

Ezra laughs the loudest, followed by Henric and Landis, who seem to find me hysterical.

The paid scribe has already written all the documentation down, our names, our ages, everything but for one small detail. For the description of my class, instead of Outcast it states, 'tailor's daughter' and 'Hugganoff' in the most elegant calligraphy I have ever witnessed. My mother's actual occupation is a seamstress, the same as her mother and her mother before her. My father, whom I have no memory of, studied to be a priest before he fell into disgrace by marrying my mother.

Finally, the priest turns toward Ezra, his raspy voice barely above a whisper. "In a fortnight, I'll send the paperwork in."

Ezra's face freezes. He steals a worried glance at me before raising his voice. "I prefer you didn't wait."

I rub my temples, trying to get my bearings, but it all flutters like a whirlwind. My mother chatting away with the priest, who keeps filling his goblet with wine, not bothering to conceal a bewildered shake of his head every time he so much as glances in my direction. The other couples nodding politely. And Ezra. Ezra glued to my side, pressing the palm of his hand faintly against the small of my back so that his warmth emanates in a way I find the most distracting of all.

It can't be happening, and yet it is. Ezra signs the document and offers me the pen. I look down at the ink forming one perfect circle of blackness on the blotter that seems to spread. I think of a puddle growing into a pond, turning into a river that becomes the sea. What stands before me is an ocean. Vast, untamed, but mine. Watching my trembling hand as if it belonged to someone else, I sign my name. And with that, my fate is sealed.

I am no longer Outcast.

My heart thumps loudly as my mother congratulates me with a dry kiss. Her rough lips scratch my cheek, and it takes everything in me not to wipe it away. Instead of embracing her, Ezra nods politely, then signals the driver to make haste, his arm still snug against mine.

My body is tingly and weak. My limbs are not my own. How did I not realize that I had my wedding-day stockings already on my feet? That single thought plagues me as I stumble outside of my home, accidentally turning in the wrong direction. Ezra, sensing my state of mind, patiently guides me toward the carriage. Unfortunately, we have Cassia and Henric's betrothal vows before crossing the deep waters to the mainland.

Where I will live. Bonded with a complete stranger I have no recollection of ever speaking to before today.

Against the scorching sun, I step uneasily into the carriage, the scent of fine leather and horse more pronounced than before. Ezra gently helps me up against the sagging cushions, making sure I have ample room.

A sharp rap on the carriage precedes the constable's untimely arrival.

Short with a protruding belly, he leers his pointy chin in my direction, faking his best smile so that all his teeth glisten. "All is well?"

Cassia hisses under her breath, "As soon as we get out of here."

Henric nudges her, his icy glare silencing her at once. But Ezra's attention is on the gate. My broken gate.

I squirm, sensing what he's about to do but unable to stop it.

"As soon as you fix the gate," Ezra commands. "You should be ashamed of yourself, letting the neighborhood fall apart like this."

Not finished, Ezra stares out the door, pointing to the nailed Prince's Proclamation, which rustles tattered and blistered by the sun.

"The Prince's Proclamation of Protection hangs like some discarded piece of trash. It needs to be etched in stone as the law decrees."

The constable's jaw drops; he obviously believes the task unworthy of his time. He's about to complain and refuse to comply when a miracle happens. The air seems to electrify as Landis steps forward, his shoulders squared. On cue, Henric rises and barks, "It's not a request."

For the slightest moment, I don't feel Outcast.

Too shocked to speak, I drink in the sight of the three of them, tall, blond, and handsome, power emitting from every pore on their bodies. They're like three gods descended from the heavens to subdue the earth, and completely out of place in this slum.

Almost tripping over his feet, the constable falls to his knees and starts pulling up the broken gate, searching for the bolts to screw in place.

Henric and Landis enter the carriage, with Ezra moving closer to my side. He smiles, seeming pleased with himself. "Better than a horseman carrying you off?"

It's meant to be some sort of joke. Something to make me laugh. But what he doesn't realize is that the constable will have the last laugh. This injustice won't go unpunished. As soon as our carriage is out of sight, there will be some sort of retaliation. I doubt if the Prince's Proclamation will ever be etched in stone, and if it is, my people will bear the cost for it.

My people.

I poke my head out the window and search for one familiar face wishing me well. The image of the gazebo and the crowds gathered to marvel over the chosen adorned in scarlet sends a wave of envy down my gut. I squint, thinking I spy something, but it's only a ball of tangled weeds rolling in the breeze.

Dismayed, I sit back and realize the truth. Not one soul troubled themselves to wave and properly send me off. They're probably all huddled in their homes with sagging roofs and broken windows and not nearly enough food to fill their bellies, obviously too busy to worry about the girl known as Neliem.

The carriage takes off with a lash of the whip, the driver anxious to get back to a more familiar part of town. One that doesn't reek of filth and desperation.

I trace my finger on the glass, and for the first time in my life, I want to do something I have never once succumbed to. Not even when rocks and thorns cut into my flesh or dogs attacked me, nipping on my heels as I ran home, did I break.

But now, I do. I want to cry and cry until there isn't a tear left. Through a cruel trick of nature, I have become Untouchable. My sworn enemy.

4

It is well past midnight by the time we reach our final destination: Playa Del Sol, capital city of Perla Del Mar, where my betrothed resides. The bright, friendly lights of every lamppost gleam, as if in welcome. The notion is more than absurd, it's preposterous. Things like this don't happen to girls like me. And yet, here I am, still wearing my wedding gown, the scent of orange blossom clinging to my flesh as Erza's private carriage climbs the steep hillsides toward his house.

Ezra, having succumbed to sleep, slumps over his seat, mumbling restlessly. Some nightmare plagues his slumber. I wince thinking that we at least share that in common. Terror.

A shiver runs down my spine. I shift my gaze, peering at anything other than Ezra. This carriage is newer and cleaner, more spacious than the previous. The cushions are a royal plush velvet, soft to the touch, and coat the walls as well as the floorboard. I frown at such lavish display of wealth and sink deeper into the cushions, inhaling the cool, salty air. Outside, the cloudy moon greets me like a tireless lover, reminding me what lies ahead. The prince will awaken soon.

Painstakingly slow, we travel up the winding path, every turn of the wheel rocking the carriage into a steady rhythm. The ferry ride took longer than expected, the waters deemed too dangerous to travel at full speed. Even then the familiar ghosts lingered, hovering to and fro. Their misty forms materialized throughout the ship, never finding rest. Ezra had adamantly refused to pay the small fee for protection, calling it an old wives' tale. Landis, not hiding his disdain for Tanya, who'd fallen fast asleep as soon as we'd boarded, had agreed, assuring us his ancestors would sooner murder us in our sleep than protect us. Cassia'd turned beet red with fear; only Henric's assurance had contained her as she'd moved far away from me while swearing under her breath.

Opening the carriage window, I inhale sea and air and sky. And beyond that, lingering to its outer edges as if a fringe, freedom. Even as a small child I had dreamed of escaping my home, of traveling to far and distant lands. But now that I have indeed escaped, all I think of is my own bed with my mother in the next room, humming as she sews until the crack of dawn. Once, my mother had been kind and good. I'd never felt the hard slap of her hand or the pinch of her tight fingers until after my first blood. My father had been alive then, I think. And my brother as well. Small and white-haired, tucked safely in a cradle by the fire. I'd played with his chubby cheeks and curly hair, teaching him how to say his name. My mother hummed as she cooked, the rich aroma of delicious food surrounding us. That was back when there was more than enough to eat.

A sharp jolt from the carriage brings me back to the present. Ezra stirs, still half asleep, and rubs his jaw.

All I know is that we are no longer anywhere near my old home, or town, or anyplace I've ever stepped foot in, for that matter. We are clear across the bay on the mainland, and everything reeks of the cold, dead sea.

Not one other familiar soul in this town knows my name. I am faceless, my identity altered, a stranger. For the first time in my life, I am truly alone. The thought is both unsettling and, if I am completely honest, somewhat welcome. There will be few who miss me. Etta, perhaps Jerris, but the others might not even register me gone. My mother will, of course. She will worry in that way of hers, but other than that, no one.

My skin prickles at the thought, the spot she pinched still tender to the touch.

I could be on another planet as far as anyone was concerned. Whisked away in the wind, fluttering above the heavens, like a faded story from long ago.

The entire way here, I've been a ball of nerves, my senses heightened due to the unfamiliar terrain, the strange fragrances in the air, the dark looks, and, most of all, Ezra's constant scrutiny of me.

The only blessing is that Tanya and Cassia are already tucked away in their respective homes. Between Tanya's mindless chitchatting and Cassia's fake sincerity after her own nuptials, I'd had just about enough. My nails were clawing the previous carriage cushions so fiercely that I'm positive that whoever is saddled with the tedious job of cleaning up will think someone poked a knife repeatedly in the fabric.

I tilt my head and stare out the window. It is too dark to even make out the road, only the roar of crashing waves leading us forward. My weary eyes finally grow heavy, and I find myself finally drifting off before Ezra's gentle snores startle me awake. His warm hand reaches instinctively, holding mine protectively.

For a moment, I allow it, somehow reminded of a child holding another child's hand. The truth is, though I would never admit it openly, his touch isn't as revolting as I would have imagined. I thought the mere touch of an Untouchable hand would scorch me like acid, sizzling my flesh. Ezra's touch is warm and sweet, however. If it wasn't for the spark of energy that jolts between us, it would be somewhat like Etta's.

Just thinking about Etta makes my stomach knot. I never had a chance to say a proper goodbye. My one friend, and she's gone. I glance back in the direction of the ferry, wondering what she thought of my sudden departure. Was she truly happy to see me with an Untouchable? Her kind gesture of a kiss and wave at the schoolyard, when no one else would trouble themselves to wish me happiness, makes me ache to see her again soon.

Ezra's persistent hand finds me once more. His grip tightens over mine, reminding me that even in his sleep he won't let me go. How very little he knows me. Instead of staring at our intertwined hands, I decide to devise a plan. One that involves my freedom. His torn nail scratches against my palm and draws my attention. It tickles more than hurts, which bothers me for some reason. It doesn't fit with his perfect hands. He must have gotten into a fight, which brings up a slew of unanswered questions. Who would he fight? He's so rich and sophisticated. People like him don't fight. At least not with their hands. They overpower their adversaries with the advantage of their wealth and power. No need for physical exertion.

Trying to focus on anything other than Ezra, I gaze thoughtfully at the hidden moon, cloaked behind a thick curtain of fog. I wish it were bright and full so that I could know precisely where I am.

My stomach growls sharply, and I take a sip of water from the water gourd before guzzling most of it down. When the carriage unexpectedly comes to a halt, Ezra's eyes snap open, and he sits up prepared, his fists clenched. Quickly, he surveys the carriage, then me. A slow, easy smile escapes his lips as he rubs the sleep from his eyes, the sense of alarm dissipating.

"Already here."

He sounds too happy. The driver opens the squeaky door, and Ezra proffers me his elbow.

My throat hitches, knowing what the next few moments hold in store for me. Not even the sweetness in the air lifts my spirits. I wait anxiously, dreading every step toward the house that will seal my fate.

Ezra studies my arm, and without knowing it, rubs the tender spot. "You didn't rest."

Ignoring him, I compulsively seek the dark moon as if it alone holds answers. Unable to find even a sliver of crescent; however, my thoughts once again run wild. No matter what, I will never succumb to his charms, not that he has many. Politeness will never be enough.

I will fight him off. That is certain. Submission isn't an option.

Sucking in a deep breath, I cautiously step forward and, as graceful as a gazelle, he moves at once to help me out. When both my feet are firmly planted on solid ground, my strength returns. Even in the darkness, I make out the shape of columns and the massive outline of the courtyard. A trickling water pond lies directly before the threshold to the house, various statues framing the path. I let out a small sigh, already devising a plan. There are plenty of bricks and sticks to use as weapons. Also, I am fast.

The second he places his hand on mine, however, pinpricks of tension spike in every nerve of my body.

Facing us is the sea, the muted moonlight glittering gray against its stormy waters. Lightning flames in the distance, accenting the scene as something from a familiar nightmare. Darkness and despair. Two old friends. The waters from below splash violently against the steep cliffs, with only the one house framed perfectly against them. His.

And it suddenly dawns on me that he had no business in my small town of Anaith. Not when he lives here.

"I don't understand …" I whisper.

"Oriana?" He leans in, his breath soft against my hair.

I frown; I hadn't meant to say it out loud. I don't want this Untouchable to know anything about me. Not what I think or feel, especially about his people. But he holds his ground, standing tall, waiting for my reply. "You live here and yet went to the town school in a small village to find a … bride?"

He shrugs, his voice faint. "My father moved us to Anaith years ago to conduct his business. It's always held a special place in my heart."

"And your mother?"

"Dead a very long time." He winces a bit before turning his gaze away.

My fingertips falter against his touch, and I immediately cast my eyes down, my heart pounding. I know what comes next. What's expected of me, or rather, what my mother has been not-so-subtly lecturing me about—husband and wife relations. Something I'd never thought I'd ever endure before today.

I cling to one thread of hope. We are not quite married yet. Two weeks remain for bonding. The priest said as much.

But one glance from Ezra makes me question this. He doesn't seem the type to wait.

An ocean away, my mother's shrill voice haunts me. "*Close your eyes. Pretend it isn't happening.*"

The boys with lustful eyes at school I could handle. And handle them I did. A swift kick to the groin or twist to the elbow was all it took to send them scampering like whimpering imbeciles to their mothers.

The more persistent ones got a jab to the eye too, as well as a few bruised ribs.

The pulse in my throat throbs. Bracing, I prepare to tear his eyes out, despite the fact that where he just touched me tingles a bit.

Ezra's voice lifts above the crashing waves. "Have you been kissed before?"

His question catches me off guard. I hesitate. Once, in a different lifetime, I imagined a kiss. A soft one. Years and years ago by a boy who reminded me of the sea. The one who'd taught me to fight, to never give up. But that was just a dream. A fantasy.

Then I remember my dagger with the strange markings.

HAVAYA

"I … I …" My cheeks burn. Clumsily, my hands try to hide the blush burning on my face.

When I lift my chin, I see that his eyes are a calm blue. No storm. Just sky.

Sliding closer, he offers his hand. "Would you like to see your new home?"

The way he says this makes me freeze. My home. As if it belongs to me. I stare at the golden doorknob, unable to move. Without waiting for my answer, he opens the door with a quick turn of his wrist. Impulsively, I step back, allowing him to lead. I pray there are no more questions about kissing.

With only the glow of faint candlelight to light the way, the house seems like something out of an Untouchable fairytale. Walls made of marble hold small enclaves at every corner. The gods of plenty, Wealth, Prosperity, and Health, are all labeled accordingly. Hugganoffs have followed them for eternity. I was forced to study them at school, though I spent the time imagining ways of subduing them.

False gods. Idolatry.

Forbidden.

When I dare peer closer, there isn't one idol occupying any enclave.

Just empty niches in the walls with pointless titles.

Strange. An Untouchable home without protection.

I finger one enclave suspiciously, thinking perhaps it's a trick, and find a bit of dust clinging to my finger. My eyesight hasn't failed me. Not one deity of deception occupies his throne. Instead, the small candles my people use for the end-of-the-week blessing as we take our day of rest lie about. By the looks of it, there are enough for months.

Not sure what to make of any of this, I turn around. The house is crammed full of works of art. I squint at one painting of the sea and a field bursting with flowers. Nothing depicting debauchery of any sort.

My shoulders relax.

Taking his time, Ezra guides me through the corridor, allowing me to process the house. Every door has been flung open as if to say, 'I have no secrets, come take a peek.' I frown. This was also planned. Every aspect of today was calculated to the smallest detail: my dress, which I still wear, the ceremony, and now this. His home, with too many rooms to count, prods me to trust him, to forget everything I know and to believe that he's the exception to the rule.

I dig my nails hard into my palm so that I don't forget exactly who he is.

Gliding smoothly out a glass door, he lingers in front of an enclosed balcony over-looking the massive cliffs. The clouds covering the moon lift on cue. Moonbeams glisten through stained-glass windows, illuminating every pathway in waves of muted light.

He turns his back to the wonderment, his gaze fixed on me. It takes everything in me not to step closer and inhale the sea and float away.

"Take all the time you need."

I stop my reverie to focus on Ezra, who's as much a mystery as when I first laid eyes on him. I scrutinize every detail: his broad shoulders, his tilted head with a halo of blond hair that needs to be trimmed, if not cut. Outcast men never wear their hair like barbarians.

"Your hair's too long," I say without thinking.

He smiles, turning his gaze toward the sea before chuckling. "You should cut it, then."

I gasp at the fact that he would arm me with a pair of sheers. As if having no clue who I really am, he strides casually to my side. I turn to what appears to be the living room and try not to gawk at all the marvels: fine furnishings, marble stairs, windows with screens and drapes, and thick carpets. A rich man's home.

My home.

Every inch of it screams one word. *Untouchable.*

And I know one thing: I do not belong in this house with these things or this man who thinks I should cut his hair.

He hovers closer, startling me. "You don't like my hair?"

I shake my head, then remember how I wondered how it might feel. Soft and silky, probably, like rose petals.

Ashamed of my wayward thoughts, I lower my gaze. "I don't know."

It's a half lie. And considering everything I've gone through, it's allowed. Part of me still expects to wake up from this dream where I live in a mansion. None of this can be real. Not for the girl everyone calls 'Neliem.'

"It's a lot to take on, at first. But you'll get used to it." He steps closer so that I catch a glimpse of his bashful smile. "I did."

His fingers reach for me, lingering dangerously close to my arm. I know what he wants, for me to grasp his hand and feel his pulse, which I could now probably identify easily. It takes me a moment to realize that I've been tracking his pulse like I would an animal I found injured in the woods. It seems familiar, the steady beat of his heart, the way his Adam's apple bobs and his throat constricts. I'm not sure when I started noticing; perhaps in the carriage. His gaze lifts upstairs just as his breath catches. Instantly, I realize why. The bedroom must be upstairs.

A rush of adrenaline sweeps through me, shaking me momentarily off balance. Everything's happening too fast. It's too dark to get my bearings. And I've lost my nail. That was inexcusable. Ezra's touch startles me, guiding me slowly upstairs as if I were blind and in need of help. As we move through a hallway adorned with several sculptures that I can't distinguish, I stop to stare at one that looks like a mother holding a child. Ezra tugs at me urgently, and although I can't read the expression on his face, I don't have to. His heart hammers harder, a bead of sweat escaping behind his ear.

Before me, wide open double doors reveal a bedroom.

My stomach falls.

The bed is enormous. Outside, the cool sea breeze drifts through the French doors, the moon full and high and much brighter than before.

My feet, like lead, are too heavy to move. The bed stares at me, taunting me. It could fit twelve people, though I don't think that is Ezra's intention. In this case, this bed is only meant for one skinny girl with an enamored suitor.

53

I stammer, for the first time in my life too afraid to act. This is it. What my mother and aunts have been warning me about since my first blood. Husband and wife relations.

But even now, I refuse to whimper like a coward. Instead, I focus out the open patio doors to a balcony that leads to the sea, where I might possibly find refuge. I step cautiously outside, counting the steps to the ledge. The crisp air sprays a faint wave of seawater, and I wonder how much rope it would take to scale the walls to freedom. I close my eyes and breathe it in, cursing myself for not eating enough.

Days ago, marriage had been but a dream that had evaded me. Now, I've transformed from a discarded spinster to the betrothed in less than a blink of an eye. I think of the school matron's pale face, the plastered smiles, the blatant looks of scorn. They thought nothing of me.

Neliem gnaws.

Ezra approaches hesitantly, almost missing a step. It's as if I am some wild animal he strives to tame and make domestic. Perhaps this is all I really am for him. A challenge.

He steps closer still, and I can hear his tiny inhales and steady exhales, as if he was falling asleep. I think of a baby in a basket, slumbering sweetly. The thought relaxes me, so much so that I barely register the touch of his fingers trailing down my arm, guiding me back inside.

He lets go of my hand only for as long as it takes to close the patio doors and return to my side.

Instead of resuming his previous position, he sits on the edge of the bed. "Are you hungry?"

I shake my head, lying again. "No."

"There's fruit in the bowl." He motions before taking off his shoes. "I would have someone bring you up a tray, but," he sighs, "I've let the staff off for the evening."

He says the last part too casually, as if it wasn't of any consequence. There can be only one reason the staff is gone. No witnesses to hear my screams for mercy while I fight him off.

"Is that right?" My voice manages to find that edge that I'm so famous for. I flex my fingers, but when he approaches, he sticks an apple in my palm.

I stare at the fruit, my hunger getting the better of me. I take a bite. It's so sweet I might be biting into candy. I take another bite and before I know it, the apple is down to a thin core.

"Thank you."

He nods and returns to the bed with a raised eyebrow. He knew I was lying about not being hungry. So, he's not as stupid as he looks. And I suspect under all those rich man clothes, he's extremely fit. I was mistaken before when I underestimated his strength. He's no gazelle, he's more like a lion. Which means he's fast. Attempting to subdue him might not work.

But I am also strong. Fit and cunning. Give me a dagger, and he might be a worthy opponent, not someone who goes running to his mother with the slightest cut dripping blood.

I'm so engrossed at the thought of spilling blood that I almost don't hear him when he begins to speak. "I went back to your school last year for a few weeks." He waits for me to say something. When I remain silent, he lets out a small moan, his neck sagging. "You probably don't remember."

The look on his face is one of sheer defeat. Either he was expecting something to happen or he didn't take into account something crucial. Once again, his remarks have caught me off guard. And I realize two things at once. He might be strong, but something at the very core of his foundation is frail. Breakable. Two very conflicting parts of his personality.

"I don't talk to … Untouchables." My tongue catches at the last word.

His face jerks up. "You must never use that word here. Understood?"

The alarm behind his words piques my interest. "Why? That's what you are."

Getting up, he shuts the blinds on the furthest window. "We don't call ourselves that. Only your people do. It's a dead giveaway."

"Because I'm no longer Outcast." My throat dries.

"In two weeks, you won't be." He's thinking how the priest wouldn't process the paperwork, offering an easy out.

The thought makes me sick. "How can that be?"

I steal a quick glance. He stands there, the master of his own fate, never knowing a moment's worth of pain or suffering. Fed, praised for accomplishing nothing, and arrogant to boot. Nothing like me. Which begs an answer to the one question plaguing me since he first offered his hand.

Why me?

Reading my thoughts, he answers, "You're the same as me. No different."

He pauses long enough to gauge my reaction.

Except what he says isn't true and never will be. We're absolutely nothing alike. Not only in looks, but in the fact that his ancestors came from some brilliant cloud in the sky and trampled all over the earth searching for the nectar of the gods. Not finding it, they instead chose to oppress my people and anyone else they came into contact with. My people never descended from a cloud. But there was a cloud, one they not-so-wisely chose to spend forty years following in a desert in search of some promised land. Regretfully, they later found themselves scattered like lost sheep, and a small remnant made their way to the island of Madera.

Some promised land. Starvation and servanthood. And countless Untouchables.

Ezra sits down and waits for some reaction. Maybe he thinks that I should be grateful. But nothing could be further from the truth. All I want is to go home and forget this ever happened. My mother, I hope, will not cast me out.

"You are the same as me," he repeats before tilting his head toward the glistening moonlight as if debating something crucial. When he looks back up, that spark of energy between us flares. The one I can't place. His voice strains, "Anyone who says differently will have to contend with me, and my family."

To stress his point, Ezra yanks off his socks, tossing them carelessly aside. One hits a chair, the other falls on the floor. Appalled, I stare at his careless act. My mother would've pulled my hair if I'd dared such an act of disobedience.

I openly glare at him, wondering if he can detect my scorn in this dim light. I also wonder if he has any clue to the depth of my hatred for him and his people, although he can't possibly understand, or he wouldn't be sitting right before me completely unarmed. There's not even anyone to come to his aid when I stab him with the scissors, he so confidently thinks I should use to cut his hair.

My feet move closer. "Why did you pick me?"

Before I throw him off the balcony, I need to know the answer.

"It's a long story." He rubs his eyes, unaware that each breath brings me closer to my target.

"I have time."

He abruptly shakes his head and stands. "You're not ready to hear it."

Even in bare feet, he looms over me. My head barely reaches his chest. Taken aback, I stammer, "When then?"

It comes off too soft, as if I'm asking for permission. Quickly, I realize my mistake. I lost my advantage the moment he stood up.

"Soon." His lips curl, his voice gentle like the breeze. "Trust your feelings, Oriana …"

He speaks in riddles. I trust no one. This means he has no clue what I'm capable of. One simple thrust to his chest and a head bump and he'd be unconscious for the better part of the day. By the time his servants found him, I'd be long gone.

I smile sweetly, edging closer. Without warning, Ezra unbuttons the top two buttons of his shirt and gazes longingly at me. My focus shifts to the tiny cluster of curly hairs on his chest. Skillfully, I crack my knuckles, reminding myself to be careful not to get tangled in the shirt when I rip it off him to tie up his hands.

For a second, I debate which way will be the most painless. The thought stuns me. Never have I wished not to inflict the maximum amount of harm on an Untouchable.

My temples throb. Rubbing them, I try to stare anywhere but into his eyes, but it's no use. Something about Ezra troubles me. It takes me a moment to figure it out. An annoying question causes me to betray my thoughts. "Why did you come back to the village school last year?"

"I thought it was obvious." He sighs, then laughs. "To see you again."

I stop. See me again? My scalp prickles like I've fallen in a thistle patch. The sensation spreads down my neck. This fool speaks in too many riddles. And he's lying. Before today, we'd never spoken.

Ezra casually collects his shoes and socks and stands by the patio doors in deep contemplation. I don't make my move. It's the perfect opportunity. His back faces me, and there are no witnesses. He's unarmed and distracted.

My feet feel as though they're encased in cement. As it is, I can barely manage to move my hands. The way I'm panting, anyone could hear my breathing from four rooms away. This is all wrong.

I can't hurt him.

It's not like before when I was hunted. That was self-defense. The most alarming thought yet crosses my mind. He's Untouchable, yet he doesn't wish me harm.

Impossible.

The fist I've been clenching relaxes. I take a step back, wanting to run, to escape this mayhem of confusion.

I need to get home. Now. And never look back.

He moves swiftly. All grace and perfection. I'm so distracted by his stride that it takes me a moment too long to notice that the door closes and he's facing me. And with it, my chance to escape is narrowly missed.

I wince. "Why am I here?"

"I … " He stops, tilting his head in that way that means he's not sure how to answer. He does it a lot. Or perhaps, it's only with me that he's not sure how to speak. He had no difficulty ordering his cousins about, or the ferryman who demanded six coins to ensure the wrath of sea gods didn't drown us. His eyes burn into mine like candles. It makes me shake in a way I never once have before. Not in anger, not in hatred. Something else. Something worse.

"Who kissed you?" His voice has lost some of its sweetness. The timbre is definitely darker and slightly intimidating.

I take a precautionary step back, feeling the heat intensify. It's a game. By asking me this, he wants control, which I'll never give.

I force out a laugh. "An Untouchable; jealous? Who would have thought?"

With effort, Ezra maintains his stance, the muscles in his arms flinching. I can tell by the way little beads of sweat glisten against his temples that I've crossed one of his lines. He steps alarmingly closer, his eyes blazing. "I've told you not to use that word. And I'm still waiting for your answer, Oriana."

The way he says my name shows he's serious. Good. He's not all sweet smiles and longing looks. That he actually cares about the boy from my half dream who once kissed me makes it all the more intriguing.

"Who is he?" This time, his eyebrow arches in a way that some people might find menacing. Or attractive.

"I …" For some unexplainable reason, the memory's too painful to speak of. Too raw. I squeeze my eyes shut, praying that the tears don't spill, knowing the truth that I've denied for so long. It wasn't a dream. It wasn't a dream. It was so bittersweet, so real. And so unbearably painful.

The apple churns in my stomach like sour milk. I stumble backward against the bed and sit down, trying to steady my breath.

"An …" His voice breaks. "An Outcast boy?'

He seems just as upset to say the word as I am to hear it. Outcast. That's what this all amounts to. No matter what's written on any piece of paper, I will always be Outcast.

Not wanting to give him the satisfaction of seeing how upset he's made me, I shake my head furiously.

"A relative … someone you've known forever? One of those pale, skinny boys scared of his own shadow?"

He's just described Jerris and Rathe to a tee.

I glare at him, ignoring the sting in my eyes, and steady my voice. "No. Nothing like that."

He waits like a king on his throne. Majestic and all powerful. The last bit of strength deserts my body. This Untouchable has this uncanny ability to make me suddenly weak and sniveling. Next, I'll be whimpering like a dog begging for scraps. For this and so much more, I should kill him.

And I won't need a weapon. My hands will do just fine. I flex a muscle, prepared to strike. "Are you through?"

He's ten paces away from two sharp edges. And there's always the balcony. People who say stupid things have been known to crack their skulls against marble when they slip.

A trace of a smile crosses his mouth. "No. But it's late." He sweeps away from the wall. "And I've upset you which is … unforgivable."

The sorrow that pours from his eyes is no show. And it can't be just for my benefit. The emotion he bears has but one name. Empathy.

My mouth drops. "He's dead, the boy … he died during the fever season."

"Are you positive?" It's as if he's pouring salt on my open wound, on what is left of my shivering heart.

I cringe; not wanting to confess the extent of my obsession of finding the boy I've convinced myself for too long never existed. After I'd miraculously healed from the fever, I went half mad looking everywhere for him. Like a maniac, I searched in every room, every closet, and under every desk at the schoolhouse for any indication as to where he might've gone. Then I took it one step further. Dressed like Neliem himself, I snuck at the crack of dawn into the Untouchable section of town, which we are forbidden to enter. I scourged the marketplace, the temples of their false gods, the fields, the hills, our cave, any place I could think of, going as far as to risk my own life for weeks to find him. Just for the chance to see him and touch him again, I would've done anything. Me, who hated to be touched, ached for this boy the way a dying man aches for water in the desert.

And even now, after all this time, I can't as much as whisper his name. It will destroy me to utter that name again. The name I buried so deep in my soul that even I can't find a way to retrieve it.

"I went to the Dean of schools ..."

"You went to the Dean of schools?" There's marked disbelief in his voice. And I know why. He must know what it means for an Outcast to approach the Dean. The well-used whip covered in our blood is proof enough of that.

I brush a tear that's leaked out of the corner of my eye and push the truth out. "He died. I looked everywhere."

Ezra's eyes never leave mine. Something unspoken is furrowed in his brow.

I don't have the words to explain how, once, a very fat boy with warts and kinky hair held my heart completely. That once, in my dreams, there was no Outcast and no Untouchable. That through the hate and disease that contaminated every inch of Madera, we, two children, found each other. And it was perfect.

Until it was not.

The dead burned for days. Their ashes filled the air.

Ezra's shoes drop on the marble floor, and he steps closer. But I can't fight him. Not now. My anger's all but wiped away, leaving only the scared girl who nearly died from fever so long ago. The girl who would be buried in some unmarked grave if it hadn't been for an Untouchable boy who saved her at the cost of his own life.

Just thinking how I survived and at what price makes me so ill that I barely have the strength to sit upright and look him in the eye.

Dropping to his knees, he carefully extends his hand. It's like watching someone reaching out to a rabid dog. With graceful calm, he moves his hand over my fist, unclenches it, and places a small object in my palm.

It takes me a moment to realize what it is.

My nail. The one I dropped.

I stare at it, dumbfounded, unable to move.

Softer than a feather, he whispers a kiss that feels like a prayer across my temple. "Goodnight, Oriana."

And once again, I'm struck speechless. My heart races wild, my blood pulsating so fast that a tidal wave of emotion rises.

When he reaches the door, an old, familiar pain awakens. Hot and sweaty, like the time the inferno burned in my chest. But this time, it's far worse. Without realizing it, Ezra's dug up my past. And with no barrier, it festers hotter than the blistering sun. An old wound that never completely healed because it couldn't.

Because I wouldn't let it.

From the pit of my gut, I speak in a strange voice, "Za-Za."

He turns abruptly, his shoulders nearly touching his ears. The blood rushes to my head as I lower my eyes and confess, "His name was Za-Za. The boy who died, the one who kissed me. And," my throat burns with acid, "he wasn't Outcast."

Unable to face him, I crawl up to my enormous bed and fall into the cushions, praying for a quick death. Even a slow, agonizing death would be better than this.

I'm sobbing so hard into my pillow that I don't hear the door closing.

If someone had told me that this is how I would spend my first night betrothed, I would've laughed. Right after I kicked them in the gut and made them vomit out their lunch.

I wander listlessly in the upstairs den, which is different than the dining area and the main living room, which are reserved for entertaining important guests, such as diplomats, politicians or the occasional curious relative desiring to take a closer look at the newest addition to the family. As it is, those rooms don't get much use. Other than Landis, no one calls or visits, and no brightly-wrapped packages arrive at the door.

Not that I wait for them.

For the few days following Outcast weddings, people call and bring all sorts of special foods and gifts. Compared to Hugganoff standards, nothing spectacular or lavish. A simple token; a wedge of cheese or perhaps some spices or good cloth to sew. Once, our neighbor's daughter received two yards of the prettiest lace and a small goat.

I had fingered the lace obsessively, inquiring to what use she would put it.

The betrothed girl, Zinnia, thought she would make a baby christening gown, which made me even greener with envy. "Not that you, Oriana, will ever have to fret over such things."

She meant it as a taunt. Because even back then, everyone knew that no one would ever pick me. I wept for a full night in my pillow, letting her words poison me. But the following season, there was no baby gown made from the fine lace. She died a painful death during childbirth, with neither mother nor child surviving.

The lace was later sold to a merchant visiting from another town, then turned to hem several dresses, which, when they got old, were ripped out and made into curtains. The very same curtains that covered my own cracked windows back home.

The story reminds me that nothing is always as it seems. There are countless roads and paths which could easily alter the course of someone's life. Now, I do not live on the island of Madera, in the town of Anaith. Instead, I live in a lavish home in Playa Del Sol fit for twenty. A staff of four women tend to my every whim, as well as a cook, and a girl who does the dirty work that five able-bodied women, with plenty of time on their hands, cannot manage to do.

And there is more food here than I have ever seen in my life. I could eat for days and still not have my fill of all the desserts and pastries and fish and roasted chicken. As children, we were taught to eat quickly, without even bothering to taste the food lest someone steal it right out of our mouths. Here, it is different. Food is to be enjoyed. First stared at, then sniffed, then rolled around on your tongue. Only if it is deemed worthy is it allowed entry down our throats. An insane notion, but nonetheless the way it is done.

Neliem grumbles and reminds me that there is more to life than a full belly. The need for strength and speed counter years of near starvation. I count my bites and swallow slowly, trying not to appear too eager.

Instead, I study my new prison.

Other than the household help, there is also a very large groomsman, though I'm not exactly sure what he does, and a driver, the same one who picked us up at the ferry. Additionally, two boys work in the stables who reek of sweat and horse and sometimes fresh dung. They don't look anything like Hugganoffs. With their dark features and strangely alluring pitch-black eyes, they seem out of place in this world of tall, blond gods. They are definitely not Untouchable, causing me to think that they're perhaps the natives of these islands. The ones long subdued by Ezra's people. I had thought the original inhabitants long wiped out, but like my own, a remnant seems to have survived.

What bothers me most is that I can't get their names straight to save my life. All I manage to remember is that Elsie is the cook, Ralio, the driver. There's also Sasha, my handmaid, who has yet to lift her head to look me in the eyes. Ralio likes his wine red and strong and, some evenings, breaks into song for no apparent reason. I like him immensely.

Due to my sudden elevation in stature, I've had fourteen dresses commissioned to be designed for me to wear. An unheard-of luxury. Four are to arrive early tomorrow morning with the prestigious Señor Frantango, a designer like no other who travels with not one, but two assistants at his beck and call. I've overheard that he prefers his wine red and chilled to perfection and has the nasty habit of snapping his fingers. All his designs are original works of art; masterpieces. And no two women in Perla Del Mar, where I now live, will ever be dressed alike, if he has any say about it.

Ezra, who has spent little time with me since the first night, was once again called upon to attend to urgent business in the morning. After dinner, he made his excuses with only a chaste kiss to my forehead and a firm but too brief squeeze to my hand, which still aches for the cool steel of my dagger. For the first time since I set eyes on him, I wanted him to stay.

For days now, his ritual of planting the softest kiss on various parts of my face, holding my hand, and sometimes offering an awkward squeeze has felt more than sufficient. Like water dripping from a ladle, the impulse to lash out and throw something at him has all but trickled away. A minor miracle.

But tonight, for some unexplainable reason, I feel adventurous enough to sneak into his room, just to see if I can. There's a lock on his door that a child of five could master within seconds. So, the challenge is not to just get inside and investigate, but to pretend that the door had been left ajar.

Much to my disappointment, not only does he not register that I've entered his rooms, he makes no indication that he even cares who might wander inside. His back straight, he sits on the bed going over papers and absentmindedly unbuttoning his shirt. Holding my breath, I tell myself I just want to see how long it will take for Ezra to figure out I'm peeking.

Part of being Neliem is knowing how to still your heartbeat so that your enemies might think you're dead. A small gasp escapes my throat, however, as yet another button pops open, followed by three more.

Transfixed, I watch as his fingers glide effortlessly, a strange quiver pulsating below my waist. The truth is that I have never once seen a man with his shirt off. My mother always rejected my assistance when men came to get sized for suits or shirts. Instead, I was sent to do backbreaking work like milking the neighbor's goat or feeding chickens before hauling countless buckets of water back home.

Anyway, all those men were old and flabby with flesh that hung like drapes.

Nothing like Ezra.

The moment his shirt falls to the floor, his perfect tight abs revealed, I moan. It's a stupid move unworthy of Neliem. It happens so fast that I have to pretend I wasn't spying. I stroll in casually and try batting my eyes the way those silly Untouchable girls do.

"I was wondering ..." I stop dead at the threshold to his bedchambers, my jaw dropping. Up close, he's even more attractive. His face is tanned and chiseled like one of his statues. The heat spreading from my face down my neck is no act.

The scoundrel doesn't even try to cover himself. Instead, he throws a towel over some picture on his end table and moves toward me, a mischievous smirk forming on his lips. "Yes, Oriana, what can I help you with?"

I scramble to think of something. "I wish to go to town

tomorrow … after my fitting, may I borrow some money?" As soon as the words are out of my mouth, dread washes over me. I'd wished to keep this secret to myself for the time being.

He eyes me suspiciously. "We have credit at most shops … and you don't have to borrow it. It's yours, whatever you need."

I'm positive that Ezra wouldn't be happy what I intend to use the money for. I quickly counter with, "I wish to see what the street vendors have to offer …"

"I should go with you then. But I won't be back until late."

"As you wish. I just wanted to see the city a bit and have a look around." My only goal now is to leave quickly and hope he forgets the entire ordeal by morning.

I haven't so much as taken two steps when he closes the distance between us, breathless.

"Are thirty coins enough?"

I freeze in my tracks. Are thirty coins enough? That's more than my mother makes in five months of working her fingers to the bone through all hours of the night.

Positive that he's jesting, I take a step closer. Allowing my gaze to linger on his chest in the most inappropriate way, I whisper, "Yes, I think so."

His gaze drifts from my feet to my face, scrutinizing every inch of me. His fingers trail a hot path from behind my ear to my shoulder in one move. "I think you're up to something."

Ezra doesn't seem upset. If anything, he studies me as if I was some rare, exotic bird that he has never seen before.

I purse my lips. "Ezra, I'm always up to something."

"Is that right?" He leans dangerously closer; so much so that I can almost taste that familiar scent in his hair. So delicate and fragrant, but I'm still not sure exactly what it is. It smells like rain and something else. Something that makes my heart skip a beat.

Like a wave, it hits me.

Ezra smells like the sea.

I stammer, "You smell like the sea."

The corners of his lips lift. "Like rotten fish."

"No." Nothing like rotten fish.

He sniffs my hair. "Squid?"

Our noses nearly touch. I shake my head, holding his gaze, knowing what this is. A contest to see who would blink first.

There's just something about him tonight. Ezra is beautiful, granted; anyone with two eyes could see that. But now, with the taste of salt in the air and faint candlelight casting shadows, his soft eyes illuminate brighter. Heat travels all the way to my toes despite the cold draft in the room.

His neck scoops down like an eagle, but he holds back. I follow his eyes to see my small hand between us. A stop signal.

My breath hitches up in my throat.

He'd stopped because I'd wanted him to.

Without thinking, I step on my tiptoes and kiss him, barely brushing my lips against his scratchy cheek. When I start to pull back, his hands lace around my waist, pressing me against his chest. Excitement spreads in the pit of my belly, every sense heightening. A servant climbs the stairs, taking her time to lift each foot, and horse stalls are being mucked, sending fragments of hay and hair traveling in the air.

And yet, standing in front of me, Ezra waits for some signal. His jaw is clenched tight, as if he's using every ounce of strength to hold back. Then the energy between us shifts, electrifying. Tempting fate, he exhales, taking the smallest step closer.

He caresses his hand over my face, as if committing it to memory. And then, just when I'm sure he'll let me go, discard me as not worthy, he lifts me in his arms, his lips grazing my neck, inhaling every inch of me.

"You smell like a field in springtime, like wheat and rain and sunlight."

No one has ever described me like that before. Springtime.

It's the most exhilarating and terrifying sensation. His face moves perfectly over my head, breathing me in. The most insane thing about this moment is that, instead of plotting my escape or attack, I want more. For the second time in my life, I want to be kissed and held and loved.

Unexpectedly, out of the corner of my eye, I see servant appear. I'm not sure who. Startled, she drops the towels and falls backward, hitting her head hard against the wall.

Ezra snarls like a lion, "And what does a locked door signify?"

She rushes away, leaving the towels, and I can't help it. I giggle. I'd been the culprit who'd unlocked the door.

"I think you scared her." My hand tangles in his sweaty hair.

The tension leaves his face, and he smiles, nuzzling closer. Slowly, deliberately, his soft lips find my cheek.

I close my eyes reflexively.

He abruptly stops. "Why did you close your eyes, Oriana?" Answering his own question, he continues, "You're thinking about that boy, aren't you?"

My eyes snap open, the lie easy on my tongue. "It was a long time ago, Ezra ..."

He takes a small step away, rubbing his temples.

"I mean," he stammers, "it wasn't wrong to care about him ..."

He searches my face for an indication of what I'm thinking. But I can't explain why Za-Za is so important to me, even now, after all this time.

"He was my ..." A lump forms in my throat.

"How is it that you loved him so much that even now you can't ..." He inches closer, and I dart back. Without meaning to, Ezra has dug up my past. A past best left buried. Blood pulsates near the surface of my wound, threatening to erupt at any moment.

I have to leave before I start crying again. It all comes back to Za-Za, the boy I can't have who still owns my heart. And perhaps even more.

"I'm tired, Ezra. I need to go to bed."

His hand finds mine. "Stay in my bed tonight. Please; I swear I won't touch you."

"I must look a mess." I turn away as my hand finds the doorknob.

"No." Sorrow pierces his voice. "Never have you looked more beautiful."

My hand trembles as I close the door.

That night. I dream of wind and rain and dark stormy clouds. I dream of butterfly wings, fluttering slower and slower until they stop beating, and of two children, doomed never to see the sun.

My very first thought when I open my eyes is of Ezra. I wish he had waited to leave until I got up, so we could discuss what had happened, or rather what hadn't happened, last night. The poor servant girl is missing. No sign of her. When I finally get downstairs, I can't help but feel a twinge of guilt over her poor timing. It had been my fault for unlocking his door.

If it hadn't been for her intrusion something definitely would have happened between us. Was he angry, frustrated, or worse? Was he debating sending me back home without a second thought? There's still time. Eleven days.

The most troubling thought is that I'm not sure which would be worse. Staying here with Untouchables or being sent home in disgrace to face my mother and a sound beating.

The servant girl whose name I can never remember, Velaria, appears without warning. I thought for sure she had been fired after last night. I'm not sure how she sneaks up on me so suddenly; either I'm getting lax in my stealth skills, or she's part phantom. Either way,

I need to keep my eyes open around her.

I narrow my eyes into slits and ignore the breakfast before me, which has gone cold. Velaria's face is freshly washed, but I detect a slight puffiness around her eyes and nose, indicating that she cried herself to sleep.

She steps forward and bows, her voice hoarse, "The dresses are here. Whenever you're ready, my lady."

I'm not in the mood for dresses or ribbons or lace. Anxiety builds in my gut, and I know why. I've stopped my training and found my belly soft for the first time in my life this morning. Reluctantly, I abandon breakfast, stuffing two rolls in my pocket, and stride into the parlor to inspect what Ezra has spent a minor fortune on.

Namely, disguising me to pass as Untouchable.

Frantango and his dressers wait patiently in the smaller receiving room for me to finish my morning tea so that I might marvel over his accomplishments and compliment him ceaselessly. On close inspection, two of the dresses are passable, the stitching not up to my mother's high standards but good considering the rush order. But the other two are plainly hideous. A different patch of inferior material has been attached to the bottom of one of them, as if I wouldn't notice. Far worse is the last dress, which gives me the chills. Based on what my mother worked on previously, it's something from last year's style with too much lace, which doesn't complement the trim. And the fabric's faded.

"These two are fine, not excellent by any means, but passable. These two are an insult."

I toss them aside as if they smelled of spoiled egg. The highly-paid tailor frets, glaring at his assistants as if they're to blame for his sloppy workmanship. They might have been the ones sewing until the dawn's first light, but he's the one in charge.

"And I would suggest, Señor Frantango, that if you wish to be employed by us, you consider this a warning. Your motto states no two women will be dressed alike. So, never bring me some leftover dresses as if I work at a fish shop and don't know the difference."

Not waiting for his reaction, I turn heel and leave him with his mouth hanging. Elsie, the cook, and the other staff have overheard, no doubt, and are wondering exactly who Ezra has brought home to be his wife.

I think of one word. Neliem. That's who.

Velaria bows respectfully, holding a small knapsack containing the coins I requested last night. "Master Ezra left this for you."

I weigh the sack in my hand. Thirty gold coins. Exactly what I needed. My fingers twitch, eager for some diversion from this tedious morning of inspecting frocks.

Velaria's bulging eyes widen, her voice hitching, "Would the lady of the house be in need of anything else?"

I nod. "Yes, as a matter of fact, I would. Bring me every sharp knife you can find."

Velaria's face turns white. "And why would you be in need of knives, my lady?"

I am already unbuttoning my dress as I climb the stairs toward Ezra's bedroom in search of a pair of loose-fitting trousers and a shirt he wouldn't mind gaining a slight tear or two in.

Without stopping, I call out, "I need to do some target practice."

On the bumpy ride to town, I find myself more anxious than I ought to be. The soles of my new boots tap anxiously and my gloved hands, smelling of lavender, can find no rest. Even in my newly-fitted gown that makes me look like an Untouchable, Neliem's wiggling to be set free and do something daring and unpredictable.

The target practice was exhilarating, but it didn't come close to releasing the built-up tension from last night. I practiced several times with the knives, suspecting that Elsie was holding back on me. Surely a man of Ezra's wealth and power is in possession of more than ten butcher knives.

But regardless, I hit the haystacks head on and dislodged all ten bottles the stable boys kept posting for me. They scurried around like kitchen rats, cheering wildly with each blow.

One even asked me to hit an apple off his head. I hesitated when I saw the color drain from Elsie's face, and promised the ambitious boy that we would try later, away from prying eyes.

The coach comes to a halt in the middle of a cobblestone courtyard surrounded by small shops bursting with wares. Coffee and spices and bronze pots and pans and fancy bonnets and dresses. Oh my, the dresses, in creams and peaches and pinks, in silks and satins with matching parasols. Marveling at all the sights, I fling the carriage doors open, not waiting for Ralio to help me down.

He rushes ahead, waving his arms as if I've overstepped myself by simply opening my own carriage door and taking two steps unassisted. Although he doesn't do much other than eat and drink and sing, when he drives, he seems to take it seriously, especially when it comes to my safety. I sadly suspect that it has something to do with Ezra's orders.

Ignoring him, I point to the closest shop, just ten steps away. "I will be in there for an hour."

He scrutinizes the tacky jewelry shop with a lifted brow. "An hour?"

The pungent stench of bitter herbs turns our attention down the alleyway, where strange fumes funnel through the entry of a darkened shop. His eyes bulging, he crosses himself over and over.

"I have no interest in sorcery." I hand him a coin and try to sound as innocent as possible. "Have a drink; I don't need you to accompany me. If the packages are too big, I'll send word for you."

And I smile. The one I've been practicing in the mirror. I almost have it.

He nods toward the tavern across from the shop. "I'll have one glass and check up on you."

"Thank you, Ralio." I scurry away before he changes his mind, knowing one thing for certain. One glass translates to two bottles for Ralio. With such a diversion, I'll have ample time to do what I need and be back in time to help him up the carriage and drive us both home.

Trying to steady my steps and not appear too eager, I approach the shop, remembering to turn around and wave. He narrows his eyes, probably thinking about my earlier target practice and wondering what else I might have up my sleeve.

Hurrying inside, I approach the saleslady and buy the first thing I see: a scarf sewn with glittering gems. I have it placed on hold and give her instructions on where to have it sent before asking a slew of my own questions. Namely, I need to know how to get to where I'm going and be back in time to avoid rousing suspicion.

The salesgirl's the friendly sort. She smiles a bit too much, trying to get me to buy more frivolous items that I have absolutely no use for. At the mention of my new last name, which still feels funny on my lips, she nearly stammers, then collects herself, clutching her heart. Without asking, she takes me on a guided tour of the shop, taking special care to dwell on a glass case containing overpriced jewelry. The only thing that catches my attention is a jewel-encrusted dagger.

"That one."

"Rubies ... "

I have no use for rubies as she unlocks the glass drawer displaying the dagger, which turns out to be only for show. Its blade is dull and too heavy to be of any practical use.

I frown. "Don't you have anything sharper, with no stones?"

Her forehead creases as she redirects me to some costly rings. No matter how flowery her speech, I keep reminding myself if she had met me a week ago, she personally would've tossed me on my rear outside before flinging dirty bathwater to teach me a lesson.

I practice my smile, finally getting the information I need.

Without wasting a second, I race out the back and slip through the alley, pressing my sleeve over my nose not to inhale the foul stench. Carefully following the salesgirl's directions, I cross down two streets and pass a naked statue of a man eating what appears to be a tree. Then I stop. I need to cross the town square before heading down the ravine near the channel, then make a sharp left.

Easy enough.

But with my bad luck, it's market day. The streets swarm with shoppers and vendors selling all sorts of foods in addition to their usual, worthless trinkets. I count four stalls that specialize in skinning apples before one especially aggressive shopkeeper slams a potato peeler in my face, practically scraping the skin off my nose.

Next, a piece of ripe fruit's jammed before me, so I hasten my step. Forcefully, I wave everyone away and turn a corner to avoid further harassment, only to bump right into none other than Henric's backside. He stands unassumingly outside of a teashop. His back registers that someone has struck him, but for some unexplainable reason, he doesn't bother to glance in my direction.

Without wasting a second, I dart away, hiding behind some coffee crates. His sole focus is on a very pretty girl in the process of scolding him.

She shakes a finger at him. "You can't just do as you please and think it's acceptable. It's disgraceful, and I won't have any of it."

My interest piqued, I press closer and continue to eavesdrop.

Her pretty features stiffen. "I think it best that we don't associate any longer. I will not take your calls or messages, so you might as well stop troubling yourself."

This girl has no qualms speaking her mind. By the look of her uniform, complete with a crisp, carefully ironed apron, she's employed at the teashop.

"This is ridiculous … " Henric's voice breaks, and his fist clenches and loosens. "You know this match was agreed upon due to the family's financial situation. Landis and I were both forced into this."

"My mother informs me that Landis had the courtesy to not cash the dowry."

Startled, Henric steps back, his face flushed. "Confound it girl, it's only for the spicing rights. Would you see us impoverished?"

The girl snaps, "I think perhaps you'll find yourself with two wives, not only one then."

His face reddens, and he starts to protest, but she gives him no opportunity to respond. Instead, she disappears, slamming the servant's entrance door firmly behind her.

But what's even more amazing is that Henric stands there with his jaw dropped, at a complete loss for words. For the first time, he isn't lashing out or taking action. He remains frozen, like an errant schoolboy taking his punishment.

I smile to myself. Whoever this girl is, she has the power to silence Henric, which, given everything I know of him, is a major feat.

But time is ticking.

I scurry back the way I came, collect my bearings, and cut through the main square. I immediately sense that someone is following me. Not closely, but too close for comfort. I literally feel his hot gaze sizing me up as if I were something on display.

Maneuvering far from the old gypsy with a glass eye promising ghostly vengeance against your enemies with no trace brought back to your household, I scurry on ahead.

Luckily, I've been followed, chased, and preyed upon most of my life. I slow my pace a fraction and stop to admire some cheaply-made lace. Carefully, I position myself near a window so I can spot the culprit and size him up.

At first, I think it might be Ralio, the wine not enough temptation for his pallet. But I'm proven wrong when a tall, exquisitely dressed young man also stops to admire some hideous woodwork across from where I stand.

Not Ralio. Not even close.

This man is quite handsome, alarmingly so, and most definitely not in any hurry to pounce. Instead, he takes his time to digest the setting, mood, and climate of this intricate game of cat and mouse he's playing. He seems to take keen interest in my appearance, tilting his head and allowing his eyes to scan every inch of me when he suspects I'm not watching. This man, whoever he might be, is no mere inquisitive shopper. He's dressed too fine and walks with ease, as if he owned the streets. Even while scrutinizing my every step, he's aware of everything around us: the flow of traffic, the more insistent vendors, and the cats pouncing up and down the cobblestones. Nothing escapes his gaze.

A carriage passes, temporarily blocking my view of him. I could easily escape, but for some strange reason, I am too intrigued.

Usually, brutish boys with little imaginations assume incorrectly that they have a chance of catching me. They fail every time, only making bigger fools of themselves for their wasted effort.

But this, this is different. It feels strangely exciting and forbidden in some dark way that I simply cannot resist. I check my timepiece and allow a slow exhale. There's still some time, and the fact remains that I've wasted too many days shut up in a high tower without any diversion whatsoever, and now a seemingly worthy opponent has crossed my crooked path by chance. I think quickly, pausing to straighten my bonnet, catching my reflection in the mirror above the cart.

Thanks to Elsie's cooking, I don't look anything like the half-starving Outcast girl of a week ago. My face is fuller, and my figure is, for the first time, shapely, not flat like a board. Allowing some curls to spill out of my bonnet, I straighten my back, making sure he's watching.

Faking a lisp, I ask the trader what it would cost for a sack of flour. To add to the effect, I suckle on my pinkie finger.

The man startles, now openly staring as he glides closer. Then, catching himself, he steps back, laughing as if thoroughly enjoying himself. A salacious gleam reflects in his eyes from the glass.

Yes, I think, too easy. Not worthy of my time. Two other men, not as nicely dressed, gawk at me openly. Their stare causes a wave of panic all the way down to my gut. I double back, dart into the first shop I spot, and race out the back way.

Undetected, I huddle against the wall and watch the imbeciles scurry in the wrong direction in hopes of catching up with me. Then, making sure the path is clear, I fumble my way back to the direction I was going. The thought that I've wasted precious time wreaks havoc in me. Time is ticking away.

I get to the market, making sure the two brutes are nowhere near, when I nearly slam directly into the good-looking man, my original stalker. I catch his face and put it to memory. With intense blue eyes, he's even better-looking face to face. I hadn't even noticed the handsome mustache before. Steadying my nerves, I pretend that nearly ramming into him is of no consequence.

"Good day, my lady." His voice is as smooth as satin.

"Sir."

I gulp, bow, and briskly away, hoping this is the end of it. But when I turn in the direction of the nearest establishment, his hot glare causes goose pimples to ripple down my arms. Faced with two options, giving up on my secret plan or playing this little game out, I choose quickly.

There's nothing like a little adventure to still my nerves and guarantee a good night's sleep. So, without hesitation, I entice this nameless scoundrel further down an intricate web. No doubt he's unaware that the game has changed, and it is I who will be setting the rules from now on.

With the assurance that I'm like no victim that he's ever encountered, I slow my steps, acting the part of the innocent schoolgirl marveling over the sights of the big city. Without glancing back, I stroll to the front of a vendor selling pagan god statues so he can get a better look at me. Velaria took great pains to fix my hair this morning. Carefully, I loosen the bonnet and allow my hair to unravel. An audible gasp emits from his direction.

From the mirror above the vendor, I spy that he's spinning in my web, inching closer and closer. Then, taking hold of reason, he lingers by a disheveled bookseller desperate to sell him a set of history manuals.

I catch their conversation from my side of the lane.

"This is something every fine young man is in need of."

He gazes inattentively at the fourteen-volume set. "How is that?"

"To read in bed, at night. Countless hours of pleasure."

He raises a skeptical eyebrow. "For pleasure, I have something entirely different in mind."

I stifle a grin; this man doesn't mince his words.

Lingering, I pick up a statue, trying to place its name. I believe it to be one of the Untouchables' fertility gods. They have too many to count. The toothless merchant smiles, holding up one with a maiden with five breasts.

"For a girl, that one, but this one will give you a healthy boy … maybe two."

The price for a boy is nearly doubled than for a mere girl.

I widen my eyes, gasping, "I wish to have three girls … nine months from now. Do you have a statue for that?"

A guffaw erupts loudly behind me. The stranger obviously finds me amusing. Perhaps now he will let me be. The choice to give up his pursuit is ultimately his. But he doesn't waver. He picks up another book and pretends to read, fascinated over a cookbook on the best preparation for all types of beans.

He lifts the book to bookseller. "If I eat these beans, will I be able to impregnate my wife with three daughters?"

I laugh, not bothering to conceal my merriment.

From this angle, my admirer resembles one of the Untouchable gods that they worship in harvest season. I forget the name. He's undoubtedly rich, as well as handsome, and something else. It takes me a full moment to place it. Then his eyes sparkle and I see it clearer than day. That mischievous, naughty side of him, the one that tempts the hand of fate.

I shudder, almost dropping the fertility god statue. The merchant scolds me, taking it back before I can do permanent damage. Admonished, I turn to the next vendor. One selling handwoven mats.

As I finger the intricate pattern, a million thoughts plague my mind. Who is he? Where is he from? But most of all, I marvel over the fact that I've caught his eye, which seems nothing less than preposterous.

Suddenly self-aware, I check my dress to see if there's anything that sets me apart from the other Untouchables frolicking about the square. I brush a spot of dust off my gown and move steadily through the crowd, giving him plenty of opportunities to finally give up his frivolous pursuit. Like the dog he is, he follows.

This stranger undoubtedly wishes to corner me in some deserted alleyway and have his way with me. He doesn't seem in need of robbing me of anything other than my virtue, nor does he seem to want to inflict bodily harm, per se. Seduction seems to seep from every pore of his tall, handsome frame, so consumed with this conquest that he can't see this for what it is. A trap. And it is his undoing. The forbidden notion of having a midday rendezvous has made his mind dull and stupid.

My heart hammers faster, my pulse racing when I stop abruptly in front of a sweetshop and buy an oversized bag of candy. My admirer halts, nearly tripping over his shoes. I smile to myself. This will be easier than I thought.

I tip the boy generously while tucking the small blade he left unattended up my sleeve. The boy's too busy counting his change to notice. I have but seconds to disappear before he lifts his head and detects it missing.

My feet glide quickly over the cobblestones.

The alleyway is off to the right, secluded and dark. And quiet enough to teach this thrill-seeker a lesson that he will not soon be forgetting. Not only will I slice his fine vest in half, I just very well might rob him to compensate for the time he's cost me from my mission.

Delighting in this appropriate punishment for his stalking, I imagine him explaining to his wife how he came about not only losing his purse, but the countless gashes across his fine clothing with every single one of his gold buttons lost. Perhaps I will keep a button as a souvenir of my conquest. Something to treasure in the days to come.

Neliem stirs.

I approach the alley, pretending stupidity. Lifting a piece of paper too close to my face, I pretend to read. This has the desired effect. He inhales sharply, now caught in my web.

Right at my heels, his hot sweet breath directly above my ear, the scoundrel speaks, "Might I, perchance, be of some assistance?"

That's all he manages before I twist around, knife in hand, and throw him against the wall so hard that his hat tumbles into the gutter.

His stunned expression was well worth the cost of buying an overpriced bag of candy. But then he turns the tables on me. With a jerk of his hip my knife falls, clanging to the ground. Like a snake, he twists, reaching with an unfathomable dexterity until I am pinned against the wall. One of his hands is firmly placed against my waist, the other grasping both of my hands above my head.

He leans in, and I see it in his eyes. Something so familiar.

A first.

I blink, concentrate, and go limp. Forcing a quiver to my limbs, he releases just enough. It's all I need. I kick from my side; it's not easy in an expensive dress, but I manage to do the move justice and plant him against the cobblestones with a crashing thud.

Startled, it's his turn to stammer as I launch on him, straddling him with my full weight. Unfortunately, I don't have the knife to do the slashing, but I can still steal his purse. He deserves as much.

I glower pleasantly, the rush exactly what I needed to lift my dark mood. My body awakens at full force.

Neliem.

Then he laughs, amused. "Well, I had hoped to get you in this position but without this fine dress ..." He tilts his face toward the traffic. "And with a bit more privacy."

My cheeks flush, but I keep my concentration and strain my arms against his so that he can't move an inch.

"Oh, my lady, you do not fight fair ..." And he's mocking me. That smile, those lips ...

"You fight like a child ..." I hiss. "A weak, pathetic babe."

He bites his bottom lip in the most irresistible way, which sparks a flame in the pit of my belly. And for the first time, I realize that I'm not sitting on his money purse as I had previously thought. It stirs, then moves again.

Horrified, I get up too fast. Flushed and desperate to never lay eyes on the scoundrel again, I straighten my dress and layered petticoats, glaring toward the traffic. Luckily, we weren't discovered.

I anxiously wait for a break in the foot traffic to return unnoticed, when he dares speak. "Did I miss something?"

He stands so alarmingly close that for a moment, I forget what I was about to say.

"No, go away. Stop following innocent girls through town. Your wife won't like it." I adjust my ruffled collar, trying to hide the blush burning on my face.

"Alas, I am not in possession of a wife." He says this solely for my benefit. This type of man probably has several wives and more children than he can count.

"Well, that's too bad. I think you need one to beat you soundly every night."

He grins like the devil himself.

I turn back toward the street, trying to gather my bearings and figure out what possessed me to play this ridiculous game. But my stalker isn't quite finished. "The knife was clever. For the first time in my life, I admit to letting down my keen stealth abilities."

His fingers reach for my chin, but I scuff him off. Part of me wants to inform him this is what happens when one thinks with an organ other than his brain. But just staring at him makes my knees wobble. My face feels hot and chilly. Slowly, I realize why. My bonnet's missing.

"Go away."

He makes no motion to move. Instead, he stares with eyes that flicker beams of moonlight through me. At a loss, I busy myself with finding my missing bonnet.

"And if given the opportunity," he continues, his eyes burning into me, "I would advise your father not to let his virgin daughter out of his sight for a second. Certainly not in that dress and definitely not with that body."

I find my bonnet in a dirt pile and beat off the dust. I would rather be giving him a sound whipping. "Good day, Sir."

He shakes his head, battling against some unwanted thought. For a moment, he seems much younger. Not the menacing stalker wishing to have his way with me in some dark alley. Checking his timepiece, he sighs, contrite, and his shoulders relax. "Tell me where you need to go. I will make sure that you get there safely."

Adjusting my bonnet, I narrow my eyes, not giving his offer a second thought.

But he doesn't relent. "I swear on all the saints, I won't touch you."

I gasp. Surely, he is jesting. Untouchables have no regard for saints.

"And why should I trust you? You assaulted me."

"If I recall, you held the blade and threw me against the ground. Not that I didn't thoroughly enjoy it." He doesn't bother to hide the smile playing against his lips.

Unamused, I cross my arms and move past him.

In two strides, he pins me against the wall, our noses practically touching, "There were two other, not-so-nice gentlemen following you when I spotted your loveliness across the square. So, it would seem that I am not the only one captivated by your charms. I gave it five minutes until someone raped you. So, I won't ask again; where are you going?"

The forceful way he speaks, combined with that intense flicker in his eyes and his ragged breath, both hot and sweet, makes me believe him. Plus, if he wanted to assault me, he would have done so already.

Somewhat sullen, I relent with a whimper. "I was just going where the Untouchables keep the orphanage."

His eyes blaze, then immediately darken. "What did you say?"

I stammer, losing my ground. His voice is barely above a whisper, but so menacing that I tremble. "The school for the …"

Gripping me fiercely, he huddles me deeper into the alley, his eyes scanning the balconies perched above us in neat rows. He doesn't release his grip, his gaze burrowing into mine for what feels an eternity. Only when he is positive that we are not being overheard does he speak, "What are you?"

When I don't answer, he shakes me. "Tell me now."

His attention shoots up to a balcony where a woman sets her wash on the line. Moving like Neliem himself, he guides me further into the shadows. "Do you have any idea how dangerous it is for you to be here?"

His face loses all color. Gone is the playful man flirting with me just minutes ago. What faces me is something dangerous and feral. My pulse quickens, adrenaline searing through me.

My senses heighten. Water drips from the woman's wash. There are two exits in the alleyway. The way we came and down back, where crates are being hauled off the back of a wagon. And then there's always lunging and scampering through an open balcony door before escaping through an apartment.

But for some unfathomable reason, I'm not scared of this man who holds me with the glare of his eyes and a vise-like grip.

Another wagon approaches. Men's husky voices laughing and joking break the silence as the eerie sensation of spirits close by chills me to the bone. A heavyset brute hovers above the wagon, tossing a crate to a lanky man. "And so, I found an extra passenger trying to cross …"

His cackle sends dread down my spine as a familiar hovers alarmingly close, mimicking his very moves.

"Outcast … typical …" The other signals the driver to continue before hopping back on the wagon. "They fester like rats … worse than rats if you ask me."

"Bet you showed her what happens."

The crate falls, crashing against the slick cobblestones, cracking my nerves as the spirit dissipates into the brute. At once he lashes out, nearly strangling the man who dropped the crate. A struggle ensues, with other spirits entering both men.

My protector wastes no time in guiding me to the other end of the alley. Quickening my step, I digest what this all means. I am in a foreign land surrounded at every possible turn with evil people who enable spirits to harm others. Especially my kind.

Quickly I realize that this isn't a game any longer; I am in real danger. Helplessly, I squirm, looking for a way out, inadvertently pressing against him.

"Because I'm …"

He presses a finger to my lips, his eyes never leaving mine. "Do not say that word here."

His stands protectively over me as if he were holding the key to my salvation. For a moment, an insane thought creeps in my mind: all I need would be to ask, and whatever it was, no matter how impossible, it would be given.

His eyes lift, his stance still looming over me as if shielding me from all unknown enemies. And just then, a wave of relief washes over me, awakening a memory so far back that I can't quite grasp it. A voice murmuring me to sleep, a gentle hand stroking my hair. A glimpse of pale, curly hair. My father. Someone I'd forgotten about completely. Someone once long ago actually protecting me.

A couple passes, and he lowers his face as if we are locked in an intimate embrace. The second they turn the corner, he releases me, but his gaze never shifts.

"I am taking you back to wherever it is that you're staying, and I suggest strongly that whoever brought you here returns you to your home at once. Do you understand?"

I hold my ground, raising my voice. "I'm going to the orphanage first."

To prove my point, I turn to walk away, but he blocks my path, his feet calculating every step. "And why would you do that?"

Lifting my head, I scoot past him and pace ahead, not bothering to answer. He matches my stride, all humor and merriment gone, his body rigid, perceiving everyone as a possible threat.

Emotions stir deep within me. The most pronounced is confusion. Who could this man be? And even more bewildering, why does he even trouble himself to bother? Surely, he must have better things to do than follow an Outcast girl around the city.

I glance up at him thoughtfully. By his dress and manner, he's a product of wealth and privilege. But something else as well. There's something lurking beneath the surface that I can't quite place my finger on.

Against my better judgment, I tell him the truth. "Because once, it was me."

He gives me a quizzical look, undoubtedly seeing only the fine dress and bonnet and styled hair. Not the true me; the girl who has had to fend for herself every day of her life. The one ridiculed for wearing hand-me-downs so worn that you could see my flesh. The girl who ate scraps and went to bed hungry most nights.

"I was that girl, in ..." It hurts to say it, but I feel compelled to share the part of me Ezra would love to hide. "In rags, hit and beaten, poorer than everyone else, who everyone hated ..." I stutter uncontrollably for a second, but force it out, "And then, once, a nice lady in a pink dress and parasol with the prettiest face came and gave me a gold coin."

It feels as if a weight has been lifted from my chest.

I tighten my fist and finish, not daring to watch his expression, which, right now, scorches like hot coals. "That is why I'm going to the school or orphanage or whatever you Un— " I lower my voice, feeling danger lurking around every corner. "You people call it to return the favor."

When I gather the courage to look him in the eye, I prepare myself for scorn in speaking such blasphemy. Perhaps he will toss me aside, or worse, notify the authorities about my true identity. What I don't expect is to find something altogether different: shock.

He drops his hand, and it quivers as his breath catches. His steps are unsteady, so he braces himself against the wall for a moment. My stalker now blinks, the flare in those brilliant eyes dimming before closing altogether.

Outside the ally, fashionably-dressed people stroll, but all I can dwell on is the memory of the kind lady in the pink gown. It is too vivid to have just been imagined. She came three times to the school to pay a visit and make sure that our rooms had all the proper materials and that we were being treated as well as could have been expected. It was during the first three years I attended the schoolhouse. The ones without — . My stomach clenches, and I force the thought out of my head. Instead, I focus on how the gold coin felt in my hand. Heavy, so full of promises. A thousand promises and more. And something else. The lady's kindness had made all the difference to a girl with no father, who went to bed sobbing into her pillow, hungry for much more than merely food.

I take a deep breath. I'm calm on the outside but seething on the inside. I hadn't wanted a soul to know what I intended to do, and now this stranger has somehow forced it out of me. Plus, he knows my secret. The one Ezra warned me too many times to count that could wind up fatal. What I really am under this fine dress and bonnet with matching gloves. Outcast.

But the expression on the man's face doesn't seem violent in the least. And much to my relief, he doesn't seem to be searching for a constable or gathering an angry mob to call me out. If anything, he seems slightly annoyed, and his brow furrows in a way that makes me want to laugh. It takes me a moment before I place it; recognition. And most shocking of all: awe.

He speaks calmly, "There are no Outcasts on the mainland. You should've known that. And whoever brought you here should be caned."

My resolve falls. I should have suspected as much. It was a stupid, careless mistake. One that could easily have cost me my life. I hold my head higher in defiance. "I'm still going …"

The point is that the children are in need, not their lineage.

He stares at me as if weighing two completely different outcomes. Part of me can't help but wonder if one involves swaddling me and carrying me off to have his way with me. Just like Neliem on his horse.

But perhaps, since he now knows what I really am, he has no appetite for that. My shoulders sag at once. I know I should be relieved, but part of me is battling with being thought less of, which shouldn't matter, but somehow does.

Obviously upset, he shakes his head, his curls tossing, his mind made up. "Fine. But I'm going with you. And I'll carry the money. There are more pickpockets here than fleas."

Forcefully, I press the bag of candy into his arms. "You'll carry the candy."

He stares at the pouch, the amusement spreading to his eyes.

"Really?" He presses his lips together, I suspect to keep from laughing. Before I can change my mind, he hails a cyclist cab, and we go to the orphanage, which happens to be nowhere near where the saleslady told me.

When we finally arrive at the orphanage, it is lunchtime and the children are sitting down to the most unappetizing bowls of porridge. They are much younger than the children at my school and appear not nearly as healthy, which seems impossible.

I sit down at one bench and make inquiries about food and health, only to be told that funds are limited. Especially now, with the strike in the neighboring island preventing sugarcane from being transported. Sugarcane effects nearly every aspect of Playa Del Sol's economy. Workers come from all over to attempt to make their fortune from the harvesting and trade. But it's the orphans and poor that really suffer whenever there's a strike or natural disaster.

The orphans stare at me with wide eyes, their faces gaunt, their little hands and legs resembling twigs. The sisters of Divine Mercy who tend to them seem well-meaning enough, and I can't help but notice that not one child withers at their touch.

Recalling the task at hand, I go about and give each child a gold coin, and across the tables, my stalker hands out candy. Too quickly, I run out of coins.

My knight in not too shiny armor arrives just as I hand out the last one. "What's the matter?"

"I've run out of coins. I brought thirty, but with the cost of the candy … I thought it would be enough."

He raises an eyebrow. "How many more do you need?"

"Three."

He hands them over without a word. Then, the smile reaching his eyes, he laughs. "Well, you have officially turned me into a good Samaritan. My sainted mother in heaven is now rejoicing. Will you at least tell me your name?"

I stop. Untouchables don't believe in heaven. Just my people. Letting this bit of information sink in, I skid to the remaining children, handing them their coins before informing the sisters that I would like to make another visit in the nearby future. They are delighted to hear such good news, and hug me a bit too tight, their genuine warmth lifting my spirit. When I glance up, I am delighted to see that even my admirer gets thrown into a warm embrace. One of the tiny sisters reaches on her toes to pinch his cheeks and give his bottom a smack.

Embarrassed, he shrugs it off. But I can tell he was touched by the sincerity of their appreciation. I hide my grin while he collects himself and proffers me his elbow. We walk casually outside, my feet absorbing the texture of the cobblestones that lead directly toward the open water, where dozens of tiny bridges intersect.

My mouth falls open. There are more bridges than I can count, all interwoven to create the most breathtaking view. Channels, open waters, tall and tiny homes seemingly suck together. I openly marvel at the splendor, which escaped my notice when we rode from the opposite side of town here. The view is breathtaking. Playa Del Sol, the capital, is indeed a masterpiece of art and style.

The aroma of spices and roasted meats carries in the breeze, assaulting my senses. My stomach rumbles, the distant memory of breakfast too far away.

My admirer raises an eyebrow. "Hungry?"

I'm starving but would sooner wither away than admit it. He isn't fooled, however; he just shakes his head, winking his eye in a way I find extremely disarming.

"You're stubborn; I like that."

I'm too preoccupied with the lavish architecture and the way the walls of one building lend to another. At the center of the canal, something chiseled in stone catches my eye. The Prince's Proclamation.

"Defender of all People. It's one of his titles." I detect a sense of awe in my admirer's voice. As if what is written is perhaps more than the ramblings of some entitled Prince with too much time on his hands.

"There are some who would wholeheartedly disagree."

Behind the writing is a colorful mural of what appears to be a revolution, complete with blood pouring down these very streets. Curiosity gets the better of me; there seems to be more to this city than I previously thought. Secrets whisper in the wind, flowing in the breeze through the hidden passageways and alleys.

"Some say that it was old magic that won the Prince these lands. He was in the minority. Five hundred of his soldiers against thousands." He points to the steeple in one building. "He was held up there for a fortnight. No food, no water, his men and the faithful few worn ragged, and yet they prevailed."

I strongly suspect that everything about this fine city is magical. The water stretches out as far as the eye can see, the old Embrian castle ruins still clinging to the furthest cliff. Magnificent and thrilling are but a few of the words I can use to describe it. The channels surround the city with numerous bridges that connect all parts of the city as if a gigantic jigsaw puzzle. I marvel at it all, the statues of the false gods with familiars lurking about, the shops selling teas and coffees from foreign lands. Pungent incense burning at every corner. Meats and spices cooking openly for prospective customers. The enormity of it is staggering and utterly splendid.

And, best of all, in the open water directly before us, there's a child's boat race in process. Without thinking, I rush to the water, my heart beating with excitement. All types of boats, big and small, race from one end of the dock toward the other.

I'm so carried away, I barely note my admirer's presence as I twist through the crowd to get a better view.

"You owe me money; who are you?" He tilts his head, becoming playful. I openly gape at the boat race, all but ignoring him. He tugs at my sleeve like a little boy. "You will tell me."

I can't help but smile. His good humor is contagious. And to think I thought him a stalker. Perhaps he is, but something tells me that there is much more than meets the eye with this one.

He leans his back against the railing, I suspect to get a good look of me without drawing attention. "Where are you from? You owe me that, at least."

"Madera."

His sharp eyes, which don't miss a thing, narrow, scanning the crowd. But fortunately, no one's paying any attention. The crowd's mesmerized on the race, not interested in the slightest with the attractive man talking to the Outcast girl in the pretty frock.

Unexpectedly, he places his arm protectively around my shoulder. "You've never seen a boat race?"

I only answer with my own question, shrugging his arm off me. "Is it just once that they race, or do they turn around and go again?"

"It's like watching a babe discover her mother's milk." He plays with a stray curl that's escaped my bonnet, twirling it around before resting his warm hand against my cheek.

"Don't ..." I stammer, shaking him off politely.

"What?" His eyes widen.

"I don't like being touched."

He stares at me with a quizzical look that reminds me of someone else. Before I can put my finger on it, he laughs, almost doubling over.

Just below us, one of the boats accidentally hits the wall and crashes. The little boy wearing the same colors drops his flag and falls into a fit of tears against his mother's chest. And I feel this child's pain. To have something you love taken away.

My face flushing, I step backward, the lump growing in my throat. That strange sensation I'd convinced myself didn't exist trickling down, plaguing my thoughts.

Za-Za.

I startle, noticing that he's even closer than before. "What?"

"You." He whispers sweetly and non-predator-like. With those wide eyes and soft lips, I would probably confuse him for a saint if I didn't know better. He plays with the rope on the ledge before explaining. "Watching you, I like it."

His gaze seems to convey two emotions, sincerity and a trace of confusion over his confession. The city clock strikes, and I wince. I've been gone for too long and Ralio will be fretting right about now. Perhaps he's already in the shop, discovering that I fled soon after I entered.

The crowd's loud cheering and yelping distracts me. I press up to the railing to get a better view of the race.

But I am not alone. He follows like a hound, right on my tracks, not letting me out of his sight.

"I'm Tristan." And he grins in that irresistible way.

When I turn my attention back on the race, his hand for the briefest second brushes against mine and a sudden tingle ignites, a current linking us. I ignore it, using every ounce of strength to focus back on the race.

Another boat capsizes as a smaller boat speeds through. It's exhilarating, and I find myself squealing uncontrollably.

"Look, Tristan, at the small red boat; it's so fast!" He frowns, but just the same turns to get a better look. The expression on his face alters. All intensity washes away, and he beams as if a small child, thrilled with the excitement of the race.

"I used to have one of those."

"I had an eagle once. I bet my eagle was faster than your boat."

"An eagle?" He stares at me in awe.

"Some …" I scan the crowd, avoiding using the word Untouchable. "Boys had killed her mother, but I saved one egg and hatched it …"

"You did not."

"I raised her, fed her worms and fish. And when she was ready, she spread her wings and flew away. And she was faster than any boat."

Tristan nudges closer, his arm slinking around mine before he remembers. He lowers it and lets out a shrill whistle. "But my boat, The Lady, won every race."

I raise an eyebrow, teasing, "The Lady? How very fitting."

He throws me an innocent look. "I have absolutely no idea what you refer to. Now tell me your name."

And the scoundrel has the audacity to tickle me.

I fight him off playfully, but he doesn't back down. "I told you mine."

Something in his eyes flicker, and I stop playing. This is neither overly-passionate or overly-protective, 'I'll-carry-the-money-purse,' Tristan. If, in fact, that is what his name is. It might very well be Sergio, and he has a wife that beats him black and blue and five hell-raising children at home, waiting to tackle him the second he steps foot in his house.

But then again, I might have it all wrong. Because the Tristan standing before me, the who follows me around like a puppy, is all sweetness and shy smiles, so playful and boyish. He's laughing and doing that thing with his eyes to make him even that more impossible to resist.

Without thinking, I brush back one of his dark curls, and he kisses my gloved hand, embracing it as if he would never let go. I inch back, forcing my feet to move. "I didn't ask you your name."

The urge to flee intensifies with each step I take. He matches my pace, his arm sliding protectively closer. He blinks, blocking my path so that I'm forced to stop. Our faces are inches apart, his breath beating over me, demanding the truth. I sway slightly at a loss for words, dizziness overtaking me.

Carefully, as if I was made of fine china, he positions me against the wall and waits for the spell to pass, his face studying mine.

"Did someone … a man …" His voice takes on a dark, delicious intensity. "Someone in Madera, is that why you're here?"

The image of those two brutes flash before me vividly, their long red hair, the way their gaze sliced into me, cutting me, wishing me all sorts of evil. Without my dagger to protect me, the panic I should have felt then breaks free, and I've overwhelmed in terror. I close my eyes and nod my head. "But they didn't …"

His face tightens, squeezing the space between his brows. "Tell me their names, and I will kill them." When our eyes connect, I see it isn't some idle threat, but a promise. A guarantee.

This complete stranger will do this for me. Kill those brutes.

"They didn't; I got away." I barely manage to get the words out. Emotions whirl around me. At the time, I wasn't even slightly scared, but now, so far away from it, I'm frightened. When I dare steal a peek, his face is still red, but some of the tension has left his forehead. Remembering the worst part, I whine, "But I lost my dagger."

Tristan's face brightens, whether in relief or sheer amusement, I don't know. Then, without asking, he moves closer and holds me tight against his chest. It's sunshine and happiness and everything good in this world. But, more amazingly, I allow it. Like it even. In one fluid movement, he unties my bonnet and runs his fingers through my hair as if I was the most precious thing in this world. The knot in my stomach settles, and my shoulders relax, and my lungs fill.

I know without asking that he's used to touching women. And that they respond accordingly, giving in without hesitation. Unlike me.

His fingers glide up my side, possessively and urgent. "They will never hurt you again."

And I believe it. I let out a breath. "Thank you, Tristan."

He closes his eyes as if in prayer and presses closer, his body hovering over mine. I let his warmth fill me, feeling safe and secure. Everything else fades, the world, the universe, the stars. All that exists is us.

But it doesn't last. The image of Tristan touching someone else makes me miss a step. I would've crashed to the ground if it hadn't been for his arm wrapped around me.

We are face to face, and all I can think about is some other girl that he'll be batting his long eyelashes at tomorrow. The thought's unsettling, so much so that I do something I haven't done in years. I tremble. He's staring at me, pinning me down with that look, those eyes, and then he does something unexpected. He lets go.

I have to ask. "Why do you care?"

"I've made it my business to care. And your safety warrants my immediate assistance." His gaze travels down the walkway we just crossed, which is crammed full of people and merchants trading their wares. It seems that market day is over, and now the merchants travel freely up and down the river peddling their goods.

Unflinching, his gaze studies them as if reading their minds. "It's still not safe."

I glance down at my feet, wondering if he would have cared enough to have given me a second thought if he had seen me dressed in boy's clothes with my dagger. Would we have played this game of cat and mouse? Gone together to the orphanage or taken the time to stop and watch the boat race?

The answer is obvious. No, never.

The thought chills me. But regardless, I know what he says to be true regarding my safety. I was given strict instructions to never leave Ralio's side for an instant. I breathe deeply, muttering under my breath, "You shouldn't trouble yourself."

He lifts up my chin with more force than necessary. "It is my prerogative to care. And I do."

My insides quiver at his unspoken words. My breath accelerates, making my throat dry. How can he speak, implying these obvious wanton thoughts so openly, so brazenly? But most important, why does my body have to react to him as if I was on fire? Positive that everyone around us has overheard his indecent proposal, I glance at the spectators, but their only focus is watching the end of the boat race.

I gather what remains of my wits and attempt to shake him off. "Regardless of how appealing that might sound, I have no desire to birth your bastard son nine months from now."

To prove that I will not be swayed with honey words and false promises, I tighten my fist. Before, I was momentarily swept away. But now, I know better. My mother never thought to warn me of the dangers of irresistible men with blue eyes and honeyed words. But I have had life to teach me. Girls who disappeared from our village without a word of their whereabouts, only to reappear months later shattered and worn out, with a despondent look of unfathomable loss in their eyes.

With more determination, I shake off his hold until his arm falls to his side. But he doesn't seem affected in the least. He dares pout. "But he would be so beautiful." And the scoundrel has the audacity to bat his long eyelashes.

"His lack of intelligence and indiscretion would more than make up for that."

I stomp off in the opposite direction, shifting my shirts and picking up my pace. But once again, he's too quick. He easily corners me and whispers, "See, you like me touching you."

Affronted, I slap him, narrowly missing. He darts back like a boxer, prepared for another round but well-aware that I can't draw any unwanted attention. Like the snake he is, he uses this advantage to rub his shoulder against mine, a mischievous glint in his eye.

"Don't worry. I'm not ready to be a father …" He pauses briefly, his brow lifting. "At least not yet."

I'm in too much shock to respond. Not that he waits for an answer. His lips trail hot kisses down my cheek. My heart practically leaps out of my chest when he repeats the assault on the other side of my face before pressing down on my mouth. His tongue tantalizes like a thousand feathers swirling down to my core.

What's left of my mind shuts off. Instead, a foreign sensation tugs, unbridled, wild, like running full force down a hill, wind in your hair, arms flailing as if you could soar into the heavens.

Never had I imagined a kiss could be like that. Relations between man and woman were whispered to be obligations. For his pleasure, not hers. But this contradicts everything I've ever been told. Because one moment his lips are hot and unrelenting; the other soft and tame, taking me places I've never been. My body yields to his as if we were two halves of the same whole. Pure exhilaration.

Tristan's kiss ignites sparks within my belly, spreading like wildfire as his tongue claims mine again and again. But what's more surprising is that I'm matching him, caught in the same whirlwind of emotion.

He breaks hold of me, momentarily coming to his senses. "We might not make it to the Inn. And I wouldn't want to sire my son in some dark, yet convenient, alleyway."

Tristan's mischievous side is in control, panting in my ear, pulling me away from the crowd. But what's more amazing is that I let him.

If my face matches my heart, I am crimson red. My blood searing hot in my veins, a strange feeling of euphoria washes through me. My natural instinct to flee pumps fiercely, telling me this man is dangerous in a way I have never encountered before. Because in this moment, I wouldn't have to be convinced to join him in the Inn. I would eagerly race alongside him, not giving it a second thought.

That indescribable desire to throw caution into the wind and just act, not think, takes control of every cell in my body. Especially the ones below my waist.

This stranger has this uncanny power to make me forget everything. A first. And the thought infuriates me enough to shut down my wayward desires running havoc. My first rational thought is that I would give almost anything to be able to wrestle him right now. Throw him against the railing and tumble with him for hours. But being in public and making a spectacle of myself isn't something even I'm capable of. The frock will tear. My gloves soil. And there are too many spectators who would take notice and possibly notify the authorities.

From his tantalizing breath to the way his gaze sears through me, I know I must get away; escape is the only option. This Tristan is no amateur. He very well knows the effect he has on me and that I just might succumb to his charms if I don't flee with my virtue intact.

In his able hands, I am clay he could mold to his likening indefinitely, then just as quickly toss away.

An image of a broken pot flickers in my mind, as well as the faces of the girls from my village, reduced to live vacant lives with no hope of any future. The ones that don't attend the betrothal ceremonies, the ones kept hidden, working in the butcher shop late at night to wash away the blood.

Knowing what awaits me if I succumb, I pray for deliverance. I need to get away, and I need to do it now. And just when I'm ready to give up, admit for the first time in my life that I am helpless, divine intervention arrives unexpectedly in the form of a bread cart with a broken wheel.

Across the channel, a traffic jam ensues. The bridge crams on both sides with carts as well as heavy foot traffic zigzagging every which way. A freshly polished carriage halts abruptly, the driver yanking at the reins to avoid running over a pedestrian. The impact thrusts the back of the carriage against a flimsy railing that bends, unable to sustain the pressure. The carriage rattles, followed by the snapping of wood splitting in half. A woman screams just as another carriage collides with an oncoming wagon full of day laborers with pickaxes and forks. A serrated blade thrusts out of the open wagon, beheading a goat being led across the bridge. Blood splatters everywhere, drenching the ground as panic ensues. Two spirits use the altercation to enter a vagabond, who rouses the horses with a devilish sneer. The horses, tangled up in their reins, bray and stomp furiously when the inevitable occurs. The carriage balancing against the railing skids, breaking the barrier and tilting off the bridge.

Screams and panicked cries for help erupt like a tidal wave from every turn. Paralyzed, I watch as the driver leaps off the carriage. Rushing to the scene, a fishmonger has the good sense to cut the horse's reins. It happens too fast. The carriage inching backward against the crumbling divider, the driver, thinking only of himself, rushing away. The horse stomping away frantically just as the carriage's back wheels spin aimlessly in mid-air. Pedestrians watch with stunned faces; no one dares move. The last plank snaps as what's left of the divider breaks, the impact causing the carriage to fall to its side and tumble over the railing, plunging into the icy cold water.

And just like that, an opportunity to escape has presented itself. Thinking only of my purity, I run as fast as the confines of my dress will allow. Neither my bodice nor my boots are designed for speed, but I don't care. I fling myself on a passing cabbage cart and, through sheer willpower, hang on as it takes me further into the heart of the city. I cross over a bridge carrying me to the opposite end of the channel. A wide river safely between Tristan and me.

When the carriage slows, I hop off and straighten my frock. The shops seem more familiar but even as I walk away something twitches in my head. Slowing my breath, like an infatuated schoolgirl, I turn. Against the railing, pedestrians gather, pointing to the waters below. The carriage is almost completely submerged when I spot it: A gloved hand frantically knocking from inside the sinking carriage window.

Someone's trapped inside.

My stomach drops, my feet moving forward to get a better look. Knowing I might very well regret it, I gain purchase and perch up above the retaining wall. When I lean forward, I see clearly that a woman is trapped inside.

My skin crawls with dread. The door's jammed from the prior accident, leaving no means of escape. Desperately, I search for a familiar face, someone willing to do the impossible and rush to her rescue.

Without thinking it through, I climb up to the ledge and see none other than Tristan balancing on the bridge where the carriage slipped. He rips off his shirt and turns, our eyes connecting across the ravine. I want to scream at him to stop, but it's no use. I'm too far away, and even if he did hear me, it wouldn't stop what he's about to do.

One thought pounds in my head: This man, this Tristan, is more Neliem than me.

As if reading my thoughts, he bows to me and then, with that wicked grin, tosses aside his shirt and dives head first into the raging waters.

After laboring through town, getting lost not once, but twice, I finally find my way back to the shop where I started my adventure mere hours ago. Deflated, I collapse into a seat next to Ralio. Two empty bottles of wine clatter under his seat, and several dirty dishes and a half loaf of bread lay piled before him.

I breathe a sigh of half relief and half shock. My temples throb, and the heel of one of my boots is loose. It seems absurd, but Ralio seems completely unaware of my comings and goings for the better part of the day. He's stumbled against a cushioned seat with a lazy smile playing on his lips, his cheeks rosy after so much drink and good food. The server arrives with a roasted chicken and steaming hot potatoes, which he places with a polite bow before me.

Dutifully, Ralio, ignores the food and checks his timepiece, making a motion to adjust his jacket. "Did you find everything you needed?"

The thought of uttering one syllable makes every nerve in my body quiver. And, if I were completely honest, out of something other than fear. Me, who has escaped capture too many times to count, was nearly ensnared by nothing more than honeyed words and a pair of brilliant blue eyes.

My cheeks flush hot as I reach for a goblet of wine. Ralio's eyes perk up, his speech slurred. "Quite a day, Madame."

He stuffs a chicken leg into his mouth, sucking it to the bone.

Instead of answering, I gulp down my drink in one swig. It's all the answer he's getting. With a boisterous laugh, Ralio pours himself more wine and swigs it down, none the wiser.

8

It's been three days since my adventure of adventures, and thankfully, Ezra's still in the dark about how Neliem I truly am. Blissfully unaware of what he has sought as a future bride, I play the part of the innocent maiden before him, hoping my anxious fingers don't give me away.

Under his careful gaze, which seems to follow my every step, I act the part, quiet and demure, keeping my secrets locked tighter than my hope chest, well hidden from prying eyes and loose lips. Never do I reveal the power I yield to attract the attention of a fellow Neliem, the one who sought to bed me in a neighboring inn.

But that is the least of my problems. The spirit of Neliem himself has awoken, possessing me, making my waking thoughts more irrational and reckless than normal. I practice my fighting skills before the first light of dawn, kicking, punching and stabbing bags of flour for hours, then feigning innocence when the cook demands to know who has been tampering with her food supplies.

Loosening my collars, I feel caged, trapped in the confines of the huge mansion, the adjoining gardens, the ponds, and even the apple orchard. I take scorching hot baths in attempts to squelch the flame and distract myself with long labored walks on the beach, finding my gaze drifting toward the city at unexpected times. I have sworn never to set foot there again.

The thought of running into Tristan, even by accident, sends my heart racing and my head spinning in a way that's both intoxicating and infuriating: A fellow Neliem resides in Playa Del Sol, of all places. With all my willpower, I push away the image of Tristan ripping off his shirt and diving into the channel. Instead, I focus on how to somehow fit into the role that will be mine in a week's time. A wife to an Untouchable.

The word sticks heavy to the back of my throat.

Ezra, gauging my mood the way a lion tamer does, is even more polite than usual. He takes me on a tour of his library and selects some appropriate reading material to calm my flailed nerves. The servants attempt to teach me how to weave a basket for the poor, but my fingers are all thumbs. I try and try and try until I explode, and strands of straw and ribbon fall everywhere. It's no use.

I would no more fit into this role as than a painted monkey pretending to be queen.

My dreams haunt me nightly. Glistening blue eyes and Neliem himself ride up against a dark stormy moon. But this time, I search for him, rushing to find him, to feel the warmth of his flesh against mine.

During my end-of-the-week prayers, I find myself lighting a candle for Tristan right alongside Ezra and Etta's. My rapid heartbeat betrays my innermost thoughts. Covering my face, I rush through the words, hoping for some semblance of peace that I cannot find.

At times I catch myself racing too fast down the stairs or walking too close to the cliff for Ezra's liking. Without scolding me, he pulls me into the safety of his arms, which feel somewhat familiar but still foreign. What is more amazing is that I allow it. I allow his touch. A major feat. I close my eyes and pretend this is how it should be. Why this stranger has chosen me, of all maidens, will never cease to amaze me.

Other dramas, much more compelling, are unfolding within the household, making me cautious and apprehensive enough to try to rein in my spirits. Ezra's receiving strange telegrams at all hours of the day, which has put him on high alert. His forehead furrows in unnaturally, and his lips form a hard line. On the telephone, which has just been installed, I catch phrases like 'warehouse shipment.' Something about a fire. And a fleet of ships that bring goods from foreign places that are not where they should be.

When I press, he forces a tight smile and tosses the correspondence in the fire so that I can't later retrieve it and know for certain what is happening. He instead turns the tables and asks his own questions about my latest areas of interests, which I'd hoped to keep secret.

Some sniveling coward thought to expose my fondness of knives and other forms of cutlery. And because of this, all forms of weaponry have now been secured with lock and key that only Elsie is privy to. She wears it around her neck and shoots a hostile look at me when she sees me gazing toward her bosom for too long.

But still, I try for an ounce of freedom and bribe one of the stable boys to let me ride. I do so with more reckless abandon that I thought possible, causing the stable hand to laugh so hard that he has to hold onto his ribs. We ride early in the morning and race with more fervor, crashing into the waves so hard that the poor boy nearly falls off his saddle. Terrified that he might tattle and therefore ensure that all horses are also forbidden, I offer him another gold coin for his promised silence.

I have not only stooped to bribery. I am now an unofficial expert on lock-smithery, so I can secure my weapons of choice. I am beneath nothing. And revel in it.

But today, I cannot do one thing wrong. Today, I meet all of Ezra's family, which sends cold shivers down my spine and makes my palms perspire so much that I have to change my gloves twice. We will be staying with them for the rest of the week, until the betrothal period ends, and our bond is sealed. At that point, we'll be blessed, and I will have my ring.

But that's not what keeps the hairs on the back of my neck standing.

It's wondering what type of pagan household I'll be subjected to. Even though Ezra assures me there are no familiar ghosts or spirits in any of his homes. He paid a priest years ago to vanquish all spirits, both good and bad. I still don't look forward to meeting his family. Landis is in better spirits and visits without Tanya. I keep the secret overheard when I bumped into Henric, that Landis is casting her aside as we eat our supper.

But later, I overhear them talking in the den when they think I've retired to my bedchambers. Ezra's brother will be a problem. One I'll have to endure, knowing full well that he stopped short of murder to keep Ezra from going to Madera to select me as his intended.

Ezra goes to great lengths to convince me that it is nothing more than a formality. "Oriana, it is nothing. Don't worry."

I play with another locket he has given me. I have four now. They are kept on my dresser, polished every night until they glisten and catch the light just so. This one is in the shape of a heart, exactly like the image captured on the wall that I still insist is a lump of fat.

Two lovebirds engraved in gold.

He places it around my neck gently, clasping the chain, his eyes staring into mine in the mirror, sending tingles down my flesh. His breath is sweet, causing my mind to drift and my shoulders to relax. "The week will go by quickly. There is really nothing to it." But I catch a glimmer of sadness in his eyes and know there is more to it. Disapproval from his family might mean a one-way ticket back to Madera, this charade over and done.

"And your brother?"

Refusing to meet my gaze, he shrugs and laughs. "Knowing my brother, he won't even show up."

"Perhaps I should stay here." I don't say 'home.'

Wrapping his arms around me, he makes a silly face to settle my nerves, but it doesn't work.

I smile politely, knowing the truth. This is nothing less than a test. The hardest one I will ever undertake. After all that's happened, I find that I do in fact care, if it means Ezra's happiness. Ezra's extremely fond of his family, especially his aunts and his Uncle Anton. He speaks of them often and always has a trace of a smile on his lips that's not for show.

As we sit down to breakfast before leaving, instead of his correspondence taking his time like normal, he's free of all business and hums a tune that I can't quite place. The newspaper laid out in front of him rustles gently, the Prince on the cover with a beautiful lady.

"The princess is quite beautiful."

He clears his throat. "She is not the princess."

There are three grown children strategically posed before them. Attractive, well postured. The article states a state visit is planned in six months to Playa Del Sol, where the Prince will meet with his advisor's families. The name Mercer jumps out.

"You know the Prince?" I startle.

He takes the paper, folding it. "Women in my family do not read the paper. But yes, my father was his advisor during the war. He secured Playa Del Sol and the neighboring islands."

I remember Tristan pointing out the steeple where the Prince was held up.

"It's nothing to worry about. It's a state visit. There will be over a hundred people invited. We'll dance …"

My stomach drops. "I don't dance."

"Never?" He seems amused by my confession.

"Only barbarians and pagans dance."

"I dance quite well." He stands up, displays a quick bow, and glides on his feet as I watch in awe. "I'll teach you."

"I don't think so."

"The Prince might request the honor of dancing with you."

"There might be a second revolution if he does so."

Ezra laughs so hard he needs to brace his weight on the back of the chair to keep from falling. I think it is, perhaps, the best time to propose something that has been on my mind for a few days. His good mood is all the incentive I need.

He returns to his paper as I choose to strike. Not like a cobra, but more like a demurred lamb with a fractured foot.

"I was wondering if I could have a personal maid."

He lifts his head slightly from the paper, a look of amusement framing his handsome features. "You need another maid?"

Good; he didn't scoff at once or mention money.

I spread the marmalade carefully on my toast, just the way I like it. Extra thick with the butter already melted. "One to help me bathe and help with personal necessities." My voice drops at the word 'necessities' and my cheeks burn.

Tilting his head, his eyes scan up and down, gauging my mood. Then, he exhales, immediately softening. "Of course. I will personally see to it that a few girls are sent for your approval. Will one suffice?"

I twist my fingers, anticipation quivering in my gut. "I already have one in mind." I force the words out. "Etta would be well suited …"

I don't have a chance to finish before the paper comes crashing down on his plate, upsetting his toast and eggs. His eyes glare dark and stormy seas.

"She's the girl from my former school, the one you spoke to …"

"I know perfectly well who she is, Oriana." He turns to see if anyone's within earshot, before studying me like he would a slug. My heart races, my pulse throbbing in my throat. "And it is perfectly out of the question."

His verdict spoken, he returns to his paper, rustling the pages with a snap.

"Why not?"

"It's illegal." He doesn't even bother to look at me, as if I'm some disobedient child that he can't trouble himself with.

"Then why am I here?" The hurt leaks from my voice.

"Oriana." His hand reaches for mine. It's the first time in four days he's touched me like this. Not a brotherly hug, but different. Intimate. Since the night I refused his request to sleep in his bed, he has been kind but distant. And always careful.

His voice is soothingly gentle, attempting to soften the blow of denying me one of the two things I desire most. The other is impossible. To see Tristan again and explain my strange disappearance before parting as friends.

"If I could, believe me, I would. For you, I would." His eyes are pleading, but all I can think of is poor Etta starving amongst all those horrible Untouchables, and of the things they do and get away with, when another, more disturbing thought races through my mind.

"What about my mother?" Panic itches in my throat.

He glances behind him apprehensively. Only when he spots no one lurking about does he graze his teeth across his top lip. "Of course, I will arrange for you to see her, if that is what you wish, for that celebration thing." He speaks of our Outcast holiday, where we fast and then celebrate for three days. It's one of the few times there is plenty to eat, and all strife is momentarily forgotten.

The thought of never seeing my own mother except for a day or two out of the year has an unexpected effect. I feel torn in half. "But when we have children ..."

Honestly, it's the first time I've given it any thought. Children. Certainly, Ezra wants a son. Maybe two. He mentioned several distant cousins with several children. Untouchables love to procreate; it's how they subdued my people. Their vast army of tall, blond giants crossed the waters, claiming everything in sight.

Our children will legally be Hugganoffs. My ancestry all but denied. The blood rushes back to my head, I stammer, "I mean ..."

He nibbles on a piece of bread, taking the time to think it through. "Children are an entirely different matter."

Relieved, I smile and reach for some juice. When I glance up, I see something on his face that I wasn't expecting. The tension that was in my body just seconds ago seems to have transferred to his. "Ezra, what's wrong?"

He's still staring at my hand when Ralio arrives to tell us that the coach is ready with everything securely packed. Ezra nods and slowly, almost painfully, turns back to me before standing up.

He stares at me with a stone face that I can't read. Holding my breath, I wait until he mutters in a strained voice, "I thought you understood, about child—"

The phone in the hallway rings unexpectedly. Startled, I nearly jump out of my skin.

Ezra ignores the call, closing the door carefully before latching it. He faces the doorway, pausing painfully slowly before turning, and for the first time, I am terrified.

"Oriana."

I gasp, thinking maybe he doesn't find me attractive or even slightly interesting. No wonder these people wait two weeks for the bonding to be sealed. Two weeks to change your mind and send the almost bride back home devastated, wondering for the rest of her life what she did wrong.

So, there can be but one meaning.

We will never have children because I am to be sent back.

By reflex, I pull back, ashamed, staring at my feet, my hands, the crystal goblets reflecting the perfect sunlight on the table. Anything but the man before me telling me that I'm not good enough. The room, with its marble floors and plastered walls and rich furniture, is stunning. Beyond anything, I could have imagined growing up in Anaith and living in a shack with a broken window and cracked walls that swayed with the wind. The sensation of almost freezing to death in the winter and going to bed with my body drenched in sweat in the summer was a constant reminder of what my life would always be like.

Until Ezra offered his hand.

But now it feels like sand slipping through my fingers, here one moment, gone the next. My heart thumps wildly as my legs move, but I don't know where I'm going. I haven't planned an exit. I've laid down all my defenses for the first time in my life and become lazy.

I am utterly useless.

Of course, he's changed his mind. It was merely a matter of time. He'd grown weary of the silly Untouchable girls that bat their eyelashes and chat away like ninnies. He thought to try something different. Something wild and dangerous, with enough spirit to give him a run for his money. But now he knows better.

Now there will never, ever be someone singing for me. No groom choosing me.

My legs go heavy, as if weighed down with stones. The doors open, and somehow, I'm climbing up the stairs, my pace quickening with every beat of my broken heart. I'm not sure where I'm headed, perhaps to my room, which is no longer my room, or to a balcony to find relief from this nausea of utter worthlessness.

I keep telling myself it doesn't matter. That I'm better off without him. That I never wanted to leave Madera or live in Playa Del Sol.

Every inhale of breath stings; my lungs betraying the truth.

I will miss this life that could've been mine.

But that's not half of it. It's the fact that Ezra finds me unsatisfactory. His pronouncement labels me Outcast in every imaginable way. I fling open the balcony doors and nearly collapse, the weight of my body pressing against the railing. The waves crash violently below my feet, too close, but not nearly close enough.

I lean in, reaching out my hands, imagining them wings soaring far away into the heavens. My eagle soaring to me. The spray of the waves sends a cold shiver on my flesh, but it feels so good. Intoxicating, heavenly, like throwing myself down a hill at full speed. And for a fleeting moment, I feel as if I could really fly, all I need is to take that first leap.

A loud gasp startles me out of my dream. "What are you doing?"

Warm hands pull me back. But something in me ignites, and I struggle out of reflex, my arms and legs flailing.

"ORIANA!" It takes me a full moment to register that it's Ezra. His face is flustered, his breath hot and ragged.

I wiggle out of reach and trip against the cool concrete, my backside hitting the marble with a crack. A scream erupts, then something crashes. Somehow Velaria's hovering over me, her eyes wild with fear.

Ezra screams, "Mistress has had a fainting spell; bring salts and towels."

My head hurts and white spots blur before my eyes, a fresh wave of seawater spraying me. Someone's holding my hand too tight. But I like it. It feels like home. A warm hand holding me tight, lifting me to the air. A cascade of blond curls.

Then I remember: I don't have a home.

"Oriana, Oriana, can you hear me?"

Footsteps snap on the marble. Velaria presses a satchel of salts to my nostril, her hand trembling. My eyes droop closed, sleep overtaking me. Somewhere, a wolf wails a hysterical howl. The chase. I need to run. I need to hide.

Velaria slaps me hard, then moves to strike me again when I grab hold her wrist, twisting her limb red. Quickly, I regain my focus, and everything becomes clear. One side of my face stings hot, but nothing like the expression on Velaria's, who appears ready to keel over.

I release her arm, and she staggers away.

Ezra, huddling over me, hisses at her, "Was that necessary?"

I lift my head, my eyesight clearing when a cup is thrust to my mouth. "Sip it slowly …"

The liquid burns hot like coals down my throat. But it has the desired effect. I arise from my nightmare.

"Darling, are you all right?" It's Ezra's voice, but the words seem wrong. Never once has anyone called me darling. Ezra glares at Velaria, reminding me of my eagle. For a second, I believe he will raise his talons and strike her. Then, with controlled restraint, he stills and swallows back what he was prepared to say. "Leave us."

She slowly gets up, wobbling a bit, giving me a lingering frown before retreating.

I collect myself, sitting up as best I can. I'm positive that I must look a disaster. My hair, which took forever to appear presentable, is probably in tangles and my stocking stained from falling. Rising, I try to sound nonchalant that I am no longer welcome in his home. "When will you send me back to Madera?"

He blinks twice, his face whiter than a ghost. "Never, never ..."

Unable to meet his gaze, I play with a button on my sleeve. "I suppose that's why my things were packed."

This morning, every stitch of my clothing was neatly folded in one large valise. It's clever. Tell your intended she's off to visit relatives when all the while she's been sent packing back home in disgrace. Very Untouchable.

"Oriana ... no, never would I send you back ..." Ezra bursts into tears, his voice breaking. "Is that why ..." I follow his gaze toward the railing. "I thought you were going to throw yourself ..."

He can't finish the sentence. I laugh. I don't know why, but I do. Perhaps it's because he just said I wouldn't be sent back home. And for the first time, I realize that I don't want to go back to Madera. That maybe, just maybe, I have a home here in Playa Del Sol with Ezra.

I correct him, pointing. "No, it's the wrong angle."

"What?"

I move my hand across the cliffside to a more appropriate spot to gain better speed to jump into the waters.

"Over there would be the ideal spot to jump. Perfect traction." His jaw drops, his face quivering, and then he laughs.

"You had me almost peeing in my pants, young lady." He moves closer in one long stride, pressing closer for what seems a small eternity. His fingers glide up and down my hair, sending a welcome tingle. Then his eyes narrow in that quizzical way, just like when he was searching for me in the schoolyard. "Are you upset at me? Please tell me Oriana ... I need to know if I've done something wrong."

"I understand Un--" I try again, avoiding the term that he's forbidden me to use. "Your people are cold. You don't like displays of affection. I will try to get used to it."

Even though it is killing me. Even though Tristan's touch haunts me day and night. Mostly nights, alone in my big bed reliving that kiss that woke me up, stirring something so primal that I'm terrified to give it a name.

When I dare look at him, he seems amused. The frown is completely gone.

"Is that what you think? That I don't like you?" Now it's his turn to sound incredulous.

This time, the smile reaches his eyes. Then, without warning, he gently holds me closer so that I can feel his heartbeat against mine, his whisper-soft voice tickling my earlobe. "I've just been waiting for the right time. That's all."

I sigh a breath of relief. "I don't want to press matters, force something … unpleasant."

He lifts my chin, then laughs. "When we get back from my relatives' home, I will show you exactly how infatuated I am with you."

A new sensation shakes me all the way to my core as our hands intertwine. Outside, a bell clangs noisily, the sound vibrating through the rooms, causing the candles to flicker.

"We are quite late." Without another word, he guides me effortlessly down the stairs, where an impatient Ralio waits, tapping this boot against the steps. Through the open door, a gentle breeze of salty air lifts and all things seem possible.

Even seeing my eagle again.

A servant helps Ezra with his jacket, and a still petrified Velaria helps me with my cloak, taking the time to fix my hair. I smile to her to let her know that, despite the hysterics of the last few minutes, I am fine.

Before stepping out to the carriage, Ezra turns me to face the large mirror framed in the doorway, his chest pressed against my back. The image reflected is stunning. He's so tall and handsome with a flawless face complete with a chiseled chin. Nothing short of perfection in human form.

And for a moment, I wish to trust in it. To believe.

"We will be late." I lower my gaze, hurrying outside, my skin crawling at the thought of meeting his relatives. He takes a moment as if debating something crucial. But instead, his face relaxes as he joins me, taking the time to inhale deeply.

"Let them wait. They have us for an entire week." He rolls his eyes, lifting me in the carriage and making sure I have the best seat. "Sometimes, I hate my customs."

"Me too." I feel a spark of confidence. Maybe this will work. Ezra and me. A couple. The thought still unsettles me though. Me and an Untouchable. Or maybe just me with anyone.

Once seated in the carriage, a nagging thought prevails. It's so small that I could easily excuse it and pay it no heed. But the Neliem in me is curious, prying for more answers. Ezra now is all smiles, kissing my hand repeatedly, assuring me that all is well between us.

Ralio cracks the whip, and the horses bray, hastening forward. The jolt catches me by surprise as our carriage slowly makes the trek down the steep path toward Playa Del Sol.

Unexpectedly, the little hairs on the back of my neck stand. It's now or never, I reason. Turning to face Ezra, I steady my voice, "Then why did you say, before, about … you know. That you thought I understood …"

His hand drops down, flexes. "I was never referring to us."

Ezra turns away, and I realize that he doesn't want to talk about whatever it was that caused such a strong reaction in me. I should know well enough to leave it alone. But it's like a wasp flying too close.

I just have to swat it.

So, I count, and I breathe, and I wait. When that doesn't work, I close my eyes and squelch down the urge, willing myself to ignore the buzzing, pretending that there's nothing left unsaid. Holding my breath, the words push out of my mouth. "What were you referring to?"

"Your mother."

I wince, and concede a bit, brushing over where she pinched me. It's faded, and with it, the pain. "We weren't that close. I mean, not really. I suppose seeing her once or twice a year will be fine."

It's a big concession on my part. One that I never dreamed I would have to make. But he remains tightlipped, that troubled expression never leaving his brow. "We will be very happy together, Oriana. Do you believe me?"

I smile, pushing and pulling at the picture of our reflection in my mind so that it fits. "Of course."

He leans in, pressing the point. "And you trust me?"

His warm breath tingles over my face. He still smells like the sea, and it shouldn't surprise me that much, since he lives here, but it does. By reflex, I move one of his curls off his forehead, noticing for the first time a splatter of tiny freckles. It settles me. He's handsome, but something else. He's safe. Startled, I realize that I do trust him. I've known him mere days, but he's never once hurt me. If anything, Ezra's gentle and careful, never pressing or taking advantage. Also, he's never mistreated a servant; if anything, he's more than generous. Ralio's protruding stomach is evidence of that.

I return the question. "Do you trust me, Ezra?"

He closes his eyes and leans back, my hand clutching his. "With my life, yes."

"I suppose I trust you as well." As well as I've trusted anyone in my life, which is very few. Never my mother fully, or any of my classmates. Etta was the exception. I miss her so much it aches. But I can't bring it up again. At least not now. Later. When he's in a better mood and knows how much she means to me.

When I look up at him, he holds my gaze, his finger tracing down my nose.

I repeat it. "I trust you."

"Then you trust me when I tell you that under no circumstances will your mother ever be allowed to see our children."

Every nerve in my body quivers. As if someone has shot me. I hurl back in my seat, clutching my heart. The carriage skids and my skin crawls with dread, hot and feverish. Instinctively, I move further from him, closer to the door. At that precise moment, a fierce wind hits, rattling the carriage. I stumble hard against the back cushion. Somehow the latch dislodges and the door flares open, thumping violently against the carriage. The view outside is fierce, something out of a nightmare. Stormy winds and a turbulent sea beat in a whirlwind, my feet dangling out the door. I blink, too stunned to move as long ghostly tendrils seem to reach inside to grab me. If it weren't for Ezra's strong hold, I would be sucked out, torn to shreds off the jagged cliffs.

Ezra curses and grabs me, his leg and arms pinning me. He yanks me inside in one fluid motion. Only once I'm secure does he reach and slam the door shut with his foot, his breathing erratic and heavy.

He lays his full body weight on me, pressing me down. His voice is raw, pulsating against my ear. "Are you …"

My elbow presses into his gut, his ribcage vulnerable. The ideal position to do the greatest bodily injury with the smallest amount of effort. And it's the first time in a long time I've thought about harming him. After he just saved my life.

Ezra moves the hair off my face so that our eyes connect. "Oriana, are you all right?"

My jaw falls open, staring into that face that, for the first time, seems dangerously predatory. The image of my eagle flashes, with its narrow beak and emotionless eyes that seem to mirror his.

I try to shake the sight away.

"Speak, tell me you're …" He hugs me for what seems forever. So sweetly, like a child. The sensation of his body encasing mine makes me soften. And I can almost forgive him telling me my own mother will never once see her grandchildren.

Almost.

Only when we've cleared the dreaded steep hill does he let go. His back stiff with tension, he lets out a long breath.

Ralio veers off the road and comes to an abrupt halt, braking so fast that dust floats up the windows. Within seconds, he flings the door open, his body shaking, his bewildered face drenched in sweat. Then he breaks into a heartfelt sob. "What happened?" he gasps.

Ezra finally lifts himself off me completely. "The door, it came unlocked during the descent. We're fine."

To prove it, Ezra manages an uneasy smile.

But I'm anything but fine. My mind races, my senses more alert since leaving Madera. Ralio fusses over us like children, not bothering to wipe away his tears, proving his innocence. He checks the handle twice and finds a small piece of wood to secure it, apologizing profusely.

Ezra, the color returning to his face, sits absolutely still, like a statue, closer to the door. Holding onto my knee protectively, he steadies his voice, "We're fine." Then he orders, "Please sit further from the door."

On cue, the carriage lunges forward, Ralio taking a slower pace to the gates of the city.

Without complaint, I comply with Ezra's wishes and plant myself as close to the window as possible. Covering my mouth with a fake yawn, I inspect everything in the carriage, trying to catch what Ralio might've missed. The cushions were cleaned earlier; not a speck of dirt mars the inside except for a small patch of dark clay red. It's just a speck or two.

Finally relaxing, Ezra rests a firm hand on my thigh and closes his eyes. "We should be there soon. Try to rest."

I have no intention of resting. My pulse spikes with every turn of the carriage wheel. I see clearer, noting everything from the nick on Ezra's cheek, where he shaved too close, to that strange speck of dirt. Scuffing the tip of my boot, I bend down and wipe it on my finger. The soil is definitely different. Burnt red with an odor I can't place. It doesn't match.

Neliem snarls.

Troubled by this small discovery, I turn my attention out the window and watch the scenery dramatically change from rural countryside to a paved road that soon will turn into a lavish city crammed full of people. Now that we've reached the outskirts of the one place I've swore never to visit, the tension mounts for an entirely different reason. More dreadful than sitting on pins and needles, every sound amplifies, every jolt in the carriage making me squirm.

Ezra places a warm hand over mine, and I try to smile. Outside, the seemingly endless hills and dairy farms quickly disappear, giving way to the majestic city gates of Playa Del Sol, the capital of Perla Del Mar. Even the horses seem aware of the difference, their trot smoother and more graceful as if to prepare for the genteel. I can't help but recognize the familiar cluster of homes of various colors and styles stacked against each other. In the far distance, the swarm of bridges crisscrossing over each other sets my heart racing, forcing me to sit back and take a long, calming breath.

I keep telling myself the same thing, over and over: I will never in a thousand years see Tristan again. In such an enormous city, there is absolutely no chance of it. I have no intention of stepping one foot out of the home or being so much as a stone's throw away from Ezra.

Anyway, Tristan's not really human. The memory of him ripping off his shirt to dive in after the drowning woman proves that. He's like Neliem himself, half phantom, half legend. A vapor once extinguished leaves no mark. No trace, just the hollow whistle in the wind, a sound so soft that you can pretend it away.

One thing that I can't ignore, no matter how hard I try, is the sensation I felt when his lips pressed against mine. Countless beads of sweat drip down my neck and pool between my breasts as I drown in the memory.

Too soon, we arrive at Aunt Cora's lavish home. It is called 'The Equidus' after some horse from some battle that probably wiped out half my people. I scan the surroundings for some indication that an atrocity was committed against my kind, but there's none. All I spot is a lavish courtyard the size of three fields, various statues framing the walkway surrounded by a massive pear orchard. A royal entrance fit for a king. My palms sweat and the corset Velaria laced tight hurts—directly before the carriage stands a statue of my namesake, Neliem. But he's not alone. Under his arm he carries some flowery maiden, her mouth captured in a screech for eternity. My senses sharpen, my gaze narrowing. This rendition of him seems off, somehow.

Drawing closer, it's as if he's pulsating just below my flesh. Neliem.

And he wasn't some random kidnapper. A fighter, a resister, yes. Perhaps in some ways a protector of sorts. He prevented the slaughter of hundreds in his hometown. Which doesn't fit with the image before me.

For the first time, I wonder who Neliem truly was. Many times, the Untouchables have claimed extraordinary people from their conquests as their own, renaming them and exaggerating their attributes. It is possible that Neliem wasn't a god, nor demigod. Perhaps just a man who fought well and didn't get bested during one of their battles.

Maybe he was one of my people. The thought makes me smile.

Dozens of delicate rosebushes surround the statue, as if to lessen the effect of the sheer terror of standing in Neliem's presence. Taking in the angle of his face, the gleam of his haughty gaze, the way the stone was chiseled precisely to make the weak tremble, I once again question everything I've been told.

I break out of my reverie and remember to breathe. A portly guard stands watch at the front gate, the barbed wire curled at the tops of the walls glitters in the sun, and somewhere, a ravenous dog barks for food. Security no doubt for those contemplating robbing Neliem or one of the lesser gods. The mansion's situated further from the bustle of city life, closer to the suburbs, where the upper class live away from the foul smells and persistent merchants peddling their wares.

And reassuringly, further away from any chance of running into Tristan. The tension leaves my body at once.

Ralio opens the carriage door, still apologizing when not cursing the confounded lock. He hits it for good measure. Ezra, as ever, composed and silent, stills him with a wave of his hand.

"It happens ... latches sometimes break." But even he glares a bit too long at the lock.

When our eyes connect, he lowers his voice in a way that tells me he wishes me to follow his orders without complaint. "Oriana, would you like to be seen to your rooms?"

The blood drains from my face, not sure to what he refers. Surely, he can't mean that we're to be intimate here.

Catching the innuendo, he slowly smiles, clarifying, "Do you need to rest? Alone?"

"I'm quite rested ..." Then, not forgetting my manners, "Thank you."

Lifting my neck, I maintain my composure while servants hurry from the great house to gather our luggage. It takes a swarm of them to get everything inside. You would have thought we'd packed for a month, not a mere week.

When I turn to ask Ralio a question, he's gone. The deep footprints on the soil indicate that he went through the servants' entrance out the back. I tighten my fist. In Ezra's home, there's no such formality. The servants use the front door and kitchen entrance only for convenience. As if sensing my mood, he massages my shoulder, causing the kink pulsating in my back to subside.

"What do you think?" I raise an eyebrow as he continues, "Is Ralio on his first bottle of wine?"

I giggle. "Probably."

The last of the servants, a tightlipped butler, by the color of his vest, limps when he reaches to take the last bag. He avoids my gaze a little too carefully, not like the other servants, whose awkward stares lingered a fraction too long.

Feigning shyness, I linger behind Ezra. The doorway before me spans the length of three tall elms, intimating and unwelcoming.

I don't belong here, that small voice whispers in my head. Not in this house and not in this place where Outcasts are forbidden.

Stepping closer, Ezra murmurs in my ear as if reassuring a child, "They're probably just as nervous as you."

I bat my eyes and nudge him gently. "Go ahead; I'll be right in."

He takes a cautionary step away, his eyes narrowing, just as someone calls from inside.

"Ezra, is that you …" The voice beckons him again. Torn, Ezra walks away, his boots leaving a trail of dirt and dust, allowing me to finally inspect the carriage door handle.

The scratches against the lock are fresh, obviously done in broad daylight by the way the pattern is precise with clearly defined sharp edges. Too clean to have been attempted at night by mere candlelight. A previously undetected piece of metal still curled under the latch tells me as much. Someone earlier, probably before we rose, used either a knife or sharpened tool to sever the latch almost completely off.

I glance at the clay specks on the footrest, then back at the severed lock.

All knives and sharpened objects are under lock and key due to my antics. I rule out Elsie, who I could hear from a mile away, and quickly press the clay against my fingertips. Someone not from the house did this. Then I catch a glimmer of something sparkling in the mixture. I lift it to my nostril and inhale deeply.

A sweet odor emits.

Sugar.

I scrutinize the remainder of the latch, how it was purposely not cut off entirely. When it shut, it would have appeared locked and secure.

All that was needed was a firm jolt or a sudden gust of wind to unfasten it and send anyone seated close to the door flying out to their death.

I wince, the truth searing through me and awakening Neliem from his nap.

This was no accident. Someone just tried to kill me.

9

The mansion I'm escorted into seems to mirror my own, or rather Ezra's. It's vast and showy, and I assume from the clatter coming from the outside patio that already most of the guests have arrived. Servants frantically bound from the kitchen, carrying huge silver trays stuffed with delectable roasted meats and breads cut into perfect squares, and chilled goblets of rich wine and fruited punch with little bits of diced apple and orange.

The walls are handsomely decorated in the latest Grecian fashion, which seems popular this season based on the multitude of shops in Playa Del Sol. The paint is new. I scratch a bit off and see a mulled orange beneath the pale blue and freeze.

Orange was last year's color. My mother had dozens of dresses in this very shade commissioned from the neighboring island of Odessa. She worked steadily through all hours of the night to complete the order, only to be robbed once again when it came time to be paid.

My blood boils over remembering the transgression. The dresses were exquisite, flawless works of art. In silk and satin with ruffles that would make the plainest Untouchable seem beautiful. It reminds me, once again, how these Untouchables get away with everything.

Even murder.

I glance out at the carriage, which is being cleaned by two boys who should be in school.

That's what they think of me. I've been created to serve them like a slave and be beaten the second I commit the smallest mistake. Dark thoughts coil like a snake in my head, reawakening every foul memory of what these people truly are. Despicable pagans.

Breaking the trance, I force myself to walk. Ezra's up ahead, conversing with someone equally blond. His gaze never drifts too far from me. Absentmindedly, I stare at the furnishings, but don't sense any spirits wandering about. The facing wall is adorned as most Untouchables', honoring their barbaric traditions. Several small statues dipped in gold are in full display, occupying every nook and cranny in an attempt to gain all forms of favor from their false gods. At their feet, bowls of fruit and other lavish gifts are prominently displayed.

Whereas Ezra's home was free of adornment. All his enclaves are bare, and I can't recall one statute in his courtyard. The thought troubles me as I lift up an unblemished pear and take a huge bite, juice spilling down my chin. The lifeless eyes of a golden woman with four hands and a round protruding belly glare into mine. Licking my lips, I glare back.

The memory of the merchant carts, with gods capable of producing girls, flickers in the back of my mind and without meaning to, my fingers trace a small circle on her stomach. A small shiver runs down my spine. I yank my fingers back, appalled over my indiscretion. This is nothing more than yet another one of their supposed gods who are utterly powerless. I snicker, wipe my fingers on the lace doily and return the half-eaten pear carelessly aside.

"If you're mad at me, take it out on me later, but please try to be cordial to my family." I nearly jump out of my skin. While I was busy desecrating the false god, Ezra soundlessly snuck up behind me.

At a loss for words, I blink stupidly. His words are whisper soft, but there's no mistaking his innuendo. I am to behave. Trying to think of some plausible excuse, I steal a glance to gauge his mood. He's statuesque, resembling one of his gods, revealing nothing, yet a force to be reckoned with if provoked. I see it clearly, this darker side to him.

I glare back at the desecrated altar. "I was hungry. And I think she might have had too much to eat."

My eyebrow lifts toward her protruding belly.

We both laugh, Ezra's face breaking into a beautiful open smile. The mood is contagious, and I almost sway into him. For the first time since stepping foot in this house, I relax. He finds his own customs ridiculous, which is good. His eyes sparkle a bit, his beautiful face so close. All I would have to do is lean in, just a bit, and our foreheads would touch, and maybe, just maybe ...

I erase the thought quickly.

He senses my mood shift and the space between his eyes pinch, his gaze intent. I smile back shyly, the fluttering sensation in my heart spreading so that the tips of my fingers tingle. This is all too new for me. I'm away from everything I know and in, of all places, an Untouchable home to be presented as a bride. And, for the first time in my life, being treated well. The way Ezra places flowers every morning in the vase by my bed and how his smile feels familiar and foreign at the same time. The curl of his lips and soft flutter of eyelashes before he speaks as if he's being cautious and something else: shy, just like me.

Ezra shifts his stance so that his breath ruffles my hair. But he doesn't touch me. As always, he waits for me to make the first move. "They will respect you, Oriana."

Standing so close to him, inhaling the warm honey scent of his skin, I believe. I believe I can live this life. Just as our eyes connect, a sudden chill creeps into the room. The air shifts sending a shiver down my spine. Heavy steps thump above us, echoing down the consuming stairwell.

Not a ghost.

"Where oh where is my favorite nephew?" A woman's booming voice, undoubtedly Aunt Cora, blares like a rusty horn from above.

His gaze lifts, his eyelashes fluttering anxiously as if anticipating the verdict much too soon. A weight tightens around my neck, and I instinctively loosen my collar. Surely, these Untouchables will allow me some time, some leniency, but just as the hopeful thought appears, it just as quickly dissipates.

The verdict was set in stone the moment he told them what I was.

Clenching my fists, I don't have the heart to tell him that they won't like me, no matter how hard he tries dressing me up in the latest finery. Underneath this dress, I am still that wild girl who would rather own the dullest blade than the prettiest petticoat, and spit in their faces for assuming otherwise.

He grasps my hand, kissing it quickly before letting go. "It's important."

Without another word, he glides effortlessly up the stairs to tend to his aunt, her wobbly steps straining each step with a sharp squeak. Something in the way he moves reminds me of both a gazelle and panther. But I'm not sure which.

Aunt Cora, unaware of my proximity, speaks, "Did you bring *her?*"

There is no mistaking her innuendo.

Pain quivers in my gut. Unable to stand another moment of this torture, I move stiffly to the parlor and allow a servant to take my cloak and purse. Once the servant disappears into the cloakroom, her hurried steps clicking on the marble floor, I dare peek at my reflection in the mirror. Staring at myself, I'm horrified to discover that I do look a little like one of them; rich and self-assured. My soft brown hair is adorned with pearls and a modest veil. Every inch of me scrubbed clean. I smell like lavender and those expensive bath salts that I would never have dreamed of just days ago. The uneasy sensation spreads, climbs up my chest, itching just below my collar as if branding me what I truly am.

I am still Outcast. Never Hugganoff. These people are my sworn enemies. And to prove it, I just defiled their goddess, who will undoubtedly try to punish me by impregnating me with more of them. And I owe it to myself and everything I hold dear never to forget it.

Voices echo down the hallway, the smell of delicious food wafting in the air.

My stomach grumbles, and I instinctively press my palm to still it.

I stand straighter and peer closer into the mirror and see beyond the physical. I am many things, but a puppet or a plaything isn't one of them. And if Ezra thinks for one moment, I can be turned to some silly wife who bats her eyelashes at every word from his mouth, he had best remember who I truly am.

Before I can tell him off, Ezra returns, his panther-like feet too soft, his face unreadable. He stands behind me, and lifts my chin, as if pleased with what he sees.

My fists clench, my tongue itching to tell him exactly what I think, when he does the most unexpected thing yet. He caresses me tenderly, his body spooning into mine, his warmth filling every shattered nerve and quivering muscle.

"I'm right here." His lips find my earlobe, his tongue tracing a small line making my knees weak. "But no more eating consecrated fruit."

Completely disarmed, I stammer, "I thought I was honoring her ..."

"The fruit are for her unborn children ... it's blasphemy; people are stoned for less." He lowers his voice, his eyes so huge for a moment it's as if I'm drowning in a sea. "I understand exactly how you feel."

If this were true, it would be a one-way ticket back to Madera. Heavy footsteps clatter noisily from the kitchen, causing me to draw back. A chorus of voices ring with excitement from the foyer, the sound of the front door slammed followed by the little bell tinkling.

"And you think I would be anything other than polite?"

"I know right at this moment you're contemplating unmanning me and throwing my inners to the swine." Straightening my veil tenderly, he winks. "Oriana, we're not all so bad. And anyway, my family is indebted to our good graces for their yearly support."

My jaw dropping, I blink, positive I've misheard.

"Oriana, I hold the purse strings." He waves his hand around the splendor, and the truth sinks in. What Henric said to the girl from the teashop is true. His family has no money of their own. Through some act of divine intervention, Ezra's in charge of their future. Displease him, and they risk their own ruin.

And even though a moment ago all I wanted was to scream and tear every statue down, I don't. "I will be polite."

"Thank you." His face brightens as if the sun, his breath so sweet. "May I kiss you?"

"If you must."

He plants a chaste kiss on my forehead and with the slightest edge warns, "Behave."

The voices from the open parlor doors raise in volume. With my hand in his, I follow Ezra through a glistening hallway that leads to yet another sitting room. Shimmering gold walls greet me as the palest linens cushion the sofas, love seats, and matching chairs. Rays of blistering sunlight cascade into the room through the massive clear glass window stinging my eyes. Immediately Ezra places the softest handkerchief in my palm.

"It's all for show," he mumbles, his gaze focused outside. "Think of a pony show, only no ponies."

I wince, slowing down my pace to spy out the family gathered across the patio to welcome us. They are an odd bunch. A generation of elderly white-haired aunts and uncles and the much younger generation, Ezra's cousins no doubt. The way they are paired indicates that they are obviously married, some even have children. They are all blond and exquisitely dressed in pastels that match one another.

And for a second, I think I'm staring at a painting. Utterly surreal with only one thing out of place.

Me.

My eyes narrow, registering every detail and leaving nothing to chance. Fourteen Untouchables and their three small children have assembled to scrutinize me as I am paraded around as the prize goose.

I force my teeth to stop clattering and straighten my back.

I can do this. It was me who threw herself off the cliffs, and this is too easy, too simple. My step falters, my ankle almost twisting.

Before I stumble, once again, Ezra's by my side. His touch welcome.

"May I be excused?" I know I'm asking permission, but for this one occasion, I don't care.

He shakes his head, a cloud crossing his features. "You promised to be polite."

Every nerve in my body screams to fight, to draw back my hand and give him a good shaking and only then run and hide in my room. Perhaps under the bed.

Without letting go of my hand, Ezra straightens to his full height, stepping outside. He makes a show to pause and inhale the sweet floral air as if he'd created the heavens and the earth and everything was just as he planned.

He exclaims to no one in particular, "Who ordered such a lovely day to present my betrothed?"

It's a compliment. For me. I gasp a little and tidy my lace sleeve that's become tangled and slowly let out the exhale I've been choking on.

One little girl adorned in pink giggles. For a second, I think she's laughing at me, but then I realize she's just silly. Her mother, seated on an iron chair with a fat cushion, lifts her head, that familiar tilt of her chin a signal.

My feet move. Ezra smiles and nods, wrapping his hand around my waist without being asked. I try to emulate the golden naked statue. Stiff and cold like these people. Their handshakes are cool and distant, holding nothing other than curiosity. The girls are stunning, works of art with their hair and fitted gowns tailored to perfection. One smiles genuinely, but I don't trust it.

Ezra takes great pains to repeat their names carefully, but their titles of first, second, or third cousins all whirl in my head. There's a cousin Beatrix not to be confused with Aunt Cora's eldest daughter Eloina. They look like twins but are in fact, third cousins. Everyone seems on their best behavior, with no sly comment or wiping of their hand clean after touching me. Ezra welcomes them only after they have paid their respects.

Tea is promptly served, with Ezra offering me the first cup to distinguish me as the person of honor. Everyone dutifully tips their head before taking the first sip, and the noose tightening around my neck seems to ease. I breathe in and force the corners of my mouth to lift.

The women cluster together with their mindless chitchat about the weather and colors of the latest fashionable ball gowns. And it's true, not one of them has an opinion on current events. After exchanging pleasantries and assuring everyone that the ferry ride across the channel from Madera met with my approval, I modestly excuse myself.

Ezra gets up, concern filling his face. I know he wants to object and make me stand my ground and stay.

Like a mouse, I whisper loud enough for all to hear, "Is it all right that I rest?"

He bites back whatever he wanted to say and nods. Only then do I get up and say my farewells. As I pass, one of the male cousins arches an eyebrow, but an older gentleman with bushy eyebrows scoffs it off, checking his timepiece compulsively, waiting no doubt for the allotted time to have paid his respects.

Without looking back, Ezra leads me to the doorway and places a warm kiss on my forehead. "I thought you said you weren't tired."

I stifle a yawn and profess an unnatural need to tend to the unpacking of my garments. Which couldn't be further from the truth.

"Perhaps you will check up on me in an hour or so?" I smile too brightly.

Recognition dawning, he flushes a bit and kisses my hand, allowing me to leave without any more chastisement. I curtsy and take off before anyone can stop me. Someone here is to blame for the latch being severed, and I intend to find out who.

If they think that they would so easily get rid of me, they have no idea who they are dealing with.

Upstairs, the servants are already unpacking my things in my room, which holds two narrow beds. When I walk in, they all straighten and bow meekly, inquiring how they may assist me. One maid can barely control her stutter, and her left cheek spasms unnaturally, as if I were someone of importance.

Then I remember I now am.

This fact startles me. I know I will never get used to this sudden elevation in status. Immediate respect tingled with a mixture of awe. From the hushed whispers and not so subtle stares floating throughout the house, Ezra's the catch of the Mercer clan. One that, without one ounce of effort, I've snared in my web.

Without explanation, I wave my hands over my face, pretending that I need some fresh air when in fact every window's wide open, allowing the coolest breeze to fan out the room.

Without looking where I'm going, I walk straight into a wall of solid muscle. Ezra. "Well?"

And I realize that I've underestimated him. He's not buying my act. He's not a gazelle after all, but as I suspected before: a panther.

"I just needed a moment. They're a bit overwhelming." I motion downstairs to the patio, where his family's engaged in mindless chitchat, eating until their bellies are stuffed while complaining about the most mundane things. I want nothing more than to tell him about the latch and point out the most likely culprit—any one of those blond gods—but something holds me back.

They're his family.

His blood.

Ezra notes the sleeping arrangements and frowns. "Why are there two beds in here?"

From the notecard on her bed, it seems I have been paired with the doe-eyed Tanya as my bedmate. Her open valise is in the corner already unpacked.

Ezra lifts the card with my name tightly scrawled on parchment. He glares at the servants. "Who saw to these sleeping arrangements?"

His feathers ruffled, he takes matters at hand, a little too eagerly in my opinion. He personally sees that my things are removed at once and put in their proper place, his room, which is on the opposite wing facing the orchard, not the busy avenue.

Outside, carriages are neatly lined up in the street, waiting their turn to drive into the estate. Which means more family members. The protocol is for the driver to unlatch it and allow the man out first, then the women. Not that I've been privy to this type of treatment. Before this week, I've only once been on a carriage, more often times than naught in the back of a rickety old wagon, jiggled up and down as if being flung against rocks. Suddenly, a troubling thought crosses my mind. There is a custom of Untouchable men always being seated by the carriage door. The fresh memory of Ezra always making sure I was seated closest to the window the day of our betrothal itches in the back of my mind.

The way his soft hand sends a little tingle shooting. His breath, always sweet, reminding me …

Downstairs, the massive doorbell clangs loudly, breaking me out of my reverie. Shuffling footsteps and doors snap open as newly arrived family members crowd into the foyer. A whirlwind of top hats and bonnets and enough lace to drape around the world encompass every inch of marble floor. Darling Cassia, with her familiar high-pitched screech that passes for a greeting, makes her way to the front of the line as introductions are made.

I noted her absent earlier on the patio. Interesting enough, she'd kept to her rooms until now, avoiding my official introduction to the family. A dashing Henric, impeccably dressed, bounces down the stairs. There's a hop to his step, and remarkably, if it were even possible, he looks more handsome than the last time I saw him. Of course, outside of the teashop with a look of dismay etched into his fine features is not a fair comparison. I take my time to study his movements, how he glides from one stuffy relative to the next, the air of self-assurance pouring from every cell in his body. His hair's combed back with pristine accuracy, every strand in place, his face as always, unreadable. He narrowly misses being suffocated in Cassia's embrace. But, like the predator he truly is, he avoids her like the plague, mindlessly chitchatting with a gentleman who could easily pass for his grandfather. Cassia pretends not to notice the slight and focuses on another elderly gentleman with a cane and top hat, who discusses the weather in great detail.

I don't have to turn to know that Ezra's back at my side, his gaze fixed on me. I nudge my chin. "I saw Henric in town …"

He arches an eyebrow, stepping closer to examine his flock of relations. I continue, unable to stop staring at Henric. "Outside of a teashop … being scolded by a schoolgirl. He said something about Tanya being sent back …"

"It would be best if you didn't mention that to anyone. And I do mean anyone." Ezra lets out a sigh, raking his long fingers through his hair, his attention now on the verbose Cassia, who seems to be making a show of embracing every relative as if they were her own. "You don't have to be nice to Cassia. I don't like her either."

His throat catches, as if he was about to say something else, but thought better of it. It's a tell. He doesn't trust me. And for some reason, it bothers me enough to inch away from him and avert my gaze. He catches this small movement and stops, a tiny bead of sweat forming on his top lip. I'm about to confront him about the slight when a familiar sensation burrows into my shoulder.

My eyes connect with cousin Henric. For a moment, I fear the worst. That he knows I was the one spying on him. But he all but ignores me, his gaze steady on Ezra. His lips press together as I watch a silent conversation transpire between the two.

"I guessed that," I mutter, feeling excluded.

From what I overhead earlier from the elderly aunts chitchatting as I studied my tea sandwich, wondering if poison was beneath these people, Cassia arrived three days ago. It seems they are in the midst of remodeling her home. The walls are being stripped of old fashion wallpaper and a nursery set up. But watching her now, engrossed with a silver-haired uncle, I notice how she favors her right side, instead of her left. It's just a slight inclination that most would never note. But I am not most people.

And most surprisingly, how after days apart, Henric remains aloof and uninterested. Conveying the usual cold-heartedness that Untouchables are famous for, he ignores her. Unlike Ezra, who's seemingly glued at my hip.

I can't shake the thought away. Henric's devilishly good looking and knows it. Cassia clings to his side like a tic, worming her way even closer. Ezra glances back at me, and I offer, "She doesn't bother me ..."

He gives me a knowing look, and once again, I reminded of a dangerous panther. "I mean, not that much."

I bow, excusing myself, when his hand finds mine, slinking up my arm.

"Fine; don't wander far." It's a warning. One I have absolutely no intention of following.

Ezra arches an eyebrow, his meaning transparent: no leaping off balconies, no direct combat with immediate family members, and keep away from the knives. The silverware will undoubtedly be counted twice before we're allowed to leave.

Pretending obedience, I sag my shoulders, and offer a contrite smile. It is answer enough. Excused, I stride gracefully downstairs without looking back, my head just a bit higher.

From the wide-open windows, a gentle breeze blows, ruffling the curtains and a bell tinkles. In the courtyard, two handsome carriages approach the house, their wheels crunching the gravel so that a cloud of dust forms choking the drivers. The rattle of the entrance hall doors being flung open vibrates once again. I peek from the closest railing, curious.

Even more relatives. By their attire, all wealthy. And as I previously suspected, they all look the same. Blond and pale. Some are bald and fat, but mostly conveying a style that comes from always having power and privilege.

They prance from the foyer, spreading all through the massive house like a locust plague. Servants scurry about taking cloaks and hats and jackets. Some family members scatter toward the den and others wander through the vast rooms, inspecting the silver and other valuables. Few pay homage to the false idols. One small child dips her finger into a saucer and mischievously licks the honey. I smile. It seems I am not the only one to desecrate their altars.

Huddling together, their heated whispers lift. Undoubtedly gossiping about their handsome cousin's strange and slightly alarming new addition to the family. My grin broadens, imagining the extent of their conversations. Their worst fears won't even touch the surface.

Instead of going down the main stairway, I wander back, discovering the servants' stairs, which are draped in mourning colors to signify the death of someone in service. Digesting this bit of information, I go about my investigation of who might have sabotaged the carriage door handle.

Aunt Cora has been quickly eliminated. Her plump legs can barely climb down a flight of stairs, let alone have hiked up the hill to where we live without drawing attention when she had a coronary. But everyone else is suspect until proven innocent. Then, spotting the library deserted, I stroll quickly inside and close the door so that it's ajar enough to alert me if someone approaches.

Turning on my heel, I freeze. It's a library that might have been in a college or university. Once, I found a picture of a library not half as impressive in one of my school books. My interest piques, wondering if borrowing a book about the legendary Neliem would be out of the question. My only copy is at home and is more of a child's book not the real unabridged version of the legendary hero and his countless adventures.

As I'm scanning for a copy small enough to fit in my sleeve, by accident I happen upon The Chronicles of Neliem tucked firmly on the shelf. Delighted over my unexpected discovery, my greedy fingers pry it out when a too-familiar voice filters through the open door.

"There you are."

My skin prickles, a wave of heat spreading from my neck all the way to my toes.

He can't be here is the only thought spinning in my head. But just the same, I pause mid-pull, all my attention toward the hallway. Two elderly women gathered in the corridor are fussing about the arrival of yet another guest. I catch a movement of hands brushing dust off a jacket. Holding my breath, I peek through the doorjamb too petrified to breathe.

As luck would have it, the scoundrel's back is to me. All I spot are a pair of weathered hands placing a handsome burgundy hat, probably worth more than my entire village eats in a month, on a peg. I narrow my eyes and inch compulsively closer.

The man, who cannot be much older than me, shifts just slightly, and I catch the ruffles in his shirt and immediately relax my shoulders. The fellow Neliem from town last week would never be caught in a ruffled shirt. But whoever he is, he is rich, as I previously suspected, as well as arrogant no doubt. He leans gracefully to his side to stifle a yawn, an embroidered handkerchief with a flowery M in a flaming pink. No, definitely not my Tristan and I shiver in relief. Shaking the tremble out of my hands, I tell myself that it's merely yet another rich stuffy relative here for a free meal and to scrutinize the Outcast girl.

A weight lifts off my chest as I reclaim my book. Once retrieved, I attempt to hide it when the wind shifts and a scatter of rain and brittle leaves rattle against the closed window, snapping like nails.

"Ta-Ta, we didn't think you would bother … no one's heard of you for the past five days."

The conversation barely piques my interest enough to lift my gaze. I throw a glimpse out the doorjamb, distracted by how the ladies fawn over this man, mussing over his hair, straightening his collar, and going as far as to straighten his shirt as if he were a child. It's as if they can't keep their hands off him.

"And miss breaking off my brother's wedding?"

The book slips through my fingers with a loud bang. Unable to move, I stand frozen, every nerve in my body shattered. It can't be, no, never, I assure myself. It cannot be the other Neliem from the city; my stalker, my admirer, my Tristan, who flung himself into the channel to save the woman drowning in the carriage. No, never. And the memory of the heated kiss with promises for much more ignite a flame in the pit of my belly. I pinch my eyes closed. It's a trick. I'm overwrought after nearly plunging to my death when the carriage door flung open and now being surrounded at every corner by my enemy.

The next sentence confirms every fear.

"Oh, Tristan, you will just love her. She's lovely. Very sweet, so shy. Why, she could barely lift her eyes when we were introduced."

The other elderly aunt nods her head compulsively, her hand before her heart as if swearing an oath. "It shows someone bothered to teach her right. Perhaps that school she attended."

My blood boils over her false assumption. The only thing that school taught me was to run for my life.

Tristan, in full form, snickers, "I will be the judge and jury of that."

The aunts prance off to announce his arrival while a female servant relieves him of his jacket. The way the servant divests him of his outer garment, her hand lingering on his waist, shows that she would prefer to disrobe him entirely. Even peeking from the small slit behind the door, there's no mistaking the lust radiating off her as clearly as the noonday sun.

Blood rushes out of my head, and I trip, nearly breaking every bone in my body over the book of Neliem. My backside thumps on the floor, causing a commotion that could wake the dead. Tristan momentarily tilts his chin in my direction, but the servant girl brazenly grabs his head, planting a kiss on his mouth that would make me blush to the tips of my ears. That is, if they weren't already blazing red hot.

Automatically, Tristan pulls back, his face white, his eyes intense, his hands blocking the wench.

My jaw drops as the wanton creature squeezes his thigh, licking her lips in a way that leaves nothing to the imagination. If left to her own designs, they would be disrobed and rolling on the carpet. "Is this all that master would desire?"

I slam my hand to my mouth to stop from gasping.

She wants him.

He laughs, shaking his head in that way of his. "Yes, Soriee. That will be all."

To confirm it, he backs three cautious steps away. My heart stops hammering, and I remember to breathe. He's not interested. And I shouldn't really care either way. What I should be is petrified. Tristan, my Tristan, is here, right now. Worse, if what he proclaims to be true, he is Ezra's wayward brother, the one who wants to stop our nuptials and send me packing to Madera without so much as a second thought.

Moving as quietly as possible, I lift the book to the desk and focus. There are five exits and three windows wide enough to leap out of if pressed upon. As well as a servant's exit, which perchance leads to an alley, where I can escape unnoticed. Then I recall the walls with barbed wire and the guard fully armed, most likely trained to fire at will. As well as a pair of ravenous dogs to hinder any such attempt.

Like a trapped animal, I can't move, let alone come up with an escape plan. For the first time, the spirit of Neliem has deserted me completely. I've been reduced to a sniveling coward, one who huddles behind the dark cover of bookshelves, hoping that I can slip passed unnoticed the moment the corridor is cleared.

Heavy footsteps stomp louder on the hardwood floors, and I know without looking that others have joined him. Daringly, I open one eye to spy. Henric, Landis and another fellow with equally blond hair are greeting Tristan warmly. They hit his back affectionately, swarming him, their mood both jovial and affectionate.

"Tristan," Landis lunges at him like a bear, for the first time with no mask to shield his emotions. He smiles brightly, like a star, and for a moment I'm captured in his brilliance. The mood is contagious. Even the sour aftereffects of Cassia's proximity have vanished from Henric, who follows suit, not only squeezing the life out of Tristan, but lifting him a few inches in the air as if he weighed no more than half a stone.

"And where have you been?"

"Where haven't I been?" Tristan, his usual cocky self, mocks. And it's the same self-assured Tristan that I know only too well. For a horrifying second, I fret that he might mention his latest conquest and have a good belly laugh at my expense.

The grandfather clock ticks rhythmically, propelling the wheels in my head to spin faster.

I know one thing; I can't stand here spying anymore. I need to run. Like a rat who's wise enough to bail out of sinking ship, I need to make my exit. Quickly. Without a sound, I slink to the ground, clutching my fist so tightly that my nails cut into my palms.

"Heard about your heroics …" I think it's Henric who snickers. A shiver crawls down my spine. My chest tightening, I glide across the thick woven carpet, kicking off my shoes.

"So did I, very amusing," The one I don't know adds.

Tristan laughs it off. Compelled by some unnamed impulse, I turn my head.

"Diving into a channel, this time of year? The water must've been freezing." Landis again. "Not to mention what was in that water."

"All for a worthy cause; the horse is eternally grateful."

More laughter, and I finally dare peek through the doorjamb.

"Not for a fair wench?"

I wince at the perfect opening to brag about his exploits. Namely, how I let him kiss me.

"No, but the horse and I are officially engaged …" I gasp and cover my mouth to prevent from laughing along.

Then, anxiously, Tristan's gaze drifts toward the stairs. "And where is my brother and his plain country bride?"

Landis shifts in his stance, his gaze just as intense. "She's nice enough. Pretty."

Henric, the bastard, rubs his nail up and down the banister. "Quite dull for my taste." And then lower, so that I have to strain to hear, "Everything is set?"

They all slowly nod, reading some expression on Tristan's face that I can't see. Then everyone lets out an audible sigh, a wave of relief washing over them and leaving me in the dark as to what's about to unfold.

Tristan's eyes catch the light just so. And for a split second, I'm positive that I've been caught. "So, she's quite dull, is she? As I suspected. I suppose now that dear Ezra will stop playing the monk and finally frequent a certain brothel to whet his appetite."

The anger seethes through me, pulsating red hot in my veins. Neliem springs to life as I'm ready to pounce. I scrutinize my adversaries cautiously. Two will go down easily, one will run, and Tristan, Tristan I will save for last. I relish how I'll make him suffer, prolonging the torture until he begs for mercy.

Henric laughs like a hyena, spitting out his words, "I wish I was there right now. Why haven't you been?"

Tristan eyes him suspiciously, about to say something, but collects himself at the last moment. "Missed my exquisite company?"

"Need you ask?" Henric glares. "You are the one constant in this world of inconsistencies."

For a moment, the curtain draped around Henric since we met, loosens. What stands before me seems almost human. Tender even, showing a side he hides better than choice jewels: fierce loyalty. And perhaps, if I had the inclination to scrape below the surface, something else entirely: admiration.

Processing the exchange, my gut clenches as if I swallowed sour rind. The truth hits me, almost making me lose my balance. Henric was just betrothed and already has absolutely no interest in his wife. First, there was that business outside of the teashop. That girl telling him to leave her alone. And even though I loathe Cassia with every fiber in my being, I know betrayal like the raw sting of a belt across my backside one too many times.

That little part of me that wishes for the impossible can't help but fear this is how it will be for Ezra and me. One minute he offers sweet words of devotion, the other dismissed while he seeks his pleasures elsewhere.

Landis shakes his head and laughs. "Seriously, where have you been?"

"Need you ask?" Tristan confesses, "Why, chasing my heart's desire."

It's as if all the air has been sucked from the room. Everyone grows deadly silent. Even the hallway clock seems to pause. Then the other boy, the one I don't know, speaks up, "Since when do you chase anything? I thought they all chase after you? Or rather, your purse."

It seems to be an inside joke. One that's been used at Tristan's expense quite often, I suspect.

Not in the least affected, Tristan is all sly smiles. "Ah, this one, I fear, knows how to run." He brushes off some lint that Soiree missed off his cuff. "Rather too fast."

Henric turns pale, and once again looks like a child. "Should we be worried? I mean … you …"

Landis hits him playfully, teasing, "Tristan, you said you would sooner be boiled in oil and have your inners pulled out through your nostril and left to wither in the sun than take your vows."

Tristan's face contorts as if actually contemplating this. Then that familiar spark flickers like thunder against a storm. "There is definitely something to be said about being boiled in oil and having your inners pulled out of your nostril and left to wither in the sun."

All three men stare at him, dumbfounded. Tristan turns his gaze toward the patio breaking from the circle, his pulse spiking just as mine matches his. "Enough of this; where is my brother?"

Without waiting, Tristan strides purposely outside, leaving his cousins on his heels, rushing like schoolboys after a treat. Once the footsteps fade, I unclench my fists that have turned white, my nails leaving little crescent moons embedded in my palms. My head spins so hard that I collapse against the wall to gather my thoughts, which are darker and bleaker than they were a moment ago. The ticking grandfather clock in the hallway resumes its taunt, the seconds amplified as realization dawns.

Through some cruel trick of nature, Ezra and Tristan are brothers. Brothers. The same blood, the same expressions. Those blazing blue eyes, calm one moment and the other … Like a whirlwind it all comes together; all the bits and pieces of information that should've alerted me sooner.

Frustrated, I slam my hand against the wall, upsetting a statue of a goddess swallowing a bird. Its wingspan shakes, then stills. It reminds me of my eagle soaring through the heavens. The answer to this drama is obvious. I might be Neliem, one who fights to the death, never shirking from danger, but in this situation, there is no course available but immediate escape.

As luck would have it, the library windows face a park, separated by merely a low retaining wall. Only a small unguarded gate lies between me and impending freedom. I count the steps that it would take to slip out the window and leave unnoticed.

With infinitesimal care, I tuck my shoes under the table. It will be much faster with bare feet. Then, on tiptoes, I slink toward the drapes. My fingers press the latch to pry open the window, when I realize it's stuck. The lock jammed. I hold my breath and gently jab it open with a fingernail. It creeks, moaning like an old woman in pain.

Straining, I tug harder. It shakes, then gives. But the squeaking's enough to wake the dead. Outside, the cloud cover lifts, the spring shower having subsided. Rich Untouchables stroll in the cool of the day. Ladies immaculately dressed and carrying dainty parasols and gentlemen in top hats and fine coats. In the park, children ride tricycles, some playing with colorful hoops.

The slick cobblestones beckon me forward.

All I need is another push to snap open the screen, and I'm free. In answer to my prayer, the window with a shudder finally gives. My fingers reach for the screen when a hand comes down hard on my shoulder, turning me around in one fluid movement.

Stormy blue oceans rage.

"What the dickens are you doing here?" Tristan's voice pierces. Then, closing his eyes, he embraces me tight. "Thank God."

His demeanor in the blink of an eye shifts from irate to tender. He glances behind his shoulder, then steps disarmingly closer so that our noses almost touch.

I know two things: he's happy to see me, and he doesn't want a scene. At least, not yet.

Every nerve in my body quivers. But a strange relief washes over me. I breathe. He's here, and I should be running for my life. Instead, I gawk like some infatuated schoolgirl. The same girl who averted capture her entire life has fallen into the simplest of traps. At once I realize my mistake; my back was to the only two entrances in the room.

To make matters worse, I'm completely disarmed. A stupid,

stupid mistake not worthy of Neliem.

I close my eyes in prayer. Once, not too long ago, a carriage falling off a bridge was sent from God in answer. Perchance a fire, or another large enough explosion will save me now.

By the look of sheer determination on his face, most likely not.

In the span of seconds, I pray to every saint who ever lived. Both alive and martyred. Holding in a breath, I glance toward the servant's exit, but my fellow Neliem is standing too close to attempt any form of escape, his hip touching mine as if to say, 'Try it.'

In two small steps, I could leap to safety and race down the avenue. Just as the thought crosses my head, his hand clamps down on my waist, pinning me against him.

"Oh, Tristan … is that you?" I use the smile I've been practicing, my hand carefully placed over my heart to convey surprise.

His arched eyebrow informs me at once that my act couldn't fool a blind beggar. Make that a blind, deaf beggar who hasn't eaten in a week.

The blaze in Tristan's eyes could melt lead. It isn't a storm, rather a tempest. One I'm about to be swept into. "Don't, 'Oh, Tristan is that you?' to me, young lady. Where the dickens have you been?" He points his finger accusingly, and it takes everything in me not to snap at it.

As if reading my thoughts, he darts his finger away. Footsteps recede from the foyer, distracting him. But his grip doesn't falter. With ease, he pulls me deeper into the library.

Only then does he allow his defenses down.

He takes a moment to collect himself, the relief of finding me enough of an incentive to explain, "I would have you know that sixteen copies of the frock you were wearing were sold last week. And I had to go through nine somewhat terrifying, yet exhilarating, experiences to find out that sadly, none of which were in your possession."

I stammer, "Nine out of the sixteen …"

"In various sizes, mind you. Your size had ten frocks. Nine of which I had to painstakingly interview in excruciating detail."

He runs a trail of hot kisses from my hand up to my elbow, then repeats the process on the other, frowning when he sees the self-inflicted marks on my palms. He lowers his head as if in prayer and tenderly smothers a kiss on each one as if a caressing a bud about to bloom.

And something delicious builds in my loins.

Tristan catches this, then just as quickly shakes his head. "Enough of this; what is your name?"

I cannot help it. "Oriana."

He smiles, relieved. "Thank Heavens it wasn't Prudence. She was the tenth appointment today."

Exasperated Tristan disappears and what faces me is puppy-dog infatuated Tristan. The one that I can't resist. He lifts my face and kisses my cheek. The tingle spreads, sending a path of fire down to my chest. He steps back only to watch my reaction. Satisfied, he grins, his eyes mocking in that way that makes me want to smack him upside his head and kick him down a flight of stairs.

"Thought so."

I'm too stunned to speak. It's the same effect as before. My flesh burns hot and even through I'm terrified, my body springs to life.

I stutter helplessly, "I'm glad you are well."

It was, after all, my wish. To see him again and part as friends.

Even though this is like no friendship I've ever experienced.

He all but ignores my formality, his eyes roaming all over me as if I had on nothing more than the sheerest petticoat. "And this frock I rather like. Of course, I'd love it better off."

How does he say these things without me wanting nothing better than to beat him soundly? I still don't know where to begin, but something tells me that parting as friends might not go as well as I'd hoped. "It's good to see you, Tristan. Really."

"And here we are. At a family function of all places." He rolls his eyes. "My family function."

"Yes, about that ..."

Tristan wanders toward the bar and pours himself a brandy, miraculously without letting go of my hand. He explains, "My brother is marrying some horrific fortune hunter, which I intend to abruptly put a stop to, but that shouldn't change our plans."

I rip my hand from his violently. "Really?"

His head tilts toward the door, scolding me, "Keep your voice down. Yes. But don't fret. We will casually make our way upstairs within the hour for a much-needed rendezvous. There are conveniently locks on these bedroom doors, unlike other homes." He pauses me to give me the once-over. "And I still haven't forgiven you for taking off."

Horrified by his intent, my jaw drops.

"You missed an opportunity of a lifetime." He makes a motion to nuzzle against me as I sidestep his advances. "Rescuing the ambassador's wife and resuscitating her." He leans in, and murmurs against my ear, "For the better part of an hour, mind you."

I almost spill the drink, a bubble of laughter escaping my lungs so hard that my sides hurt. "She must have been eternally grateful and rewarded you appropriately. Don't tell me, you have sired a male child. He will be impossibly handsome to make up for his lack of discretion."

Tristan's resolve breaks, and for a moment he looks so young and vulnerable. His breath catches, about to say something when he pulls me into a tight embrace. His heart hammers against mine, and for a moment, I don't wish to be any other place than in his arms. I inhale deeply, mischief and spice and storm. The lump in my throat pulsates, telling me to end it now. As it is, I can barely move, the heat radiating from his body intoxicatingly sweet. So playful, so Tristan. "She's eighty. God, I've missed you."

Outside, a door slams, alerting him that we are not alone. When he shifts his stance, I take the opportunity to move away, contemplating how to announce myself as the devious fortune hunter who's tricked his brother.

Tristan's hot gaze trickles over me like warm milk, his eyes lingering on the gown, but most likely what's concealed under the fine satin and lace. "And I'm relieved to find you once again unblemished."

Softer than feathers, his fingers glide down my face, and I'm rendered paralyzed. There's something about how he looks at me, one moment deadly as a cobra, the next as gentle as a lamb. Both equally irresistible. And for the life of me, I still don't know how he can tell that I'm still pure.

"How can you tell that, just by looking at me?"

He squints as if also perplexed. "Yes and no. There's just something about you …" He absentmindedly brushes his finger over my nose, and tries again, "It's this scent, almost, like a whiff of heaven, or what I suppose heaven to smell like."

His boyish innocence makes him even that more dangerous. Awkwardly, I stare down at my shoes, tucked under the table, which I haven't bothered to put back on. This morning, before I woke up, a box was on the empty pillow by my head. I rubbed the sleep from my eyes to find Ezra at the doorway, with that sweet anxious look on his face. I quickly unraveled the ribbon, opened the box, and gasped. There they were. The most perfect shoes on the planet, adorned with golden bows. Ezra waited patiently for my reaction, not daring enter my bedchambers without an invitation. The truth was that I was so touched, I wasn't sure whether to laugh or cry.

"May I?" And still, Ezra waited for permission.

I could only nod. He crouched by the side of my bed and with the gentlest hands placed one shoe, then the other, on my foot.

A perfect fit.

It was just another small token of his affection.

My heart bleeds.

I blink at Tristan and force my mouth open. "There's something that I have to tell you, and you're not going to like it." My shoulders arch, tightening like wires, bracing for the impact.

He squeezes the bridge of his nose, anticipating what he thinks the worst possible scenario. "Don't tell me you're friends with her? The shrew that has stuck her vicious claws in my innocent brother! You know her?"

He explodes, his natural Neliem instinct taking over. And something else, something that pulls at my heart. Streams of tears leak from his eyes, his body crumbling.

The truth hits me. "You love him."

Gingerly, I place my hand on his shoulder, torn between two very different actions. Embracing him, going as far as to allow him to weep on my shoulder or admitting that, I am that very shrew whom he detests, before inserting my foot up his arse as he begs unsuccessfully for mercy.

As if unable to bear his own weight, he collapses into a seat. "Oriana, my family be hanged, I really need to get you upstairs and bury myself in you. Now."

His words send a delicious quiver to my gut, one that stirs me even more awake. I exhale slowly, not sure how to respond. I know firsthand the tension he's experiencing. I've felt it every waking hour for the last few days, building since our last encounter and unable to find release.

And in dealing with Tristan, a fellow Neliem, I know that only blatant honesty will work at a time like this. "Tristan, I would rather wrestle with you for an hour and knock some common sense into that thick head of yours."

Tenderly, I rub at his throbbing temple hoping to alleviate some of the rage that's certain to erupt when he discovers the truth.

Unexpectedly, Tristan's mood shifts. Instead of anger, what I get is merriment. He laughs and grabs me. "God woman, how have I ever survived one day without you in my life?"

I let out a yelp as he tosses me in the air and catches me effortlessly. His smoldering eyes burn into mine just as the library doors fling open. I don't have to turn to see who it is.

I would know that heartbeat anywhere.

Ezra stands before us with a wide grin. "There you are …"

And their voices are identical. The tilt of the head, the glimmer of blue, the delicate flare of their nostrils, down to the tiny dimple at the base of their chins.

Brothers.

I don't know how it's possible that I missed this.

Ezra glances behind him, probably making sure there isn't some lurking relative about. Once sure, he sighs. His shoulders soften, the cease finally leaving his forehead, his eyes full of hope. Which makes it all the worse. He has absolutely no inkling of the monsoon about to erupt.

The air shifts, electrifying. I brace myself, my senses heightened. In the kitchen, there's a quarrel over some soup. Too much pepper. On the banisters, two Untouchables prance down slowly, speaking in hushed whispers obviously gossiping about me. My skin prickles and the hairs on the back of my neck stand.

When I look up, Ezra's glare sears through me as if somehow understanding. But Tristan still doesn't loosen his grip. His touch makes it all the more unbearable.

"Introductions would be in order, but I see that you are well acquainted." There's that lightness in Ezra's tone, that bit of boy mixed with just a hint of mischief. Panther yes, but something else as well. "And you thought, well—" He cuts short his admonition with a wave of his hand and offers, "Wonderful to see you brother."

Still unaware, Ezra chuckles, pouring himself a drink. There's something so familiar about that laugh. It tugs at something forgotten buried deep within me. A summer's day. A bowl of ripe berries and that laugh.

I pinch my eyes closed. The instinctive nature to run pulsates through every muscle, causing my hands to spasm. My anxious feet twitch, and I steady my nerves, attempting to squelch the flame. But it festers like a tornado, with every breath, matching the clock in the hall: Tristan's grip, the soft curve of Ezra's mouth, the air heavier, thicker, intoxicating sweet.

When I lift my head, I catch my reflection in Tristan's eyes. And for the life of me, I cannot open my mouth and tell him the truth. My heartbeat pounds as outside in the hall, a patter of several footsteps approach.

"Brother, I admit it." Tristan stares lovingly at me, not bothering to hide it. I blush and try to inch away. "You catch me in too good of a mood to brood about anything."

"So, you like Oriana?"

"Like her? I love her." His husky voice deepens in a way that makes my knees quiver. Ezra laughs again, having no inkling where this is headed. He wraps his arm around my free shoulder, and I am caught in the middle of two enamored brothers, trapped.

My body humming, I start to hyperventilate. Two weeks ago, two brothers also had me trapped, and the memory flashes before me like rusty nails scrapping against my flesh.

My head burns. My focus blurs.

Ezra speaks first, taking my pulse. "Are you ill?"

Tristan breaks his hold to get me some water, which I quickly accept. Ezra patiently leads me to a sofa, scattering off pillows to make ample room.

Feeling dizzy, I collapse down, the confession slipping before I can stop. "A little over two weeks ago … something happened at my village. I was collecting some apples …"

Tristan's hot gaze soaks up my every word. But Ezra shows no emotion other than a quick glance to gage Tristan's reaction, then back at me. He knows part of this story, but Ezra still has no clue. He doesn't suspect a thing; if he did, perhaps things would've been different.

"These boys … two brothers …" My voice cracks. Just like before while watching the boat race, it seems so vivid. Those brutes, cornering me like an animal. Me with only an old dagger and my wits to save my life. Then I recall the way the dagger had seared hot, as if to warn me.

My hand clenches desperate for my dagger.

Tristan breaks the silence first, "What are their names?" And he sounds like Neliem himself. All darkness and death. He flickers a look to Ezra, who just rubs his eyes.

I rack my brain but come up empty. "I don't know ... they have red hair ..."

And one is missing an ear.

Footfalls click louder as cluster of elderly ladies approach the threshold, idling before entering. But my attention's elsewhere. There are four weapons on the table, a letter opener, two marble paperweights and a pen with a sharp enough of a point to inflict permanent damage.

My fists squeeze, then release. Ezra nudges just a fraction, his breath warm against my neck. "Oriana, those boys will never harm you again. Do you believe me?" His voice is a whisper, soft, alluring. And something else. Deadly serious.

I shake my head in response. He still doesn't understand what those boys tried to do to me. But my tongue's too dry to try to explain. Without warning, Ezra gets up to greet his elderly aunts, their frail steps slowing as they approach the library.

Tristan stirs. "Listen to me, Oriana. I will hunt them down and hurt them; after I'm done, they will be lucky if they can crawl. Ever."

I look up feeling naked. He knows and yet it hasn't hampered his feelings. He protected me in the city, and now, now his gaze comforts me in a way words could never.

My voice quivers, "You would do that?"

"Yes. For you Oriana, I would. And much more." Tenderly, he moves a stray curl, tugging it around his finger with so much care that what's left of my heart breaks.

Because I know what's coming. Like a flame, the tension in his body bursts just as Ezra says, "I'm so glad to hear you love my bride. It makes our new life complete."

And I'm eternally grateful for whichever saint caused Ezra's elderly aunt to stumble, his hands quick to steady her steps. Because of this act of mercy, he's saved from the look of horror as all the blood drains from Tristan's face.

Tristan gasps, his grip turning to ice when he finally lets go. Then, just as quickly, his fists clench, a look of defiance emulating. A mixture of dark stormy clouds and disbelief.

Ezra busies himself with his elderly aunts' preoccupation over the fickle weather when there's a monsoon building in their very midst.

"Will it dare rain again? I for one cannot bear another spring shower …"

The other plump Aunt fans herself compulsively. "It's so hot … will there be enough fans in all the rooms?"

"Of course, I've had new ones delivered especially." Dutifully, he addresses the other aunt who has a chill, "I will see that there are ample blankets."

I lower my head and wait an eternity for Tristan to speak.

Finally, one word escapes his lips, "No."

When I dare lift my gaze, he resembles a small boy who has lost his mother and still waits for her. It breaks my heart all over again. It's the same look when he was watching the boat race with me. Soft and sweet. Without thinking, I reach for him, but he moves away deliberately.

"I tried to tell you a dozen times."

His jaw clenches, his voice a venomous hiss, "Don't say anything." His neck strains, the cords like thick ropes and for a moment I fear he might strike out. His fists clutch, release, clutch. Repeating over and over compulsively.

I would do almost anything for Tristan not to suffer. Not like this, not now. The worry of his family discovering this transgression is only secondary. Needing relief, I turn to Ezra, none the wiser, and shiver. When they know, it'll be over. And the thought pains me.

Finally, Tristan speaks. It comes out as a grunt, both raw and forced. "It isn't a joke."

He stares right through to my soul, and asks again, this time so clear that I would have to be stupid to miss the innuendo. "Is it?"

I shake my head sadly. "No, Tristan. I'm so sorry."

Words fail me because there are no words for what has happened. I sneak a peek but he's as rigid as a statue, the pained expression glued to his face. He whispers to himself, "Madera, the girl ..." and immediately swallows it down. "He never said ... never insinuated that you ... that ..."

Tristan shakes his head, the truth penetrating his heart. "Ironic, isn't it?" He smirks, and the façade is back. The one he hides so well behind.

Ezra turns from his conversation to check on me. I smile and realize I have the same defense mechanism; I, too, hide behind a mask of my own making and have for years to survive. It's the same face I wore when I arrived home bleeding from falling after running for my life to hide the obvious from my mother.

"The girl that I've spent the better part of my life convincing my brother not to marry turns out to be you ..." his voice trails off. "I have to leave." Tristan gets up and walks away without explaining to anyone what just happened.

A moment later, the front door slams shut with a sharp jolt, knocking the little bell off the hinge. It rolls noisily on the slick marble for what feels an eternity.

I close my eyes and count. When I open them, Ezra stands before me, a strange expression on his face. The clinking of footsteps and the clock's menacing tick are the only distinguishable sounds in the universe.

"What's wrong?"

There are no words left. I try to slip past him and follow the group to the dining room, but his body blocks mine.

Those kind eyes narrow in that familiar way, and it's as if Tristan's still in the room. Brothers. For a moment, I think I will faint.

So, I answer the only way I know how. "I don't think your brother likes me very much."

Ezra studies me with a quizzical look just when the maid announces lunch is being served. But instead of moving, he pauses just long enough to let me know that he suspects something. He's suspicious, and rightly so. Forgetting himself, he almost reaches for my hand, then stops himself, waiting for my cue. I remember a moment too late that I don't like being touched and that he's being respectful.

"You don't always have to ask." I grab his hand harder than I mean to only to find that he matches my grip, just as tight. This dispels any question that might linger. My secret is safe.

When he delicately raises my hand to his lips, I meet his gaze, pretending that all is well in the world like the liar I am.

10

Enduring the meal is like crawling through an unending pit in hell on my stomach as razorblades slash my gut. Part of you, the part not bleeding to death, knows that this pain will eventually subside. The other part has stopped caring.

I glance longingly at the steak knife at my side, the only means of escape. I count which veins will bleed out fastest and most painlessly and which ones that will cause me more suffering, prolonging the agony.

I opt for slow and torturous.

The food seems tasteless, but I force every mouthful and every swallow, counting each bite as a tally. Another survival mechanism; eating means surviving and having the strength to run another day. Ezra, at my side, is especially quiet, his gaze never far from me.

When he sees me stabbing my potato into small pieces, he whispers, "We can leave now."

He glances toward the door, giving me an out. A way to escape and cower down to these people that would like nothing more than to see me run with my tail between my legs.

From across the massive table, Cassia smirks.

I straighten my back. "It's fine. I wasn't feeling well before."

Henric eyes me coolly, murmuring to an uncle beside him, and something in me snaps.

"I think perhaps I need some special tea." Without skipping a beat, I continue, "Dear cousin Henric promised to take me to a teashop he especially loves to frequent."

The right side of the table grows deadly silent. His grandmother, Aunt Leraias, is the first to break the suffocating silence with a raise of her teacup. "Since when do you like tea, Henric?"

Henric wipes his mouth, for the second time in his life, at a loss for words. "It's nothing, grandmama. Right now, I assure you that I have absolutely no taste for tea."

Her smile tightens, her gaze dissecting me as if I were a flea. "A passing fancy then."

Under the table, Ezra tugs at my sleeve and hisses, "I told you to drop it."

I swallow a dry crumb of biscuit and choke. "I'm sorry."

But I don't mean it, and he's smart enough to know it.

"We'll discuss it later." He gives me that look again, somewhere between a storm and a rainbow.

The bell in the kitchen finally clangs, signaling the end of the meal and the commencement of yet another tedious activity. The ladies are obsessed with card games. Wasting the better part of the day engaged in such stupidity will never cease to amaze me.

My spirits don't lift when a plump maid announces that dessert will be served in the parlor salon. I can't get up fast enough, the urge to race down the marble foyer toward freedom bursting out of my lungs.

Instead, with Ezra glued to my side, we retire to the salon for hot drinks and tiny colorful cookies for dessert. I find myself seated in a small wicker chair at the center of the great room. Everyone surrounds me from all sides, the exits blocked. And the only accessible window is closed shut with a heavy latch that would take me the better part of an hour to pry.

I'm only too well acquainted with this suffocating feeling: trapped like the wild animal I truly am. Too late, I realize this is what Ezra was trying to rescue me from, The Inquisition. I'm assumed guilty, which is strangely fitting, considering that I am.

Oddly enough, relief washes through me. I have no desire now to escape. I deserve this and so much more. Anyway, my people are only too familiar with inquisitions, having survived them only to face even more grueling hardships. I've taken great pains to acquaint myself with the items of pain and suffering that were once used to subdue my ancestors. And since there is no obvious equipment of torture anywhere to be seen in this fine elaborate house, for the most part, I'm safe.

For now.

Aunt Cora, who Ezra loves dearly, begins the scrutiny. The teacup rattles like a chime in her hand telling me at once that she's nervous, but not enough to be polite and back down. "Darling, tell us something about yourself. We all want to know more about the woman soon to be married to our darling Ezra."

Something in me stirs. I actually wish to tell this old woman, this Untouchable, the truth. If only to see the expression on her face before she faints dead away.

Only too aware, Ezra's elbow gazes the back of my arm just so. Not forcefully, but with it a firm reprimand: behave.

I nod a bit in false submission, hoping this shows whatever it is that they wish to see.

"There's not much to say ..." I remember Ezra's caution not to mention the words Untouchable or Outcast, a dead giveaway of my nationality, even though everyone in this room knows my perceived origin. Still, Ezra insists that I don't need to announce it or rub salt in this wound. "I was born in Odessa and raised in Madera. I lived with my mother who is a dress designer."

"Oh, that dress you have is lovely; did she make it?"

I shake my head politely, saving the smile for later. Ezra slides his hand around mine, no doubt to show support.

"Not much in Madera ... absolutely nothing to do," One of the male cousins slyly comments, and Ezra flinches ever so slightly. I catch the look they exchange. He's asked them to go easy on me.

Unfortunately, they have absolutely no intention of honoring such a request.

"That's why I'm here," I insist, and someone laughs behind me. Feeling bolder, I take a sip of my brandy, knowing I'll need something much stronger to get through this. The brandy glass is especially thick and heavy. I envision breaking it and cutting off the tongue of the fiend who mocked me. I laugh, then smile. "Plenty to do here."

"You must have such interesting hobbies." Aunt Cora shifts her eyes toward another woman, who prods her on. "Do you crochet? All my nieces crochet so nicely ..."

Another senior aunt chimes in; I think she's Aunt Hilda, but I'm not sure. I overheard the servants mentioning how Aunt Hilda rings for her liquor bottles in her rooms to be amply stocked. Interesting, as this lady seems quite sober at the moment.

But I know only too well, with Untouchables, appearances can be deceptive. They excel in deception. The sweetest-faced Untouchable schoolgirl would have a knitting needle tucked in her boot used to poke at me during assemblies, where for the smallest infraction, including squirming, we Outcast would meet with the faithful whip. All the while, I had to sit there and take it, swallowing down the pain.

A moment too late, I recognize this question for what it really is. It's bait. Just to show off how dull and tedious I really am. How by Ezra marrying someone of my stature, he'd be making the worst possible error of judgment.

"I have many hobbies; crochet is unfortunately not one of them." I'm positive that Aunt Hilda would be shocked to see what I can do with a crochet needle. Especially to the girl that thought she would get away poking me fifteen times in the back.

Henric, who's back to being his arrogant self, sneers, "What are your hobbies?" I seriously doubt if a tone could be more blatantly menacing. He doesn't even pretend with the back-handed niceties that Untouchables are notorious for.

Ezra's hand slides down my waist. It's both a protective and defensive stance. Before I can turn and nod my gratitude, one of the uncles shakes his head, obviously disgusted over the display of affection.

Henric softens his tone by a fraction, "That is, if you are in the possession of any."

What he's doing is nothing less than taunting a starving dog with a bone. And what happens next is only fair. I have teeth. He's asked for it, and I will be more than happy to deliver.

I glance toward Cassia, who's remained unnaturally quiet and still whenever Henric speaks. Like the bully she is, she'd like nothing better than to join in with this cruel game and show off her expert skills of debasement. Instead, she flinches away. When she lowers her chin to sip her tea, I see a large red welt beneath her lace collar. I stare back at Henric, his handiwork no doubt. And with that, I remove the final barrier out of the equation.

"Well, I'm not as skilled as some, but I do have a talent or two."

Henric snickers, taking the bait and having no idea how I would love to beat the living daylights out of him, leaving him black and blue. The only question is where and which tools will be utilized to inflict the most pain possible before he passes out.

Ezra catches my predatory gaze toward Henric and shifts in his seat, drawing closer.

Neliem stirs ever so subtly, his breath fueling me. Slowly, I allow my lips to form a smile that must make me appear possessed because an elderly aunt starts frantically fanning herself.

"And yet you avoid the question so tactfully. Pray, what are you hiding?" Henric baits.

"I suppose, Henric, that you would like me to answer that I have a deep love and appreciation for cooking and cleaning, though sadly to say, I possess neither quality. But," I grin like an imbecile, "I admit I love a good fight."

A few relatives gasp, and one lady chokes on her tea, the look on her face worth the argument that will no doubt commence the second Ezra and I are alone.

Ezra tightens his grip, but I wiggle away to scratch an itch which doesn't exist.

"I'm afraid no one was expecting that answer. I apologize." I feign innocence.

Cassia looks as pale as a ghost, and I stifle my laugh. At my side, Tanya glares as if she didn't hear me correctly, "A good fight? I don't understand ... it's so brutal. Fighting, I detest it."

So is having Untouchables torment you for most of your life, I wish to scream.

Landis, who's remained deadly silent, finally breaks. "Well, I also love a good fight."

Some of the men chuckle. But the uncle closest to him playfully taps his shoulder to still him. Another girl cousin giggles and from the corner of my eye, I see Tristan step into the room. I'm not sure how long he's been there, and frankly, I don't care. My chest stills, relief washing over me.

"As do I, as well," Tristan adds loudly as he pours himself a rather large brandy.

But Henric isn't through with me. "Fighting has its merits. At times, quite exhilarating. Overpowering one's opponent. Oppressing them to the point of submission."

I bet. "I'm sorry, did I say good fight? I meant to say a fair fight with equally matched opponents."

He shifts his stance. In two strides, I could knock him down and have his head in a vise, crashing it down on the coffee table, slicing the back of his head in half. But if he moves slightly to the right, the door could be used to slam his skull against the wall. The two equally appealing scenarios are making it difficult to choose.

A wave of unease shifts through the room. Aunt Cora blushes, stammering, "Do you have any collections?" Her smile is tense, every pound of flesh quivering in her corset that must've taken three maids to lace. "I collect spoons. All sorts."

"I am not acquainted with spoon collections." I sip my tea to refrain from saying any more on the subject.

She frowns to an elderly woman, who stirs her ginger tea, glaring at me like a hawk about to swoop down to capture a rodent. Catching the look, Tristan rolls his eyes, a soft smile curving those full lips.

Tanya exclaims, "I adore dolls."

I recall her wide assortment of dolls from her room.

"I'm afraid I have little interest in dolls."

"And what will my rich cousin be buying his wife, pray tell?" Henric is a bastard, and the first chance I get, I will be throwing him from the stairs, where he will hopefully break not one, but both of his legs, and possibly an arm. I'd pay good money to see the next fight he has with Cassia, which I wager, due to his injuries, she will easily win.

"I collect weapons." The words spring out of my mouth before I can stop them. The air thickens at once, the room growing awkwardly still. No one moves, no one breathes. Aunt Cora's teacup is frozen before her round face as her three chins tremble.

Someone behind her gasps.

I elaborate, "All sorts." I wink at Ezra, hoping he finds some humor in my confession. "Perhaps my rich husband will buy some for me. They didn't let me bring any from Madera."

I bat my eyes like a stupid schoolgirl. "I don't understand exactly why."

Ezra whispers loud enough for anyone to hear, "Under no circumstance will your rich husband be arming you in any possible way."

Unaffected, I serve myself a large portion of almond cake clustered in dried figs.

Someone laughs hard. When I look up, I'm relieved to see it's Tristan. Tears glisten in his eyes. "I would love to see your weapon collection."

"And I would love to show it to you," I respond. "That is, when I have one to show."

Tanya reaches for her slice of cake, pursing her lips. "I detest weapons. They're so violent."

I offer, "I know; you like dolls," and everyone laughs at her. She blushes and turns to Landis, who ignores her but stares at me in awe.

Aunt Cora tenses before finally releasing her ironclad grip on her teacup. "She's teasing us. A joke. Tristan, don't encourage her; she had me frightened there for a second."

Ezra hides a smile, and I can't help it, I laugh and make a face at him. When he smirks, I stick out my tongue.

Henric isn't finished; he has to have the last word, "You must have earned so many nicknames with your quick wit, Oriana. Pray tell us some ..."

I cover my mouth politely as I eat my cake. "I only had one nickname my entire life."

Tristan looks up, intrigued as well.

"Neliem." And everyone bursts out in laughter. It's contagious; I laugh along as Ezra shakes his head once and stirs his tea.

Aunt Cora clutches her heart. "That's from our history, Oriana, not a nickname for a girl as sweet as you." She sips some tea with a forced smile, explaining, "Neliem is the god of war."

"That's Feret; Neliem is not a god, rather a spirit ..." Landis offers. "With all sorts of tricks up his sleeve, if I recall."

"I might have some of those as well," I murmur under my breath.

"More of a phantom, roaming the earth ..." Another uncle corrects. "Once a prankster ... yes, held rank in an Embrian court legend has it."

I press my lips tightly to refrain from uttering another word while Henric slithers to a corner to sulk. It seems that I've won everyone over except for him. It's obvious, and I relish in the power it brings me. Perhaps breaking only one leg will suffice. Imagining him hobbling around in crutches, at the mercy of others, is somewhat comforting.

"Must have had a ton of admirers with that wit," he snaps.

"Not really," I snap back, before I remember to flush and bat my eyes.
"Don't be coy."

Ezra and Tristan stand up at once, speaking at the same time,
"Enough, Henric."

Henric widens his eyes innocently. But he's anything but innocent.
He's a brute that beats up his defenseless wife. Until I notice the red
gash just under his neck, a definite claw mark by none other than his
carnivorous mate.

Impressed, I raise an eyebrow. It seems that Cassia isn't that
innocent after all.

Not lifting his gaze, Henric whirls his brandy glass between his
fingers. "Just asking a question; if she's too embarrassed, she should
just say."

He's daring me. Provoking me to confess to something lewd and
unflattering.

Unashamed, I stare back at him. "I only had one." I smile at
everyone. "I was eleven."

Aunt Cora places her fat hand over mine, in what might be mistaken
as motherly affection if she wasn't preoccupied with the butterknife too
close to me for her liking. "How sweet. He must've adored you."

"He did, and I him." My heart beats like a thousand butterflies,
and I have to stop what I was about to say to press my palm against
my chest and swallow down the stone in my throat. Why does it still
hurt so much to talk about Za-Za? And just like that, I see his fat face
with three little warts on his jaw. His frizzy white hair was like wool,
so thick my fingers would get tangled in it.

Tanya, finally interested in something I have to say, raises her
voice, "What was his name?'

"Za-Za." I say it without thinking. And once again, the room
grows deadly quiet. Three things happen at once; Aunt Cora bursts
into tears, Tristan flinches, and Ezra closes his eyes as if in prayer.
Uncle Aton hands Aunt Cora a lace handkerchief, which she uses to
fiercely blow her nose.

"That's so very sweet."

Tristan's face turns ashen, his fist clenching open and closed. He's looking for something to pounce on. I know the feeling. Seething rage. For a moment, I believe that he's angry with me. Before I can move, he stomps out of the room. Ezra leans in and plants a gentle kiss to my temple. It's the first time he's shown any such affection publicly.

"Thank you, Oriana." But I'm not sure why he's thanking me. Stunned, I catch Cassia squirming, sea green with envy, her reptilian face more pronounced than usual. Part of me wants to ask her why in a thousand years she would envy me. The other part wants to stomp on the viper.

Henric sulks like a small child, and I think back to when I saw him in town at the teashop with that young girl who'd verbally whipped him to the point of submission. As if she held his very life in her hands. I shiver just thinking about that look of loss rendering him completely defenseless.

I push the thought away, sure of only one thing.

Nothing makes sense with these people.

Cassia stiffly gets up and leaves. I can only assume that everyone's retiring to their rooms to rest.

Reluctantly, I follow the ladies, who chat merrily away. Like a gaggle of geese, we stroll past the foyer, everyone all aflutter about the newest fashion trend of having lace boots. Conveniently, we allow the men to congregate in the den to light cigars and talk more about whatever it is that they talk about outside the company of women. In what I can only assume is motherly affection, Aunt Cora takes my hand, pressing my small hand against her milky flesh. She points emphatically over the wide assortment of family portraits neatly framed on the walls.

I have only once had my picture taken. A year ago, in a borrowed dress that I had to wash and press myself and return the next day. The girl, a friend of my mother's, complained openly that I hadn't pressed it right and tossed it on the floor in a fit. When I had crouched down to pick up the dress, the girl had slapped me so hard that I saw stars before my eyes. In a flash, unaware how I did it, I had my dagger to her throat.

She left me alone after that.

And let me keep the dress.

"This is Great-Uncle Gustave, the patriarch of us all."

Someone behind me whispers, "More like tyrant."

Intrigued, I stare at the golden-framed faces of blond Untouchables. They all look alike. By the faded paper, I assume some are deceased relatives, but then I recognize the faces of the numerous cousins and aunts and uncles gathered to inspect me.

Aunt Cora's voice lightens when she points out one of a distinguished man. "That's Tristan and Ezra's father. Rol Mercer. A trusted advisor to the Prince."

"He's very handsome." I'm not flattering her; it's the truth. Both boys resemble him; tall and muscular with broad foreheads and identical noses. But the black and white photo fails to capture the glimmering blue eyes that have the effect of rendering me speechless at times and running for my life the very next.

"And, of course, our Tristan. How I wish he would find a nice girl and settle down." She waves her hand toward a picture of a tow-headed boy of perhaps seven with dimples and a smile I could identify anywhere. I stare a little too long, wondering what random thought he was thinking as the photo was taken.

Cassia striding passed us, her perfect nose in the air, sneers, "Don't count on it."

I wince, knowing the truth. He did find a nice girl, who shattered any hope of happiness by lying to him.

Aunt Cora holds up a picture of a fat baby, cooing, "Who would have thought Ezra would have turned out so handsome? His father worried that he was …" she lowers her voice, her eyes darting downstairs, where the men are gathered. "Disfigured as a child. But he was just fat."

Standing in the threshold to the den, Ezra, in the midst of conversing with his uncles, catches my gaze and smiles. My heart skips a beat, probably due to the heated inquisition. Without meaning to, I find myself smiling back, curious about his promise to never arm me. Surely, he didn't mean self-defense tools.

Another picture is thrust into my hands. A shiver as cold as ice runs down my spine.

The picture is of Za-Za. My Za-Za, with his triple chins and frizzy hair and warts. I brace myself against the railing just as my legs give out, almost dropping the photo.

"Don't worry. Most of the cousins at one point were fat. We called it healthy back then."

Another aunt remarks, "After the fever, he lost all that weight. His poor father fretted over that child … it would have killed him if he had died, like so many."

Aunt Hilda sighs as if the weight of the world presses on her. "Rol was smart; the second he heard word of the fever outbreak, he brought Ezra home. Saved his life … if only we'd been wiser …"

Unable to lift my gaze from the picture, I gasp, "Za-Za …"

When I lift my eyes, Ezra, from below the stairs, smiles that crooked grin I've always found strangely familiar. My heart stops beating. It can't be the same person. Za-Za died saving me. I saw the rows of coffins nailed shut, the Untouchables mourning, the stench of pungent incense choking the air. It could only have meant one thing.

Ezra steps out to the foyer, curiosity on his brow. My vision blurs, his face becomes fuller, his hair not straight … and …

"Look how handsome he is now. Your children will be beautiful," Aunt Hilda exclaims a little too loudly, making me shudder.

Aunt Cora reaches to touch one of my curls. "Just don't overfeed them."

But I don't hear another word. My head spins in circles and my knees cave in right before everything goes black.

O nce, I knew a boy with the heart of a lion, who smelled of the sea. Za-Za was the boy who even the Untouchables hated. And he was one of them. By birthright a full Hugganoff. Well, sort of. He looked like them. Same color eyes and white hair. But he was fat, with three plump chins, freckles, and three warts under his ear. Even the teachers seemed to grimace if he came too close. At lunchtime, he would sit by himself on a bench and eat four bags of food, eyeing everyone's lunch with a half-starving look.

"Who's that boy?" I asked out of curiosity one day. His hair had caught my attention, reminding me of someone I couldn't quite place.

School had just started for the season, and he was the only new face. I was intrigued enough to single him out. Apart from his physical appearance, for some strange reason, he seemed different than the others. He was never mean or nasty. He spoke in a voice so soft that you would have to strain your ears to hear. And the fact that the other Untouchables seemed to reject him made him seem less menacing. Even though I didn't understand how the Untouchables would reject their own kind. Outcasts always stuck together. It didn't make sense to my eleven-year-old brain.

Etta scrunched her face from her meatless sandwich, scratching the bit of mold off the edge. "Untouchable. Don't look at him too long or you'll get a wart."

I looked down at my feta wrapped in foil and picked out an olive. "Doesn't seem fair."

Jerris shrugged with a boast, "They're pagans; they aren't fair. They killed all our saints."

He shot Za-Za a dirty look, ending the conversation. Rathe scooted closer, offering one of his mother's cookies. He'd asked me earlier if he could kiss me and when I said no, he'd run away sobbing.

To show some remorse, even though I had no intention of letting him kiss me, I accepted the cookie and wrapped it carefully back in my napkin.

"Thank you."

The bell rang twice to clean up. If you were late, you got a rap on the knuckles. I got up first and went to toss my trash in the furthest bin. The one closest to Za-Za.

I threw away my trash and pretended to retie my shoe. When I looked up, our eyes met.

Soft blue. Like the sky. "Hello."

He stared at me, then looked down at once.

"Be that way," I snapped, and prepared to leave.

"No, I mean … I didn't think you were talking to me." He sighed, almost on the verge of tears. When he spoke again, his voice trembled, "Hi."

My friends were lining up in the courtyard, and we were alone. But I didn't make a motion to join them. Instead, I sat down. "Why are you so sad?"

"Other than everyone hates me, no reason."

"Here." I handed him my cookie.

"What is it?"

"What does it look like?'

He stared at it, suspiciously, his eyebrow arching. "Did it fall on the floor?"

"No." I smiled.

"Did you spit on it?"

"Not yet; do you want me to?" I inched closer beside him.

"Thank you." And he ate it in one bite.

I winced as I leaned against the wall. The rock thrown at me yesterday still hurt my back.

"What's wrong?" The expression on his face was real enough. Real enough to tell him the truth.

"I haven't completely healed." I closed my eyes, wondering where I would be hit today when I ran home. I was getting faster, but not fast enough.

"Who hit you?"

"Your friends who hate you."

"I hate them." He balled up his plump fists.

"It's not so bad." I touched his hand by reflex. It was softer than a feather.

"Don't lie to me." And he looked right at me, making it impossible to lie. Feeling ashamed, I lowered my head.

"My mother says if I pretend it doesn't hurt, it won't."

"Your mother is an idiot."

I laughed, holding my hand over my mouth. "She is."

"Where do you live?"

"Where all the poor Outcast people live." I pointed toward the south wall, explaining, "We live closest to the water to make for an easy escape. One day, I will fly away."

The second bell rang once. I got up. "I have to leave to be beaten now."

He grabbed my hand, sending a tingle down my arm. "Don't let them."

"What?"

"Today, don't let them hit you." By that intense look he gave, he meant it. And I thought how his eyes could be the sky, and if I were a bird, I would fly into them and finally escape. Pushing those thoughts aside, I hurried to the end of the line, expecting the worst. The dean took you to his office for the switch; Matron rapped your hand once or twice depending on her mood.

My head low, I followed the trail of tardy children, my hand stretched out. I felt the familiar wave of tension flutter in my body. The ruler was drenched in our blood, no longer a pale brown, but a deep burgundy. Blood of Outcasts too weak to fight back. A flame quivered in my gut, that unflinching glimmer of blue propelling me to do something dangerous.

The boy in front of me got hit twice. Just as I reached her, I darted back my hand and dared fly. "Don't hit me."

Shocked, Matron's mouth dropped. Then she did the unthinkable: she let me pass, and most importantly, she did not hit me. That she'd been caught off guard was the only explanation. Za-Za did that. He made me strong. Strong enough to take a step into his perfect sky.

My head throbs like a drum, my vision blurs. It's like being surrounded in fog, wandering about, searching for the light that I never find in my nightmares. The images I tried for too long to convince myself didn't happen flood through me, a relentless crashing wave. Over and over. I am floating, almost drowning in it, tossing aimlessly, and finally, I reach the surface. Za-Za. My Za-Za somehow lived.

Soft voices vibrate against the walls. Ones I know.

Ezra and Tristan, I correct myself, rubbing my aching temples. "Za-Za and Tristan."

Straining to sit up, I squint toward the doorjamb. It takes me a long moment to adjust my vision until I see them clearly. They're laughing in the adjoining room. Aunt Cora, seated on the largest chair, strikes her teacup with one of her prized spoons.

Like a thief in the night, I crawl out of bed and inch silently closer. Before a tended fire, she's in the middle of lecturing them as if they were two errant boys caught with their hands in the cookie jar.

"Girls aren't like boys. We are predisposed to fainting spells." She sips, then scolds, wagging her finger. "You would both do well to note that."

"Not Oriana." It's Ezra. Rather, Za-Za.

I smile, a warm tingle spreading to my toes. Aunt Cora sighs, getting up, her wide skirts rustle. "I need to see what the good doctor has to say about poor Roo. You two stay out of trouble."

Opening the door, Tristan kisses her warmly before she leaves, the floor creaking under her weight. Now it's just the two brothers alone sipping tea. Compelled by some indescribable force, I lean in, mesmerized by the sight of them.

They're both tall, broad-shouldered, and fair, the only exception that Tristan's hair has grown darker with age. But nonetheless, the similarities are striking. Obviously, brothers. Save for their temperament, that is.

Tristan pours dark liquor from a flask into their teacups. "So, my little brother finds himself in the possession of a bride."

The fire crackles, setting my nerves on edge. Za-Za dreamily smiles to himself, resting his lips against his fingers in a way that reminds me of a summer day. "It seems I have. Still upset that I went behind your back to retrieve her?"

"Seems that you not only found her but convinced Landis and Henric to join you in wedded bliss." Tristan makes a face, obviously unimpressed by both selections.

"Took some persuading." Za-Za's voice hitches, "Landis had to be forced to make his choice … at the very last second mind you. And now he's gone back on his word."

"And yet it seems that one week has sufficed for both. Or was it a full hour for cousin Henric? Dear, dear Roo … clumsy little bugger."

So, my assumptions were correct. There's absolutely no love lost between Henric and Cassia. I shouldn't be surprised. Desperate for more gossip, I pry closer.

"What did mother always say, Ta-Ta; be nice." Za-Za admonishes Tristan by calling him by a family nickname.

"Those exasperating shrews ... It's like the two, evil step-sisters from that children's story."

I press my finger over my lips not to laugh. Tristan, his brow creasing, refills his teacup, then screws back his flask with care.

"Why are you drinking?" Za-Za's voice hikes up in a way that tells me he's more than worried. "I mean, you never drink around family."

The flask clinks. "Really? And I thought I was well regarded."

"You are. Since when do you trust them?" Za-Za is gone. This is Ezra now. Ezra, who can't help but fret about the most mundane things. And without seeing his face, I know instinctively that he's lifting a suspicious eyebrow.

"Ah, I have you for that; I trust you, and that is enough." Tristan salutes him with the flask like this is all some sort of game.

Ezra motions toward the door where I'm supposed to be asleep, and even though I'm concealed, I dart back, nearly slamming into the wall.

"I don't know what to do with her, Ta-Ta."

It's sweet, his nickname for Tristan.

"What's there to do? I mean if you'd been more willing to learn from the fine establishments I escorted you to ..."

"Not that. She's wild."

Painstakingly slow, Tristan's smile lights up his face, and my knees weaken in response. "That has certain advantages."

"I've had to have all the knives in the house locked up."

Tristan yelps in amusement, hitting his knee.

"It's not funny, Tristan." He lowers his voice, "She killed a rat with a fork."

Tristan can't stop laughing, tears stream down his cheeks.

"When I went last fall to reacquaint myself, not only did she not recognize me, she did everything humanly possible to avoid me. You would have thought I had the plague."

"You have altered some …"

"She hates us, she calls us Untouchables. I keep having to tell her not to use that word …"

"Us Outcasts have plenty of reason to hate you Untouchables," Tristan mocks.

I almost gasp.

Jumping out of his seat, Ezra snarls, "You're not …"

"Our mother was …"

Ezra finally releases his fist and pours some liqueur into his cup. "I only wish she was my real mother."

"She raised you; she is our mother."

"On loan, whenever father saw fit." Ezra runs his fingers through his hair, tugging. The gaze in his eyes blur with emotion. "When I found Oriana, she was like a warrior. Neliem himself. Do you know she trains for hours every single day? Lifts weights, push-ups, pull-ups, sit-ups … I have never seen anything like it. And then I spied her caging wild animals …"

Tristan chokes on his tea. For a moment, I think he's about to have a seizure.

"I thought she was torturing them or sacrificing them." Ezra rolls his eyes, trying to find the words to describe one of my favorite hobbies. "I was terrified what I'd created. But she just fed the lame ones. The babies, the ones that would normally die. I cannot begin to tell you how relieved I was."

"She's an angel. And I am pea green with envy." Tristan gets up searching for something in his pocket when my heart stops. It's as if the door isn't between us. His gaze is like the sun, hot and all-consuming. "Let me pay respects to our dear wild Neliem before I leave."

Furrowing his forehead, Ezra squeezes Tristan's shoulder, "You're not actually thinking of going to the Capital?"

He says 'the Capital' as if it was one of the outer circles of Hell. Not where the royal family dwells in the largest most affluent city of the free world.

"Za-Za, you know very well that I have no idea what I'll do until after I've done it."

They smile broadly at each other, sharing in the private joke. They embrace forcefully, like bears, and Ezra pulls back first. "Better see to the relatives and their schemes … Uncle Gallis is trying to get me to invest in a canal somewhere …"

Sighing, he lifts his hands in prayer before heading downstairs. Once the door slams shut, Tristan speaks. "Heard enough?"

I quickly rush and hide under the covers, but it's no use. With the stealth and speed of a panther, Tristan crosses the room and stares right through me. I hold up the covers to shield me, but his gaze scorches. Heat and sweat and want. And I don't know how he does that; how he makes me feel vulnerable and breathless at the same time.

"You must hate me." The words burn like acid in my throat.

"I wouldn't be in agony if I hated you." He stands at the threshold, neither in nor out. "What have you told Za-Za?"

He pushes closer as if tethered to the wall, unable to move away, his eyes glued to mine. And it's like the horizon at twilight, blazing blue and endless.

I close my eyes. "Nothing."

I hear him shift his stance, that familiar pacing of his feet gliding just a fraction closer but then he stops, retreating. When our eyes connect, it's Za-Za's eyes. Soft and kind. No animosity. No hatred. My breath hitches, the weight lifting.

"Good; don't." He brushes further away, retrieving something in his pocket.

I have to ask. "Does he suspect—"

"No, and he won't." He says this with an air of certainty. Our secret is safe.

My shoulders sag in mixed relief and an emotion so distant that it takes me a moment to place. Guilt. Without speaking, he moves and faces the window, his back to me, and I hear the match strike. He's lighting a lantern, avoiding the electric lights, making it all the more unbearable.

"Are you really going to the Capital?" The sob escapes my throat before I can swallow it down. From all my years at school, I know the Capital is situated at the furthest corner of the mainland. Four days travel by train. It might as well be on the other side of the world. My gut clenches, needing to know yet dreading the answer.

He finally replaces the glass casing over the flame and glances toward me, where I sit like some infatuated schoolgirl. He creeps closer, pausing when those beautiful hands tremble just before brushing a speck of dust off my hair. His hand lingers, and without meaning to, I clutch it to my face. Tristan sighs before releasing me. And what's left of my heart breaks.

"Oriana, right now the Capital might be the safest place ..." His brows knit together, his jaw tight. That voice I would recognize anywhere breaks. "The best place for me."

His fingers draw the softest line down my cheek.

Adrenaline sears through me like lightning. Crawling like the wild animal I am, I dart back to the furthest corner of the bed, needing to get away. "Then go!"

He lifts his palm cautiously, the way a lion tamer would. "Oriana."

I slap it away hard. Then again and again. I don't know where this rage is coming from. Tristan doesn't move; my blows are of no consequence as he watches me with eyes that seem to know every inch of me.

"What are you waiting for?" I hiss and jerk my foot at him, which he catches.

We're at an impasse; he stares at my bare foot just as my nightgown slinks up, revealing more leg. He doesn't move but takes a cautionary step back so that only one knee is balanced and starts massaging my foot.

"Did you hear me? Leave; run off to all the girls who will throw themselves on you ..."

"Well, there is always that …"

In a fit, I throw myself on him, tossing him on the bed and trapping him under my grip.

He makes a wistful face, his lips pursing. "Oh, has someone been doing her pushups? Nice."

In one swift move, he twists so that I'm beneath him.

"But you forgot that I'm quite a bit stronger than some skinny girl …"

I jab hard with my knee and he winces. It's the only leverage I need. He falls backward, his head narrowly missing nicking the end table.

Not giving him a chance to flee, I seize the moment and sit on his chest, pinning his hands above his head. "Really? I seem to recall kicking your arse more than once."

He moves, and I'm back on my back, frantically trying to toss him off.

"That's right. Where are my gold coins?" Our eyes lock.

"Fiend, where is my knife?"

"You stole that knife, you little vixen." His breath tickles my ear, his voice husky, "Where is my money?"

He lowers his nose down my chest. "Are they here? No? Perhaps I will find them here …"

His hand curves up my thigh, and I melt. My breathing catches in my throat, my body reacting to his. Finally, his lips quiver: his tell.

Tristan looks down at me so pensive, so full of awe. "What was my brother thinking, letting you out of his sight?"

He trails his head down my chest. The little hairs of his mustache send a shiver down my flesh. "If you were mine, I wouldn't let you out of bed for a week."

Strength surges through my veins, and I toss him off the bed, unsetting a water pitcher that falls into a nearby chair. Luckily, it wasn't full.

"Only a week?"

Suddenly, Tristan staggers and pushes off the floor. His hair disheveled and eyes blazing. A beautiful exquisite mess.

And all I can think is that I want him to come back and leave me alone and go to the Capital and I don't know what else. All the blood rushing to my head, he speaks clearly, "I am leaving. This will never, ever under any circumstance, happen again. Do you understand?"

Every nerve in my body screams as he opens the door, prepared to leave.

"I was wrong, Oriana …" He stares right through me.

I wipe a tear away. "What were you wrong about?"

He adjusts his lopsided tie. "The Capital is definitely not far enough."

Hesitantly, Tristan closes his eyes as if in prayer, and then, without any further word, leaves.

It takes me but a moment to get out of bed to follow.

Downstairs, everyone gathers around a distinguished gentleman with a medical bag. Ezra carefully hands the doctor an envelope with a stiff nod. The doctor takes his leave, and the bell back on its hinge lets out a shrill ring.

The aunts and uncles all stop talking at once when Tristan prances down the stairs, still adjusting his tie.

Not daring breathe, I crawl on the carpet and spy from the balcony.

"Thought we heard something fall. She is all right?" Poor Aunt Cora once again has that pinched look on her round face, her fan fluttering too fast. "Please tell me that she didn't roll off the bed?" Her fleshy arms bounce frantically, her shrill voice hitching. "One accident is more than my poor heart can bear."

Tristan paces down the stairs with ease, his voice deceptively smooth and carefree, "Oh, that; we were just wrestling."

Ezra laughs as Tristan swoops down and picks something off the carpet and pockets it. Aunt Hilda sighs, "Poor, clumsy Roo. Can you imagine missing a step and breaking both your legs? Poor darling. I should see to him."

I barely have time to register what has happened to Henric when Aunt Cora takes her leave, waddling her plump body toward the west wing of the house. Dutifully, she pauses briefly to pay homage to some Goddess with a winged foot.

Landis arrives, making a gesture over his shoulder. Ezra goes outside to accompany the doctor to his carriage.

Two other cousins, whom I don't know, step into the foyer and clamber alongside Tristan. And I know that I should get back to bed before some servant finds me snooping, but curiosity gets the better of me. Silkily, I slither like a snake out the corridor and slip onto the landing, eavesdropping.

"So, what's the verdict on Za-Za's future bride; do we send her back to the island?"

The shorter one snickers, "Fine company, don't you think?

Tristan silences him with a glare that would turn water into ice. Self-consciously, they all look behind their shoulders, anticipating being overheard. "If Landis here formally withdraws his offer, that leaves you, dear cousin, up next. Take one for the family, eh?"

The short cousin, who can't be more than fifteen pales, stammers, "I thought we were discussing Oriana, sending her back ..."

Once they are positive that they are alone, Tristan relaxes, the smirk back on his lips. "Oh no ..."

His eyes dance up to where I'm spying as if saying, "You are caught."

I dart back immediately.

One of the cousins dares complain, "And you were so adamantly against it."

"Yes, Tristan; why the change of heart?"

He glowers, "It's quite amusing that you think I have a heart. But since you insist on an answer, I shall give you one. I approve. Adamantly. Inequitably, and if I were as lucky as my beloved brother, I would," he clears his throat, "be well acquainted with her at least five times a day."

All the blood drains from my face.

The men all laugh like hyenas at my expense. My face hot with emotion, I force back the tears welling in my eyes as I rush back to bed. With nothing to do, I resign to lay down and slow my accelerating pulse.

I convince myself that I will need every available ounce of energy to properly torture Tristan Mercer when next I see him. It will be slow and especially excruciating; one that I suspect that he will thoroughly enjoy.

I snuggle up in bed, the sheets tangling up in my legs until my mind stops spinning and I drift off to a restless sleep.

Etta startles me awake. Her tiny hands shake me viciously. Her face is hauntingly white, her eyes so large that it takes me a moment to realize that I'm still dreaming.

It's my childhood. Six summers ago. A time plagued with horrific hunger and want and little mercy, save but one. I blink back to a world I thought never to visit again. My old room reeks of musk, almost faded. The cracked walls, the faded bedspread, the tattered curtains. It's so pitifully ugly.

I open my mouth to complain, but no sound emerges. All I hear is my steady heartbeat hammering in my chest.

But interestingly enough, it's not a nightmare. No monsters or Untouchables lurk in the shadows. It's spring, the gloom lifting as sunlight pours from my window.

A bird chirps noisily outside, the remains of the plate of bread and cheese Za-Za brought me still on the perch.

"I found this!" Etta, all three and a half feet of her, is screaming at me. I turn. In her hand, she holds the dagger that Za-Za gave me, the one we'd spent countless hours practicing with. "I found it under your bed, so don't try saying it isn't yours!"

I'd just arrived home, late as usual, and had laid down for a moment before she accosted me. My mother was across the street gossiping with a neighbor, but still, Etta was too loud. Loud enough for my mother to hear and come barging in.

"Lower your voice." I close the window, leaving the plate in our spot to be filled later. Then, taking my time to draw the cheap fabric across the glass, I relax my face and take a deep breath.

"I know where you've been."

I close my eyes and count before turning around to face my accuser.

"All these weeks, all those excuses ..."

It'd taken her longer than I had thought to guess my whereabouts. All the mysterious disappearances, the large blocks of time unaccounted for. Training time. Time to learn how to hike and climb and fight. Mostly fight.

But now, staring at her small face, her hand barely able to clasp the dagger with the strange etchings, a twinge of guilt spreads in my heart.

Etta can easily be fooled into believing almost anything. I see this as an advantage as I sit down patiently waiting for this tempest to dissipate. She's small, underfed, and doesn't have a muscle in her body. I could take her down easily. One bump to the head, a kick to the side.

I shake the thought away.

"What do you think you know?" Part of being Neliem is never giving too much away, as well as playing stupid when the occasion calls for it.

She whines like a goat. "You spend all your time with him ..."

I try to act surprised, knitting my eyebrows for effect. "What do you mean?"

"When you say you're sick and not feeling well or have to help your mother. All lies to go and see him."

"Who?"

"That fat boy ... the Untouchable ..."

"Don't call him that." Anger rings in my voice, "Ever."

She nods, confused and unable to meet my gaze. "But ..."

"But what?" I swiftly jerk the dagger away, making a note to find a better hiding place.

"It's what he is …"

I shake my head, the kiss Za-Za had just given me still pulsating on my lips. Soft and gentle, tingling like a feather. I lie outright. "He's just a friend …"

"They can't be our friends, Oriana." Lowering her voice, she whispers, "They're pagans … we are believers, set apart."

"Za-Za isn't a pagan." Folding the towels my mother had set aside for me, her words send a shiver down my spine. The tension leaves my shoulders. I'd just given him my one and only prayer book. So, he couldn't be a pagan. He swore he believed in the one God.

"You could get hurt." When I look up, huge tears roll down her cheeks. Her trembling fingers reach for my hand, the one with the belt mark my mother gave me yesterday for not hurrying with the wash.

I flinch a little but allow her touch.

"He's just teaching me to protect myself and not get bullied." And gave me one kiss. But what a kiss.

"But I was your friend first."

"I know that. Look, he lent me a book …" I pull out the book of Neliem and show her the pictures of the soldier who died and how his spirit still haunted the earth.

Pointing, I explain, "He rode an Arabian stallion, look, and he searches the ends of the earth for his one true love. When he finds her, he carries her up in his arms and takes her away. Rescues her. And he has powers …"

"It's a pagan book. And …" her shrill voice spikes. Her eyes widen at the picture of Neliem hiding his bride in a cave. "Where is he taking her? It doesn't look right."

I lean over my bed and start to read, "And his spirit flows in the wind, like sand following those of pure hearts. He searches the stars for her, and his enemies tremble …" I close my eyes and read from memory, "Who dares look into the eye of Neliem and survive? Only his beloved."

"It sounds horrifying." She clutches her chest, the vein in her neck pulsating so fast that I think she might have a seizure.

"Just for his enemies. Everyone else is safe." I close the book and pause trying to gauge her reaction. "It makes me feel strong, reading this, and you have to admit I don't get picked on so much …"

"But …"

"Etta, it's just a story. There are tons of them, and Za-Za's having his cousins come visit tomorrow. Would you like to join us?" I flip through the pages when the front door slams shut, rattling all the windows. "My mother is here; decide quickly."

I hide the book and dagger under the mattress and fluff up a pillow. "Za-Za and I have decided that it's best not to discuss our friendship with our parents. So, we have to be careful …"

Her wounded look sears right through me. And she is right. She was my friend first. And Neliem always remembers his friends.

As a concession, I offer, "Come over to the little hill after school and we'll all play."

I walk her to the front door slowly, standing between her and my mother already behind the sewing machine, pins in her mouth as she tugs the velvet fabric through the machine.

My mother barely glances up. "Three orders for betrothal gowns … three."

She bites down on the pins while threading the well-used sewing machine. I keep walking, my hand possessively on Etta's skinny arm. "Etta needs to leave to do schoolwork, but she's coming back later."

"Good; there's flour for a cake. You two can bake while I sew. Now, what kind of cake will you bake?" Her attention only on the expensive fabric.

Etta starts to say vanilla, but I interrupt. "Chocolate."

Za-Za loves chocolate cake.

12

Twisting and turning, my arms and legs flail in my sleep, and I try to hold onto the dream that slowly turns into a nightmare, with bodies washing up to shore and screams and blood and smoke filling my lungs.

I cling to the dream of Za-Za. There's more I want to say. I want my mother to look at me. I want her to say she's sorry. And, for the first time in her, life acknowledge the fading bruises and worry, fret over me and weep over my pain. But most of all, I want her to see me. Compulsively, I reach for Etta's young face, but it fades. My mother's distant frown disappears, and I bolt up remembering the welt on my hand, which I can no longer pretend away.

My hair sticks plastered to my face, my nightgown drenched in sweat and fear.

I'm terrified, but I don't know why. It started off as a good dream. The day of my first kiss. The day Za-Za made plans for our future. We would escape together. He'd promised me, even going so far as to swear it on my prayer book so that I would know he meant it. My pulse slows, recalling distant memories so old that they don't seem real: The three dresses in velvet for girls who would be wed, have babies; Etta so small and defenseless, the tickle of a kiss that set me soaring.

It was so long ago, in a different world, but it somehow felt more real in this house with these people.

Untouchables.

I cringe, shaking the thought away.

The delicious aroma of hot food wafts in the cool air, filling my nostrils as my stomach grumbles loudly. My mouth tastes stale and dry, and I can't remember the last time I ate.

A dark memory flickers in my head.

For a second, just before I woke up, I thought I was back home in Madera in my old room. And I hated it.

I glance toward the drapes, half expecting to catch a glimpse of bars like the ones my mother had welded in last year. She said it was for protection. But I knew better. She probably suspected my comings and goings and wanted a tighter hold on me. But no matter, I snuck out the front door whenever the need arose, and she was never once the wiser.

Rubbing the sleep from my eyes, I inhale deeply. Other than the scent of food, the room smells like lavender, with just the hint of the bitter incense they use to worship their false gods. In our village, Outcast children would labor for hours in the thicket, getting tick bites and nettles in our hair just to collect vast quantities of the herb so we could be compensated with some stale bread for our trouble.

The best roots grew near the swamp, half submerged in dank waters, all murky and coated in green, sticky slime. The Untouchables would hang it out to dry, then burn it over their alters for days, praying for prosperity and fertility. It must've worked. All of them were wealthy, with fat bellies and healthy children who tormented us weaker, skinnier Outcasts.

And I hated being Outcast.

I squeeze my eyes shut, letting the dread wash over me.

The sour aftertaste lingers. I stare down at my hands, half expecting to see the gashes and scratches from crawling in the mire in the hopes of filling my belly with their leftovers.

Knowing where the scars mar my body, I stretch out my fingers and search for the telltale signs of my shame. But strangely, I can't feel the trace of one mark. Not even the last one, caused from the brambles when I fled those brutes.

A glimmer of moonlight flits through the clear glass window, but all I can think about is food. I want to eat and eat and eat until I'm sick and then eat some more.

Then I remember something that makes my heart stop altogether. I will never go hungry again.

Something to my side shifts.

"There she is." I shield my eyes as the light from the gas lamp flickers on.

Za-Za, I mean Ezra, is directly before me, seated in a cushioned chair that reminds me of a throne from a picture book about an isolated king living in the swamplands. It strikes me as odd that I didn't sense him sooner. I mean, I should've. Maybe part of Neliem's slipping from me. Stealthy like the darkest night, Neliem can transform into vapor that can pass through walls seeking his target, going as far as to be two places at once.

His gaze never lifting, Ezra lingers at my bedside, reading my expression. "I was worried."

His breathing is soft yet urgent at the same time. Purposeful.

As I thought, on the table rests a covered plate of food. I stare at it, blinking. The few times my mother managed to save me a plate of food, there was always a clean linen napkin placed on top. This one's covered by a silver-plated holder with an engraved lid.

"Are you hungry, Oriana?"

He seems to know me well. But part of me wonders if it really is true. That this man before me was once short and round and my entire world. I squint, once again trying to imagine him five stones heavier, his face as full as the moon, his hair frizzy white. But it's no use. Ezra looks no more like Za-Za than I do.

He lifts the lid, the soft curve of a smile on his face spreading. The heavenly aroma of roasted meat and potatoes and honeyed carrots make my mouth water.

I don't have to be asked twice. Carefully, I take a few bites, savoring each one as if it were my last. My mouth chews, I swallow, but my head still spins. And I'm glad for the distraction of the food so that I don't have to speak. When I finish, he hands me a wine goblet and our fingers touch, a slight electric charge ignites.

"You look very well rested."

I nod; by the dim light, he looks so utterly handsome, but also equally foreign and therefore suspicious. Nothing like Za-Za. But still, somewhere in there might be the boy I fell in love with. And the thought makes me tremble.

"Are you over the shock of discovering who I am?"

I shake my head. "No."

He moves the tray away and guides me off the bed, helping me with my robe.

"I was waiting for you to be ready." He says this casually, but it has the opposite effect. My lungs hurt trying to reconcile the two very different parts of my life. The skinny frightened girl that he met years ago and who I am now.

Neliem.

"You could have told me, Za-Za." The name feels funny on my lips, like a tickle. A kiss. And a promise. I blush, my cheeks burning. Thoughtfully, I touch my lips, allowing the relief of seeing him alive to take the sting off everything else that's happened.

"Would you have believed me?" He gently moves toward the door and peeks down the corridor, only turning back to plant a soft kiss on my brow. A tingle of excitement courses through my body. Then, with a glimmer of mischief, he presses a finger to his lips and guides me downstairs.

With the grace of a panther, he prowls, guiding me through hallways, secret passages until he stops and opens two large golden doors with a smirk. The hallway clock chimes one o'clock. And without realizing it, I've held my breath, both trusting and suspicious as to our destination.

I take a step forward, and my mouth falls open. Before me is a majestic ballroom. Something from a palace, with golden and crystal tapestries, sparkling chandeliers, and a shimmering dance floor.

"It's beautiful," I gasp, twirling around to breathe it all in.

Ezra guides me to the very center and bows.

"I can't dance," I confess, sweat forming on my forehead, squirming under his intimate gaze.

He presses closer, so that my body fits into his, his warm hand draped over my back. The fire from my cheeks rushes to the pit of my stomach. "Let me teach you."

And we move, slowly at first, my feet attempting to match his pace, though oftentimes failing. That is, until my breath catches and I close my eyes, allowing his heartbeat to guide me.

"So, I've altered some?"

Without realizing what I'm doing, I touch his angelic profile, still half in doubt, for something familiar. "Where are the warts?"

"You forget they weren't warts, they were moles. Ta-Ta cut them off after I recovered from my illness."

The illness. The one I gave him. The words stick in my throat, "Did it hurt?"

"I don't know; I was practically in a coma." He reaches down and hesitates. Once again, he's asking. When I dare look up, he lowers his face again, testing the waters, searching for some sign.

"Am I still your Za-Za? The one you love?"

"Yes." The word comes out breathlessly, as if I've been carrying a weight that's suddenly been released. My shoulders relax. My hand reaches and caresses his head, searching for a trace of curly wool to know that it's really him, that he didn't die.

But his hair is as straight as silk, smooth and perfumed.

Before I know what's happening, we're off again, leaving the exquisite ballroom, his steps quickening as my heart pounds harder in my chest. We arrive back at our rooms, where he brushes a soft kiss on my hand before helping me off with my robe. I hide in the bed as Ezra yanks off his shoes, getting into bed with me, his intention clear.

Panic sears through me. It's too soon and too fast. And I don't really know him. I clench the sheet over me while he dims the light so that I can barely make out the outline of his face.

"Oriana, it's easier in the dark."

My heart stops beating.

Sensing my shock, he waits, not moving. I squeeze my eyes shut and feel his pulse as if my own. Slow and steady. So peaceful and true.

And I know that he's no panther prepared to pounce.

He is the sea, his waves beckoning me closer.

My scalp prickles with tension, drops of perspiration welling up behind my ears. Slowly, I hear him remove his necklace. The heavy chain clinks. Then he wiggles off his shirt, his belt. The tension mounts and I'm not sure what to do.

I could scream. I could run. The door isn't bolted, and there are no bars on these windows. With a soft thump, his pants hit the floor, his svelte body slipping under the covers.

Pressing a corner of the sheet against my chest, my voice quivers, "Could you make it darker?"

Shuffling. The bed creaks as the flame flickers smaller until shadows engulf every corner of the room. In the stillness, I let out a breath and inadvertently wiggle my cold toes, accidentally touching his.

A spark spreads. All I have on is a thin bed shirt that's hiked up to my waist. Trying to control the tremble raking through my body, I move to lower my shirt when he unexpectedly kisses me so very gently before rolling on top of me.

My belly rubs against his strong chest, tiny curly hairs tickle me as my breath catches. I try to think of some excuse, anything to divert his attention. But all I hear is the rumble of waves, the scent of the sea wafting, drenching me.

His fingers cradle my head, and the panic subsides enough for me unclench my jaw. He smells divine, like maybe he just bathed with seaweed and salted bathwater that was freshly gathered.

My pulse relaxes.

He washed up. For me. When the outline of his face moves closer, a blush spreads down my chest. In answer, he sighs, that soft sweet breath finding my face. Easing down, he adjusts himself carefully, drawing himself down deeper into me. Surprisingly, he's not too heavy, and I adjust to his size when the mattress dips below his elbows.

"Tell me if I'm hurting you," he murmurs against my ear.

I barely manage to nod, terrified if I try to speak the quiver in my voice will give me away. He kisses me again, this time with his tongue as his fingers glide up my shirt, sending a wave of unexpected tingles.

"Could we just get this over with?" I squeeze my eyes tighter, my mother's and aunts' words of caution clanging like a rusty bell in my head. Blood, pain, and then a horrifically long labor nine months later, when every bone in my body will feel like its tearing apart. Then more blood, more pain. Possibly death.

I envision the corpses of young mothers who didn't survive. How they waited until nightfall to collect them in a rickety wagon for a speedy burial. How I crept outside to witness families mourn their lost daughter, sister, wife, as yet another lifeless body was tossed in a shallow grave and buried under the haunting moon.

The light flickers back on as Ezra gasps, "God, Oriana, you're as white as a phantom."

I blink, sucking in a breath. "I'm fine. Continue."

"I'm fine, continue?" Incredulously, he snickers. Then, his voice drops. "Seriously, I'm not a rapist."

He rolls off me, his chin tilting in a way I'm starting to understand might mean more than one thing. "Did your mother prepare you for any of this?"

"Childbirth?"

"No, intimacy ... pleasure ..." Now he's being ridiculous.

I sit up, indignantly clinging the sheet against me. "Of course not."

His face softens, and for a moment, I see Za-Za. My Za-Za.

With the tip of his finger he massages my hand, his face softening. "What do you know?"

I close my eyes seeing my aunt flailing her hands wildly, talking about losing her virginity and how she wished for a speedy death. "That it hurts, there will be some blood ... that good girls hate it. And that all men love it."

"Well, that's not true."

I raise an eyebrow. "None of it?"

He laughs. "I like it. And I would like, I mean love it, with you."

"You've done it before?" The hurt as thick as a pinecone chokes down my throat, needles prickling into my chest.

"Yes." He doesn't bother to look away and feign shame.

"A lot?" I feel sick.

"Some." He reaches over and trails a kiss on my shoulder. Sparks shoot up and down my flesh. "Do you like that?"

"Yes?"

"And this?" He spreads his fingers down my back, resting on my backside. His fingers pulsate like wings, and it reminds me of my eagle soaring in the clouds.

My eyelids flitter, my body finally relaxing. He dims down the light and gets on top of me again. We fumble in the sheets, lips and hands and want. Then he tugs off his undergarment, and I feel as if someone lit a candle in me.

"I love you, Oriana." He kisses my temple over and over until I lift my gaze toward him.

I don't know him, part of my mind whispers. Don't trust him. But my feet, for the first time, are not fighting the urge to escape. And I sense something lifting inside of me. Something so familiar that the final burst of tension leaves my body.

"Yes." And my smile releases.

"You sure?" As always, Ezra's asking. But I feel too lightheaded to answer. This is not my body, but someone else's. My hand is not the one pulling him closer.

He presses all his weight down, and it stings. He pulses closer, and it feels as if I'm being ripped apart. I gasp, the pain spreading like wildfire. My lungs heave, sweat drenching my scalp as a wave of heat consumes me.

"Stop."

He pulls back immediately. "What's wrong?" His breathing's erratic, his hair wild as my mind reconnects with my body.

"It hurt." My hands shake as I reach for the light. He's hovering over me, shirtless, only the sheet draping below his waist which is pitched up.

And he's all muscle and tightness. Not an ounce of fat.

"I'm sorry, I barely touched you ..." The look of complete bewilderment spreads as he runs his fingers through his hair, "The first few times it will be uncomfortable ..."

"First few times?" I gasp.

"It takes time; by the end of the week you'll like it."

But I'm positive that I will never grow accustomed to being ripped apart.

"It really hurt, Za-Za ..." My face is already drenched as I clutch his chest, releasing a sob. "And now you'll hate me and send me back to Madera ... and you won't love me anymore."

And saying that, I realize that's my worst fear. Going back to Madera, a prison sentence full of sadness and sorrow. My own living hell without Za-Za.

Gently, Ezra soothes my hair, whispering, "That's impossible. Who's filling your head with all this nonsense?"

"Your cousins."

His body tenses. "Really."

I can't meet his eyes. I'm a failure at the one thing he really likes.

"I'll be a bad wife, Za-Za ..."

His head shakes against my neck, his breathy voice intense, "You're a wonderful wife. And I love you very much and never would I send you back there. Ever."

"You're just saying that." I close my eyes, thinking of Tristan, wishing for the first time that I'd never met him. How could there be two brothers more different and yet so alike? Both mystify me for completely different reasons.

"I'm saying it because it's true." Turning so that our eyes meet, he looks down at me all clear skies and promise. I reach out and press my finger against his lips, for a moment believing. "Do you have any idea what you mean to me?"

"A little."

"I would give you anything to make you happy." He leans in and brushes a kiss on my forehead, before releasing a wave of kisses down my face. "Absolutely anything."

When he looks at me, the world seems soft and pure, not dark and menacing. There is no Untouchable and Outcast. No need for Neliem. There is only us, in this bed. His warm hand protecting me.

"I'm starting to remember when I met you, on the island." My lips break into a shy smile. "It was splendid."

"And you loved me ..." he says this as if he still can't believe it's true. I hug him tighter and nod my answer into his chest. Suddenly, a very selfish through crosses my mind.

"Za-Za, do you really mean it? You would give me anything to make me happy?"

His eyes glisten, a single tear escaping. "Anything."

I sit up, determined. "I would like a gun."

His body goes rigid. "No ..."

"A small one."

"Never ..." He offers no compromise. "No guns, knives, or daggers ... understood?"

"But you said I could have anything ..."

"Practical," he scolds.

"A gun is practical." For some unexplainable reason, I think of the carriage door bursting open. "I could protect you."

I must look a sight, sitting in the middle of the bed with my wild hair and rumpled bedclothes riding up my body.

A slight smile plays on his lips. I sulk a little, puffing out my lower lip like a baby. This does the trick—he scoops down and kisses me, the kiss taking on a different intensity. More urgent, less soft. Our hearts hammer in unison, our pulse matching the heat engulfing our bodies. Before it's too late to turn back, I gingerly fall out of his grip and wonder how I can convince him that a gun is really what I want.

"Fine; I'll make one."

He stops, then laughs, pinching the space between his eyes. "You'll make one? Out of what?" Wood?"

I'm amusing him, which means there's still some hope. "Yes, if I have to. I saw some elms I can carve one out of. So there. I will get my gun."

"What will you use for bullets? Do intend to shoot with it, or is it simply for purely aesthetic value?"

He's smirking at me.

"Marbles."

He yelps, then catching himself, presses his lips together. Playfully, he grabs and holds my wrists down, pressing his weight in a way that doesn't seem threatening in the least.

I don't even wiggle. "Better be careful with those smart remarks when I have my gun and marbles, Ezra."

"Oh, I'm trembling …" Then without warning, he hikes up my bed shirt even higher.

My heart stops.

"What are you doing?" I try to push his hand away.

"Something that you will really, really like." He nibbles on my ear. I blink. "But …"

He scoots down, only looking up mischievously for a second. "Trust me, it won't hurt at all."

"Then why is it that you look like a naughty little boy about to show me his snake?"

"Oriana, we'll save the snake for later." He grins, before ordering, "Now dim the light. You're up for a very special treat."

I don't have to be told twice. The light dims just as the giggling commences.

During breakfast the next morning, I have the hardest time keeping a straight face. I'm downright giggly, and I don't even count the knives or trouble myself to examine which one's sharpest.

But still, Neliem counts for me. Like the phantom he is, he hovers over my shoulder, pointing the obvious. There are four exits in the room if you include the wide window. True, it only leads to the side alleyway and has a fence that one would have to gain momentum in order to scale. Fences don't bother me, but the dogs that are kept alarmingly underfed do.

Neliem hisses at me.

Watch and learn. Your enemy waits at the gate planning your demise.

And no matter how hard I try, I can't help but notice. The maid who favors her right side and the butler who attends to the elderly uncles seem to regard me with unbridled contempt. He has a deep scar that didn't heal properly on an otherwise handsome face. A face that reminds me of someone. He only converses with certain house staff, almost as if a private club. The newer household don't seem privy to his telling looks and offhand remarks.

"Yes, Master Otis, the weather has a certain chill, does it not?"

He doesn't fool me. What he means to say is that he would sooner stab the old man with the butterknife than have to suffer another one of his requests for hotter water for his tea.

I watch. I listen. Neliem breathes on my neck. There's no doubt that my enemy is indeed at the gate, seeking my demise. But mostly they avoid me at all costs, averting their gaze as if I didn't even exist. Their hatred is like bubbling poison, leaking from their pores as if I have no right to be in this fine home, eating this exquisite food, favored by Ezra.

And it has absolutely no effect on me. For the first time in my life, I feel calm. In control.

I don't need Neliem, I sing to myself. I chant the words over and over, "Neliem be gone."

Then it happens.

A maid arrives with the smuggest expression. In her hands, she holds a silver platter, which appears empty. As she passes, she drops a medal on my plate. It clangs noisily. "She forgot this when she was dressing."

Her venom seeps rich with hatred. And for a moment, I'm transported back to Madera, once again running for my life. Under the table my fist clenches, my gaze coolly sizing up how big an enemy she is, all but ignoring whatever it was that she tossed in my plate.

Ezra's voice hitches, "What is the meaning of this?"

He lifts his chin and cups the object in his palm as if it was soiled.

Calmly, I study the maid. I know her from the hallway, Soiree, the one who threw herself at Tristan. The one he rejected.

I smile.

Speechless, Ezra opens his palm, and I see what it is.

The star of my people.

A muscle in Ezra's jaw flexes, but my eyes are glued to the star. Something about it seems off.

It's a perfect shiny silver, and I quickly realize why it looks odd. It has five points instead of the customary six. This star belongs to the goddess of peace, the one with the bird who can transform into a rose. Having been forced to study their asinine traditions, I know it's to protect one's home from invasions, not cause harm, which is precisely what it's done.

A cruel trick to expose my heritage and not only disgrace me, but harm Ezra.

Without skipping a beat, I ask, "Does not this mean the goddess seeks tranquility instead of strife?"

A wave of relief seems to wash over the room. The uncles clear their throats and Aunt Cora lets out a long breath, fanning herself nervously.

"No," the confused girl exclaims. "It's the one of her people. They worship it …"

Realization dawns on her that she's the one who's been tricked. She's been given the wrong star to accuse me with.

I look up, my question still unanswered. "Is it yours, Soiree?"

The girl gasps, "How can that be mine?"

I whisper, "You had it …"

"It was in your room, on your dresser …" She looks for support from the other servants in the room, then gazes attentively past Aunt Cora, toward the female cousins a moment too long.

Ezra speaks softly, "You found it?"

I know he's exercising every ounce of self-control while giving nothing away. Instinctively, I nudge closer.

Soiree stammers, "In her room, I mean rooms …" Her arms shake, her face turning an unbecoming shade of crimson. "It's hers, I know it …"

"Which room, Soiree?" I ask as innocently as possible.

This catches her off guard.

I explain, "My rooms were changed shortly after I arrived. I'm no longer on the East Wing."

Ezra, his back as straight as a board, confirms this with a nod. I know he wants to say more, to defend me. I feel his pulse quicken with every moment of this charade. But like a pent-up bull, he cautiously holds back.

Soiree stammers, her lips trembling, the vein in her forehead throbbing. "She's trying to trick me … It had six points, not five. Six, I counted them twice."

I ask again, "But which room, Soiree?"

She's stumped. All she can manage is to rub her hands together. Cassia lifts an eyebrow as if to prod her. "The second one, in the West Wing." She looks around the room, her voice steady, "I found it just now in the West Wing room, amongst her things … in her valise."

One uncle arches an eyebrow. "I thought you said you saw it on her dresser?"

This observation makes Soiree flush deeper, the tips of her ears an alarming purple. Desperate, she looks for support, but Cassia adverts her gaze, whispering to an aunt, "Are we going shopping soon?"

Caught in yet another lie, Soiree stutters, "Yes, on her dresser, that's what I meant to say."

Landis offers pointedly, "You said amongst her things … What business did you have searching a guest's belongings?" He winces, turning toward Tanya, who remains dumbfounded, her eyes especially large this morning.

"Maybe it's mine," Tanya lisps, blinking too fast. "I love tranquility."

Everyone laughs, breaking the tension, and one by one the relatives resume eating.

I swallow down the rock lodged in my throat. These people are so stupid they can't get the star right. What's more, it doesn't belong to me; even though I am Outcast, I've never been able to afford any type of jewelry.

The relatives chatter amongst themselves, arguing politely over the specifics over which god has which type of symbol. There seems to be a consensus that Dina, the god of fertility, also favors the star. Across the table, Landis shoots me a sympathetic look, which I ignore. I don't need help, and even if I did, I would sooner suffer fifty lashes before begging him.

Aunt Cora chimes, "Someone open a window …" She fans

herself violently, her eyes dashing about the room. This talk of stars has obviously piqued her blood pressure.

Ezra shoots her a dark look to silence her. Moving my lifeless legs, I get up, deciding that this fiasco has gone on long enough. Soiree wrings her hands on her apron, looking for support but finding none.

Aunt Cora eyes her hostilely. "That will be enough. Go to your quarters, Soiree."

"But, I …" The maid lowers her gaze, her forehead creasing.

"Now," Aunt Cora commands. Soiree rushes out of the room, leaving her tray.

Once the girl's gone, the color returns to Aunt Cora's plump white face. Her voice drops a notch, "Yes, yes … Oriana is now paired with Ezra … after that dreadful fainting spell." Then the old woman sips some tea as if that will resolve everything. "All her things are in Ezra's rooms. Matter resolved."

Uncle Otis barks, "Well then whose is it?"

I shrug, batting my eyes directly at Cassia. Tanya's big eyes widen, then she stammers, "Well, if no one wants it."

Cassia, a little too quickly, offers, "I would like to see one up close."

Her greedy hands go to clasp it when Tristan, who's appeared out of nowhere, grabs it and tosses it in the air. For a moment, I'm positive that it will come to blows.

"I favor stars." His eyes twinkle an irresistible blue. He pockets the star protectively and sits down, at which point he's immediately poured tea and served a platter of sliced meats and cheese. "They mirror my own perfection, don't you think?"

Everyone laughs, one uncle laughing so hard that he chokes on his biscuit. Two female relatives excuse themselves to their rooms, taking a rattled Tanya with them.

Ezra, who's behaving more like Za-Za, clings protectively to my side. But the damage is done; the servants seem to have a different opinion of me, regardless that the star is not mine and has five points, not six.

"If our ancestral familiars were allowed back in our homes, none of this would be happening," an elderly aunt openly complains to Aunt Cora.

Someone snickers, but as Ezra rises, Za-Za all but gone. "Excuse me?"

The contentious aunt complains as two others back her up. "We're the only ones left unprotected." She eyes me apprehensively as my gut clenches.

If it isn't bad enough, they somehow blame me for this fiasco. I didn't bring my faith into their homes, but I've been found guilty, nonetheless. I tighten my fist, wondering which of the relatives set me up. It seems a grand gesture on their part. Especially since none of them seem able to count. But I don't have to go too far to guess who my accuser is. The exchange between Soiree and Cassia is proof enough.

The rest of the meal is served without further incident. When I resume my seat, I am served last, even though the women are always served before the men. Ezra's eyebrow arches every time I'm ignored by the servants. As it is, not only is my food cold, but I'm the last to be served tea, which is weak and lukewarm, not hot. The cookies on my plate are broken, little bits of crumbles that would be fit for a dog, not the family's benefactor's cherished wife.

The tension builds like a tidal wave. Ezra's shoulders keep hiking up, building until I think he might explode.

Carefully, I ease my hand over his, whispering, "It doesn't matter."

He flinches, his words harsh; "It matters to me."

When the servants return to the kitchen, he offers a complaint to his aunt. "Is there a shortage of servants this season?"

Aunt Cora grunts and excuses their behavior with a wave of her gloved hand. "Finding anyone with references is impossible, keeping them a miracle." She exchanges a glance with an uncle, who nods. "Especially after the accident. Soiree will be dismissed."

Ezra does not lift his gaze.

She adds quickly, "At once. With no references."

He glares at her openly, and she fusses with her fan as if the room has suddenly raised in temperature when in fact a cool breeze lingers. "I try. No one understands what I do …"

She snaps her fan repeatedly, searching the room for support. She finds none. If what he said is true, the uncles and aunts, as well as most of the remaining cousins, are relying on Ezra's goodwill for their comfortable lifestyle. They are in no position to complain, and it's probably the only reason I haven't been sent packing or worse, flogged in the town square for being in possession of a five-pointed star.

Ezra's stare hardens as he sips his tea. "Aunt Cora, perhaps you will find the weather more agreeable near the seaside. The house in Odessa might be more to your liking."

It is nothing less than a veiled threat. The home he refers to is not a proper house, but rather a small cottage nowhere near the town. He mentioned that he had plans to remodel it for quite some time, but never got around to it. The foundation is solid, but the walls facing the sea need to be reconstructed as well as install indoor plumbing. Also, there is no electricity.

He would be sending her to basically a shack to suffer for her lack of discretion in hiring help who cannot count past four.

His words chill Aunt Cora to the core. With a flip of her wrist, she drops the fan but quickly composes herself when three plain serving girls return to clear up the tables. The rest of the attending staff members are excused to their daily tasks.

Za-Za nods and winks at me. I wonder if he thinks he's done me some great favor. It's almost as if he has forgotten that my entire life I've dealt with far worse prejudice. I might pass for one of them, have documents that state as much, but the truth is the truth.

I am Outcast. And these people will never let me forget it.

Dark thoughts cloud my mind. Last night, Ezra worked hard to soothe my fears and make me feel accepted, even when I failed him in the bedroom. And he did succeed. I woke up refreshed and happy. Happy enough to ignore the looks and stares boring into my direction every time I so much as lift my fork.

"Aunt Cora, I expect all the servants who were disrespectful to my wife to be dismissed."

Ezra will not be not satisfied with solely Soiree's dismissal. The room grows alarmingly still. No one daring to utter a sound.

Aunt Hilda clears her throat. "Is that really necessary?"

Aunt Hilda's the eldest aunt, a tall, beautiful woman whose blond hair has faded to a regal silver. Everything from the way she sits, her back perfectly straight, to the look of self-assurance and privilege tells me that I'm not welcome here.

But the cow won't come out and say it as long as Ezra holds the purse strings. He knows it, and they know it.

Ezra smiles easily, pouring me a fresh cup of hot tea before settling the silver teapot back. His fingers wipe a trace of water off the side. "Yes, Aunt Hilda, that is necessary, seeing as I will be visiting here often with my wife."

Someone behind me lets out a gasp, but I don't turn; I won't give credence to their worst suspicions. They sit there, smug, waiting for me to prove their foulest thoughts true. Perhaps if I throw the plates on the floor and pounce, scratching my nails on the hardwood floor and belching, they'd be satisfied in their assumptions that Ezra has brought some savage home to be his bride.

And if they despised me before, now they downright hate me.

Cassia, finally free of Henric's tight leash, relishes on the animosity seeping from every corner of the room. Her sinister glow confirms that indeed she brought the star here.

"This reminds me that Oriana and I will be in need of the master bedroom from now on." Ezra slips his arm over mine without so much as a second glance. The little hairs on the back of my neck prickle. Asking for the servants who offended me to be dismissed is one thing. He pays their wages. But this, this is too much.

The uncles break into a chorus of not-so-polite coughs, and one gestures with his hand in a way that seems to beg for leniency. But Ezra does not back down.

"Work will be requiring me to be in the city."

Aunt Hilda whispers politely, "Surely, Oriana would rather stay back at your home ..."

Ezra's neck stiffens, his voice taking on an edge, "This is my home. A home free of all unnatural presences."

I steal a quick peek at his face. In a matter of minutes, his features have hardened; his forehead is more pronounced, like most Untouchables, and his mouth is tight. I don't recognize one hair of my soft, sweet Za-Za, whose lips would have trembled with tears leaking from his eyes before using such a tone.

With hushed whispers under their breaths, the relatives turn to each other, not daring correct Ezra, while shooting me apprehensive looks. The ladies, in unison, rise and head toward the foyer, a better spot to gossip over the latest turn of events.

I'd almost forgotten that Tristan was there. He's deadly silent, almost blending into the wallpaper. And I'm not sure how I feel about him. He watches apprehensively, his face giving nothing away. The second they are out of earshot, he sasses, "Good riddance. Fat, preposterous cows."

One uncle objects, "Come now, Tristan."

Ignoring him, Tristan gives me a wink that would make me blush if I wasn't so flustered already and drops the star in my palm.

"I would sell it," he teases. He's back to being witty and distant. "And with that, I pay my respects."

He bows perfectly, and I cement my feet down to fight the urge to chase after him. Ezra's back tenses before he rises to his feet. "So soon? You barely got here."

Both head toward the corridor, and I have to strain my neck to catch a last glimpse.

"Don't want to overstay my welcome." Tristan finds his top hat and jacket and scarf in the cloakroom, calling out to Aunt Cora,

"Hang half the staff and flog the other."

But this time, his smile doesn't reach his eyes. And for a moment I am terrified if I blink, he will disappear. Just like Neliem.

On the other side of the foyer, I catch a glimpse of the remaining female relatives adjusting their bonnets and preparing for the day's exertions. The smallest, most insignificant part of me wishes one of them would trouble herself to invite me, even though I detest shopping. Tanya wraps a lovely violet bonnet around her head, the laces dancing against her slim waist.

Through the hall mirror, she catches my gaze and mouths, "What have I missed?"

Too much, I think and focus on my tea, which is now cold. The sharp edges of the star cut into my palm, reminding me of danger at every turn. Tricks, schemes, lies. They will go to any length to separate us. And yet, like the panther he sometimes is, Ezra doesn't flinch.

The image of the serrated carriage lock makes my heartbeat pound in my throat. That was no accident. Reigning in Neliem, I narrow my vision, scanning the room, even more determined to find the culprit than before.

The aunts pry Tanya from the mirror and escort her outside. Their scowling faces do nothing to hinder her mood. She smiles stupidly, not having a care in the world before being yanked forcefully outside.

So much for Untouchable affection; the girl's as much a pawn as I am.

Cassia, who lingers in the hallway, wrinkles her nose, her disgust blatant. "What is that smell?"

One aunt tightens her bonnet and scolds before leaving. "Mind your manners."

"I have a disgusting headache," Cassia whines before excusing herself from the group. She instead joins some cousins too feeble to go shopping in lounging about the sitting room, her intentions clear. She wishes to know how her scheme might fare for her later. Like me, she has a few days to prove herself, and this little shenanigan might cost her dearly.

I inhale shapely; the faint stench of something burning wafts from the kitchen, followed by a screech. Someone snickers behind me, but I keep my focus on Cassia, wondering if she would dare harm Ezra.

Like a chess piece, I study her carefully, watching how she moves her hands, how her feet seem restless, how she always has that pretty smile on display.

When Cassia steals a glance, she is met with Ezra and Tristan's hostile stares. Relieved, I relax my shoulders. They are on to her. Good.

Without further ado, Tristan mumbles something to his brother before shutting the door, the little bell sending a shiver down my spine. And I might be imagining it, but I could swear that Tristan mouthed the word, "Behave."

I square my shoulders, having no intention of behaving.

Like a dimwitted fool, I bat my eyelashes at Cassia.

"How is Henric?" I provoke. A blind mule could gage her reaction whenever someone mentions Henric. When she says nothing and excuses herself to the furthest corner of the room, I have my answer.

Landis leans into me. "He hasn't asked for her."

One of the aunts who stayed behind consoles a red-faced Cassia with an embroidery kit. The flung doors between us allow easy access, and all I have to do is tilt my seat back a bit to catch every word. "By the end of the week, poor Henric will be in a far better mood. Guaranteed."

The aunt with the large mole grins sheepishly, and I think of Za-Za's moles. Great-Aunt Leraias nods her head in agreement. "Henric got this way as a child."

Someone dares contradict her. "Leraias, he lost his mother so young."

Aunt Leraias lifts her head, in the way I think an executioner might just before bringing down the ax. "Stubborn. Willful. Disobedient. I blame his fits on his nurse; she coddled him. I, for one, have never prescribed to any lack of discipline."

I bet. Aunt Leraias seems as tough as steel. Instead of grandmotherly affection, no doubt her harsh childrearing has produced a monster in Henric. And yet I can't help but think of that look of loss he had when he stood there outside the teashop.

"Oh, that was Nula ... darling girl. Whatever happened to her?" Uncle Anton inquires a bit too loudly. A wave of suffocating silence falls like a cloak throughout the room leaking to the floorboards. It's so palatable that I suspect if I open my mouth and swallow, the taste will be like swallowing acid. And for the first time, I suspect that it has absolutely nothing to do with me. Family secrets linger like ghosts in this great house, hovering about from room to room, waiting to pop open and spread like pollen.

It's too hard to stifle the words at the tip of my tongue. "But, how is he?"

Aunt Cora sighs, then resumes fanning herself. "Just a severe sprain." I can tell just by the way her eyes flicker toward the servant's entrance that she's still rattled about being threatened into exile over a servant's poor behavior.

Ezra, now back, shrugs his shoulder, obviously not distressed in the least. "Two weeks, no strenuous activity."

Landis poorly hides a grin. But all I feel is a sharp spark of regret. I'd wished for both Henric's legs to be broken but have to settle for a mere sprain.

A devious thought trickles in the back of my head. I bat my eyes the way Tanya does when she's attempting to think straight. I call out, "You should go to him, Cassia; I'm sure he would feel much better with you there nursing him back to health."

Tending to him hand and foot. And beaten over the smallest infraction. Yes, perfect retribution. Cassia wiggles in her seat, suddenly finding her needlework fascinating.

I press, "He needs you. We all understand if you leave right now to tend to him."

Ezra, feigning boredom, stretches his arms like an eagle, engulfing me in one stroke. He leans in. "Please end this conversation right now." His eyes burn like flames, his voice stern, his intent clear. "And promise never to it bring it up."

When his gaze drifts back to his food, I feel his pulse spike. He's upset. At me. But for what, I have absolutely no idea. He doesn't care for Cassia, he said so himself. Meticulously, I pine over every detail concerning Henric's sudden fall down the stairs and the subsequent doctor's visit and come up empty. All I know is that Henric is now back home, nursing his wounds alone. And prefers it this way. That greedy, selfish child, alone in a home that could probably fit fifty easily. This can only mean one thing. He is not alone. He has company. Company that he chooses Cassia and his relatives to know nothing about.

I perfect the Untouchable smile. "Of course, Ezra."

By the look he gives me, he doesn't believe my false sincerity for a second. Clever boy.

Ezra sizes me up, before softening his face. "I'm sorry; it's … complicated."

The fact that he might actually think his explanation suffices leaves me feeling empty. I might pass for one of his people, dress like them, have my hair styled just as fashionably and even go as far as to mimic their mindless chitchat. But I am not one of them. I inch away in my seat, engrossed in buttering an ice-cold biscuit.

Ezra doesn't let matters rest. He lowers his face, his lips brushing against my ear, sending a familiar tingle down my neck. "I'm sorry. Truly sorry."

I bring my goblet to my lips and sip daintily, relishing over the instant that Za-Za whispered in my ear. He's back, Ezra tucked away. When I lift my eyelashes, the soft blue of springtime engulfs me. My skin flushes, the warmth emulating off him like the toasty kiss of the sun. Every time I steal a look in his direction, a wave of heat threatens to consume me. Attempting to distract myself, I focus on my food and try to eat. Za-Za's all smiles and sweetness, making him all the more irresistible.

And forgivable. At least for now.

Absentmindedly, I release the star, and it falls into his palm. I rub the indentations only to catch a glimpse of horror on Ezra's face. I lower my eyes to what he stares at. It's the star.

But now it has six points.

A chill creeps up my shoulders as Ezra gets up casually and tosses it into the burning fireplace. After a moment, I get up and join him, and together we watch what could have been my demise melt into nothing more than a singe of silver.

Later in the day, the ladies who remained indoors are excused to one of Aunt Cora's studies to read and sew and do other tedious activities that I have no interest in. I realize that, in Untouchable households, especially ones as lavish as these, that men tend to spend as little time as possible in the presence of their wives and female relatives, choosing instead to distract themselves with pursuits that have little interest to their feminine counterparts.

Tanya planned wisely in escaping when she could. I long for the fresh air and sweet and spicy smells of the city, the views of the channels, the bridges, anything other than being trapped inside of these four walls without a moment to myself.

After a full half hour attempting to read a rather disturbing legend of Neliem, one entailing his systematic annihilation of every inhabitant of the island of Waria, I grow listless. There are only so many severed arteries and torn-off limbs one can digest on a full stomach. As it is, the food in my gut twists painfully and I press the heel of my palm to silence it, trying not to focus on the near miss earlier.

A servant notices my discomfort and brings me some hot lemon water to ease my indigestion. I accept it gratefully and continue with my disturbing studies, making a note to never step foot in Waria, which has a blood curse. When not wincing over bloody passages, I am subjected to listening to snippets of silly gossip and a recipe for a poached pear tart described in excruciating detail over and over, with each aunt giving her own variation to the point that I think I might go mad.

"I have a bit of a headache." I rub my temple viciously to aid in my deception. Not one eyebrow lifts. All these Untouchable women seem to suffer from severe headaches at all hours of the day. Especially whenever their husbands are lurking about.

"Oh, dear, please rest," Aunt Cora insists, placing her crochet needle as far away from me as possible. I have little doubt that once I'm excused to my rooms, she will give her true opinion on having to relinquish her fine room for my occasional visits.

I smile weakly and, keeping the pretense, stroll painstakingly slowly toward the door. Rest is the last thing on my mind. As soon as I shut the door, I glance around twice, then sneak up the foyer, across the library, and to the den, where I can see the men smoking cigars and swirling cognac in large crystal goblets through a small window. Part of me wonders where Tristan could be. He keeps his own hours and didn't bother to make an appearance for lunch. All I know is that a room has been reserved for the week, but he didn't spend one hour here. His bed is untouched, and his luggage still packed.

Softening my steps so that they, too, become but a whisper, I slide through the servant's corridor directly facing the den and find a small, cushioned stool. Stooping down on my knees, I lean against the stool, pressing my ear to the wall, and listen.

It seems the men have circled around Ezra, no doubt eager to have their own questions answered far from the prying ears of their female counterparts. But the wall muffles their voices to the faintest murmur.

The room to my right holds a servant's quarters. The room is small, with only one exit, but luckily a window perched by the bathroom allows for perfect acoustics. Late last night, while everyone slept, I snuck out of bed and familiarized myself with the layout, counting all doors and windows and seeing which were better suited to flee through in a moment's haste.

My heart hammers harder in my chest, my mind whirling over every detail. There are fourteen steps out the back way to the alley and three at the front of the house. Aunt Cora sleeps in the East Wing in a suite larger than my home back in Madera, her bed the size of an average room. Lavished in silks and satins, the room seems more a shrine than an actual sleeping quarter.

While Aunt Cora slept in luxury, her daughter Eloina slept in the West Wing, furthest from her, in a room that could be mistaken for a broom closet. An interesting note.

Tristan's room was not the only one vacant all evening. Landis also went missing. Tanya, since being moved from our room, slept with Cassia, which I found unusual since these arrangements were placed well before the ill-timed accident. Having nothing better to do, I go over the lay of rooms. Now, with everyone preoccupied, is the best time to conduct my own investigation as to the truth behind these people. Henric's room is obviously unoccupied, allowing for a thorough search. I rummage through every drawer and pant pocket.

I find no proper suit, merely a few pressed shirts and a small picture of Henric as a child, identical to one displayed on the stairs of him holding an adorable baby who could've easily passed as his sister. The names on the back indicated that the child was not a relative. I stare at young Henric, a stunningly beautiful child who seemed somewhat affectionate in the way his hand caressed the baby.

Touching that even a monster could once love something.

I return the picture exactly where I'd found it, taking note that he hadn't bothered to retrieve his wallet. Four pounds and two shillings. Unusual that he was staying here an entire week and carried so little money with him. This could only mean one thing. He never had any intention of staying.

I sit down, retrieve the picture, and trying to piece everything together. The baby, perhaps a year old, is lovely, with natural curls and a distinct dimple just below her right cheek. They share the same eyes and shape of mouth. But not a relative. The name on the back my only clue. Nulence Valiente, dated sixteen years ago.

Nulence. Not a Hugganoff name, and certainly not Outcast. Someone had mentioned a servant named Nula. Staring at the photo, it snaps into place.

Henric's holding his nanny's child. A child that is somehow connected with this family, based on the way Aunt Leraias squirmed at the mention. No doubt this baby is the product of some illicit affair between one of the uncles and the servant Nula, who now must be the proprietor of the teashop.

Nula's Teas and Gifts. The same establishment that kicked Henric out.

When the floorboards in the hallway creaks, I startle. I return the picture and quietly sneak out through the bathroom door. When I find the hallway clear, I go about my spying. Everyone else in the household I find at work, and the servant with the strange rash to her face is cleaning the outside sewers. She plunges the waste with a shovel, jabbing in a way that seems more fitting to gutting a goat. The fury emulating from her tight body one of pure rage. My interest piqued, I go and recheck her drawers, though I find nothing noteworthy. This only spikes my interest. Servants always have a small amount of money they wish to hide. This woman carries no purse or means of identification. So, I fish around until I find her money purse hidden behind the dresser stowed in a hole in the wall.

Fifty-five pounds in coin.

A fortune for a woman in her position. I count it twice. Then, I do the unthinkable. I steal it. No good could come of this woman possessing such a large amount of money. I tuck my loot in the last unoccupied room, and only then do I pay an unexpected visit to Uncle Anton's quarters. He has the disturbing habit of sleeping with a revolver under his pillow. To steal it would only rouse unnecessary suspicion, since I'd aired my fondness for weaponry. Instead, I disarm it before making my way back downstairs with no one the wiser.

Now continuing my habitual snooping, I scurry to the small corridor and pry open the marbled glass window, allowing me a bird's eye view of what the men are up to. They continue to circle Ezra, laughing merrily. But this laughter doesn't ring with familiar Untouchable sarcasm or hostility. This heartfelt humor beats genuinely, warming my skin with only a trace of self-abasement tingling at the edges. Unlike the prior inquisition of last night, I sense that hard liquor and the stench of cigar smoking might loosen a few lips.

These men seem quite different than their women. True, there are the bullies from the village, whose lascivious gawks haunt me even now. But perhaps in this close-knit group, far away from the underprivileged and Outcast, they've no need for such drastic measures. Or maybe not.

Now the group gathered chuckle and carry on as if there was no tomorrow, exulting such warmth and merriment that for a fleeting moment, I completely forget that I'm but a fly on the wall.

I adjust my seat to get a better look. They are in the middle of toasting Ezra, their expressions inviting. Not grave and menacing like the women in the other room, crocheting and gossiping like bored schoolgirls. Part of me fears that this domestic monotony will soon become my daily life, attempting to knit while forced to endure cup after cup of lukewarm tea. Losing myself even more as I suffer the company of women I have absolutely nothing in common with, far away from a husband who will soon tire of me.

It is a life I have no desire to live.

A cry pierces, and my ears prick up instinctively.

Some freshly-arrived cousin cloaked in a fur coat and sable hat hugs Ezra warmly, offering him a cigar, which he pockets.

My shoulders drop in relief. Tristan's among the group, as dashing as ever. He leans against the wall solemnly, the only one not drinking, his gaze cast down. But I know better. He's paying very close attention to everyone else, going as far as to refill their drinks.

One of the male cousins is missing, as well as dreaded cousin Henric, who's having his physical therapy later that day to alleviate his pain. Further, a cast was set as a cautionary note, limiting movement.

"Poor Henric; some board games were brought to his home in attempts to occupy his time since he's immobile," Landis says without malice. But his demeanor seems off. As if his mind isn't on Henric at all.

Part of me wonders if Cassia would be so compassionate a nurse mate. The cut on Henric's neck indicates she isn't the understanding sort. But what caused her to flare is beyond me. All I know is that he's at his home and she's here. A bottle of champagne explodes, the cork hitting the ceiling before splitting in half. Tiny icy bubbles cascade over the bottle as Ezra's toasted and patted down affectionately.

The fine glass flutes clink, chilled champagne poured generously.

"To our married cousin."

"In four days' time," Tristan corrects mildly.

For a second, it strikes me odd that they only toast Ezra, not Landis, who frowns, not bothering to lift his glass. Perhaps his plans to rid himself of Tanya are already in motion. Not cashing the dowry indicates as much. Then again, if his fortune is tied to her family's spice business, perhaps not.

"Who would have thought?" A cousin chokes under his breath, before lighting a cigar.

The men seem to take great enjoyment in this bit of information for some strange reason. Landis jitters on his feet, unable to find a comfortable place to stand. When he steps back, he nudges Tristan directly under where I hide and whispers to Tristan, "Have you secured her passage? And that of her family? She's prone to seasickness; I want to make sure she's comfortable."

"She's already safety landed in Odessa. Forging the paperwork was a bit troubling. The family name had to be altered a bit. But her parents have work, not menial. A tutor has been selected. The house is let under my name, as agreed." Tristan rakes his hand thought his thick hair.

I don't need it spelled out for me. Landis has somehow found himself a mistress. A young one at that.

"If it wasn't for the past debt the family had incurred, she'd be my wife." Landis scowls.

Tristan barks, "You believe marriage is an option here?"

"Za-Za married Oriana in mere days; anything is possible ..."

Tristan glares in response, silencing him. Chewing on my lip, my eyes to start to water. Who is this mystery woman, or rather girl, that Landis wishes to lay claim to? Someone he has forged papers to move her and her family to Odessa? Someone he can't rightfully marry?

Of course. I could kick myself for not thinking of it sooner.

Over a week ago, I'd entrusted a reluctant Velaria with the simple task of posting a letter to a distant relation in Madera, when in fact it was to Etta. It was the the same day Landis came by for an unexpected visit. I'd foolishly risked exposure yet again by bribing one of the stable boys to post yet another, right before we came to spend the remaining week with Erza's family.

Landis, the scoundrel, went beyond what I had intended, and taken matters one step further. He must have delivered the letter directly to Etta.

Cautiously, he looks behind his shoulder, an unfamiliar glint in his eyes. Underneath his cool demeanor, he's seething, his gaze narrowly missing me. "I still say I should meet with Tanya's family and explain myself. I didn't take the vows lightly. It nearly killed me going through with it, but after spending time with Etta these last few days, all I can say is to hell with a spice empire."

Tristan's voice gets suddenly harsh. "Don't say another word." He steps forward, raising his empty glass, "To my brother …"

Everyone lifts their glass in unison, drinking down the fine champagne as I lose sensation in my legs.

It can't be. Not Tristan. But if he's plotting Etta's dishonor, what else is he capable of? Surely not … the severed lock flares before my eyes. No, never. Not my fellow Neliem planning Za-Za's demise.

Landis lets out a long exhale, his focus razor sharp as if expecting something dangerous. Perhaps Tanya's family demanding recompense. Blood curses are common amongst the southern Hugganoffs. These people known to take their vengeance into the next life.

A glass crashes to the ground. At once, Landis flinches. Tristan, calm as ever, settles him with a look, then slowly an easy smile crosses his lips.

"Look happy." It's an order, one which Landis follows with a painted-on grin.

One of the cousins teases Ezra, who looks especially sheepish this morning. "Well, we heard a lot of giggling coming from your room last night."

Tristan's face pales just slightly before he finds a seat. "How is Oriana?"

I tremble at the sound of my name.

Ezra shrugs while Tristan prods with a fiendish grin. "Well rested?"

I don't need an interpreter to guess what he alludes to. It's plainly written on his too-handsome face. His eyebrow arches just so, and my fingers tingle, wanting nothing more than to slap him silly. He dares ask if I'm still pure.

Ezra answers causally, taking his time to light up a cigar. "After the shock of discovering that I'm her long-lost sweetheart, there was much to be amused about."

"Ah, she was caught unawares …" One cousin seems a bit smug, in my estimation. He should shut up or risk finding his boot positioned in a very uncomfortable position when he wakes up tomorrow.

Ezra shakes his head, not falling for the bait. "Oh, that would be telling." He inhales deeply, savoring his cigar. "But I will share that she's quite ticklish …"

A roar of laughter erupts.

I scoff; he's sharing intimate secrets and should know better. I prepare to sneak away when the scoundrel adds, "I just don't know what to make out of her continuous pleadings for a gun as a wedding present."

Landis, back to being normal, grabs a piece of candy from the crystal dish and pops it into his mouth. "I, personally, would be wary." But he snorts and gives Ezra's arm a tug.

Tristan ridicules them both. "For her, I would open up the Prince's armory and let her run rampant."

"You would be dead within the week," another cousin offers. I honestly can't tell all these blond cousins apart. There are too many to count and only a few distinguishing features, such as a slightly longer nose, or broader forehead with a shatter of pale freckles. Although Henric might be the better-looking one, Landis most definitely comes in a very close second. The only one set apart is Tristan, with his chestnut locks and smoldering blue eyes that seem to change as frequently as his moods.

"Perhaps, but it would be well worth it just to see the glow of satisfaction on her face." Tristan laughs genuinely for the first time in what seems a very long time. I remember the stare he gave me before he dove into the icy waters to rescue the woman. Defiance and arrogance and something else.

Neliem.

My heart pounds in recognition. For a moment, the distance between us dissipates. There is no wall dividing us, no blond cousins that I can't keep straight. Just Tristan and me.

I close my eyes and recall the sensation of his lips against mine. His breathy voice murmuring my name, those eyes lighting up like candles. It takes me far away, soaring in the clouds, chasing the dawn.

The noonday bell clangs twice, breaking the spell. Everything in me feels raw and more awake than before. When I open my eyes, my hand clutches my gown so tightly that the fabric's wrinkled. Easing my grip, I release my hold and tell myself to breathe.

Tristan cannot be guilty.

Etta is a different matter. As soon as I retrieve where she's staying in Odessa, I'll send word to her to keep on her guard. And to keep her legs crossed.

In tune with my emotions, Tristan's shoulders drop, a soft glow flickering in his eyes as he steals a glance toward the ceiling.

My breath catches. His gaze burns where my rooms are. I know he's thinking about me and it makes my heart swell with joy. I can almost forget the insulting remark what he would do if he were my husband.

More jeers flood the room.

"Was she pure?" It's Landis asking, and I wonder what has stirred this topic of conversation up. I really had no idea how highly Untouchables regarded purity. I thought only my people went to great lengths to prove a girl's virtue. A thorough examination before a betrothal is mandated before any announcement of an engagement can be made. And on the eve of the wedding, elderly women are sent to inspect the bedsheets carefully.

The memory of the two boys who tried to capture me makes my throat go dry. Their salacious stares and outstretched arms clawing for me. To have expected anything else from a people marred with perversion, sordid orgies, and mayhem deeply woven into their culture, makes me even more stupid.

Ezra's voice rises above all others, "As pure as the day she was born."

I cringe. Not only was I pure, I still am. But I've had enough.

It's one thing to share this with a beloved brother, who may or may not be behind a plot to kill you, but to openly disclose such delicate matters with relatives, whose names I can't even keep straight, is completely different.

Tristan shifts his stance, his forehead cringing in a way to be in deep thought. But for the life of me, I'm not sure if he's relieved or disappointed.

Some wayward cousin bellows out a snort, gagging hysterically so that Landis has to hit him several times on the back.

So that's what they think of me. Some foolish Outcast girl who loves a good fight and is pure as the driven snow. Well, good riddance.

I return to my rooms furious. The maids scatter about, trying to appease me with a pot of tea that I have no taste for and lowering the shades so that the entire room dims, reflecting a cool rising from the clouded noonday sun. One offers to soothe my aching feet, while another fans me gently. But no matter how hard I try, I can't find peace. I should have accompanied the ladies on one of their frivolous diversions. Later today, it's shopping for china tea sets. Last season it was lacy dollies, which Aunt Cora stockpiled in the upstairs cabinets. I counted forty-seven.

Feeling more alone and utterly miserable, I excuse the servants and immediately take out the fifty-five pounds I retrieved earlier and recount it. There is an extra shrilling that I missed twice. A small mistake, but still a mistake. I place the money under a loose floorboard, thinking I will show it to Aunt Cora and tell her I saw the maid acting suspiciously, followed her, and discovered the money.

Then, quickly, I devise a better plot.

I pour the money inside of one of Ezra's boots that he doesn't wear, stored in the room across from ours. The soles are practically untouched, the soft leather polished perfectly. The anxiety builds like a tidal wave rising with every tick of the hallway clock. What I need is physical excursion to take this edge off, to squelch the fever threatening to erupt from my veins.

Finding no means of an outlet, I return downstairs, cut across the servant's quarters, and get some cool water to quench my thirst. The water refreshes my soul and clears my mind. It's a good thing that the home has ample running water. A luxury, since right now, I am in need of plenty to drown the flames ready to combust. I wash my face and neck and scrub under my pits and lavishly use the lavender soap until I am scrubbed pink.

Only then do I dry myself and place back on my blouse, refreshed enough to face anything. Even taunts over my fondness for weaponry.

Unexpectedly, voices echo from the ladies waiting room. Carefully, I lower myself to the floor and press my ear to the doorjamb.

"They can't be trusted; it's simple." Cassia's shrill voice is unmistakable. "Five hundred years of history should prove something."

Aunt Cora sips her tea, saying nothing, when her sister chimes in, "The men seem quite taken with her."

She looks around the room, baiting for more.

Another elderly aunt stirs. She appears to be balancing on a ledge; one wrong step and she'd go flying into the waves. "As long as she knows her place and keeps to it. I have no serious objection."

Aunt Leraias hisses like an old goat that I would love to cook on a skewer. I know she wishes to say something vile, but I also know what makes her wince and swallow back her poison. Her finances rely heavily on Ezra's large fortune.

My only half-ally, Tanya leans back on her seat, fanning herself. "I like her. We should invite her to go shopping."

The same aunt chortles. "I notice Landis keeps a watchful eye on her. I would proceed with caution. Those … you know … women have been stealing our men for centuries."

Aunt Cora hits her with her fan. At once, all eyes are glued at the door.

The wrong door.

Behind the opposite wall, I lay crouched on my heels, listening like a rat from the servant's entrance.

"They brainwash our men."

My heart lunges, the need to run intensifying with every pound of my heart.

The aunt with the mole sighs. "Well, I never meant him ... Rol was Rol. No one could tell him anything."

She refers to Ezra and Tristan's father. Immediately, I feel protective.

"I have nothing to be worried about, thank you," says the girl who cannot even lure Landis with a spice empire. Tanya gets up, wrapping her scarf around her shoulders. "And I am bored." Looking anything other than bored, her eyes dance. "And since no one wants to go shopping, I'm going for a walk."

One aunt whispers to her sister, "Another one?"

Tanya prances away without a coat as Cassia turns to the others, the malicious sneer that I know so well engraved on her face. "It is an ill-fated union. It's what everyone thinks, even if they won't say. She has a look about her, haven't you noticed?"

Cassia stops abruptly, watching the door carefully, and her voice drops, "Like she's reading your mind, knowing your most intimate thoughts ... looking for any weakness."

One cousin laughs. "Like Neliem ... just like him ..." She quotes, "*I know your innermost thoughts and fears, and I shall shower them upon you like the morning rain. Beware those that dare cross my path. For I am like the wind; I am everywhere. I will steal into your chambers and claim my own.*"

The silly girl breaks into a fit of giggles, and I can't help but smile. I am Neliem, and they better watch out because I do go around discovering their innermost secrets; I have fifty-five pounds to show for it.

But Cassia isn't finished. "I had to let her into my home for the ceremony. My neighbors witnessed her entering. My home, an Outcast ..."

Everything goes quiet at her words. Their silence condemns me. I get up, unable to listen any more.

They all hate me. So much for defending Cassia to her abusive husband last night. But I suppose it serves me right for rubbing in the fact that she's here when he's at their home obviously keeping company with someone else. Board games. My mind spins over this bit of trivia.

Aunt Cora finally lowers her teacup with a clang that almost shatters. "It was not expected. Tristan has been begging him not to go through with it for ages …"

Everyone nods and sighs in agreement.

She hesitates, spilling some tea, before continuing, "When Ezra went last fall to Madera, we all hoped this foolish obsession would be done with. And it seemed, for a time, that it was."

Aunt Hilda chimes in, "We knew nothing about her. Even less now." She huffs, "Weapons."

"Can you imagine what his mother would think? That thing, in her house, touching her belongings, walking about in Eugenia's home … it's too painful to imagine." The aunt who's never uttered so much as two words chimes in.

Someone else whispers heatedly, "You know what she thought about …"

Aunt Cora throws her a harsh look, which immediately silences her.

Looking taller, Cassia smirks, "I'm glad we're all in agreement."

Fresh pain washes through me. Nothing from like before. That was bullying and being chased by strangers. This is family. I swallow down the lump of poison turning everything darker. No matter how clever and cunning and prepared I might think myself, I'm not wanted here, nor will I ever be. When I look down to turn on the faucet my hands are shaking.

Everything in me breaks.

I'm no longer seventeen and in possession of the spirit of Neliem.

I am a sniveling eleven-year-old Outcast girl perpetually running for her life. Sickened over this realization, I suck in a long breath and stare at my reflection. I don't look anything like Neliem, the prince of fear, he who fights until death. I am a skinny girl with rosy cheeks and a strong constitution with an unnatural fondness for weapons. I can run, hike, and sprint on most terrains, and my skirts hide most of the muscles rippling through my legs. I have long soft brown hair that flows like rose petals in the wind and eyes the colors of sapphires and earth. At least, Za-Za once said as much.

But now, with the disapproval of his family, what faces me is a one-way ticket to spend the remainder of my life branded as the Outcast girl tossed aside. The image of the old woman limping to clean out the septic tank flutters before me. How could I ever have imagined my fate any better than hers? What I've done is simply prolong my suffering.

Raising her china cup, Cassia lips curl into a malicious grin. "He should send her back; there's still time."

And with this pronouncement, I am doomed.

I dry my face and hands and apply a generous portion of rich cream all over to wash the stench of filth from this disgusting house with these evil people.

From the corner of my eye, I spot movement and turn sharply, my hand reaching for a pair of scissors left unattended.

I'm ready to draw blood when I see who it is.

Ezra.

At once, the scissors fall.

He stares at the door left ajar before firmly shutting it. With one fluid movement, his hand braces my shoulder, guiding me out. Only when he's positive that we are alone does he speak. "Were you spying?"

"Yes," I confess, breathless and strangely relieved.

His gaze softens slightly. "I can only imagine what you heard."

"Their true thoughts. Yes, it was quite enlightening."

His eyes darken, just like Tristan's. "And what did you expect? A standing ovation? Applause, gratitude over my choice?"

The words stick in my throat. He seems upset, and I've never once seen Za-Za upset. "I thought they liked me ..."

His shocked expression nearly blindsides me. He actually stammers, "Let me enlighten you, then. They don't like you! And that you thought anything else makes you foolish."

He darts closer like a predator, his body alluding both grace and sheer force. Hypnotized, I gawk. "But you said you wanted them to accept me ..."

"Yes, and to your face to be respectful and kind and considerate ..."

Like Neliem himself, he's looming right before me, so tall and blond and handsome. Nothing like my Za-Za.

"Just to my face? What about behind my back?" I spit.

"They are jealous of you, Oriana! Don't you understand that, or are you so stupid you think that I bring the most desirable, witty, beautiful, captivating girl on this earth to their home and expect them to not be seething with envy?"

I think he's just complimented me. But I'm too furious to back down and actually listen.

Ezra wipes the sweat of his forehead, trying to control his breath. "All the men in my family can't stop talking about you, about how you're nothing like those dimwits sipping tea all day and spending money on silly dresses."

"Yes, I also heard what they had to say about me. Truly inspirational ..."

He smirks. "So, this is a continual habit with you? Listening in through open doors and windows ..."

"I have to find out what everyone is thinking ... thank god for it ... oh wait, that's right Ezra, you believe in the wind, the rain, the fire...flowing through the air, what else...Horse manure?"

He makes a poor grab for me, but I rush out of the room, a fire flaming so hot in my gut that I might explode.

Without thinking, I race out from the kitchen and step right into a pile of chicken waste. The foul stench reminds me how I just insulted Za-Za. No, not Za-Za, I remind myself, but Ezra. Ezra, who cares more about pretenses than about what is actually in the heart of people.

And Ezra's a jackass if he thinks I will ever forgive him for this.

I'm so busy scraping the poop off my shoe that I don't pay attention to where I am going. I've passed the courtyard and crossed the orchard, looking out to what seems miles of rich fertile land.

The stables are situated toward my left. Curious, I walk by an open stall and come to face to face with an unattended young filly. Her coat shimmers chestnut waves, her ears pricked up as if expecting me all day. Something about the animal soothes me, and without thinking, I comb my hand against her rich mane. She smells of apples and grass and horse. I smile and press my head so that I hug her with my entire body, one thought fluttering like the wind on my back: That I could be a horse and run away from all of this.

Then, a gasp from the stables startles me. My senses heighten, Neliem awakening. The grunting seems to be coming from the furthest stable, the one facing the orchard. And it seems to be escalating. Stepping over scattered leaves and hay, I cautiously inch closer, both terrified and elated to discover what may await me.

The sound muffles, and at once I crouch low and crawl on my hands and knees toward the open path. And by the moaning, it's definitely not an animal. I peer closer.

The sight before me makes me freeze. I press my lips stifling the gasp threatening to erupt.

Before me is Tristan, and he's not alone. On her knees, Tanya's positioned in front of him, ready to do what Ezra did to me last night.

The only saving grace is that Tristan appears to be bored. He rolls his eyes as if asked to do a tedious math problem at school. "Tanya, please stand up."

Tristan, thankfully fully clothed, is not amused. By the way he stands, a grimace on his lips, he's either very upset or embarrassed. Or possibly both.

Tanya's bodice lays open, sweat dripping over the tops of her ripe breasts, which heave with excitement. She bats her eyelashes suggestively, making no motion to rise. "You want to do it standing up?"

He yanks her up by one arm. "How many times do I have to tell you that I'm not in the least bit interested?"

Breaking away, she rubs her arm, pursing her lips. "That hurt." Her eyes narrow, the green flickering. "I thought you were playing ..."

Tristan's gaze drifts back to the house. "Get yourself presentable."

Indignant, Tanya pats off some dust and straw from her petticoats, tying her bodice too tight. "What's with you anyway?"

"What's with me? My favorite cousin's betrothed wants to pleasure me, and I offer objection?"

"Last summer it didn't stop you."

"Last summer you were a friend of a friend visiting ..." He turns, making a sweep of the stable as if suspecting someone listening. The weight of his stare penetrates through the walls, so I dart back and hold my breath. "... from a faraway island, who I hoped I'd never have the pleasure of ever running into again."

"I can be discreet," she purrs.

"Not interested. Try Henric ..." Then, thinking better, he corrects himself, "Anton has always had an eye on you."

"He's eighty!" she screams, her eyes a deadly brown.

Unaffected, Tristan tosses Tanya her outer gown. "Get dressed, and I will forget this ever happened."

The corners of Tanya's mouth lift. "So, it's true, you are taking your vows."

Tristan's halfway out the stable when he turns abruptly. "What?"

"These past few months, I hear you don't frequent the brothels ..."

Tristan snickers, "Are you afraid they'll go bankrupt?"

He pauses to scrutinize her. "Don't fret - when you are dutifully employed within an establishment of your choosing, there will be undoubtedly ample patronage."

She throws on her gown and hisses, "I was pure with you."

"I was the fourth, perhaps the fifth." He barks, "Lucky number five."

"I hate you!" Her fists pound his chest, but only a flicker of amusement crosses his brow.

Carefully, he removes her hands from him. "Oh, yes ... you disrobe and offer favors to all men you hate."

Unable to counter his remark, she scurries off. "Rot in the seven sands, Tristan."

He watches her go with a look of apprehension before tilting his head toward my hiding spot. "Heard enough?"

I press down into a stack of hay, hoping he's addressing the pregnant mare in the stall right next to me.

He stomps closer, but I can't look past his black boots. He scoots down so that our eyes are level. "Did you think I was talking to the mare?"

That familiar tug pulls at me. The one that defies reason. Just a hint of those blue eyes and everything in me awakens. Playing with a piece of hay, I finally nod. "I was praying that you refused Tanya in order to not insult the mare."

And that smile I've memorized breaks like the dawn. Tristan, taking great care to be tender, fingers one of my curls before tucking it back in place.

"Oriana." He closes his eyes as if in prayer, his voice so tender.

I blush, stammering, "I ..."

He looks past me to the house, some thought lingering. "You seem upset."

I refuse to acknowledge what just happened when his hand finds mine. They're larger and tan from the sun, like my people. His skin, my skin. The similarity is oddly comforting. Someone in this horrible place is just like me.

"You can't have secrets from me," he scolds.

"Why did you interfere with my friend Etta? And her family?"

He doesn't deny it. Instead, he brushes his hair off his face. "It's what you wanted for her."

"Not Landis ... not that type of a life ..."

"He won't so much as touch her unless she agrees."

Trying hard, I force the sob back down my throat, willing myself to be strong and determined. But right now, sitting on the hay with Tristan staring right into me, all I feel is foolish.

"What now?" His words coax out the truth.

I wipe a tear that I didn't realize I'd shed. "Everyone hates me."

He gently shakes his head and sits alongside me. "That's not true."

"Outcasts don't belong here."

He blinks, the color leaving his face.

"I didn't mean you."

"If it fits." He eyes the house apprehensively. "What did the vicious bitches do now?"

"Za-Za says they're jealous."

"They are." Absentmindedly, he traces a line up and down the back of my palm.

"It's so easy for you, for them to love you, admire you, want to be you ..."

He leers a bit. "No one wants to be me, Oriana."

"You fit in." It's the truth.

"I don't." He stares at me, the ball of energy between us, drawing me closer. My pulse escalates.

"Is that why you refused Tanya?" Part of me is scared of what he might say.

"I can't stop thinking about you. Ever since you told me about the pretty lady coming to your school and giving you a gold coin." He places my hand over his heart. "Maybe even before."

I start to speak, but he stops me with a look so tender that it takes my breath away. "She was my mother."

His eyes melt into mine, sending a quiver to my gut. This beautiful creature, part Neliem, part Outcast, part me, utterly takes my breath away. Almost as powerful as when Za-Za offered me his hand in the schoolyard. The reminder sends a wave of nausea to my stomach. Za-Za; my Za-Za, who I loved and lost and somehow found again.

I bolt up, panic fluttering in my head too fast. I cannot do this. I cannot allow myself to fall in love with his brother.

Tristan collapses down in the hay, his head a mass of chestnut curls and stares at me with eyes that promise everything. Then, without a word, his hand finds mine.

"Ezra will send me back to Madera. There is still time left ..."

"Ezra is never sending you back to Madera, and if he did, I would fly the seven winds to find you."

And I believe him.

I scoff, "Taking the ferry would be faster."

He lowers his face so that it's almost touching mine. And it's there. That spark that turns my blood to fire.

"Cassia and Tanya will be returning to Madera later tonight."

"What?" This is news. Welcome news, but unexpected. Especially the way they're treated, as part of the inner circle of venomous vipers.

"Landis never cashed the dowry. He knew as soon as he got off the ferry … and Henric … well … it took him the better part of the day. Personally, I think they deserve each other. But regardless, they entrusted me with the funds, which have been properly secured."

A light shines on their previous conversation. This is the plan that Tristan has been keeping secret from the others. But it's still puzzling. "I don't understand. Why go all the way to Madera, to only change your mind and send them back?"

"Untouchables don't make sense, Oriana. Stop attempting to understand anything these people do." He checks his watch and winks. "By tomorrow, it'll be done, as if none of this ever happened, all monies back in their families' hands."

I suppose it's easier this way, secretly sent back without warning and without any potential family interfering.

"What do you know of poisons?" Tristan stares at me, and I explain, "I'm serious; I found a book under the butler's pillow. At first, I thought it remedies, but … well."

I pry the book out of my pocket with the pages marked for toxins. He bites his lip, fingering the worn book. "Only one reason to have such a book."

Someone is either being poisoned or is about to be.

His breath steadies as he turns the leather cover and reads an inscription. "What else has my sweet Neliem been up to?"

"I found quite a bit of money in a servant's quarter."

He laughs loudly. "Opening purses … I should've suspected after you stole that knife."

Affronted, I gasp. "It was wedged in a hole in the wall behind the dresser."

Tristan glares toward the servants' quarters. "We need to inform Aunt Cora and have them discharged at once."

"Why not wait to discover their motives?"

He looks at me, perplexed. "They wish harm, Oriana. Someone might very well wind up dead. Za-Za won't take it seriously. At least, not as much as he should."

"Oh." I'm not sure informing Aunt Cora is the best solution. I steal a glance. Tousled in the hay, laying so close that I can count each inhale, he's more beautiful, more intoxicating than ever.

"Can I ask you a personal question?"

His arm slips over mine. "What is it now?"

"Why don't you frequent the ... the ... brothels?" I try to sound disinterested, but my voice hikes up at the last word.

"Za-Za going back last autumn to seek you out. I mean, it was more than an obsession, it was madness. Our father sought to disinherit him, and no one even suspected your origin then. Still, the boy wanted his heart's desire. It made me think. The thought became a dream, and the dream became a desire, which became a possibility. Don't look at me like that."

It takes me a moment to realize that I've been glaring, a small puddle of drool escaping my mouth.

He wipes it away. Then, gazing deeper into my eyes, he pulls me so that I'm seated aside him, my undone hair cascading like waves over him.

"And?" My heart hammers, my pulse racing. I'm more terrified than I've ever been in my entire life; scared of what I'm feeling for this complicated man.

His fingertips stroke my face. "And I wanted that. Crazy as it sounds, I wanted that obsession that would drive me to the brink of insanity to possess it. Not knowing, not having a clue that it was you who he'd found." A shadow of sadness passes his eyes, before he jerks and grabs a handful of hay and tosses it down my shirt.

I scream and throw him down. Hay is flying everywhere, and we're swimming in it, his shirt collar comes undone, and his bare shoulder sticks out.

I gasp.

His eyes follow where I stare.

"It's a birthmark." He tugs his shirt over it.

The blood drains from my face. It's looks like my heart, the one from the wall when Ezra and I poured the water over the coals. Only it's slanted and smaller.

"A birthmark." My throat's so dry, I can barely force out the words.

"I think it resembles a lump of fat." Tristan smirks.

A lump of fat. My heart. It can't be.

His eyes soften toward the house, lingering. "When he was little, they thought Ezra was deformed. He had a mark ..."

He makes a gesture around his face.

I gulp, dread spreading down my arms.

"His mother had the maid toss him in the garbage." He gages my reaction.

"What?"

"His birth mother, the bitch, had Za-Za tossed into the trash. They consider disfigured children an abomination. A curse."

Suddenly, a layer is peeled back from my comprehension of Untouchables, about why they are all strong and healthy. How, with minimal effort, they conquered my people and countless others.

His finger twirls a pattern of a diamond on my palm, his voice whisper-soft. "A compassionate maid dug him out of the dumpster and brought him to my mother."

I hold back the tremor in my voice. "She saved him."

It's not a question as much as a statement of admiration. I love Tristan's mother for saving Za-Za, who in turn saved me. Tristan heaves, his shoulders sagging. "I was four. My mother, our mother, tended to him. The birthmark faded ... but he was always beautiful to me."

His beautiful smile drops. "We should leave tonight, Oriana."

I stammer.

At once, the conviction to do the right thing snaps. I push him away.

"I've gone over it a thousand times …" Like Neliem himself, Tristan doesn't let go. "It will take some time, but he will forgive us. The train leaves tomorrow. We can be on it together, and never have to see this place or these people again."

Struggling, I push away, but he only tightens his hold. He's so much stronger and more determined than I could ever be. Here he's telling me to leave the one person who saved my life, who I owe everything to. And even though I strain every muscle in my body, I cannot fight him off; it's like pulling my own limb.

"We'll be married in the Capital and after five years …"

"Five years?" I cannot possibly move to the Capital for five years.

"The years will go quickly. Being away will be a fresh start, a new life."

He looks at me with those pleading eyes. "He will eventually forgive us."

I'm in too much shock to tell him the truth. It's not Za-Za forgiving me that I'm worried about. It's forgiving myself for destroying my one true friend's life.

Za-Za, my Za-Za, took me to the cave as soon as the fever hit. The quarantine was already in place, with the harbor crowded full of ships denied passage. Flocks of people had gathered, demanding to be allowed to leave, but the army held them back, firing shots in the air at first to subdue them. Then, they fired into the crowds.

We'd been playing in the river, the one that led to the caves. Za-Za was teaching me how to master jumping from one stone to the other to cut across without falling into the water with the dagger clutched between my teeth. Tired, I'd leaned on him for support as we walked toward my home, Za-Za's arms the only thing between me and earth.

Next thing I knew, I awoke to the smell of mold in pitch darkness. I'd fainted.

Za-Za had carried me to the cave. It was safer, he insisted, especially with my mother on another island for a wedding. Better than staying at some neighbor's, who might not want to help. I was too delirious to counter that my mother would whip me raw at the thought of me being held up in some cave with an Untouchable boy.

Already my eyesight blurred, and I could barely hold my head up. He moved me further into the cave, on his back, apologizing every time his feet tripped or he stepped wrong on a rock.

"Are you feeling better?" He kept asking, waiting for me to say something, anything.

He left me in the cave, which was already stockpiled with a cot and water. My body an inferno, my mind drifting out of consciousness. All the while, he held my hand, his blue eyes so full.

"Za-Za ..."

"Don't speak." He fed me broth he'd stolen from his cook when she wasn't looking.

I obeyed, barely clinging to life. He brought blankets and pillows and food and took vigil telling me old Embrian stories. My mind held on to the snippets of these wonderful, courageous People of the Talent, while Za-Za forced Untouchable medicine down my throat to fight off the flames ravishing my small body.

But it was what he didn't say that made me love him more. That the sickly were being tossed in rowboats and sent adrift into the waves to die. Their anguished cries carried in the breeze until silencing completely. And this was the only reason that I didn't die like so many other children. Outcast and Untouchable.

Because my Za-Za saved me.

And then Neliem's words called to me. "*I am like the night, all powerful and encompassing. I ride in the seven winds and conquer the seven sands. There is no escaping me.*"

I wanted to hear more. It was terrifying and yet utterly compelling. Deep in my soul, longing awoke, my spirit restless, desperate to hear more. The way my lungs heaved for air, my burning body seeking relief, my mind clung to every syllable.

"What is it that you're saying?"

"It's another story about Neliem ..." Za-Za sitting on a stool, paused, and for a moment it appeared as if he wasn't by my side, the soft curve of his hand on my brow. I blinked, and it seemed that he was ravished with fever in a bed with those lights that didn't need a flame. He cleared his throat and pressed a cool rag to my forehead.

"He can be several places at once. Especially if someone needs him, someone he loves."

It sounded impossible, but for the fact that I knew of someone who also was capable of such feats. "My God is like that, Za-Za."

"He's not God, he's something different. Perhaps he has God in him, if that makes sense," he murmured, pressing until his plump body encased mine. "Some say he was a trickster, a magician; does it scare you? That we don't know who he really was?"

I opened my eyes for the first time in what seemed days. The cave was bare; no cot, no food, no Za-Za. I was dying and utterly alone. "I'm dying Za-Za."

His voice echoed, "I won't let you die, not ever ..."

"Tell me the story again."

"Neliem rises with the waves, his horse rips through the sand ... and he finds her, like I found you." His ice-cold exhale touched my face, squelching the fever. "It means that you won't die, not for a very long time."

The imprint of his stubby fingers trailed down my face, through my hair, and it felt true. Every word. "He's strong, and you have to be strong."

"Be strong for me Za-Za."

"No, Oriana, you need to be strong, like Neliem. Fight back. Use the dagger; never leave it out of your sight. Promise."

I closed my eyes and imagined the all-powerful Neliem riding in the waves, his hair fluttering like ribbons in the wind. He feared nothing, and I feared everything. There could be no two people more different.

Za-Za's soft blue eyes buried into mine. "Every single time, you'll fight back ... promise."

In a state of panic, I barely managed to shake my head. Here I was in a cave, unable to move, let alone kill a fly. "I can't."

"No, Oriana, you can. You can be anything you want ... Ta-Ta tells me all the time I can be whatever I want."

"He's never met me …" I held back a sob, hot tears spilling off my face.

Za-Za's eyes lit up like candles, his voice fading, "I'll come back for you soon…"

"Don't leave … don't ever leave me." I reached out, clinging to him.

"I have to."

Music lulled me to sleep. The fever pounding in my ears, vibrating to the point that I must've been hearing things. A music box played a sweet lullaby, footsteps shuffling up and down floorboards. Jasmine and orange blossom in the air.

"But I will come back, and I'll marry you. I swear it…" Za-Za whispered in my ear, as if it could be true.

It seemed impossible. But, so did an Untouchable boy risking his life to save mine.

"Really?" Shadows danced on the walls, the cave eerily cold with only a sliver of moon peeking inside.

"Yes, but …" His voice broke, quivering. "You'll meet Ta-Ta."

He was no longer beside me. His shadow turned, his shoulders hunched. His body quivered as he stifled the sobs.

"Why are you crying?"

"Because you'll meet Ta-Ta and love him more …" His round face held more anguish than I had ever witnessed.

I reached out and, using every ounce of strength, wiped his tears.

"That's impossible." And I meant it. I might not have known this Ta-Ta, but I knew I could never feel about him how I felt about Za-Za. Ever. "Come here."

"Why?"

"I want to kiss you."

He hesitated. "You're too weak."

"Not for a kiss." I reached up and brushed my lips against his wet cheek.

"There." And I smiled. The fever didn't feel so hot, and I could wiggle a little. "It proves I love you, Za-Za." I sighed, feeling better. "Forever."

He touched the spot where I'd kissed him, fingering it. Then without warning, he threw his warm arms around me and hugged me close.

"I will get better; I'll be strong and fast and unstoppable, like Neliem. But most of all, I'll only ever really love you until the day I die."

Gently, he scooped down and kissed the top of my forehead. "Oriana … I swear I will come back for you. I swear it on your saints and on your God."

Exhausted, I rested my eyes, safer and happier than I had in my entire life. The next day, I awoke to find myself in my own room. My fever had broken during the night, and my mother returned none the wiser.

But the worst part is that I might have lied to Za-Za.

I do love Tristan.

The bell clangs twice, signaling that dinner is served. It rings, vibrating like some harpy, clanging until I'm positive I shall go mad. In the foyer, dozens of newly arrived packages collect, waiting for servants to distribute them to the correct rooms. One girl, who can't be more than eleven, fills her skinny arms with a box too big. Without thinking, I relieve her of it with a simple, "Thank you; I will see to where it's going."

Reading the tag, I carry it upstairs to one of the female cousins' rooms and toss it on the pink satin bedcover.

Down the hall, I hear arguing. The porter arrived earlier with tickets for Tanya and Cassia back to Madera. Tanya's mother is deadly sick with gallbladder stones, and since Cassia is conveniently available, she will accompany her, as well as Uncle Anton, who has some pressing business on the island.

The crumpled telephone message said as much. Now the servants rush to have supper ready early so that two girls, who've never so much as skipped a meal their entire lives, won't leave on an empty stomach.

For what it's worth, it's a clever lie. With everything that's happened, Cassia would never have believed that her mother or father were ill. But conveniently, Tanya's mother has no telephone and it fits that she would need someone to go back with her. Uncle Anton will no doubt have an urgent message right before the ferry leaves, which will require his immediate attention. With fake sincerity, he will offer apologies for such an untimely interruption.

Two Untouchables girls will be dismissed without a second thought.

But this news brings me no joy.

Through the doorjamb, I can see Tanya's bag's packed for a day. Cassia paces about, her eyes never resting. "Why do I need to accompany you?"

More pacing. A pitcher lifts, then settles. "I shouldn't even be here. I should be in my own home. Henric should've sent for me."

"He will; you have your entire lives to be together ..."

The bed creaks, the rusty springs squeaking.

"Why can't *that one* take you?" Cassia won't even dignify me by addressing me by my proper name.

"Oh, you would rather Oriana escort me?" Even from outside the door, I can hear Tanya's clear disdain. She was wise to hide it so well. And I have to give her credit; by taking my side, she appeared sympathetic and kind. Clever girl.

"Tanya, I didn't mean it like that ..." Cassia's voice breaks into a pitiful wail.

"Cassia, stop worrying about stupid Henric. What you should be focused on is finding a handsome lover." Something thumps to the floor. "I have."

"You have not ... who?"

"A handsome brother ..."

My cheeks burn. Tristan, she means Tristan. My Tristan.

I move past the door when the servant girl from downstairs clears her throat politely. It takes me a moment to realize why.

I finger a coin and offer it freely. "For your trouble."

She curtsies in a way that reminds me of Etta. Soft and jittery, not meeting my eyes. And when her thin fingers graze over mine, I think of Etta's wonderful yellow eyes, wondering how much better life in Odessa will be for her. Later, when I confronted Landis, he shared that a position as a lady-in-waiting to a rich woman in Odessa had been secured for Etta's mother. The lady was already taking a liking to her as well as Etta, who now had a private tutor twice a week, seeing to her education.

Downstairs, the family's clustered like chickens before the dining hall, greedily waiting for the doors to open.

What we had for breakfast and tea alone was more than I would eat in a week. And yet these scavengers demand more.

"Why do they always make us wait?" One immaculately dressed cousin, who can't be older than me, complains bitterly. She catches my gaze and presses her lips closed, as if speaking ill of the servants is something she's been warned not to do.

I watch the group carefully. The two elderly uncles stand back with their canes, impatiently tapping the marble floor as if to make the doors magically open. The aunts tend to their daughters like mother hens, picking and fussing to make sure they are possibly less detestable.

Backtracking, I go down the servant's stairs. The aroma of something burnt turns my stomach. The entire kitchen's fogged with some stench as maids scurry about, opening all the windows to let in a fresh breeze.

In the kitchen, a harried cook, tendrils of long hair coming undone from her disheveled bun, wails, "She burnt the curry, the dimwit."

The scurry maid, a fresh welt on her face, huddles in a corner. "It isn't my fault."

A memory flashes before me of my own mother doing the same thing, slapping me for burning some small morsel of food or for refusing to eat something so rotten that I gagged. If it hadn't been for Ezra, I would be her. If not cleaning the school, at some Untouchable home being worked to the bone. The hope of love or a family a mere fantasy. An ice-cold shiver runs down my spine.

The two maids mock her before retreating to the dining room.

With renewed interest, I observe the poor girl hunched over, weeping on the kitchen floor. Above her lies a blackened pot of curry, which the cook scrapes off.

"Barely enough for anyone ... stupid girl ..."

I close my eyes and breathe out of my nose. It takes everything in me to resume my descent down the stairs, dread piercing my gut. Part of me wants to shut it all out, like I have most insults. It's nothing new to be called stupid, or ugly or useless. But since arriving here, I've been treated better than I have for most of my life.

My heart lunges just watching her. Her hair's come undone and rests in long red curls around her drenched face as she continues to sob into her sleeve.

The cook admonishes her further, "Milly, get off your arse before I slap you silly and cut some tomatoes ... marinade will have to do ..."

A step below me creaks, and the girl catches my eye and bows at once. "Ma'am."

I nod and try to think of what to say. If it were Etta, I wouldn't hesitate to tell her to stand up for herself and give the fat cook a piece of my mind.

I smile.

A good sock to the eye would silence the cook for a while. But such an impulsive action would grant the girl's immediate termination, plus a call to authorities.

The fact remains that I alone can do nothing.

I help Milly to her feet. She's pretty, and if given a chance to wash up and put on something clean, she might shine. "What happened?"

The cook, knee deep in stirring the soup, shakes her head. "Nothing to trouble yourself about."

"It was the other one." Milly swallows. "The very pretty one, she wanted to know how the curry was made."

The cook edges closer with a wooden spoon. It would take two moves to disarm her and have the said spoon up a very uncomfortable place. Catching my expression, she wisely backs down.

"Lady Cassia?" I ask the trembling girl.

"Milly," someone screams from outside, and the poor girl rushes away before I can probe further. The salvageable curry is quickly placed in a silver container for the family. What's left of the burnt curry is scraped onto a bowl for the stray cats.

Deep in thought, it takes me a moment to register the back of my neck prickling. I would have to be blind, dumb, and deaf not to feel the intense gazes of Tristan and Ezra. One of them is bad enough, but two. My knees wobble. Holding up my head, I turn.

Ezra chuckles, "Sweetheart, learning the finer points of domestic bliss?"

The two lift their hands at the same moment, and once again I'm dazed over how similar they are. As if threaded by the same string, their heads cock toward the alley where the ravenous cats are being fed and let out an identical sigh. Almost as if they're the same person in two forms. Za-Za all goodness, and Tristan with his dark smoldering looks pulsating the very essence of Neliem.

Forcing my feet to move, I follow them, trying desperately not to lean to either side. The dining room's prepared for the late-day meal. And there's still evening tea later.

If I stay with these people, I'll be too enormous to walk on my own two feet again. I glance down at one elderly aunt's plump feet; Aunt Mildred. She has a wart on her nose and obviously can't find proper shoes that fit. She wears soft slippers and complains incessantly about the cold, which is ridiculous. If anything, it's cool, with a pleasant breeze throughout the house. These people have no idea what it is to endure a bitterly cold winter or a scorching heat that fries your skin as you labor for miles to fetch warm, murky water to drink. They wouldn't last one day in Madera.

Politely, Aunt Cora nudges my shoulder, and I take my place across from Ezra. Unfortunately, I'm paired directly next to Tristan, whose hand finds mine under the table too quickly.

I flinch, suddenly aware of every blue eye in the room.

Tristan whispers like a cad, "Stop fretting; you'll get wrinkles."

I purse my lips and stomp on his foot before popping a fig in my mouth.

He releases my hand and stifles a grunt. Ezra's eyes are on us as he's served the shrimp cocktail, which I won't touch.

Ezra raises an eyebrow, trying to determine what's wrong. He tries his best at a smile. "Fig too dry?"

Tristan moves his foot a safe distance away. "And surprisingly hard …"

Cassia and Tanya are the last to arrive, and I can't help notice, for a girl whose mother's about to die, she seems a little too chipper. Batting those strange eyes, Tanya gushes toward Tristan. "I love figs … Tristan, tell us about Cortos. Those figs you brought back last summer were delicious."

Ezra peers from his untouched plate. He's divided his food and plays with one half as if trying to find a perfect balance. "If I recall correctly, Tristan was seven the first time he picked figs there. He always brought the best back for me."

Tristan winks, and cuts into his meat. "Mother made fig marmalade."

A wave of tension spreads amongst the elderly aunts at the mention of Tristan's Outcast mother. But the rest of the cousins seem oblivious to the slight.

Tanya licks her lips. "I bet it was delicious."

She's openly flirting, and Landis just allows it as if nothing is out of the ordinary. And I know why. He can't let on that she's being sent back. The promise of a spice empire is not enough incentive to entice him. Instead, he's set his sights on poor Etta.

Cassia darts me a glance, then returns to her meal to sulk in silence. She tried calling Henric earlier. I heard the phone ring back twice, but she wasn't put through. Some nonsense about the wiring. Obviously desperate, she went as far to try to sneak out of the house to see him but was caught and sent to do some embroidery while all the aunts marveled over her accomplishments.

That was the tell. They flattered her too much.

The ancient timepiece ticks noisily and one of the fans must be broken because sweat is collecting under my armpits and down my legs. The tension is as palpable as bitter herbs as I pull on my collar. My feet twitch to run and never stop.

I fidget in my seat as Landis turns with a fake smile directed toward Tanya. "He was eight …"

Tristan chews his steak. "I was five." He reaches to fill his goblet with wine.

They share this little smirk that sends a shiver down my spine. This is all some elaborate game for them. Playing with these girls and discarding them as easily as broken toys the moment it best suits them.

The heavenly scent of freshly baked bread wafts through the kitchen door as servants usher in platter after platter of food. Meats with sauces, chicken, duck, quail. My stomach twists. There are already three baskets brimming with mouthwatering bread, enough to feed forty, not twelve, with all sorts of butters and jams to drench our palates.

Tristan playfully flirts back with Tanya, and I think that he might be trying to make me jealous. "I'll bring you figs next week …"

She blushes, and I find myself wincing. There will be no figs next week, nor the week after. Tanya will be back in that beautiful house she hates with a mother who hits her for not being pretty enough to have ensnared a rich, Hugganoff husband.

Landis, the first chance he gets, will be off to Odessa to seduce Etta, who frankly won't need much persuasion. But he'll have to marry eventually. Someone no doubt with a bigger purse and maybe a bit more sense not to flirt so openly.

All the melodrama distracts me from the choice at hand. Ezra or Tristan. Tristan or Ezra. The clock ticks in rhythm. I get up, then sit down just as quickly. I need to decide now, before tonight.

One distinct pair of pale blue eyes burn down on me. I glance up at Ezra, and it's as if he's never left me.

I swallow down a dry piece of bread and nearly choke. Tristan's warm hands slink up my back before I squirm away. "All better?"

Ezra pours some water and, like a gazelle, lifts the goblet to my mouth. Soon, I have downed the entire glass. My chest heaves. The inexplicable need to confess everything pulsates. My Za-Za I could tell anything to. But maybe, just maybe, he already knows.

He shifts his steady gaze to Tristan. "I believe my brother has an announcement."

And something unsaid passes between them. Some unspoken language forged by years together, and miserable ones apart.

When Tristan doesn't answer, pin prickles of tension sweep down my back.

"Yes." Tristan focuses on folding and unfolding his napkin as we all wait. Cassia even looks up, momentarily not overwhelmed with her unexpected trip to Madera.

"What is it?" She turns to Ezra who remains unreadable.

"After much thought, I have decided that a change of scenery is in order." Still, he doesn't elaborate. It's maddening. Ezra, on cue, clears his throat.

"I will be accepting the invitation of the Ambassador and accompanying him to the Capital." His eyes lock on mine. "Alone."

A stabbing pain twists through my gut. Tristan finds my hand under the table and I surrender to it, finding a comfort I never thought I could. Overwrought with emotion, I squeeze my eyes shut so that tears don't burst out.

Tristan releases my hand and gets up to accept congratulations from family. Tanya hugs him too tight, the fret on her face speaking volumes. With difficulty, Landis pries her hands off of Tristan and offers him a firm hug.

It's as if all the air has left my lungs. Ezra lingers at my side, his face strained. "It is for the better, don't you think?"

Moments ago, I was seriously debating a life apart from him. But now, the choice is ripped out of my hands. It's too much.

Outside in the courtyard, Milly scrapes away the last of the burnt curry. Stray cats mew obsessively, licking at the tin plate.

I play with my food listlessly and stare as one scrawny cat breaks into convulsions. Another cat starts vomiting and three others start choking, gagging up green phlegm. I stand up and, without thinking, grab the silver platter of curry and take it to the kitchen, where I pour it out under the faucet, the hot water nearly scorching my hand.

The murmurs and gossiping from both staff and family follow like a storm about to break. I ignore every heated whisper, instinct taking over. Heavy footsteps echo behind me, but I don't stop until the dish is washed perfectly clean.

I flinch toward the open window where six cats now lie dead, a swam of flies infesting their carcasses. An upstairs maid with a crisp blue apron arrives with clean linens, a frown marring her fine features.

"The curry was …" I see a trace of clay on her sleeve, just like the one in the carriage, and freeze.

Before I can finish my sentence, Ezra appears like Neliem at the doorway. No sound, not even a hint of a footstep. "What's wrong?"

My hands shake at the thought of what nearly happened.

Ezra stares out the window, and I catch the back of Tristan as he enters a coach. He doesn't turn or wave. The driver whips once and the horses trot away, until only a flutter of dust remains.

"He didn't say goodbye," I whisper.

Ezra takes the platter out of my white-knuckled hands and sets it aside. "I will escort you back. Everyone's waiting. They are under the assumption that you were having yet another fainting spell."

There is no possible way I can go back and pretend that everything is normal. Not even Neliem could manage this.

But Ezra doesn't give me a chance; with a firm grasp, he places me back in my seat with a smile to his family that would fool the devil himself. He takes Tristan's seat and places his napkin on his lap as a servant offers him a clean plate. "Ta-Ta had urgent business with his trip. And I'm ravished ..."

He cuts into his meat like a predator.

Tanya moans, "He promised me figs."

Ezra smiles his best smile. "I am positive they have figs in the Capital."

One elderly uncle grumbles, "Politics," and blows his nose loudly.

The male cousins, who look too much alike, snicker. Tanya blushes and starts peeling a tangerine to pieces. The juices smear on her lacy sleeves, and I just watch. I've had enough. There is no way I can stay in this house with these people and pretend.

"I have a horrible headache," I explain, getting up.

Aunt Cora nods, with a sympathetic look. "You've overextended yourself."

Of course. By doing absolutely nothing and forgetting my daily exercises and combative techniques, I'm overwrought.

I prepare to slip away, but Ezra's at the door by the time I reach it. He wraps an arm around me and, playing the part of enamored lover, escorts me upstairs to a room across from ours, which they use to store our excessive clothing. The second the door closes, his grip around me tightens, his eyes a stormy sea.

He knows.

With care, he locks the door with a snap. I gulp and am about to explain that I'm in no mood for company when he double bolts the top latch.

My nerves shatter the moment the top latch fastens.

He pants like one of those ravenous dogs that used to chase me out in the woods. The gashing of teeth, the scent of blood in the air, the earth pounding, the need to escape intensifying with every breath.

After what seems an eternity, he turns and faces me. Gone is my sweet-faced Za-Za.

"What was that about? You ... flirting with my brother."

The floor drops beneath my feet as I stumble against the bed.

"There's something going on between you two ..." He approaches like Neliem himself. Dark and dangerous. And so alluring.

I edge back, forgetting that I know how to defend myself, forgetting everything.

"You were in the stables with him." Seething rage emits from every pore in his body, making him more attractive. More like Tristan. Before I can deny it, he hisses, "Do you deny it? That you got down on your knees before my brother?"

Now, it's my turn to laugh. "That was Tanya!"

Sense registers on his face, and the murderous gleam softens. "Tanya?"

"They had a thing last summer."

"I am well aware that they had ..." He stops, still suspicious. "But you were there."

"I had to speak to him."

"About what?"

I then confess my early morning spying. My continued suspicions about the carriage latch being tampered with. The butler with the scar, the maid who couldn't meet my eyes. The poisoned curry. The only thing I leave out is knowing Tristan a lot better than he suspects.

To prove my case, I pry the bag with coins out of his boot.

His eyebrows perk, but still, he doesn't speak. I remember the other maid with the clay smear. But it still doesn't quite fit. She works only upstairs, not in the kitchen.

When I look up, the most intriguing expression fills his face.

Calmly, he takes the money and unlocks the door. "These schemes have led to nothing. As they always do."

"But …" I scramble to think.

"The servants in question were fired earlier." He tosses the bag in the air, the coins clinking together. "Theft will be added to the charges."

I can't remember ever being this angry with anyone. "You don't believe me."

"I didn't say that. But with everything that's happened, you will stay in bed and rest."

I'm too infuriated to speak.

Ezra opens the door, then closes it. "Am I understood?"

I stare at him, wondering when he became so strong-willed and determined. Maybe he always was, and I failed to notice. By the way he speaks, it's not a request but a command. And he makes Neliem breathe fire, filling my lungs with rage.

"Don't tell me what to do, Za-Za."

He tilts his head in a way that would tell most people not to press the point. But I am not most people.

"You say you don't want me to be like those other girls, and yet you treat me the same."

"Those girls don't go around slicing boys' ears off and talking to daggers and caging wild animals."

I'm too stunned to speak. He knows what happened in Madera.

"Mark my words, Oriana. If I have to chain you to this bed to make sure that you remain inside of this house, so be it…"

It's a threat, and also a lie. He has no chains. Neither in this house or his other one. I should know. I've scoured every inch of both homes in search of anything to subdue my enemy.

The air leaving my lungs, I cower, hugging my knees. "I never spoke to the dagger."

Before I can will them away, tears leak out, finally able to confess my deepest secret. "I was talking to you, Za-Za. It was always you."

His jaw drops. I think he'll turn around, get down on his knees and beg forgiveness. But he doesn't. Ezra opens the door and leaves. The bolt outside the door snaps into place sharply.

I wait for him to come back, to say this is some sort of joke, locking me in a room that would only take me seconds to escape.

The minutes tick noisily, tick, tick, tick, and still, there are no approaching footsteps or the faintest creak to tell me someone's outside.

Then I notice that in this room the only window is barred, and the bathroom has no exit.

Impatiently, I rattle the door handle but find not a trace of a hole to poke a needle through. Also, the hinges are facing the wrong way.

I swallow hard and realize the truth.

For the first time in my life, I am trapped like the wild animal I truly am.

16

Against the blood moon, a horse's hooves click clack against the drenched cobblestones. A bird rustles in the branches as brittle leaves scratch against the window. The carriage taking Cassia and Tanya to the ferry arrived hours ago. By now they're probably halfway back to Madera.

I swallow the inevitable. Tristan will go to the Capital and be spectacular. He will win the hearts of thousands and probably be elected mayor and have the perfect blond wife and children. He'll be blissfully happy, without me.

"It's for the best," I whisper, praying that one day I believe it.

The thought makes me almost fall back on the stairs, disturbing my plans of escape. Ezra was called away for some pressing business moments ago. When the servant unlocks the door to see that I was well, I ask her to draw me a bath. The minute her back is turned, I steal the key, which she absentmindedly left in the lock.

Equipped with a knife I borrow from the pantry, I slink through the corridors until I reach the servant's entrance and escape out the alley.

The streets are hauntingly empty before dawn. The gaslights flicker, casting shadows that roll up and down like lingering ghosts with nowhere to go.

I waited impatiently for the carriage to leave with Cassia and Tanya. Cassia dragged her feet like a cow to the slaughter, thinking of every possible excuse. Uncle Anton had to practically yank her into the carriage and sit against the door to make sure she didn't try to escape. All the while, the old man reassured her that she could take the ferry back the very next day if she didn't feel like staying.

Interestingly enough, I didn't take any pleasure in the spectacle. I had more pressing issues at hand. Someone is trying to kill Ezra. And there is only one other person in Playa Del Sol who is cunning enough to help.

The one Untouchable I loathe more than any other in the entire world.

The lock to his kitchen door is so easy to pick that I'm inside faster than I thought possible. The warm aroma of honey biscuits makes my stomach quiver. With everything that's happened, I'm starving. With the knowledge that nothing in this kitchen is poisoned, I help myself to bread, meat and four glasses of chilled milk.

When I cut across the downstairs corridor, I notice someone has upset the china display, and all the contents have spilled to the ground in pieces. Shards of broken china and glass outline the floor.

Reigning in the spirit of Neliem, I slink up the stairs and cross the main hallway when I notice a door left ajar. Without thinking, I ease inside.

The girl from the teashop lays fast asleep in a pretty pink room. The one that screamed that she wanted nothing more to do with Henric. Obviously, she's had a change of heart. From the faint odor of fresh paint and the pristine furnishings, this was the room being decorated. Not a nursery as Cassia was led to believe, but a room for Henric's new acquisition, a mistress. His former nanny's child.

I wince as I stare down at her angelic face, so transfixed that I detect the heavy breathing behind me a moment too late.

"What the devil are you doing here?" He speaks in a mere whisper, but the threat is clear.

I nudge toward the door, and he follows, using his cane for balance.

Softly, he shuts the door closed and only then does he release the full extent of his disdain for me. I almost laugh. Those all too familiar blue eyes sweep up and down, attempting to disarm me, but it has the opposite effect.

I shrug, my attention back to the sleeping girl. "She's too young, Henric."

He winces, offering no objection. Then, unexpectedly, he sighs. "I know."

The silence between us throbs like a tainted knife wound, the poison leaking into veins, the contamination rendering one immobile.

Every instinct says I should never have come. But I've ignored common sense so far, and there's no turning back. Scanning the massive corridor framed with art and family portraits, I move toward the stairs. A moment too late, I realize walking down might be impossible in his condition. And I don't want to prolong this conversation any longer than need be.

He interrupts, "Are you going to tell me why you're here?"

"Someone is trying to kill Ezra, and I need your help." I hold my breath, then add, "There is no one else."

He shakes his head, in either disbelief or sheer astonishment. "Why should I help you? I don't like you. It was a mistake for him to go fetch you from that confounded island." He stammers, and I catch a bit of a lisp.

I've stopped listening. A dagger too distinct to be mistaken for any other lies abandoned on the end table.

My dagger. The one Za-Za gave me. The one that saved my life too many times to count is in, of all places, Henric Mercer's home.

I pick it up, transfixed. "How did you get this?"

Henric leans against the wall, rubbing his forehead. "I told him not to, by the way. Beating those boys senseless was pointless. You'd done an impressive job yourself."

His voice hitches up on the last part. Quickly, I reign in my emotions. Those boys. My attackers? That would mean that the brutes who attempted to rape me were the cause of Ezra and Henric's injuries.

"He hurt them?" I ask, still not believing.

He confirms, "Not that you appreciate it."

I wonder what he suspects of Tristan, but I find myself unable to ask.

"Tristan has gone to the Capital."

"I know; I was there when he got on the train." His voice wavers, "Well, he might have been coerced."

Without asking, I know that he's left much unsaid. My heart racing, I slink to the floor.

"He's risked everything for you, you know." Then clarifying, Henric adds, "Ezra has gone to hell and back. And to see you not appreciating it one bit ..."

This explains his hostility from the start. I finally manage to meet his gaze. But what I see isn't an arrogant Untouchable wishing me harm. It's someone as broken as I am.

Unable to face him, I hide the dagger in my boot and stare out the window. "I know that no one likes me. You don't need to remind me. But he's asked a lot in return."

"What has he asked, other than respect?"

"My mother will never see my children."

With difficulty, Henric balances on his cane. "He didn't tell you, did he?"

"Tell me what?"

His face flushes. "The dowry ..."

I'm about to ask what money, since my mother has none, when he hisses, "She asked for four hundred pounds; four hundred. In our culture, the woman's family pays for the privilege of marrying into a good family. Especially ours. I intervened and got the sum lowered to two hundred. Cash, non-refundable. I only got one hundred for

Cassia, two years ago. Do you have any idea of the stigma this will cause us?"

It's nothing more than a lie. "How dare you ..."

"I was there. She drew a hard bargain. He begged me never to repeat what had happened. The woman was out for herself. And she beat you, when she wasn't starving you."

I stumble against the wall. "It's not true ... he's prejudiced against my people."

Hearing this, he roars like a lion. "Ezra was raised by one of your kind. He, as well as all of us, loved Lania Mercer ... she was a saint. But your mother," he shakes his head, "is something entirely different."

And it fits into place. Why Henric disliked me from the beginning. He thought I was taking advantage of Ezra, his beloved cousin. I narrow my eyes, giving nothing away. "I cannot help what my mother did or didn't do. But the fact remains that his life has been threatened now three times and I need you to help him. Not me. Ezra."

Outside, a splatter of rain sprinkles against the glass windows. Soon, dawn will break, and Ezra's in more danger every second I linger here. I stare outside to the colorless sky, wondering when his attackers will strike next. Perhaps today, or tomorrow. The frequency seems to have intensified in the last few days I've been here.

Carefully, not leaving out one detail, I explain all that has happened and show him the bit of red dust I've collected.

Interesting enough, he doesn't scoff or call me stupid. With an intent gaze, he examines the dust and does something even I didn't think to do. He tastes it.

"Cinnamon," he exclaims, his eyes widening a fraction.

"It must have something to do with the embargo ..." He attempts to sit down, the pain in his leg evident as he stumbles and without thinking, I reach out and steady him. He stares at my hand which I carefully retract before taking a step back.

"But it doesn't explain why Cassia tried to poison him."

"Cassia?"

"Yes, I know it doesn't make sense."

By the incredulous look he gives me, I'm sure he doesn't believe it.

"Cassia? Poison? I don't think so. Mind you, she has a temper ..." His eyes roam toward the broken china and glass. "She nearly killed herself with her fit and took me down with her."

Clear as day, I see it. Cassia furious at Henric. Breaking the china and getting harmed, then attacking Henric.

Impressed, I shrug. "She did that?"

"The vixen is as transparent as glass."

"Tanya is in love with Tristan," I blurt out.

His face reveals nothing. "For the record, every woman in Playa Del Sol imagines Tristan in love with her."

Including me. Henric scrutinizes me for a moment too long, and I realize that we're sitting too close, almost as if we're friends. "Unfortunately, he has only eyes for one. Himself."

"Tanya will be very disappointed."

He smiles, and I think it's the first time he's done that.

"Undoubtedly, which brings us back to Ezra. It was very daring of him starting the embargo. I mean, I'm not judging, but ... he has made many enemies because of it."

My eyes widen.

"Don't get me wrong, we've all profited. The family fortune restored. But now, will all the cane coming in, we can't find enough workers to process it. Who could've possibly foreseen a strike?"

The countless faces of the orphans scraping the bottom of their empty bowls shake me to the core.

"People lost their homes. It went on for far too long. They wanted blood ..." Henric rubs his bloodshot eyes, the bags underneath indicating he hasn't been sleeping. "I would never have agreed to it if I had thought for a moment ..."

My skin crawls listening. I honestly don't think I can bear to hear another word. My Za-Za would never have caused people to go hungry, which brings up another ugly thought. "What happened to his real mother?"

He studies me as if weighing how much to say. "What has that to do with anything?"

"She was cruel. Like mine." I swallow down the bile in my throat.

"Much, much more." His face holds some unspoken horror.

"I know she's dead ..."

"He killed her ... inadvertently."

I hold my breath.

"And her servant ..." When he glares at me, for the first time, he's not taunting or fueling a need to retaliate. "The fever." He shakes a thought away. "We lost three cousins; Landis's brothers. Somehow Za-Za contracted the fever ... no one knows how."

I remember the quarantine. Flocks of people frantically trying to escape the island, some going as far as to attempt to swim to another island. All boats were grounded with no means of escape.

Everything in me breaks as the truth dawns. I gave Za-Za the fever. "Za-Za had the fever before he left the island."

Henric shakes his head. "His father couldn't have brought him over ..."

"Henric, he saved my life ... he stayed for days on the island and nursed me back to health." Shame washes over me.

"One day he was fine, the next ... his father kept him here in this very house ... at death's door." He looks around incredulously. "Even in his state, Ezra wouldn't let them take him anywhere near his mother. No one knew ... his mother came here to visit, not suspecting a thing. From what I was told, she wasn't even in the house an hour with her servant. By the next day, both of them were dead."

"But what of Za-Za?" My voice breaks, remembering how he took great pains to tend to me hand and foot as I lay incapacitated. Placing himself in danger, risking everything.

"Tristan's mother nursed him to health. But the damage was done. His own mother was cremated, as well as the child she was carrying."

"That's terrible." I hold back a sob imagining Za-Za's baby brother burning.

"It's divine justice. She was a bitch if ever there was one, she and her brother …" I can tell that there is a lot more he wishes to say. But he doesn't. Restless, he gets up. "I will go to the docks. With the strike over, I will see what I can find out."

Another thought plagues me.

"Why would Ezra risk so much with the blockade?" A shiver crawls down my spine as I answer my own question. "The dowry he owed my mother."

"We will leave at once; let me get some clothes on."

Something forces me to my feet. "Henric."

He turns sharply, his eyebrows arched.

I motion toward the bedroom. "Henric, if you care for her …"

He catches my gaze.

"If you care for her, you will marry her."

He pauses for what seems an eternity. For a moment, I'm positive that he will lash out, or at the very least kick me out. But he does neither. Balancing on the cane, he returns to his own room and gently closes the door.

I remain on the stairs a long time, contemplating everything that's happened. Henric swears that Za-Za was brought back to Playa Del Sol before the quarantine. Which somehow makes sense if the harbor was closed. Madera was shut down for months. But if that's true, how did he save my life?

The image of Neliem flashes before my eyes. His promise to be there for his beloved.

Frustrated, I quickly prance down the stairs, dread washing over me: it was my illness that killed Za-Za's brother. When I get to the bottom of the stairs, I hear a metallic rattling. Using the electric chair to glide down the stairs, Henric, looking fresh and dapper springs to his feet, the cane by his side.

"Sad to see that neither leg was broken?" he teases.

It's an honest question so I give an honest response. "I'd hoped for an arm as well."

He nods. "We are not friends."

"No, we're not."

Then, as quietly as possible, we slip out of Henric's home, taking the trouble to lock the door behind us, only one goal propelling me forward.

Keeping my Za-Za alive.

The avenue that leads to the docks is thick with hovering ghosts. Some stop, gazing blankly before continuing their aimless path. The streets so slick with rain that I nearly skid twice. Henric calls a coach, and we silently enter, not daring even so much as gaze too long at each other.

It seems strange to find myself with Henric, of all people. All around me, the city awakens slowly, like a slumbering child. A harried housewife on her hands and knees scrubs the pavement before her home with bleach. Dutiful shopkeepers display their freshly slaughtered meat like trophies at the doorway. Traffic jams narrow streets as an assortment of dairy trucks clang a little too loudly up and down the avenue making their rounds. I poke my head out the window when one zealous merchant offers me a piece of fresh cheese. I gobble it down greedily before remembering to say thank you.

A cart with a wobbly wheel pushes alongside the path, pots and pans clatter noisily, my mind spinning.

One: Za-Za caused a shipping embargo on cane sugar.

The price went up, and he is rich. Very.

Two: he went to Madera to find me. Paid my mother off and brought me here. In three days' time, the bond will be sealed, and we will be man and wife.

But the real question still haunts me: will I be in fact choosing him?

The doubt sears through me like the dull blade of a knife.

There is no chair ride to the gazebo, no one singing for me. And there never will be.

People died because of the infection I gave Za-Za.

I swallow the guilt down, hoping my rage will cover these confusing emotions. But sadly, I come up more miserable than before.

The carriage brakes by the outer edge of the main square, the scent of sea too distinct to be missed. Right before us, a paperboy unwraps a newspaper and thrusts it in my face.

Henric tosses him a coin, and the boy rushes to the pavement to collect it, leaving the paper in my hand. The headline blares bold and black: Sugarcane quadruped in value.

A good picture of Ezra opening the factory doors while migrant workers cheer him on.

"Are you going to buy that?" The newsstand owner glares hostilely.

Henric moves me aside. "We already paid for it."

The newsstand owner grabs the paperboy by the collar and starts thrashing him.

Henric hisses under his breath, "Bastard." And tosses another coin on the street.

Painstakingly slow, the carriage moves, making little gain toward the docks. Henric raps with his cane on the carriage door for the driver. "Can you get us closer?'

The driver shouts, "There's traffic."

Unpersuaded, Henric shouts back, "A pound if you can get us to the docks ..."

Henric rubs his leg, and I almost feel sorry for him.

"I can go alone," I offer, finally making out a bit of the bay.

"Absolutely not. I'm in enough trouble as it is. I should take you back to Aunt Cora's and be done with you."

I sit back as the carriage rolls up the sidewalk, people frantically moving to give way. With nothing better to do, I flick through the newspaper to find a small announcement of my betrothal. It lists the date as two weeks ago and that I'm a childhood sweetheart. My first name is listed, but conveniently not my last. Ezra took the trouble to add his prematurely. According to the paper, I'm a student and my father a professor in the island of Gretos, which is nothing short of a lie.

I crumble up the paper and toss it aside. Henric raises an eyebrow. "It seems my father is a professor."

He just shakes his head. "He is."

I refuse to say another word. The streets are starting to fill, and I'm not sure which way is faster. Using his whip, the driver's bent on getting to our destination. But if I were to slip out of the carriage, I could travel much faster.

Henric clears his throat. "Not that it's any of my business, but who would you choose, if you could?"

Startled that he knows more than he let on, I counter, "You're right; it's none of your business."

Part of me wants to ask Henric about Tristan's birthmark that resembles a lump of fat. But terrified of the answer, I press my lips together.

He nods stiffly. "You believe Ezra to be in danger and you sneak off to save him."

I twist my head to glare. "Your point?"

"Just that, Tristan is like the sun and the stars. He's always shined brighter than the rest of us."

"And?"

He lets out a sigh of exasperation. "We all reflect in his glory. Even me."

I remember how the mood in the hallway shifted when Tristan greeted his cousins. How, for Untouchables, they seemed happy and festive. But another memory pierces my gut. The day at the schoolyard when Ezra offered me his hand. That look in his eye. Determined, yes. But something else. Something that's stayed with me every waking hour since then. A cloak of sorts, warming me, causing me to smile at almost any given moment.

Our eyes lock, and I'm the first to turn away.

I close my eyes, certain of something else—Ezra deserves someone much better than me. Someone who was not responsible for the death of his unborn brother. That debt can never be repaid.

When the carriage rounds the final corner, a commotion filters from the docks. The stench of smoke and rotten fish stinging my nose, I get to my feet and scan the bay.

Dozens of boats are on fire, thick curls of smoke blackening the sky. A crowd of fishmongers has gathered as rescue teams dressed in shocking yellow are assessing the damage. Lines of tiny lifeboats cloud the horizon as victims are being hauled over. Ghosts flutter everywhere.

"What happened?" But even as the words leave my mouth, I have no doubt what has occurred.

My nightmare has come to life.

Without a word, Henric gets out, offering me his hand. He tosses the driver a gold coin and tilts his head. "We've come too late."

One man, donning a large apron smeared in blood answers, "Early this morning, the ferry capsized. There were several fatalities."

A shiver runs down my spine. "No."

Desperate to learn more, I press against the spectators to get a better view just as the lifeless body of a girl floats to shore, crashing against the waves. All the air escapes my lungs as I recognize a familiar pink skirt.

Hiking up my own skirts, I push closer, delving into the icy water, just in case it's a trick of the morning light and I'm imagining things.

But this is no mirage. My eyesight clouds as I recognize the dress, the unmistakable blond hair now tangled in filthy mats. The betrothal image of the burnt incense on the wall of her house showed a boat with ribbons floating, spinning out of control.

Everyone thought it a sign of a happy life.

But now I see it for what it was. The deep gash to her skull has stopped bleeding, only one smear of blood seeping down her mouth and nose. Her body is shockingly white, with the exception of a web of blue veins.

A large woman smelling of sweet bread weeps, her shoulder touching mine as she reaches down and lugs Cassia to the shore. "Poor darling, she mustn't have known how to swim."

I close my eyes, as someone behind me gasps.

When I look up, Henric hunches over, clutching a handkerchief to his mouth.

"My god ..." He blinks, then steps forward, his gaze in the waters. "Tanya was on the boat."

Panic fills me. "Ezra ..."

Ezra left before the crack of dawn on pressing matters.

Kicking off my boots and grabbing my dagger, I race faster into the waters, pushing past the crowd to find a familiar shape, a tousle of blond hair and feet that move like a panther. My pulse in my throat, my heart hammering hard, I race. Like Neliem himself, I quicken my pace, biting back the pain of sharp pebbles stabbing into my feet. I gain in momentum, turning one lifeless body after another but still, I don't see him.

Henric, still standing next to Cassia's lifeless body, shouts, "He isn't here ... come back ..."

My body shivers from cold, my dagger burning hot, guiding me toward the harbor.

Moving deeper into the water, Henric braces on his bad leg and grabs me. "You are no use to him dead."

I'm about to argue when I recognize a flash of white blond hair on a small boat about to leave the harbor. Brown dust covers the deck, glistening like diamonds in the sun.

"Za-Za!" I scream and push off Henric, who tumbles into the water. I climb back onto the dock praying that I'm not too late.

Because of the commotion, the pier's jammed with stalled vendor wagons and crowds of curious spectators, some still in their nightshirts. Someone steps on my foot as I fight to maneuver the best way I can against an upstream of people, getting jabbed in the ribs more than once. Perching up on a crate, I see that it's pointless. It will take hours to cut across the traffic and get to him. And I'm barefoot, making it all the more difficult.

Frantic, I jump over one crate, then another, scaling them as I did the jagged rocks of Madera. I land near the port and unbalance a man who holds on to me for support, his fingers digging into my flesh. I tug away, barely escaping as my bodice rips. Two men tumble, falling into the water. Their heads bob like apples as more lifeless bodies float into the harbor.

Tucking my dagger into my pocket, I gasp, digesting the enormity of the disaster.

Countless bodies mar the harbor, washing to shore on both sides of the bay. Spirits leave the departed, adding to the number of restless ghosts clouding the sky. But Ezra's helpless on some small boat heading out to sea if I don't save him.

Squeezing my eyes shut, all I see is Cassia dead. I detested her, but the sight of her lifeless body nauseates me. I retch into a trash bin, vomiting until nothing is left but the burning acid in my throat. When I right myself, a whirlwind of bodies presses too close, the stench of smoke and fish and death. Glaring, their glimmering blue eyes drinking me in. One arm grabs my shoulder and tightens like a vise.

I try to pull away, but the hold intensifies to the point of hurting.

"Let go of me ..." My feet kick out, breaking the hold and I move forward, struggling to get to the boat and following the scent of cinnamon. Gaining traction, I leap and land on the vessel.

Like a pile of rags, he's face-down on deck, soaking wet. His chest heaves, and I don't think, I act. Using every ounce of strength, I heave his body into the small life preserve and toss him into the water.

A splash, a moan. Then our eyes connect. It isn't Ezra's face. It's Landis. The deck under my feet pushes into the harbor. My head spins, unsure what to do.

Landis, his eyes rolling, gasps, "Get off the boat, Oriana."

I look back, turning in all directions. "Where's Ezra?"

Pushing back to the bay, the current takes him farther so that I can't make out what he's trying to say. Blood pours out of his mouth. "Tanya ..."

I strain my ears to catch what he's saying. "Trap ... Get off ..."

In my pocket, my dagger burns blistery hot. Pressing my slippery feet to the edge to dive off, the tremor of footsteps pounce hard on the deck. I hold my breath to dive in, when a sharp pain jars my head, and everything turns black.

But still, I fight. I fight and fight and fight.

I wake to a boat swaying. At least, I imagine it to be a boat and not the hammock my mother sometimes set in our small backyard to rest and catch some sunshine. My head throbs from the blow to the back of my skull, my eyes seeing double. Forcing myself to move, I manage to lift my face.

The motion of the boat turns everything upside down, making me gag. I still my nerves and breathe. The air tastes of salt and blood and sand.

I stare down at my torn dress coated in blood. My blood, I think. When I reach down, I don't find a wound. I lay back, somewhat relieved I'm covered in someone else's blood.

Neliem stirs and prods. My hand reaches and retracts the dagger that's gone ice cold and wait.

By the full moon, it's nearly midnight. And it's the first welcome sign since forever. Neliem strikes his enemies by the light of a full moon. The stars have once again aligned in my favor.

I know this moon; it's the same one that lit my way to the apple orchard when I awoke with hunger stabbing my gut. Where I found my eagle egg and rescued my beautiful bird. It delivered me there and will deliver me now.

Voices echo outside and my dagger jolts into life. Za-Za's close by. I inhale sharply and force myself to sit up, ignoring the throbbing pain in my head. I close my eyes and try to sense Za-Za. There's an unexpected chill in the air. Not of the sea, but of something else.

The hair on my arms stiffens, and I peer out the window. Something is amiss. I try to feel for Tristan, wondering if he really got on that train. I could sense it if he were close, I tell myself. My heart reacts just thinking about him. Perhaps Henric was lying just to gauge my reaction.

My hand trembles. I cower down and check my pulse. It's weak but steady. I look around and face the inevitable. I will need to kill to survive.

Heavy footsteps precede a gentle clicking on the floorboards. Expensive boots.

I collapse to the floor before the door opens.

Pink patent boots approach, then falter before my face. For a split second, I think she'll kick me in the head, and my hand tightens around my concealed dagger.

Instead, she sighs, and I squeeze open half an eyelid.

It's Tanya, crouched over me, very much alive. Carefully, she runs her gloved hand over my face. "I told them not to hurt you."

Every nerve in my body wants nothing more than to lunge and strike. But I force a pathetic moan to escape my mouth as if I'm weak and afraid.

"To think I used to envy you, Oriana." She says my name like it's a disease.

I shoot up with my dagger, pinning her in one fluid motion against the wall. Stunned, she drops her handbag, her mouth hanging open.

"Scream, and I'll slit your throat. Where are we headed?'

"Waria."

The hot dagger almost slips from my hand. Waria, birthplace of Neliem.

Suddenly, the boat rattles and a gust of wind howls like a demon. But I hold tight and stare into those sad brown-green eyes.

"Where is Ezra?"

The boat quivers, this time the image of a smoky ghoul crossing the room. As it goes through the wall, he takes a huge bite of the plaster, and the entire boat shakes violently. These are not normal spirits, but something else. My hands tingle in dread as I push her in front of me, the dagger digging into her neck.

"They've already started; you see them, don't you?"

I shake my head, forcing myself to remain calm even though the boat is filling with deadly ghouls and demons. Or perhaps the devil himself.

"They've started the blood curse … summoning the destroyers … it's just a matter of time now." She shivers as if having a dagger to the throat is of no consequence. The fear pulsating from her eyes is directed at the ceilings and floors, everywhere except for me. "You weren't part of the plan. It was Ezra, not you. He's the one they wanted."

My mind flashes to the carriage door lock. The cats convulsing in the alley.

I push her harder against the wall. "I know it was you. They got you to poison Za-Za."

Before she can form a lie, I press my blade tighter against her throat so that a trickle of blood drips down her neck.

"Why? He was good to you!" I spit out.

Her shoulders sag, her lips trembling. "My uncle made me accept Landis's proposal. Even though I wanted Tristan, I couldn't say no."

Another phantom stops right before us, lingering until I lift my dagger and it vanishes.

Released from my grip, she explains, "The disease he brought back from Madera. That's what started this. It killed my aunt, lady-in-waiting to Ezra's mother. They've waited for years for this revenge."

Exhausted, I step away, angling toward the door. "You were here last summer; why not then?"

"I had to earn their trust. They had to believe that I was one of them." She touches her neck compulsively, the look of dismay covering her pretty face. "We didn't count on you."

"It had nothing to do with the embargo or the strike."

Tanya stumbles against the wall. "Everything went wrong; you were never where you were supposed to be. It was maddening. We had people trying to get you last week, but they failed. Then he started posting guards ..."

The memory of the two men chasing me through the market the day I met Tristan flashes before my eyes. It all makes sense.

"We tried to kill him a dozen times, but he just wouldn't die." She stares at me in complete bewilderment.

Another phantom crosses the room, dissolving into the wall as the lanterns flicker, the wind howling.

"So, we had to do the spell to get the spirits to come and finish it."

Rage bubbles up in my chest. Grabbing her by her hair, I yank her out of the room and cross the small corridor toward the deck. Losing my footing, I nearly stumble over the bodies of three men, all cut up with precision. I don't have time to waste to figure out who did it as two phantoms hover over the bodies, gnawing on their flesh. I don't as much as blink. When Tanya tries to speak, I press my dagger harder against her throat, when she points to the wall.

A lump lays covered in the corner. A tangle of blond hair peeking through a blood-soaked mat. His hand dangling out. That torn nail, that ring.

Za-Za.

I can't think. I can't breathe. Za-Za.

A wail rips out of my lungs. Part animal, part anguish as I reach down and grab him.

In answer, Za-Za's heartbeat pulses. His forehead creases, a hint of blue eye blinking.

He's been beaten almost to the point of death, blood oozing out of his side, too weak to move.

Tanya bats her eyes, her face contorting. "It's too late! They're coming for him."

A phantom with blood dripping from its mouth moves between us, and she screams.

Hysterically, she tries to push Ezra off me, but I slap her so hard that her head spins. Her necklace breaks, tiny beads popping everywhere as she flails like a wild animal caught in a snare. A door to my right vibrates, its hinges creaking open. I turn just in time to see Tanya rushing down the corridor as two ghouls make chase after her.

I don't think, I act. Lifting him, I brace Za-Za against the wall and scan the deck and pray. In answer, a small boat knocks against the hull.

Using every ounce of strength, I carry Za-Za on my back, my dagger warding off the evil seeping over every inch of the ship.

Throwing Za-Za into the rowboat, I use my dagger to cut the ropes, and the boat plunges down, splashing into the raging waters.

The impact of the boat hitting water makes every bone in my body shatter. Za-Za, coming to, lifts his head. "Oriana …"

His shirt in shreds, I finally see it. What I should have known was there all along. The heart that materialized on the wall the day of our betrothal is on his shoulder. It shines against the moonlight large and perfect and bright.

The lump in my throat throbs as tears sting my eyes.

Our heart. Unmistakable.

Staring into his sleepy eyes, I tighten my grip on the oars and push. But it's as if we're trapped in quicksand. The boat isn't moving. Something in my peripheral vision makes me stop. A ghostly arm claws one of the ropes, preventing us from escaping.

I swallow hard and hold up his face to mine. "I pick you, Ezra."

He opens his mouth to speak, but no sound comes out.

"I pick you, Ezra Mercer, as my intended. To love forever and ever."

Fighting off my tears, I grab him as if it is the last time and kiss him. "It was always you Ezra, my first love, my only love. I would've died a thousand deaths if you had not been in my life … let me now return the gift. My life for yours."

I set the oars next to him and climb up the rope, the dagger clenched between my teeth, and sever the ghostly hand with one slash and jump up, catching the net.

Bracing myself on the deck, I watch Ezra drift away in the rowboat. Someone shouts, "He's getting away; go after him."

I prepare to cut the last rowboat loose when a mob of evils spirits tears it to bits, wood flinging in every direction. Not wasting a moment, I race out the back only to nearly collide with two men with guns racing toward me.

I don't hesitate. I yield my dagger and escape through the side, where I find Tanya huddled in a corner, weeping. A fresh gash on her forehead oozes blood over her hair and once beautiful dress.

She mopes, "They were supposed to kill Ezra, not us ... I don't understand."

I would laugh if it weren't for the fact that I will most likely be dead in the next few minutes. All the decks are filled either with men with guns or ghostly phantoms tearing down the ship. And there is nowhere to go. We are out at sea, the outline of a small island miles away, with no means of escape.

Yanking Tanya to her feet, I use her as a human shield just as the men, joined by four more, gain upon us.

A phantom lunges toward me and I slash it with my dagger until it dissolves into ash.

Behind me, someone screams a blood-cuddling moan as his arms are ripped out of their sockets, blood splattering everywhere. I turn in all directions to witness the enormity of death and destruction. It is as if every demon in hell has been set free.

A shot erupts.

I twist my body so that the first shot hits Tanya in the arm. The second shot fires, and then a third. A burning sting in my shoulder makes me almost drop the dagger.

Balling tight, I roll and jump as a phantom arrives and drives a bloody stump into one of the men, pushing out his pulsating heart.

At the sight of the beating heart, Tanya collapses. I clench her limp body against mine, seeking cover behind a barrel as another shot rings and cinnamon fumes explode above my head.

This is it.

I am going to die. I swallow hard.

One man grabs a tight hold on a rope forming a noose, lacing it over the mast, and I see my fate too clearly.

These are the same men from the market. Their sinister faces are marred with hatred. I settle my nerves, knowing that I should start praying for deliverance. The words hitch up in the back of my throat. Only one escapes from my lips. "Tristan."

It floats away, carried in the wind as I close my eyes and prepare to die.

A soft thud hits the boat. An unexpected fog setting in.

Tanya, coming to, moans. Clutching her arm, her green eyes blaze open. Staring into them, I know one thing truer than ever. I am nothing like her. And her poison of hatred will not stain my last breath. Some force stronger than myself multiplies, and I do what I could not before.

I forgive her.

The sensation of flight washes over me, and I inhale the sea.

Za-Za is safe, I convince myself, and he knows that I picked him, my one true love.

Suddenly, the men about to attack heave, their chests ripping open. I blink as they collapse in a heap lifelessly on the floor. Their blood floods like a rivulet until the floorboards are soaked slick and wet.

A form resembling Tristan materializes and steps forward, his arms open, a look of calm resolve over every inch of his perfect face.

Tanya stirs alert, then breaks into a run, racing toward him, her face elated. "I knew you would come, I just knew it." She ignores her bleeding arm, burying herself against him. My lungs heave for air, but there is no air, no light. Only the sound of my heart slowing.

The boat jolts, hitting against rocks. Someone has lit a fire, fumes filling the boat. I cough, and through the porthole, make out jagged cliffs.

For a moment, the image of Tristan blurs. Like a dream unfolding.

Like a tempest, the wind bursts, seawater spraying all over, rocking the burning boat violently.

I struggle against it, fighting to gain purchase with my feet.

The image is somehow behind me, guiding me to take one more step into the unknown.

Below me is water. But I don't understand. I search his face for the answer.

"Oriana, fight."

And then he does the impossible. He lets go.

His form alters. His frame fading.

I barely manage to keep hold on the railing. The wind drowns his voice. But it's his lips I'm staring at, I see the words float out of his mouth and touch me.

"Swim."

His warm breath tingles my skin, jolting me awake as I plunge into the icy black waters.

My arms and legs move by instinct, fueled by the warmth of his body propelling me forward.

Seawater fills my mouth, and his fingers run through my hair. And it might be the wind, but I swear when I look to the sky, I see his face, the stars in his eyes.

"Don't leave …"

He winks one last time. "I'm already gone."

And like a vapor, he vanishes. I don't focus on anything but keeping my head above water.

Not on the dead bodies on the galley crashing into the rocks. Or the pit in the middle of the sea sucking up howling phantoms. Or Tanya, hysterical, rambling about ghosts and spirits and the undead, before getting tangled in the noose and choking to death. Drops of her blood scattering in the wind, washing over her body.

Instead, I swim.

18

Someone is touching me. Someone with warm fingers who smells of fresh mint.

"Shouldn't she be awake by now? It's been days."

Cool water rolls down my face, trickling down my chest.

"She's alive. The god Mulock has heard your prayers."

My eyes fling open, correcting the tiny woman, "God ... one God. No fine jewelry."

I smile weakly, every muscle in my body throbbing. The sting of antiseptic tells me that I'm in some sort of hospital, not the boat. Relief washes over me as a familiar face pries too close. "My lady, do you know where you are?"

When I try to shake my head, pain sears through my shoulder.

The doctor snaps his bag shut, his voice stern. "Plenty of rest and fluids ... no physical exertion until I check back on her next week."

I collapse back in the cot, never in my life so relieved to see an Untouchable. "So many dead in Playa Del Sol ... it will take forever to straighten up this mess. Last we heard, Lord Mercer's missing, feared dead, and now this."

Alarm seeps through me, and I struggle to sit up. "Ezra Mercer was on a rowboat ... "

The nun adjusts my blanket. "Only you washed ashore … we thought you dead. But you are so strong, like Neliem; you defied death."

She nods toward a small statue of my namesake. Neliem. But this rendition has a gentle smile on his face as he holds a dagger similar to my own.

"You honor what is dark and dangerous?" I swallow hard, scared of the answer.

A smile lifts from her tanned face, and I remember where I last saw her. The orphanage in Playa Del Sol. "There are many versions of that story. Some say Neliem was a saint who, after the murder of his beloved, roamed the earth seeking pure hearts to aid. Going as far as to be in two places at once to defy death itself."

Which explains how Ezra was able to save me in the cave while laying sick in Playa Del Sol.

Another nun, fitting sheets on a cot, adds with a cluck of her tongue, "Sister, he fashioned a blade to defy death itself. With it, he fights the demons and sends them back to their fiery eternal death."

I shiver, seeing the phantoms all too clearly being sucked back into hell, and reach compulsively toward my dagger, which is missing.

"You are from the orphanage … what are you doing … " The air escapes my lungs as my head spins. Bracing on my good elbow, I scan the room. Bare walls, a few cots with threadbare blankets, broken toys scattered on the dirt floor.

"We come here to collect the unfortunate."

From outside the open window, small children play in the sand. Some are brave enough to race toward the waves before pulling back and letting out a heartfelt scream.

The distinct smell of sea and salt flutters everywhere. Sunbeams glisten brightly as my eyes start to close.

I am alive.

And in, of all places, Waria. Home of Neliem. Who, it turns out, is not all death and destruction, but something entirely different.

In the days that follow, I'm informed of all that has occurred since my ordeal. After the explosion that destroyed the ferry, civil disobedience ensued. The entire harbor in Playa Del Sol has closed. Thankfully, the riots have been curtailed, but at a cost, with hundreds dead or missing. The good sisters of Divine Mercy had just left on their monthly excursion to retrieve orphans as armed guards seized all vessels, placing the city in lockdown. It will take weeks, if not months before we can return, with only medical personnel allowed passage.

My heart stings over the news.

When I am strong enough to walk, I'm allowed to pace the beach. At first, just short distances with the children flocking around me like chicks, begging for a story or tall tale about my adventures.

They ask continually about my eagle. The one I nursed only to free her right before the betrothal ceremony. I elaborate some, going over how the dagger led me to the last egg, and how she was terrified when she hatched, covered in her own blood, unable to lift her head. And yet, when the time was right, she soared into the heavens, her wingspan pushing me to the ground.

"But someday, she will return," they insist and search the sky for a sign.

"Yes, one day my eagle will return," I whisper under my breath.

I put that story aside, sometimes wondering, with everything that's happened, if it's something I made up. Instead, I grow stronger, forcing myself to eat when I have no appetite. After a week, I manage a mild trek to where the seaweed washes up and collect seashells. Sometimes the children follow me along the reef, the patter of their little feet picking up sand, eager to hear about the city and how I am a great lady who offers compassion for the poor.

It seems ironic.

At night, in my small cot, I try to push aside the fact that my fate lies in the hands of my worst enemy. Henric has undoubtedly fabricated some story to add in the deception of my disappearance.

Landis, if he survived, for all I know might be in a coma. And, even if he does recover, he will recollect nothing of me pushing him off in the life preserver in an attempt to save him.

I cannot bear to think what has befallen Ezra. My one love, who might be half dead in a rowboat adrift at sea.

I stare in awe of the statue of my namesake by my bed, wondering how I could ever have been so stupid to have doubted the pure love that Ezra offered so freely. The same one I, time and time again, stubbornly cast aside.

One early morning, after I wake and assist the nuns with the children, I find myself wandering out toward the horizon, past the bay where the small fishing boats flock like seagulls against the waves. The urge to move, to run is but a distant memory. I close my eyes and wade into the white foamy waters barefoot, banished to live alone, without Ezra, far from everything I've come to love.

But today, the air seems sweeter. I travel further up the beach as if I can cross the wide abyss. In the far distance, one of the nuns waves frantically from the orphanage. I ignore her until cloud shadow falls over my face.

It is not a cloud, however, but the wingspan of an eagle, flying so close I can feel the faint wisp of her feathers against my head.

I swallow hard, the air leaving my lungs.

My eagle has returned.

I look down, goosebumps covering my arms.

When I dare lift my eyes, a boy strides purposefully up the beach.

I spot the small boat that's washed ashore a moment too late. A larger vessel is anchored out in the bay.

The sun stings my eyes as tears pour down my cheeks. But even then, I blink, unsure who has found me.

It is not until Ezra stands before me, his broad shoulders shielding me from the blinding sunlight that I dare inhale sky and sea.

My heart hammers harder in my chest, the words tangled up in my throat.

He smiles, half Za-Za, half Ezra. All goodness and strength and love. Everything that I've ever wanted still waiting for me.

His hair, much longer, brushes against his face, and without thinking, I reach out and touch it, never wanting to let go. "Your hair is too long."

"You promised to cut it." His voice cracks, and it is my undoing. I close my eyes and let the whirlwind of emotions consume me.

With the gentlest touch, he lifts my chin, still waiting for my answer. "Oriana, my love, tell me why you are crying?"

I move first, encasing my small body perfectly into his, allowing his scent to wash over me. Because against all odds, a miracle has occurred.

When I wasn't looking, a chair ride to the gazebo arrived for the girl known as Neliem.

THE END

Acknowledgements

Neliem would never have germinated from a seed to a fully grown garden without the inspiration of my paternal grandmother. Nonna's face and laughter were my earliest memories. Sitting at the kitchen table as a child, eavesdropping on how she'd persevered through so much, inspired me to eventually write this story about overcoming the harshest obstacles, without losing your humanity.

The amazingly spectacular Georgia McBride gave my story wings, with her faith and patience. Thank you from the depth of my heart. I am indebted to Month9books' amazing team, Dr. Emily Midkiff, Christine Hogge, as well as a huge hug to Danielle Doolittle for her amazing cover!

None of this would have happened if my agent Liza Fleissig hadn't taken a chance on me and *Neliem*. And my friends Saida Staudenmaier, Susanne Wright-Nava, and Erin, who have been reading, and rereading, my stories forever. I love you all.

But most of all, I owe everything to the unconditional support of my family: Forrest, Edmund, and Oliver.

Writing is a tough path, many lives crisscrossing and intercepting, sometimes for a moment, with others taking hold. As for supporters, I wouldn't be here without the amazingly talented Stephanie Gordon and Judy Enderle, both who've been cheering *Neliem* on since page one. As well as Steve Bjorkman and Lee Wind. Steve, thank you for going out of your way to encourage me during our yearly lunches. Lee, thank you for telling me to rewrite the beginning 50 times until I got it right. You all offered a spark of hope when everything seemed its darkest.

Thank you and bless you all.

Claire Di Liscia

Born in Queens, New York, **Clare Di Liscia** moved to California as a small child and grew up in the hills by Dodger Stadium. Constantly roaming the woods, she took to embellishing on the stories of Peter Rabbit and Jemima Puddle Duck to fill her imagination. To her horror she soon realized there was no way to fit a miniature tuxedo on a frog. Fortunately in sixth grade, Clare won a short story contest with the grand prize of fifteen happy meals. She would like to point out that two of those meal tickets were missing by the time her mother handed over her prize.

After traveling extensively throughout South America and the Caribbean, Clare attended KU Leuven, in Belgium for University where she studied Dutch and French. Clare graduated from Cal State Northridge Film School, earning Dean's List recognition with a BA in TV/Film.

In 2006 she placed in the prestigious Academy of Motion Picture Arts and Sciences Nicholl Fellowship in Screenwriting beating out 4700 other applicants.

After joining SCBWI, Clare won 1st place HM in the Sue Alexander for her YA novel, now entitled NELIEM.